50 PIMP PHILOSOPHIES

FOR ENRICHMENT
IN THE GAME OF LIFE

KUSHAQXI

Publisher's Cataloging-in-Publication data
50 PIMP PHILOSOPHIES: FOR ENRICHMENT IN THE GAME OF LIFE
AUTHOR: KUSHAQXI

Contents

DISCLAIMER

This work is a work of fiction. Any resemblance to real persons, living or dead, or actual events is purely coincidental. The characters, organizations, and scenarios depicted herein are entirely the product of the author's imagination or are used fictitiously for the purpose of storytelling and creative exploration.

While this work draws inspiration from historical narratives, cultural references, and the documented philosophies of individuals associated with various subcultures, it does not claim to be a factual representation of any real-life events, people, or organizations. Any insights, philosophies, or strategic principles referenced within are drawn from widely available literature, memoirs, and sociological analyses on the subject, including but not limited to works by authors such as Iceberg Slim, Donald Goines, and others who have explored these themes through a mix of experience and creative expression.

This book is not intended to glorify, promote, or advocate for any illegal, unethical, or exploitative activities. It serves as a work of pulp literary and philosophical interpretation, offering a blend of social commentary, street wisdom, and storytelling.

Readers should approach this material with discernment and an understanding of its fictional and thematic intent.

Note:

The use of the word **"Negus"** in this work is intentional and rooted in its original meaning—not to be confused with any offensive or derogatory language. In this context, **"Negus" symbolizes nobility, authority, and self-mastery.**

"Negus" is a royal title from Ethiopia, historically used to refer to **a king, ruler, or emperor**—particularly one who governed over a region or province under the larger imperial structure of Ethiopia. The title dates back centuries and carries deep cultural and historical significance tied to sovereignty, leadership, and divine right.

Throughout this work, any reference to "Negus" is meant as a celebration of identity, legacy, and the greatness that lies within the bloodline. It is a reminder that royalty is not always about lineage—but often about mindset, movement, and mission.

For a deeper dive into the origins and cultural significance of the word Negus—from its royal Ethiopian roots to its reinterpretation in the diaspora—see titles such as **Negus: Majestic Tradition of Ethiopia** by Miguel F. Brooks, **The Negus: The Life and Death of the Last King of Kings** by Angelo Del Boca, and **The Negus: An Anthropological Construction of African Diasporic History** by Shema Rismay. These works unpack both the historical lineage and the modern symbolic power behind the term.

DISCLAIMER

Again, this should not be mistaken for the distorted and bastardized misuse of the term in its derogatory context elsewhere.

Introduction

Imagine you're the CEO of a Fortune 500 company, a city councilman with a PR crisis, or a high school principal barely holding it together before third-period chaos erupts. Maybe you're the founder of a team lead at a startup hemorrhaging money or a small business owner staring down an IRS audit like it's the final boss in a video game. No matter your title, the common denominator is this: life and business are tag-teaming you in a steel cage match, and you are losing—in a real way.

You've read the self-help books, binged the TED Talks, and even tried meditating (twice), but nothing is sticking. Every piece of advice sounds like a vague horoscope: "Trust yourself. Be adaptable. Align your chakras." Meanwhile, your problems are multiplying like rabbits on spring break.

Then, one fateful holiday gathering, while half-listening to a cousin ramble about their long-winded vacation story and his twins, your uncle asks how you've been holding up. With little thought, you let it slip—life's been kicking my ass. You're not expecting much. Maybe a nod of sympathy. A generic, "That's life" or "That's tough, nephew." Maybe even the classic, "Keep your head up."

But instead, your uncle—the former pimp who's lived ten lifetimes in under fifty years, the one with stories so wild they sound like urban legends—leans in, smirks like he knows something you don't, and starts dropping gems. Not in riddles. Not in clichés. But with raw, unfiltered, straight-no-chaser wisdom. The kind of wisdom that comes from a life of making things happen—sometimes the hard way, sometimes the smart way, but always with a finesse that defies logic.

What started as a random check-in and vent session over plastic cups of cheap wine has now become a master class where unc began spitting from an endless reservoir of game that flowed with passion, like sacred scripture. At first, you try to brush it off. But then, somehow, against all logic, his advice is making sense. It doesn't sound like theory—it sounds like solutions. And real ones.

Before you've even finished your second plate of vegan turkey—which is surprisingly bussin, with the mushroom gravy and such—you've already solved three of your most complex problems—via text, email, and sheer confidence that you didn't have an hour ago. By the time the sweet potato pie is served, your entire perspective has shifted, and you've made a play that's got your Coinbase wallet looking healthy AF.

This Book, Cousin, is that Uncle.

Welcome to **50 Pimp Philosophies for Enrichment in the Game of Life.** A collection of wisdom so sharp, so undeniably effective, that it doesn't just make you think—it makes you move. In these pages, you'll find the kind of philosophies they don't teach in business school but should. The kind of rules that could save your career, your wallet, and maybe even your soul.

Each principle, rooted in a corresponding philosophy, unfolds through a rich narrative that sets the tone, leading into a monologue-style lesson from that one archetypal uncle who's been through it all—delivering the game in a way that's impactful, easy to absorb, and ready for real-world application.

For the literary purists, take note: what may appear as grammatical errors are, in fact, a deliberate rendering of voice—rich in culture, cadence, and character. This story also uses shifting narrative perspective, blending first- and third-person narration. This intentional approach draws contrast between internal experience and external observation, capturing not only how things feel but how they look and are. In short, if you read, " one-hunnid and not "one hundred," it is intentional.

As you read, you'll likely start to hear a voice behind the words—gritty, raw, full of character. Let it speak. That voice is what brings the story to life. Imagine a living, breathing presence behind each line. Whether it's Sam Jackson, Denzel or even Jason Statham's voice you hear—Read it with that tone in mind, and the whole experience hits different—the rhythm, the world, and the weight of what's being said will come through like someone sittin' right next to you, lacin' you with raw, uncut game.

In our exploration of strategic and personal development, we will delve into several principal areas essential for cultivating a profound understanding of individual, social, and business growth. I'd also argue spiritual growth, ultimately, seeing as currency is energy and energy is spirituality. While there were

countless topics explored, these specific topics have been meticulously chosen to provide a comprehensive overview with ac-
tionable insights into the dynamics of professional and personal
advancement.

We will cover several, including those listed below.

- **Business Acumen** - Understanding the fundamentals
  of business operations and market dynamics.

- **Financial Management** - Mastering the art of financial stewardship and investment.

- **Adaptability** - Cultivating the ability to navigate and
  thrive in changing environments.

- **Leadership and Influence** - Developing skills to inspire, lead, and influence others effectively.

- **Strategic Thinking** - Enhancing the capability to
  plan strategically and think several steps ahead.

- **Personal Development** - Focusing on self-improve-
  ment and personal growth strategies.

- **Communication Skills** - Honing the ability to communicate clearly and persuasively.

- **Self-Empowerment** - Building confidence and autonomy to make empowered decisions.

- **Risk Management** - Learning to identify, assess, and
  manage risks effectively.

- **Practical Wisdom** - Applying practical knowledge

and common sense to everyday situations.

- **Self-Reliance and Independence** - Fostering independence and self-sufficiency.

- **Social and Relational Dynamics** - Navigating social interactions and understanding relational networks in business and personal life as well as exploring the complexities of interpersonal relationships and their impacts.

Each principle will touch on various aspects of the above topics and is designed to provide valuable insights and practical skills that are crucial for success in both personal endeavors and professional settings.

While love may not have a place in the pimp game, my affection for you, the reader, compels me to **include 15 additional bonus principles.** That's right, 15 extra on top of the 50. This ensures you are well-equipped with the necessary game to eat in this world. I am excited to explore these themes with you and aim to furnish you with the essential knowledge and skills required to excel.

Each principle, rooted in a corresponding philosophy, unfolds through a rich narrative that sets the tone, leading into a monologue-style lesson from that one uncle who's been through it all—delivering the game in a way that's easy to absorb, impactful, and ready for real-world application.

So, pull up a chair, clear your mind, and let's chop it up one time—albeit from the perspective of someone who gives it to you straight, no chaser, with a splash of tough love. If you're the sensitive type, this ain't your lane. Might as well gift this game to someone with the backbone to stomp ten toes down—and ready to polish and bejewel their crown.

Preface

From the time I could walk, I was called a pretty boy and was told the ladies loved me. Maybe it was the way I smiled, my charm, or something deeper. Fast forward, my mother, unfortunately, crossed over when I was still very young, and I believe that loss sparked an endless search for a special kind of love or nurturing. Apparently I sought it in the attention and beautiful smiles of women.

I soaked up attention and admiration like a flower in sunlight, thrived in fact from the energy fed to me from those who adored me. He's going to be a lil pimp when he grows up, they'd say. Or, "you must be a player," the girls would remark while smiling. It made me feel good, special even. The energy was reminiscent of the vicarious reflections experienced as joy, pleasure, and excitement some get when served or from serving others. Call it "Altruistic Euphoria," "Empathic Fulfillment," or even "Emotional Transference." Call it whatever you want, but it certainly wasn't the Ism—not yet anyway.

I wouldn't learn of Pimp-ism or the concept of *pimping* until my first year at Tri-Cities High in Atlanta, Ga. My New York homie 'Daryl' put me on game. We were both fed up with school, with being broke, and with watching students walk the halls in a mindless shuffle like extras and non player characters (NPC's) in the matrix. I remember Daryl scanning the crowd one day, then locking eyes with me like he had just uncovered some ancient truth.

He blurted out with no warning, **"Man, I'm about to start pimpin'."**

He had already given it considerable thought, actually. I, of course, greener than a California bud," *had* no idea what TF he was talking about. I was more square than a Rubik's Cube fresh out the box.undefined—a couple weeks later, Daryl was gone—Out of there. I never saw him again. His conversation stuck with me though.

Around that time, Atlanta's cousin Memphis produced some young kings called 8Ball & MJG. Yes, " it take's a negus that's hard from the start, you gotta have heart, to meet a bih. . .   if you know, you know. Oakland had Too Short, who was born to mack and telling freaky tales that he told so well. All of them schooling young heads through hip-hop about pimp culture. As weaponized as it was becoming, hiphop was always a tool for spreading information—street wisdom, wrapped in poetry, bouncing through subwoofers, shaping minds whether people realized it or not.

I was now in the tenth grade, where for a short time I shared Mr. Morton's science class with Antwan Patton, better known to the world as Big Boi of Outkast. Both of us quiet, calculating, not doing a lick of work yet masterminding—it's no surprise, however, that we didn't cross paths much, being in different grades but the same class. What I admired though was not long after that season, he and Dre3K were pushing their own brand of game through the Dungeon Family, stacking awards, saying something and shifting the culture.

Their first LP sprinkled bits and pieces of pimp game just as $hort Dog, 8Ball & MJG did, as well as UGK. By then, however, I was long gone from high school. I was hardly in class when I was there. Some days, I'd stand up in the middle of the lesson, chuck deuces, tell the class and teacher it had been real, and was on my way. Teachers had already written me off as a lost cause, so there was no repercussion. I'd like to imagine Mr. Morton would say, 'Have a good day son, and be safe out in those streets,' but I'm sure that was not the case. More a silent look of disappointment.

I only came to school to get at chicks, hit all three lunch periods, beat on the lunch table while freestylin', and go to Mr. Stiggers TV production class before convincing some young admirer to skip class and bounce with a young player—most likely to Lenox Mall to eat free samples from all the restaurants. I once got caught smashing outside in the baseball dugout during one of these excursions by Dr. Robinson, *(the principal)* and his colleagues, but that's a story for another day.

I was already on my own, kicked out of the home early, running from pillar to post, crashing at older rap homies' spots, or being tucked away in dorm rooms at Morris Brown, Clark, Spelman, or some young sista's furniture-less apartment somewhere in Atlanta for a few nights. I didn't have to run game back then. They just understood my story and my babyface sealed the deal. By eleventh grade, I already had an apartment of my own and a son. I thought I was grown. Years later, during chance meetings, I ran into ole Mr. Morton and Ms. Scott—two of my most impactful former teachers—and without hesitation, they both told me the exact same thing: *that I was ahead of my time.*

The real highlights of those days, however, aside from being a young father, were the pimps on Stewart Avenue, one of the top tracks in Atlanta at the time, now known as Metropolitan. I'd hit the strip selling mixtapes, sock's, and incense, confident the OGPs—'OG Pimps'—would show love and chop it up with me. They were my first stop because I knew I had guaranteed sales everytime, but more than the money, I was there to soak up major game like Major Payne. 'What you got new, young blood?' They'd call out as I approached. We'd lean against a money green Seville or a champagne-colored Jaguar, smoking Newport 100s, in what looked like an abandoned skating rink parking lot if not at Pleasure's—discussing the rules and repercussions of the Game—which apparently translated to all areas of living, I was often reminded.

If there's one thing I've learned, it's that pimps love to talk, especially if you've got the gift for understanding the Ism and could keep up. I flirted with the idea of stepping into their world, but certain ones would often tease and say I didn't have the heart for their profession. They'd say I was a bona fied player, but not a pimp—yet they certainly recognized that I would never be a payer or a muthaphukin simp. They dug my curiosity and loved how I interpreted the game. I asked a lot of questions about the life, pulled out books, and talked psychology and human behavior. One OGP even started calling me Lil' Scientist. They conveyed a sense that I was capable of much more, provided I put in the work. I'm sure had I come off the coin thing's may have gone a lil different as high level game is sold and not told.

At the time, it stung to hear them say I wasn't built for their life, but they were right. My empathy wouldn't let me break anyone. I mean, I could break some bank and check some gas out a tank, but I wasn't built to break someone's soul no matter how broken it already was. If I were a polygamous Imam with four wives, ten Airbnbs, thirty-five Turo car rentals, and real estate spread across the hottest cities across America, with my wives running point, and managing various aspects of our operation, that would be different. But to take a woman and grind her down to the worst version of herself could never be in my cards. My gift is to make people the absolute best version of themselves in every way—now if they decide they want to pay, who am I to say I ain't gone play? Not a whole lot of sympathy, but a gang of empathy would be my way.

Still, I learned a lot of practical plays from these men. From real-life P's to every book and documentary I could find, I absorbed game like a sponge, honoring every second of it. I respected the trials and tribulations of the game. All these men walked so others could run, and I made sure to learn as much as possible from them, even the ones I never met. Their lessons could make boys into men. You'd learn how to check wisdom out of sin—no matter the terrain, if you knew what to listen for and how to apply it.

The ultimate lesson learned? Adaptability breeds abundance.

That same mindset carried me beyond conversations on the blade into different schools of thought. I studied men like Mystery, Neil Strauss, and Ross Jeffries—PUA strategists who dissected the psychology of attraction and influence. From the streets to corporate boardroom suites, the laws of the game remained the same.

Today, the battle of the sexes rages harder than ever, and the wisdom from the game has never been more crucial, and **"The I Am the Table Mentality, "** book goes deeper into the roots of these social dynamics and is a recommended read. This book here, however, is different.

'50 Pimp Philosophies for Enrichment in the Game of Life', is a blueprint. A collection of principles that started as street wisdom but have been translated into universal laws for survival, success, and strategy. Most of the rap in this book is public domain game, sayings passed down through generations like scripture. Others come from documentaries, interviews, yet mostly from firsthand knowledge imparted upon me by those living it.

Artfully written in the format of fiction, most of the game bestowed here is my own personal brand, refined and perfected over the years. I first drafted this manuscript in 2012 and held onto it, letting time shape it. What you have now is the upgraded, refined script, brought to you almost fifteen years later—because everything happens in its right season.

While I wish I could credit every source behind some of the quotes shared, they have circulated so widely and have been repeated so frequently that their origins are now indiscernible.

To all the P's, both known and unknown, I extend my deepest gratitude. Wherever you are, if you have ever contributed wisdom to the game, know that I salute you. There are no scripts or copyrights with street knowledge. It's not regulated like comedian's with stolen jokes. Once you hear the wisdom, it's yours. You internalize it and apply it when the time comes; you spit it with your own finesse just like the greats before you. If you don't understand the principles and can't deliver them with confidence, charisma, and precision, you're mouthpiece is invisible either way.

What you can expect:

I've gathered, refined, and remixed insights and ism's learned from the game—worldwide, time-tested, and battle-proven—then broke them down into a digestible format, turning streetlight into spotlight so the blind can see, and the lost can be found for making their way back to solid ground.

Each principle, rooted in a corresponding philosophy, unfolds through a rich pulp fictional noir narrative that sets the tone, leading into a monologue-style lesson from that one Uncle who's been through it all—delivering the game in a way that's easy to absorb, impactful, and ready for real-world application.

This ain't just a book—it's a lifeline. Mark my words, it'll soon be sittin' next to soups and honey buns in every commissary, turning prison stores into mini Barnes & Noble. Send a copy to your people inside to help them come home right. But don't get it twisted—this ain't just for those already locked up, read it now if you're still free, so you never have to sit down at all. Prevention beats penitentiary every time.

This book does not seek to reach everyone; it speaks to those who may not otherwise encounter these ideas or the language that can ignite greater ones. Told through the lens of creative fiction, it transforms complex concepts into something highly palatable and easy to grasp. And to the critics—if you're not raising the same objections about violent blockbuster films or the top 100 rap and rock hits, then miss us with the shenanigans.

Knowing that Grandma and-or the youngins might get ahold of your copy—or end up overhearing while you're listening to the audiobook—I've aimed to keep the message as universal as possible for commercial reasons, and yet, it's still a rustic kind of read—unpolished, authentic, and intentionally unfiltered, right down to the punctuation and grammar. It helps to view each chapter as a journal entry—capturing a specific day and the meaningful lesson it left behind.

>> Most Importantly, throughout this manuscript, you'll find **'Bolded Words'**—these are hidden jewels, clues to the principles and philosophies being shared. **Hunt them down** and jot them in the journal section I've provided at the back of the book as if you are creating your own *Index*. Every time you spot one of these Easter eggs, capture it with a pen and place it in that section.

This is important, and you'd be cheating yourself instead of treating yourself if you didn't.

When you've completed the book, return to that section in the back where all those jewels are waiting. Now, it's your turn. Break them down, build them up, notate and lace them with your own brand of game, definition, and insight. This isn't just about absorbing knowledge—it's about shaping it into something uniquely yours.

Sprinkled throughout the text in bolded print as well, are powerful book recommendations—gems for those sharp enough to collect and absorb them with savant-like focus. Those who lock in will find themselves on a path to unimaginable wealth. You won't just be well-read—you'll be well-fed. And by default, you'll be rich beyond your wildest dreams—mentally, spiritually, and materially.

Write it down on real paper with a real pencil and real intent and watch it get real.   ~Ms. Wright

Study these philosophies, contemplate the principles, and absorb the translations. If you do it right, you'll be well on your way to mastering the game of life no matter what it throws at you.

EPIGRAPH

Life's turns can be unpredictable.

Sometimes, the richest lessons are hidden
in the least likely encounters.

With Uncle, wisdom flowed whether he was fresh off the Yac,
reflecting post-meditation, or just after sealing a deal. You never
knew what you were going to get, yet his perspectives came sharp
and seasoned with a lifetime of wisdom, insight, and a gang of
experience.

Unc has a way of circling back, repeating, and reiterating the same
truths until they sink in. He'll tell you the subconscious learns by
repetition, not reason, or remind you that repetition is the mother of
learning. At times it feels like the rhetoric of an old man, but hidden
in the rhythm is the revelation because somehow—out of a hundred
slick lines—there's always one or two that land just right. And when
they do, it's the jewel you didn't know you needed, the one that
shifts your whole trajectory in a single moment and changes
everything.

What follows are dialogues spanning a little over two years, ignited
by a simple holiday meet-up, each one a deep dive into life's complex
tapestry.

~ Nephew

One

Pimpin' Ain't Dead, Y'all Negus Just Sc'ed

The throne's still here, but most too shook to sit on it. A few do, but most rather shyt on it.

*T*he festive spirit of the holiday gathering permeated every corner of the house, where the aroma of soul food filled the air—succulent fried chicken, sweet candied yams, and collard greens seasoned to perfection. Laughter echoed through the rooms, mixing with the lively beats of soul music that spilled from the living room speakers. Children dashed through hallways in a blur of excitement, their shrieks of joy punctuating the air as they played tag, dodging between legs and around the clusters of relatives.

In the dining room, a boisterous game of spades was underway, with aunts, uncles, and grandparents bantering over each play, their voices rising and falling in a rhythm that matched the soulful tunes. Nearby, a group of cousins leaned into a deep conversation about the ups and downs of life, their stories weaving through topics of love, work, and dreams, all shared with an earnestness that only family could evoke.

Uncle sat quietly this evening at the corner of the sofa, observing with amusement the stories the younger generation told themselves and each other, as well as the old-timers gossiping over cards and tipsy recollections. He noticed how much had changed—faces he'd never seen before now belonged to his family, reminders of the many years spent chasing ambitions far from home.

Perhaps it was the alcohol or the satisfying fullness from the hearty meal inducing a state of comfortable drowsiness known as "the itis," but he resolved quietly to visit more often, cherishing the simple, priceless moments shared in this atmosphere of warmth and kinship. Half-nodding as he took it all in, he soon found himself drawn into conversation by his sister's boy, his nephew, whose initial casual chatter soon gave way to deeper exchanges.

Uncle had long noted his nephew's sharpness, wit, and innate intelligence, seeing clearly that the young man held great potential that merely awaited the right push to truly flourish. Their conversation moved swiftly from general pleasantries to matters of substance, each word exchanged forging a deeper bond and mutual understanding. After some spirited and insightful banter, the nephew leaned in over his plate of onion smothered pot roast, his expression curious and tinged with seriousness as he asked, "Unc, is pimping dead—or is it still true and livin'?"

Uncle, his face a mask of reflective experience illuminated by the flickering glow of the big-screen television playing some random movie in the background—yet drowned out by the music, paused thoughtfully. Recognizing this as an important moment to impart principles transcending mere gamesmanship—principles of adaptation and survival—Uncle weighed his response before answering:

I mean, is a pig's pussy pork? Just cause you put a wig on a pig, and the pig work a gig on fig, don't mean it ain't what it is, yuh dig. I aint gone hold ya nephew, pimpin' ain't dead, you Negus jus' sc'ed! You should know the game is alive and kicking—it didn't vanish; but it might as well be Spanish. It's a foreign language to a square—but I'll get you fluent.

Pimpin' just evolved, nephew. It's still prowling the streets, still making waves, but see, the environment's tougher now. Cats are more wary, more strategic, because the stakes have skyrocketed and the boys in blue are prowling harder than ever. They'll have you caught up with a trafficking charge just for flying your girlfriend in for the weekend and turn you into a **13th Amendment Slave** before you can click ya gators together three times, talkin-bout there's no place like home. But, dig deeper, Todo; it's also about guts, the raw nerve to live by the hardcore dictates of the game, no matter yuh situation, yet moving as stealthy and as legal as you can, which ain't never been for the weak-spirited.

So, when I say "y'all just sc'ed," ain't nobody throwing shade—it's straight-up truth. It's acknowledging that not every player is built for the high tension and high risk of the life. Pimpin' demands audacity, tenacity—an unapologetic break from the usual, stepping into the arena with the wolves and lion's when others step back. That's the heart of the mantra. You got to know how to operate on a high functioning level to really just pimp anything in this world. A lot of people sittin' on million dollar ideas but sc'ed to plot a course out of the so called safety of a job they hate, to create a life they dream of—a life they deserve.

Now, take you, nephew, you already maneuvering through a corporate gig, talking 'bout stepping into tech investments, scouting partners for that startup vibe. You're dropping names like Y Combinator and other 'start-up accelerators,' dreaming of bagging **Angel Investors** and **VCs**—whatcha call'um—venture capitalists. You're eyeing that Mark Cuban swag and dreaming of Bezo-level bread. But here's the raw deal—that's just it—you just talking. It's time to stop hesitating, and start innovatin' and creatin'. Stop dabbling in what-ifs. You gotta channel that same boldness you admire; pull the trigger on those big moves already.

You're already mastering the corporate game, got a big social media following, and you already running major LLC side hustles, two or three in fact—that I know of—but you holding back from going all-in on the real deal. Don't get me wrong, nephew, I'm proud of you. A restaurant here, a laundry mat there. A little bit of this and a little bit of that over there. But all you keep talking about is this billion dollar corporation type money, so I know you ain't 100% happy.

It's not just about takin' action; it's about seizing command, embracing the high stakes with the confidence of a seasoned hustler—pimpin' every opportunity you get like you the most diabolical pimpin' ass muh-phuka the world has ever seen. This ain't just about making moves; it's about making monumental moves. So, what's it gonna be? You gonna keep playing it safe, or you gonna step up and claim your throne in this high-stakes game?

Don't just aim for success; be relentless, be fearless. That's pimpin' at its finest, and it's time you live it fully, not just fantasize about it. Remember, in this game, you either play big or go home cause' suckas aint made for no thrones. So, go ahead, nephew, make those power plays, because those who dare, win. And that's real talk—pimpin' in this new era ain't just about survivin; it's about thriving and slidin' without being conniving.

See nephew, you think pimpin is limited to the streets, and you think I'm talkin' bout some girls. Essentially, what I'm talking about is **'Leadership Presence'**. Leading ain't just about being in charge; it's about taking charge and owning every room you step into. The essence of pimpin' is leadership and knowing how to lead. Aint no way around it. It's about projecting confidence that resonates, that makes folks want to follow, invest in, and believe in your vision. Leadership is the subtle art of persuasion, where your vibe, your voice, and your vision align to command respect and compel action. It's about embodying the kind of presence that don't just suggest authority but magnetizes it. It's about the grind.

They say work smarter, not harder, and while that's true, it definitely aint easy. That's why so many people are scared. They get stuck in a comfort zone. A pimp is what you'd call a risk-tolerant individual—like CEOs, Navy SEALs, and other elite players, this kind of person moves comfortably in uncertainty, thrives in danger, and embraces unpredictability. They look for challenges and enjoy the game. Some are thrill seekers, adventurers, and adrenaline junkies.

Yuh' commander and chief once said, "Money was never a big motivation for me, except as a way to keep score. The real excitement is playing the game." And then he put out that book, 'The Art of the Deal,' breaking down how this shyt is an art form. See nephew, most people choose to play it safe, but there ain't no real reward without risk, ya dig?

Just like entrepreneurship, the average man ain't got the stomach for pimpin'. It's too much like holding down a CEO position. I be watching that *School of Hard Knocks* joint on YouTube, and every time that young brother asks a CEO if most folks could be entrepreneurs, they don't even hesitate. They hit him with a quick, "Nah." And I get it, because truth be told, leadership ain't for the faint—and running a business, that's pressure most folks ain't built for. Same with pimpin'. It sounds pretty till you're the one making the plays, taking the losses, and still gotta keep the whole operation moving like it's sweet.

And just like folks out here playing house or dressing up like they Mr. Businessman, you got a whole crowd impersonating and imitating the pimping. They talk the talk, wear the coat, quote a few slick lines, but they ain't built for the burning. See, there's a difference between presentation and position. A lot of cats look the part, but when the game gets heavy, they fold quicker than a card table at a church fish fry. Pimpin' ain't a costume—it's the Constitution. And most of these imitators couldn't walk a mile in them gaiters without crying for a refund.

True leadership presence is cultivated by stepping out of your comfort zone and taking those risks that terrify others. It's about showing up, not just as a boss, but as a beacon—a guiding light in choppy waters. This means being the calm in the storm, the strategy behind the hustle, the vision behind the grind. When you lead with conviction, with that unmistakable swagger of someone who knows where they're headed and how they gettin' there, people can't help but stand up and take notice.

They'll wanna' join you, support you, and elevate you. You represent that version of themselves they can't quite tap into. They feel like they can't do what you do—but they'll do it with you. Piggy back pimpin—ridin yo wave. It'll get'em a lot farther in the long run. If they ain't got a vehicle yet, they got three choices, walk, catch the bus or stand still. If they got any sense, and see you drivin' that bus, they'll hop on that bus with you and ride it like a surf board on a Hawaiian wave.

Remember, nephew, the game's about more than just playin' with pussycats; it's the money game, the power game, the innovation game and it's full of cut throat competition from every angle you can imagine. You got to leave n impact so indelible, so potent, that it shifts the landscape of whoever you touch and leave an outstanding impression. Embrace this, embody this, and watch how the world bends to your beat. Them partners, VC's and angel investors aint gone chase you down and beg to be led by you. You got to ask yourself, do you have what it takes to take risk and be a leader, or are you just a useless eater and a mutha-fudgin mouth breather.

Halfway through Uncle's talk on the evolving nature of the game, amidst the lively beats of music, the rich aromas of home-cooked soul food, and the sounds of children playing with reckless abandon, nephew leaned in closer to hear Uncle chop up game on life. Uncle's colloquial dialect and vernacular took nothing away from his brilliance; cultural expressions in language never diminished intellectual capacity or lessened one's intelligence, and so nephew listened on.

I'm giving you the PG version for now because there's kids around and I'm not sure you can even handle the real deal but let's slice through the sweet talk and drop some heavy game, nephew. Back in the days, if you ain't have ten toes stomped down on that blade, you definitely wasn't no pimp. Nowadays you can hoe hustle on the internet and in the newspaper amongst other places. Yet, It's still all about that streetwise charisma, that magnetic mojo that pulls success towards you like gravity.

You gotta glide through the crowd with that assurance, that swagger that says you own the block, the boardroom, and/or the business deal. It's that energy, that unspoken command that separates the players from the spectators, the chiefs from the chumps. When you embody this type of charisma, you ain't just moving through spaces; you're defining them, commanding them.

My man *Naval Ravikant* said "Read what you love until you love to read. All the returns in life, whether in wealth, relationships, or knowledge, come from compound interest—and learning is the most powerful form of compounding." So look, nephew, if you really wanna' learn this game and understand the pressure of real-world pimpin' and what it takes to be on top in the world, dive into **'Executive Presence: The Missing Link Between Merit and Success'** by Sylvia Hewlett and **'The CEO Next Door'** by Elena L. Botelho and Kim R. Powell. They'll break down how to navigate the corporate game. And for a taste of how things use to go down in my world, explore any book by **Iceberg Slim** or grab **Pimpin' Ken's '48 Laws of the Game'** to get the raw truths of the streets. Comprende?

Pimp game, Business game, Money game, War game—it's all the same baby boy. If you Know one, you know them all. It's like code switchin' through different languages and cultures. Pimp game just get a bad rap 'cause of the goofies out there misrepresenting the pimpin'. There's two things a bona fide, verified, and certified pimp will never take: that's somebody's ability to choose, or their life. People know they can either choose up or lose up, 'cause it's always by choice and never by force.

Pimpin' offers a service so hoein' ain't gotta be on the blade nervous. My job is to protect and serve from the trick and the perv, and after work, I love, guide, and provide. See, I'm a finesser, not an aggressor. Or at least I used to be, before I gave my life to the master pimpin' called Christ, ya dig.

I aint Kilo Ali and it aint 1992, but im bout to lay on you the got'damn truth—Pimpin' ain't dead, y'all ninjas just sc'ed. It's definitely alive and well and just waiting for the brave to claim the throne. Only the bold ride the wave of the game—in whatever form it take, yuh dig what I buried.

And—Just like that, Nephews first few lessons had began, and they definitely wouldn't be mthe last.

Two

The Name May Change, But the Game Remains

All capitalistic pursuits are parallel to pimpin. You just didn't know 'cause you didn't pay attention in the kitchen. New label, same recipe—real players know the flavor—they'll cook up and can it, then sell it to they neighbors.

O*n a random Tuesday night, feeling a touch of restlessness, Nephew decided to visit a cigar bar Uncle had praised for its chill atmosphere. Sharply dressed and sporting one of his first Rolex watches, he headed out, eager for some downtime. Upon entering, he unexpectedly spotted Uncle, who greeted him with arms raised, as if to say, "Ayyee, Look what the cat dragged in." Uncle, alongside a comrade, was comfortably ensconced in the plush leather chairs, both enjoying fine cigars while their attention flitted between sports on one screen, stocks on another, and election coverage on a third.*

Nephew approached with a grin. "I won't even ask who you're voting for, knowing you," he teased. Uncle, slightly tipsy from the whiskey he savored, chuckled and responded, "It's all the same game, nephew, just two sides of the same coin." As they settled deeper into their chairs, the ambient light from the television screens above the bar cast a warm glow on their faces, Uncle leaned back and began to share his insights in his typical candid manner.

"New levels, new devil's—The name may change, but the game remains," Uncle mused, his voice carrying smoothly over the blend of bar chatter and soft jazz in the background. "Whether it's pimping or politics—chart's, stocks, or sports, it's all about readin' the plays, understanding the strategies, and knowing how to position yourself."

He paused, taking a slow drag from his cigar, allowing the smoke to spiral upward as he locked eyes with Nephew.

*"See, every decision, every vote, every investment—it's about **leverage** and foresight. It's not just about what's happening now but about anticipating the next move before it unfolds." You can call it whatever you want, **rebrand** it however many times you see fit—but it's all the same game.*

Nephew listened intently, Uncle's words striking a chord as he contemplated how these principles applied not just to their current setting but also to his broader ambitions. As the evening progressed, Uncle's stories and analogies unwound further, each one reinforcing the enduring truths of life's complex game. The tipsy slur in his delivery didn't dull the weight of his words—they still landed, clear and heavy as the game began to pour.

Now listen up, nephew; let me paint you a real slick picture. See, when I say, "The name may change, but the game remains," it ain't just about what you call it—it's about what it truly is. Rebranding of the same ole product. It's like those cats out there code-switching from the streets to the boardroom—it's all the same hustle. It's about adapting and evolving without losing the essence. You could be slinging in the alley or closing deals downtown, using the same strategies, just different geography. The tools might change, the scene might shift, but the core? It stays the same. It's all about seeing through the new packaging to the timeless truths inside.

Adaptability, that's the real name of the game. It's not about who's playing or the cards you're dealt; it's about how you play them. It's reading the room, the market, the street—it's knowing when to push, when to **pivot**, when to hold back. Adaptation, nephew, is seeing opportunity where others see obstacles. It's being a chameleon in a world that loves nothing more than to pigeonhole you. Every mogul you idolize, every empire that stands the test of time, has this in common—they adapted, they sacrificed, they overcame, they evolved. I don't have to mention how many billionaires and multi-millionaires slept in their cars—technically homeless while on the come-up.

And here you are, talking about shifting your game from currency exchange and stocks to crypto, wondering if it's the right move. Hear me out: the landscape is going to shift a hundred times over. Your job ain't to stop it; your job is to ride it like the wildest bronco in the pen. You adapt by staying true to the hustle, not just the hustle as you know it today, but the hustle as it might be tomorrow, next year, or next decade. Think bigger, think broader. If you've seen one chart, you seen'um all. Whether bull or bear, up or down, by the end of the night, somebody gonna be wearing a crown.

Alright, nephew, let's chop it up about this thing called **strategic fluidity**. That's your ability to adapt rapidly and effectively to changing circumstances—kinda like how a hustler needs to switch gears on the streets to stay ahead of the game. It's all about being able to move with the times, changing your tactics and strategy without losing your core focus or getting shook by the unexpected. Just like on those street corners, you gotta stay loose, watchful, and ready to pivot at a moment's notice.

Now, take that concept up to them high-rise offices downtown. It's no different there, nephew. Those suit-wearing hustlers gotta be just as agile, man. They reading the shifts in the market, sidestepping pitfalls, and flipping strategies like a seasoned street vet. Whether you wheeling deals on the sidewalk or leading board meetings, strategic fluidity means you keep your operation flowing smoothly, no matter the bumps. You keep that mindset sharp, your plans flexible, and always stay ready for the next move. That's how you maintain control, whether you're dodging cops or clinching corporate deals.

See, drivin' a tractor trailer, you steer and counter-steer... but in the sky? You roll, rudder, and ride the air. It's all about how you handle the drag baby, adjust the trim, and counter every crosswind life throws at you. You bank and balance, trim and correct—ya dig? Just some lil' shyt I picked up when I got my pilot's license. You ain't never met a pimp pilot, have you?

They laughed. Nephew chimed in, "Soon you gon' have a plane to match the boat and the Bentley, huh, Unc. "God willing," said Uncle.

He continued, **Adaptation** is your golden ticket in this high-speed train we call the game. It's about leveraging every change, every twist in the tale to fortify your fortress and expand your empire. Whether it's hustling tech gadgets today or space tourism tomorrow, the spirit of the game remains. You gotta keep your eye sharp for the shifts, and most importantly, keep your flavor original.

What's the quote you was always telling me from ya man Wall Street trapper, " we use to buy the shoes and drank, now we own a piece of the company because we own stock in it." Now that's that game I like to hear you talking about. See, whether you selling puss-or-pounds, bussin nuts or rounds, playing stocks or on blocks, XRP and Crypto always going up or down. If you know what to look for you can ride that wave any which-a-way, and you still gonna come out with the pay, and on top cause its the same game with another name and the same rules as the last hustle.

So, here's the clincher, the juice that'll getcha loose: Keep cooking up that special sauce, nephew. The market, the players, the haters—they gon' keep changing. But what do we do? We keep our recipes tight, our pots hot, and product ready to serve. Because no matter the name on the door, the game—it remains. And in this ever-evolving hustle, only the slickest, the quickest, the most adaptable stay feasting. Remember, it ain't just about surviving the changes; it's about owning them, leading them. So step up, adapt, and let them know—new label, same damn delicious recipe. That's how real players do it. The name may change, but the game? Oh, it remains, more robust than ever—like a king pigeon wearing peacock feathers.

Hey, nephew, swing by the spot when you get a chance; I got a few books lined up for you that'll sharpen your mind real nice. First up, I got 'The Art of Strategy' by Anavash Dixit and Barry Nalebuff—it's like a playbook straight from a game theorist's mind, perfect for mastering those business moves. Then there's 'Adapt' by Tim Harford, this one's all about learning from the swings and misses, you dig, how every fail is just a step closer to nailing it. Trust me, these reads are like tools for the mind, sharpening your hustle from the street to the suite. Come on by the spot and grab'em off me, so we can level up that game of yours.

Three

Pimpin' Ain't Easy, But Somebody's Got to Do It

The game ain't for everybody—some preach it, few teach it, only the real reach it.

A couple of weeks had passed since the night at the cigar lounge—which was just days after the family gathering where Unc first laid down the street-smart gospel that had been living rent-free nephew's head. *The echoes of his advice lingered, especially during a particularly tense boardroom meeting at the day job. The company faced a complex issue, one that nephew's own startup could handle effortlessly, yet the executives seemed lost in a maze of ineffective solutions.* Their misplaced confidence stood in sharp contrast to the chaos they carried. The mention of break time was music to our ears, casually dropped by one of the associates with perfect timing.

On a brisk afternoon, the city pulsated around me as I stepped out of the glass monolith of corporate towers and into the crowded street for lunch. The sounds of traffic blended with the distant hum of conversations drifting from nearby cafés, wrapping the block in a familiar urban symphony. Pulling out his phone, Nephew dialed up Unc—not with a plan, just a need to connect. As he weaved through the bustling sidewalk, he found himself replaying his uncles old tales from the track—stories laced with game, full of unorthodox answers to problems that once felt unsolvable.

Reaching a quieter corner beneath the shade of a tall building, he paused and waited for Unc to pick up. He didn't have a clear agenda—just calling to touch base, not necessarily to ask for advice. They chatted about this and that, and Nephew mentioned the predicament back at the office almost as an afterthought. He was curious about Unc's take, but didn't expect a solution. It was just one of life's little puzzles, shared in passing.

*Well, son Pimpin' ain't easy, but somebody's got to do it," Uncle finally said, his voice deep and resonant, filling the call with a sense of gravity. "Just like in the streets, in the boardroom, you've gotta be sharp, nephew. You gotta see the angles others miss, act when they hesitate, and always, always stay ahead of the game." He paused, letting the words sink in, then continued, "It's about control, about maneuvering with precision and being relentless. It's about **execution**. Whether you managing corners or corporate giants, like I said before, the principles remain the same.*

As the conversation progressed, Uncle shared tales from his past, each story threading through the complexities of street and corporate hustle. Nephew listened, captivated, realizing that the essence of Uncle's teachings was about mastering the art of leadership and strategy, essential for anyone determined to make their mark, regardless of the arena.

Yeah, it definitely ain't easy, but who's gone do it when it got to get done? You? suzie Choosy, or Frida Fluzy. As soon as Nephew asked, "What does that even mean, though?" Unc went in.

So you ask me what does it mean, Aye. When you hear me saying, "Pimpin ain't easy, but somebody's got to do it," understand this—it's not just a slick line; it's a testament to the grind. The game, my nephew, is ruthless and relentless. It ain't for the lazy or the lackadaisical. It's for those with the grit and the gumption to push through when the going gets tough. The real game, the true hustle, it's about persistence, about keeping your eye on the prize even when the odds stack high against you. It's about that steadfast dedication to your craft, to your cause, no matter the storms you gotta weather. You think rain gon' stop a stomp down hoe when the track got stacks on stacks from the front to the back. The lazy ones go home but tricks known to roam, specially on a cloudy day. You betta get that money.

Now, let's talk brass tacks. Persistence, my boy, is what separates the dreamers from the doers. You talk about diving deep into tech, about playing in the big leagues with the heavy hitters of Silicon Valley. But talk's just the start; execution is where it counts. See, talk is the teaser—execution's the feature. If you ain't ready to film, don't rent the theater. You got to transform those sparkling ambitions into solid, tangible outcomes, ya dig. Every mogul you admire, every titan you aspire to emulate—they didn't just stumble upon success. They built it, brick by painstaking brick. They persisted, even when the path was obscured and the climb was steep. And that's what you gotta embrace.

To persist is to command your destiny, to hold the reins of your future so tight that every no, every failure, every fall just fuels your fire further. It's about harnessing that raw, relentless drive that I see in you, that fire that needs to burn past the barriers. Remember, the hardest trials will temper you the toughest, crafting you into a force formidable and feared in any field you forge into.

So, as we chop it up, keep this game in mind: the hustle ain't just about keeping pace, it's about setting the pace. It's about leading with the kind of compelling charisma that can command a room, a revenue stream, or a revolution. It's about that indomitable will that doesn't just aim to play the game but aims to redefine it entirely. So, nephew, wear your persistence like armor and wield it like a weapon. It's a tool that'll carve your name not just in the ledgers of success but in the legends of the game. Persist like real pimpin stepped in a boardroom—sharp suit, sharp game, sharp aim. If life's a pitch, then make 'em buy the name—and that's got ta' come with a hefty choosin' fee.

Persistence is the playful partner of progress, twirling through troubles with a tenacious tango. Picture persistence as a crafty chess player in a never-ending game, where each move is methodical and every setback is a setup for a comeback. This crafty player flips the script on failure, weaving wits and will into a winning streak. Remember, a persistent player plots and plans, then plants their feet firmly in the future they fashion—flowing forward, never faltering. Persistence, in its purest form, is the art of turning the impossible into the I'm-possible, making magic with the mundane, and mastering the marathon of the mind.

"GodZamn Unc, slow down," said nephew. "Sound like you need to keep up," said Unc.

Remember this, young blood, pimpin anything from products, services, hoes, or clothes—that means retail to heaven in a hoe-tail—ain't easy, but it's got to get done. So, who's going to do it? Somebody's got to do it, right? Might as well be you. Let the spectators spectate while you innovate and dominate. 'Cause at the end of the day, it's the ones who push past the pain, who persist with purpose, who reach the peaks.

And that's the real talk—The game ain't for everybody—some preach it, few teach it, only the real reach it. I'll say it again—It ain't easy, but somebody's got to do it. I wanna see if you pickin up what I'm puttin down, nephew, cause' my time is valuable. If you ain't heard nothin' else, tell me what I'm tryin' lay down. In fact give me in two words what it is and what it's gotta be.

Newphew wasted no time. Persistence and Execution, is my muthaph*kn solution. Im'ma make a contribution by going up in thei office and starting a revolution. Let'em know that I got the resolution and then bust this game in they mouths like I got a lock on distribution.

"Hot-damn, the boy's on fiye,' said uncle. I'm hip. They both laughed.

Uncle continued, Knock every sucka up in there for that contract, nephew; make'um choose you. Show them that outsourcing it to your private firm is the smartest move they could ever make. Make'um feel stupid for not doing it. May yuh next move be yuh best move, nephew. Hollah at me later and let me know how it went.

Oh, and nephew, if you serious 'bout stackin' results and not just ideas, you need to soak up—**The 4 Disciplines of Execution** by Chris McChesney, Sean Covey, and Jim Huling, and **Making Ideas Happen** by Scott Belsky—'cause real game ain't just spoken, it's studied, scribed, and applied. That's high-ticket game.

Fuh'sho Unc, said nephew—and in his 'K. Dot' voice from the 'TV Off' song, nephew belted out, "*Pimpin aint easy, but somebody gotta do it,*" just before hanging up.

Four

The Game Ain't Told, It's Bestowed.

The game is to be sold and not told but you already know so hold or fold for the gold.

On a crisp Saturday morning, as the city began to stir beneath the soft light of dawn, Nephew headed to Uncle's upscale downtown condo. He wanted to catch Uncle before he left for his more secluded lake cabin, hoping to discuss a potential motivational lecture for the currency trading collective Nephew headed up. In the plush living room, surrounded by sleek modern decor and floor-to-ceiling windows offering a panoramic view of the city, Nephew broached his idea.

"Unc, could you swing by and give the crew a little pep talk? Maybe explain why it's crucial they keep investing in themselves by sticking with the collective?" he asked, hopeful.

Uncle paused, adjusting the strap of his leather duffel bag, and frowned thoughtfully.

"Time is money, young blood," he began, his voice firm yet affectionate. "The game is to be sold, not told—and Ted got ta get

paid, if you wan't TED to Talk." He walked over to the expansive glass that framed the city's skyline, gesturing broadly.

"You're family, and I'm all about enriching our family trust for generations to come. But the group needs to understand—they need to contribute something, to invest, if they want to reap the dividends. That's how the game goes."

He turned back to Nephew, a slight smile playing at the corners of his mouth. "I'll show you how to make it count. Make a donation to my nonprofit. You can write it off as an expense, and that way, it benefits us all—keeps the IRS happy too."

Nephew nodded, absorbing the layers of strategy Uncle wove into every decision. Uncle chuckled and eased into a leather chair as the morning sun cast long, warm beams across the hardwood floors, highlighting the intricate details of his art collection on the walls—each piece a testament to strategic acquisitions over time.

"Alright, sit down. Let's chop this up proper," Uncle said, patting the seat next to him. As Nephew settled in, Uncle began to unravel his take on

the principles of investment and return, as well as strategic money movement, but first using the time to explain why old players insist the game is to be sold, not just told.

First off, game is never simply told, it's bestowed," it's deeper than what you might think jack—it's about **knowledge transfer** and the value of what's passed down. See, something bestowed? That's a gift, but not just any gift—it's one given to those deemed worthy, to those who've earned it and those who've shown they can handle it. It ain't about just spilling the beans to anyone willing to listen; and not come up or make the necessary investments into themselves—ya know, earnin their seat at the learnin' table. It's about recognizing who's ready to carry the torch, who's ready to run with it.

To bestow is to grant something valuable with a certain kind of ceremony—it's an honor, a privilege. It's like knighting someone in the old days; you don't get the sword just because you show up—you get it because you've shown your worth, your mettle. In our game, knowledge, my boy, is that sword. It's not handed out freely; it's earned, through proving you can handle the weight of it. Money? Sure, it comes in greens and digits, but the real currency in our game is the trust, the respect, and the insider know-how that you can't just find lying around. A billion dollar mentor aint about to just be having coffee and croissants with any ole geek off the street, ya dig.

Now, dig this: selling the game. It ain't just about making a profit; there's a whole other level. The art of persuasion and making believers out of skeptics is the flip side. It's selling ice to Eskimos—convincing them they need what you got, even when they're surrounded by it. That's the supreme game, nephew. It's about presenting the game so slick, so enticing, that they can't help but buy into it. Why would someone entrust their body, their time, or their loyalty to you? Because you've sold them on the idea that the trade is worth more than gold. You've shown them a vision so vivid, so compelling, that they're ready to bet it all on your word. Salesmanship beyond your wildest imagination. That's the true measure of this game being sold.

Spittin' game like a wordsmith, with a mouthpiece like an Uzi fresh out a jacuzzi—now that's a whole different breed of craftsmanship. Craftin' moments, curating experiences, and creating opportunities most folks can't find on their own. Openin' doors they ain't never seen, let alone could open. Making sure that when you say the game is to be sold, not told, it ain't about just selling secrets—you're offering value, building empires in minds before they even hit the ground. I'm talkin' turning your words, your plans, into their dreams, their goals. That's how you get followers, loyalists, believers who will stand by you when the chips are down.

You ever seen the movie Wolf of Wall Street when the guy says, "Sell me this pen?" That's what I'm talking about. You can't just tell somebody; you got to sell somebody. This game here got to be sold, not told. The average cat couldn't sell his wife on having intimate relations half the time so he definitely couldn't sell this game here to a broad in the pod. When you only got three seconds to keep someone's attention who could potentially fund your next enterprise—what they call an elevator pitch—whatchu' gon' say, and how are you gon' say it? If it's me you're talking to, I aint trying to hear you from the jump but if you look like you about something, you got two seconds to spit and it betta be lit. The first second is already gone because your presentation started from the moment I saw you—from the way you look, to the way you cook, I'm usually not impressed. You got to be the world's greatest marketing guru in that moment or times up.

And then their is the obvious, if you tryna' get like me and become a street king with the power to move mountains out a bihh ass, and convert it to cold hard cash, then cash is the culprit. Prove your worth and fill my purse, and I just might bestow the game of pleasure, passion, and pimpin upon a young P'.

On the real though, nephew, remember, knowledge is more than power—it's potential, it's profit, it's promise. But it's also responsibility. You don't spill it and reveal it, you sell it—for a profit and sell it with your chest like a bulletproof vest. You don't just share it—you shape it into something so valuable, they'll line up just to get a whisper. That's the art of the hustle, the essence of the game. It's why we don't just blabber to any ear that listens; we gauge, we judge, we measure twice, and cut once. We bestow our knowledge like a crown, and we sell our secrets like jewels. Cautiously too, it could be a C.I. or double agent you spillin' the beans to.

This here game we're playing, it's what the sharp minds call **intellectual property**, a treasure chest of insights that can flip your whole life script—elevate you to new heights or drop you down low if you mishandle it. It's that potent kind of capital that don't just jingle in your pockets; it jangles in your mind, setting the rhythm for your every move. It's the philosophers stone from **The Alchemist**. Handle it right, and you're crafting a legacy, a dynasty that'll outlast the flashy bling and quick cash. But slip up, get sloppy with your strategy, and that same treasure can turn into a trap, setting you back further than you started. It's all about how you play it, how you protect and project your most valuable assets.

So you asked me how you can spit this game for a hefty fee but make your followers feel like they getting it for free. You wanna bestow this game till ya pockets catch a flame. Alright, check this out: Intellectual property ain't your usual storefront, it ain't bricks and mortar. It's that digital gold—info, media, code, contracts—that lives in the cloud, but weighs heavy in value. Now, in the streets, you might be pushin' tangible products you can touch, but in this high-tech hustle, what you're movin' is invisible assets. This is next level pimping, where your riches don't clink, they click.

Having, keeping, and leveraging intellectual property—that's how you play the long game to wealth. This ain't about making a quick buck; it's about setting up a revenue stream that flows longer than the Mississippi. Think about it like this: you could be slangin' your secret sauce like a subscription—yeah, like them streaming services where folks pay monthly to get what you got. That's passive income, nephew. Money while you sleep.

But here's where it gets slick: copyrights, trademarks, patents. These ain't just fancy legal words; they're tools. Tools that lock down your creations—your beats, your designs, your unique sauces—so nobody else can bank on your hustle without cutting you a check. You lock down your intellectual property right, and it's like planting money trees that keep on giving.

So, if you wanna get rich and stay rich, you wanna get your hands on some of this intellectual property game. You wanna own the blueprint to the money machine, not just the coins that drop out. Real pimp talk, you sell access, not just assets. Licensing deals, royalties, residuals—every time someone clicks, copies, or cues up your work, you're stacking chips. And the beautiful part? It scales. You ain't trading hours for dollars no more; you're earning on every share, every use, worldwide. Why you think pimps go into business for, just to talk shyt and swallow spit alone, no sir, we in it to eat every morsel off the bone.

This is how the smart money plays it. Not just hustling harder, but hustling smarter. Intellectual property lets you control the board without even sitting at the table. Digital assets—game sold—you set it up once, protect it right, and watch it pay off again and again. Look, your game's gotta solve a real problem. That's the entry point. Folks don't care about your ten modules or your fancy workbook—they care about what it's gon' *do* for them. Sell the result, not just the content. That's the difference between pushing info and delivering transformation.

See, it's bigger than just dropping a course and walking off. That's old news. What you're really building is a whole ecosystem—education, brand, and community all working together like gears in a watch. It ain't just "post a course and pray." It's about building something that grows legs, moves without you always being in the room, and still adds value every step of the way.

You got your books, your videos, your PDFs, the workbooks, the quizzes—those are just the tools. Then you elevate that with VIP coaching, group sessions on Zoom, one-on-one access for the high rollers who want your undivided time. That's where the real bread gets baked. And don't sleep on the power of a private community—forums, Slack groups, Facebook circles. Somewhere folks can chop it up, share wins, ask questions, stay plugged in. That's retention, that's culture, that's brand loyalty in real time. Webinars? Man, you should be running those like clockwork. Warm 'em up, serve some sauce, close it down with confidence.

Now here's the money part—upsells. Coaching programs, masterminds, retreats, done-for-you services… all them lanes that take what you started and make it deeper, more personalized, more valuable. And on the back end? Monthly recurring revenue. Memberships, exclusive access, ongoing game. That's that residual bag. And not everybody ready for the big ticket. That's cool. You meet 'em where they at—mini-courses, templates, eBooks. Low friction, high value. That's your downsell. At the end of the day, you ain't just a course creator. You becoming a creator, an educator, a consultant, and a certified authority in your lane. That's how you don't just make money—you make a mark.

speaking gigs, where you just stand on stage and spit game for fifty stacks, imagine that, Jack. This goal to sell intellectual property, it ain't just knowledge—it's power, potential, and your ticket to the big leagues. So, treat it like the crown jewels; every piece you hold could be the key to your kingdom or the lock on your downfall. At the end of the day, if you want to lead, to truly run the game, you gotta be more than a player—you gotta be a kingmaker. And that's the real deal, the true game. It ain't just about having knowledge; it's about knowing how to use it, how to sell it, how to make it so invaluable that they can't help but buy in, all in. Remember, nephew, the game ain't told, it's bestowed—and always, always sold, never told.

Peep game! **Product Launch Formula** is broken down in a book called **Launch** by Jeff Walker. And if you want to position yourself as an expert, check out **Expert Secrets** by Russell Brunson. And if you try'na build demand for your knowledge *before* the product even drops, **Oversubscribed** by Daniel Priestley is a must-read.

For the legal side of things, **Intellectual Property: Everything the Digital-Age Creator Needs to Know** by Aaron X. Fellmeth offers a clear, no-fluff breakdown of copyrights, trademarks, patents, and trade secrets—especially for creatives, entrepreneurs, and digital builders. And **The Entrepreneur's Guide to Law and Strategy** by Constance E. Bagley & Craig E. Dauchy covers all the legal moves you'll need, from forming your business to protecting your IP and navigating contracts with confidence. Awww, and I can't believe, I almost forgot, The Automatic Customer: Creating a subscription business in any industry—by John Warrillow. I just listened to that whole book on Audible, and I loved it.

"Damn Unc, what you some kinda savant or somethin?" How you remember all them book titles like that? said Nephew. Uncle responded with, " Prison Poverty and God are my only fears, so I do what I got to do to keep it pimpin and never simpin.

Five

Come Off The Coin Before You Join

Be apart of something elite and exclusive. This pimpin' euphoric and blissful, them other negus abusive and elusive. Fiscal focus then fun--, prioritize profits and the pleasure gone cum.

*N*ephew and Uncle sat tucked away in a cozy corner of the old Waffle Shack, an eatery steeped in the aroma of fresh coffee and sizzling bacon. As they waited to meet a potential new business investor, Uncle watched Nephew sprinkle salt and pepper on his scrambled cheese eggs, a thoughtful frown creasing his forehead.

"So, is your lady cool with you getting close to this new investor?" Uncle asked, eyeing Nephew with a mix of curiosity and concern.

Nephew paused, his fork mid-air. "Yeah, we're in an open relationship, but honestly, we hardly ever act on it. We're both so wrapped up in our work that we mostly just enjoy each other's company. But this—this could be different. I'm thinking about getting to know ole' girl a bit more... intimately,"

He confessed, the last word hanging between them as the clatter of dishes filled the brief silence. Uncle leaned back, his expression serious as he absorbed Nephew's words.

"Listen, young blood," he began, his voice low and steady over the hum of the diner,

"This kind of decision could cloud things real quick. You're walking into a potentially sticky situation. Always remember, purse first, ass last." He pointed his fork at Nephew for emphasis. "Get the money, secure the investment, and keep it strictly professional until she's proven her value. Don't mix business with pleasure until you know the ground you're standing on is solid. If you tryin to put some of yuh pimpin in her life; she needs to come off that coin before she join, comprende?"

Nephew nodded slowly, absorbing the gravity in Uncle's advice. The air around them buzzed with the sounds of the diner, the occasional sizzle from the kitchen, and the muted conversations of other patrons, grounding the moment in a slice of everyday life.

But soon as you see her, you'll know what I'm talkin-bout Unc, she supah bad, and rich AF.

"Don't be slow, nephew; that purse is all you wanna focus on. Let me school you real quick before this broad show up and spins you sideways like a trick who thinks with his dick.

He leaned forward, his voice dropping to ensure their conversation remained private amidst the clinking of dishes and the low murmur of the diner.

Listen up, nephew, never forget 'purse first, ass last,' it's all about the bread, baby, not the pizzazz. They got to put it in my hand to make me understand. That ain't just some catchy lil Ism—issa creed, a way of life, a doctrine carved in the hustler's handbook long before your granddaddy's granddaddy was trickin' off his first dollar. You gotta secure that bag before anything else. They gotta socket to yuh pocket with the speed of a Space X rocket, ya dig. It's the cost of doing business—call it an **Operating Cost.**

It's the golden rule of the game—you don't get caught up in the honey without first seeing the money. It's 'bout business over pleasure, always. This game? It's commercial, straight up—money drives everything. You put the cash in play before the play gets underway. That's how you keep it all about the bankroll and not about the bedroom, you feel me? I ain't never seen a man lose ass chasin' cash but I seen a lot of men lose cash chasin' ass.

Now for me and my cohorts and consorts, it's gonna mean a little something different than it does for you. This ain't just about gettin' paid—it's about establishing order, setting up your priorities so that the game feeds you instead of you feeding the game. Those that follow my lead got to come off the coin before they join with the fruits of my loin. See, too many fools out here leading with lust, chasing tail instead of chasing treasure, and that's why they end up broke, busted, and disgusted, living hand to mouth, waiting on a break that never comes.

Now for you, when I say "purse first," I'm talking about structuring your life so that financial stability comes before fleeting desires. In business, in investments, in any move you make, your priority should always be securing the bag before entertaining distractions. You ever wonder why some rich folk say if they loose it all they'd make it back—cause they got the mindstate.

You think the CEOs you admire out here making billion-dollar deals worried about happy hour and weekend flings before locking in their next quarter's revenue? No, sir. They managing their assets, making sure their money is multiplying before they even think about indulging. That's what separates bosses from busters—discipline in their decision-making, knowing when to lock in and when to let loose.

This right here is about **Priority Management**—because, nephew, your energy, your time, your focus, and your finances all work together like gears in a well-oiled machine. Mismanage one, and the whole system breaks down. Imagine having a stable and you let one of ya assets catch a free ride, you liable to have chaos in the kingdom.

A real player understands that indulgence is a privilege of the prepared. You don't spend what you ain't stacked. You don't play until you've put in the work. You don't entertain what ain't bringing in gain, cause like the playa potnuh Pimpin Ken say, you got to pay my ransom if you think I'm handsome. Without that coin you get's no groin. This pimpin like a slot machine, you got to drop that spend if you wanna win.

These ain't my rules—this the Pimpin. The Ism is here to keep everything in order. I ain't tryin' to be mean by taxin' but a player got his own operatin cost too. I can't dole out this good game that's gottum' livin like a rockstar if they ain't droppin that coin. If I take the ass first and the purse last, we'll all be out here livin under a bridge drinkin' from a flask.

Operating costs? Pssh, that's just the overhead of the game, nephew. (Unc leaned in, eyes sharp like a calculator dressed in gator shoes.) "See, the pimp game—like any business—ain't just about what you bring in, it's about what it takes to keep that whole show on the road. You got your flash—that's marketing. Gotta look the part to play the part, right? Suits, shoes, cologne that smell like success. But that ain't just flossin'—that's branding.

Then there's your whip, your travel, your phone, your time—all expenses. You payin' for presentation, transportation, communication, and preservation of position. That's operating cost, baby. Even energy is a cost. Mental bandwidth. Emotional labor. If you ain't budgeting for that, you already bankrupt in spirit before you see a dime.

Bottom line? The game pays, but only if you know what it's costin' you to stay in it. And if you don't track what it takes to operate, you ain't runnin' a game—you runnin' from one. So don't just count what come in. Count what it cost to keep it comin'. That's real business. That's real game.

Whether it's business, investments, relationships, or even just daily habits, your money and mind should always be working towards building, expanding, and securing your empire. You know what happens when you focus firstly on ass and put that purse last? You end up chasing broke situations, drowning in debt, stretching your last dollar just to impress folks who wouldn't loan you a dime if your life depended on it. That's how a man finds himself investing in liabilities instead of assets, sponsoring temporary pleasures while sacrificing long-term prosperity.

See, the weak-minded don't understand that discipline today is the price for dominance tomorrow—can you afford it? If you got a hundred dollars and you blow ninety on nonsense, you ain't got a hundred—you got ten dollars and a regret. But if you put that hundred into something that generates another hundred, now you got room to play without ever feeling the pain.

Just then, a young waitress, seemingly new and still adjusting to the rhythm of her duties, accidentally spilled coffee on the table behind them, eliciting mild frustration from the patrons. The diner, filled with the heavy aroma of greasy breakfast foods, buzzed with morning activity.

As the door chimed once again, signaling new arrivals, both men turned sharply, their focus sharpened, ready to engage the potential new investor and nephews new crush with a clear, calculated approach. Their tense readiness eased momentarily as they noticed it was only a delivery man with a hand truck, navigating through the crowded space with boxes of fresh produce.

Nowadays, you youngsters have way too many avenues not to take advantage of. You can make 'em pay your choosing fees across several platforms. You got Patreon, OnlyFans, Substack, and Buy Me a Coffee—even Instagram, Twitter, and YouTube got paid subscriptions that let you charge to choose up across the board and around the clock.

Don't get me wrong, there's a lot of free info out here, and I highly suggest you and all your potnuhs stay learnin so you can keep earnin. There are way too many podcasts that can keep you growing so you ain't got to keep hoeing–on somebodies job that is. They teach you how to become an entrepreneur so you ain't got to stay in the sewer. But be careful, because if you ain't paying for the product, you are the product.

Now, let me lace you with some serious sauce—if the opportunity is elite and exclusive, it ain't free, nephew. You gonna want access? I tell'um, you got to come off the coin before you join. That means investment before enjoyment, foundation before celebration. Ain't no real seat at the table for the empty-handed, and ain't no VIP treatment for the visionless. The price of admission into real success ain't cheap, but the cost of staying broke? That's a tab you don't want to pay.

Peep game, nephew: It shouldn't be hard to understand because sometimes you got to come off the coin too. Investing in yourself for real, don't look like flexing on the 'Gram with money phones alone—it's about coppin' that VIP pass to the knowledge vault. You gotta be willing to drop some serious coin on mentorship and guidance, 'cause that's your direct line to the code book, the cheat codes that can launch you straight into the stratosphere. It's like this: when you pay for the time of someone who's already mapped the stars, you ain't just buying their words, you buying their wisdom, their war stories, their wins and their losses.

You're purchasing a fast track to finesse your own hustle. It's a hefty price tag, but the returns? Out of this world. Even I had to drop some coins on a mentor to help me get my business acumen up. Her name was Joi and she was the prettiest lil thang you ever seen and she put me up on major game. If she wasn't so pretty, I might still be fumbling around in the dark like a cave man trying to figure out my next level of the business game.

Don't shy away from shelling out for that caliber of counsel, 'cause the right guidance doesn't cost you—it pays you, multiplying your investment in ways money alone never could. And when you have it all wrapped up and marinated inside, put a bow on it and let it slide–for a fee–because remember, you got to sell it and not tell it cause it aint free. They gone have to pay you for it first and then y'all can get to generating and celebrating.

Now I'm sure this lil lady friend of your's is a real looker, could be the prettiest thing you ever seen. Get yuh cock harder than a rock. But the lack of self control? When it comes to making decisions from your root chakra versus your crown chakra, it can have you livin' out of a 24 hour gym locker.

'Matter'a-fact—I was just thumbing through **"The Tao of Sexology:** *The Book of Infinite Wisdom"* *by Dr. Stephen T. Chang,* just the other day, and nephew, it had me thinking 'bout you. Should've slung that book your way. You need to cop that **"Semen Retention MONK MODE***: Unlocking the Power Within" by Prana Man,* too, or scoop up any read about holding down that seed. It's all about keeping your juice and stacking your power high. Them books will school you on keeping your game tight and your spirit right.

But all in all, do like the P's say and get that purse first and that ass last, nephew. Make sure they come off the coin before you let'em join yuh fine pimpin program. Because when you handle your priorities right, you ain't got to chase. The game gone find you, respect you, and, best believe, it's gone pay you.

As they spoke, the bell above the diner door jingled again, signaling her arrival. Uncle gave nephew a knowing look, a final nod to cement his advice as they prepared to turn their attention to the woman who could potentially change the stakes. "Real talk, I might have to take that off your hands though nephew,' uncle said with a sly grin just before she sat down.

Goodevening gentlemen, said the smiling woman in the red dress.

Six

If It Don't Make Dollars, It Don't Make Sense

Cash flow confirms the convo so count it up or count yourself out.

*A*s Nephew cruised through the winding roads leading to Uncle's secluded lake cabin, he dialed his uncle on the car phone to give him a heads up. "Hey Unc, just letting you know I'm on my way over to drop off that bread." Money from a play the two of them went in together on. "22 stacks infact, was uncles cut."

The line crackled slightly before Uncle's voice came through, relaxed yet authoritative, "Good to hear, nephew. Just leave it in the trunk of the benzo; I'll be out on the boat catching some of these rainbow trout. Ain't nobody gonna mess with it out here in these woods."

Nephew chuckled, the car's speakers carrying Uncle's confidence smoothly over the hum of the engine. "It paid out pretty good, Unc. Easy twenty grand for me just for a few clicks.

There was a pause, then a low laugh from Uncle. "Reminds me of my gambling days, but with a lot less risk involved." His voice then sharpened with that streetwise sagacity Nephew had come to respect deeply. "Just goes to show, if it don't make dollars, it don't make sense." Nephew added, "I'd rather get strait to the money than foolin around with all them goofies that was trying to get us involved with they shenanigans. How'd you even hear about this play unc? '

The line hummed with the weight of those words, setting the stage for a lesson, bridging the gap between old school hustles and modern-day business acumen.

When you out here in this money game, the rule is simple: cash flow confirms the convo. You gotta count it up or count yourself out, because in this world, profit isn't just a goal; it's the confirmation, the metric—the proof that what you're doing ain't just noise. Most plays, will have you withdrawing rather than depositing. Every move either prints paper or proves you ain't ready cause' you either buildin' interest or stayin' broke paying it. Hell, ain't no point playin' the game if the scoreboard don't change.

See, it's like this: money talks, everything else walks—without it, you might as well be outlined in chalk. You can have all the ideas, all the charm, all the swagger in the world, but if the cash ain't stacking, what are you actually doing? Spinning wheels? Nah, nephew, that ain't the game. The game is about turning every hustle into a profit. It's about making sure that every move, every decision, every risk is calibrated to not just break even, but break banks.

Let's put it straight—every deal you step into, you gotta be asking, 'Where's the dollar in this?' If you can't spot it, then you might be the dollar, and that's a bad look, my man. In this fast-moving world, where everyone's trying to eat, you gotta be the chef, not the dinner. It's about keeping your eyes on the prize and that prize is always gonna be that paper. Because money, nephew, it ain't just currency; it's the scorecard that tells you you're winning. It's the metric that says your electric. Why do you think they call it currency? Because money is energy. It's a current that ebbs and flows.

Imma keep it a stack with you—a whole one thou-wow—cause you my sistas boy and I love you—plus I want you leading with financial freedom. It boils down to one thing, the principles and philosophies surrounding **'Profit Focus.'** Profit focus means keeping your eyes on the prize—those sweet dollars. It's about strategic hustling where every move, every decision is weighed on the scales of potential gain. This ain't about chasing every opportunity that glitters; it's about discerning which moves will fill your pockets without draining your resources.

Think of it like a chess game where every piece you risk should bring you closer to checkmate—the ultimate payoff. In the world of business, whether you're dealing in stocks or storefronts, the bottom line is king. Your goal? **Maximize returns** while minimizing outlays. It's about being shrewd, savvy, and always a few steps ahead. Stay focused on the profit, and you'll navigate through the noise straight to success. **ROI** ain't no lie. Most young men your age aint thinking bout' no return on investment. Everything they touch is a liability. Every woman, every frivolous scroll down a rabbit hole and everything they focus they attention on. Their like energy trick's—trickin' off they energy, focus, and attention on everything under the sun with no return on they investment of time and currency—and they stay energetically broke as a joke.

Now, I see you, you're smart, got ideas about tech, about moh'startups. You bout that flippin' properties and stocks life, or whatever your hustle might be. That's all good, but remember this: each of those hustles needs to turn a profit or else you just playin business man. Lot of brothas' out here playing business and playing house. They play toys and lil boys. You not in this to make friends or impress people with your spend—it's about building empires, stacking assets, and securing futures. Funding trust and policies for generational flow, ya dig. You gotta strategize like a general in the field. Every move has a cost and a payoff. Your job? Make sure the payoff is always heavier.

Invest wisely, negotiate fiercely, and always, always make sure the cash flow is right. This ain't charity; it's capitalism, baby. It's survival of the fittest, and in this jungle, the lion doesn't just need to roar; it needs to eat. You keep your financials tight, your overhead low, and your revenue high. You keep your deals clean, your promises solid, and your deliveries on point.

And here's another piece for you: money is also about momentum. Keep that cash flow moving, and it grows—it's like rolling a snowball down a hill. But the minute it stops, it starts melting away. So, you gotta be agile, sharp, and always ready to pivot. You see a market trend? You jump on it. You see a downturn? You find the upside and exploit it.

Lastly, remember that money is also a tool. It's a key that opens doors, a bridge that connects you to the next big opportunity. Use it to invest in yourself, in your growth, in expanding your horizons. Money ain't just for flaunting—it's for fortifying. It's the shield and the sword in the battle of business. A toolman with no hammer is a fool-man and a bama—got to have yuh tools if you wanna make the rules.

Im'ma keep it one-hundun here. Getting emotionally hitched to any single hustle can lead you straight to the poor-house. It's like this—cling too tight to anything that ain't paying it's way, and you might as well be tossing your dollars into a burning barrel. A smart player knows when to hold, but a wiser one knows when to fold and roll out. This ain't just about pride; it's about profit. Hemorrhaging money on a dead-end deal is worse than bad business; it's self-sabotage.

In my young days, I'd see a P' keep a broad around because he was thirsty for action, knowing full well she was a liability. Up the road when time passed, she wouldn't get knocked; she'd knock him and his whole stable by settin the pig on him. The broad moved like a C.I.—a goddamn agent. You can't be that thirsty for some action that you don't know how to cutt'um loose. Too$hort say, Ill give you a bihh, and would'nt give you a joint and P' Ken say they look betta goin' than they do comin. I say, I approve this message.

Even the Buddha said attachment is the root of all suffering. if you cant release your attachment, whether it's a chick, some money or a deal, then, you're playing yourself. Take, for instance, when you're trading on the Forex or the S&P 500, playing the market like it's Vegas—pushing chips after a little win, doubling down to chase losses—you're setting yourself up for a knockout. Down goes Fraizer. That's emotional trading, nephew, and it's a straight path to having Johnny Knuckles knocking at your door, looking to collect on behalf of your friendly neighborhood bookie. You gotta stay cool, detached, like ice. Wins and losses—they're just part of the game, and the game is all about staying afloat and staying ahead.

Trading in the Zone by Mark Douglas, **The Psychology of Trading** by Brett N. Steenbarger, and **Fooled by Randomness** by Nassim Nicholas Taleb—those are all solid scripts for the mind when it comes to keepin' it right and keepin' it tight.

Here's the real deal—stop while you're up. Count those losses as the cost of doing business. Pivot, adapt, move with the kind of cold calculation that keeps the sharks swimming. You gotta live to hustle another day. It's not about the hand you're dealt; it's how you play those cards. Remember, nephew, never let your heart lead your wallet. Keep your head when those around you are losing theirs, and you'll not only survive, you'll thrive. That's how you play the game smart, stay liquid, and keep stacking that paper.

So, keep this law close, nephew: If it don't make dollars, it don't make sense. Stay hungry, and above all, stay profitable. Because at the end of the day, it's the winners who count their winnings, they not counting losses. Make sure when you talk numbers, they're always adding up to more. Cash flow confirms the convo, so either count it up, or count yourself out of the game.

Seven

Are You a Player or a Payer—A Square or a Sphere?

A player secures the bag while a payer covers the tab. A player flips profits while a payer funds pockets. A player makes the play while a payer pays to stay. I could go on and on till ya game get strong-but I digress, it'll cause me to much stress.

*I*nside the luxurious confines of the suit shop, the air was thick with the subtle scent of polished leather and fresh textiles, setting a high-quality tone all around. At this upscale Italian family-owned tailor shop, it was clear that an arrangement between old friends was benefitting both Uncle and Nephew. Uncle was being measured; the soft clicks of the measuring tape and the gentle rustle of fabric provided a smooth, calming backdrop for an important conversation about to unfold. Uncle subtly hinted, "You're getting a firsthand look at fine tailoring, thanks to an arrangement with an old pal." His friend *was repaying a debt by offering bespoke services, turning it into a learning experience for Nephew.*

*Uncle's gaze swept across the shop to the rows of impeccably arranged suits and the quiet professionalism of the staff. "Now, let's talk about that pretty face who's offering to handle your finances because she's giving you a deal," Uncle continued, smoothing the fabric of his new jacket. "That's a quick fix, nephew. You're setting yourself up to get played. You gotta school yourself first, learn the ins and outs. Then you bring in a heavy hitter—a **licensed CPA**, or even better, an (EA) **Enrolled Agent**. Don't let a pretty face with a slim waist control your bread." First it was the investor, and now it's an accountant.*

He leaned in, lowering his voice for emphasis. "Are you a player or a payer?" he challenged, giving Nephew a sharp look. "Sounds like she's tricking you out of yuh money because she knows you're soft on her. I understand wanting to give new business a shot, but damn." You lucky the investor was solid and you made the right decision and handled it like a champ, but whats up with this new girl? Do you really trust her to handle your books and be all up in yuh numbers.

The soft murmurs up front in the suit shop and the occasional whir of a sewing machines in their section enriched Uncle's lessons on financial literacy and personal responsibility. Each piece of advice was woven into the fabric of their afternoon as tangibly as the suit being tailored to fit—not just Uncle's frame but also his philosophy of self-reliance and strategic foresight.

So dig this: when I ask, Are you a player or a payer?" that's no rhetorical question! What is it that you think I'm asking you, nephew? That's really like me asking you if you are a

'Crediter or a Debtor. Listen up, young blood, as I school you on some real game. You see, in this life, it's only two types of people: pimps and hoes. Essentially, you either a player or a payer, creditor or debtor—ain't no middle ground, ya dig?

Now, a player, that's a man who orchestrates the whole symphony. He's the maestro of his destiny, commanding respect and stacking his paper right. He ain't just participating; he's creating the waves others are just riding on.

Now, a payer, that's them tricks out there. They the ones getting hustled. They come with their wallets wide open, ready to drop stacks on a moment's pleasure. These the cats always coming out of their pockets, spending their hard-earned money chasing after fleeting thrills. They think they's in charge 'cause they got the cash flow, but in reality, what they're really doing is feeding the game. They just fueling the players' rise. They caught up, never really pulling no strings; just loosenin'em.

So you gotta ask yourself, nephew, what's it gonna be? You gonna be a player, master of your fate, making the moves that count? Or you gonna be a payer, caught up in the flash, losing your grip on the green? Remember, every choice you make sets you up as one or the other, it's all about how you play your cards in this grand old game of life.

You look confused nephew like it's flying over your head. Let me slow it down, yet, take it a little deeper. Players always putin juice in the game. They're the **secured parties** securing the bag, not just holding it like a scarecrow or strawman. A real player is the **executive of his own trust** and **sovereignty** over simpin is a muthaphukin must.

A player moves with purpose, with precision, orchestrating every step towards securing that victory. In contrast, a payer? Well, they just keep the game going for everyone else, footing bills and filling others' coffers without ever calling the shots. Real pimpin' play those; they don't pay those—and if you know, you know.

On the flip side, you got your Payers. Now, these cats, they're just in it to pay out. Covering the tab, funding someone else's pockets, but whose pockets? Not their own. They always a step behind, reacting instead of acting. They stay gettin taxed from every direction. They don't read the small print—don't cross they T's and dot they I's. They write O's when it's suppose to be zero's and zero's when it's suppose to be an O.

They're paying to stay in the game, not playing it for the change. They're the ones always catching up, never leading the pack and always being taxed. It's a cycle of spend, not a path to ascend. Now, don't get it twisted; every player pays at some point, but the smart ones turn those payments into platforms. They invest in assets that appreciate, in ventures that multiply, in connections that convert. That's how a player stays playing, not just paying. The game rewards the bold, the brave, the strategic—not those who just stay, pay, and pray. Most folk go broke payin' attention—to the wrong things that is. Always withdrawing it and never depositing it.

Now, here's how you gotta see it: being a player means owning your actions, owning your outcomes. Accountability is more valuable than a platinum Rolex Daytona Rainbow with an ice blue dial, fully encrusted in diamonds. And the cold truth? Some of the so-called richest men alive still can't afford it. Being a Payer? That's a hard road, my man. It's like a steady passivity, letting the game play you instead of you playing the game. Always a step behind, always a dollar short. It's like being in a boat with no oars, drifting wherever the current takes you–just like a damn sheep being herded to the hotel to get at some ho's tail.

In the thick of it all, as the two chose ties and cufflinks to match their tailored suits, the quiet clinks of metal and silk rustling against each other filled the air. Uncle looked at Nephew, holding up a sleek tie. "Think of each accessory like the details in your financial planning," he suggested, tying it back to their ongoing conversation about financial acumen. "Small touches make the biggest impact, just like the right financial advice can define your portfolio's success."

Now if you can pick up what I'm laying down let me lace your crown with some level up sauce, ya dig. You ever heard of Robert Kiyosaki? Yeah, the man who wrote **Rich Dad Poor Dad** and broke down the **Cashflow Quadrant?** Well, that's where the game starts to flip for you. In his book **Loopholes of the Rich**, Kiyosaki drops knowledge about how the rich operate on a whole different level when it comes to money management–which is life management.

He shows you how you can expense most of your daily operating costs, just like a boss, and avoid losing all your bread to the fed. See, the game ain't just about making money—it's about keeping it, protecting it, and using it strategically to build wealth. You cant have every Tom, Dick, and Harry plus Suzie screw screwin' you. People treat you how you let'em and if you lett'em tax you they gone stay taxin you to the wheels fall off.

Then you got Tony Robbins, another heavyweight in the game. In his book **Money: Master the Game**, he lays it all out for you, showing how the rich don't just work for their money—they make their money work for them. He teaches you how to flip the script on your financial situation, and how to leverage everything you got to put you in the driver's seat of your future. This is real life playerhood, where the gettin is good versus being a puppet payer paying it out like only a pawn could.

So, I ask you, nephew, which are you? It's time to decide. Do you want to be the one calling the shots or the one chasing the shot callers? A player don't just participate in the game; they dictate the terms. They're the architects of their fate, the authors of their fortunes—and a payer gone pay like they weigh—every single gotdamn day.

Remember this: every choice you make ain't just about now; it's about setting the stage for what's next. Are you setting up plays, or you just paying dues? It's about leveraging what you know, who you know, and what you're willing to do about it. Invest wisely, play the long game, and flip every opportunity into profit. It's not just about having resources; it's about **resourcefulness**—making more out of less, turning pressure into diamonds.

Remember, a player is proactive; a payer is reactive. Flip the script, secure the future, be the player, not the Payer—cause in this game, nephew, it's all about making sure when the music stops, you're the one with a chair, not the one looking for a chair.

Eight

Mookie and Pookie will Die for the Coochie

A Fools will trade his freedom for fantasy, but real ones play for keeps, not kicks—chasing thrills can cost you real deals.

*N*ephew's phone call came in just as the evening was settling in, his tone a mix of frustration and urgency. "Unc, can you swing by and scoop me? Me and my lady just had it out over something dumb; I just gave her the keys and bounced," he explained, frustration lacing his words. Uncle, never one to shy away from imparting wisdom and sensing the distress, agreed immediately, rerouting and steering his whip toward downtown.

The cause? A nearby couple's argument had spiraled out of control, ending with the guy getting cuffed and carted away by the cops. Nephew and his lady had found themselves caught up, taking sides and clashing over their perspectives on the debacle.

As Uncle pulled up, Nephew slid into the passenger seat, the tension from the argument still palpable—his expression clouded—His voice tense but measured. "Man, Unc, you should've seen it. We were just bystanders, but somehow, it got us going at each other too," he vented, frustration lining his words.

"Man, we were out having a good time, and this couple nearby started going at it, real nasty like," Nephew recounted, shaking his head. "Dude lost his cool and ended up in cuffs. Me and Bae got into it too, picking sides."

Uncle nodded, pulling away from the curb smoothly. "Sounds like you two caught a bad case of **energy transference** to me, nephew," Uncle observed as he navigated out of the neighborhood. "Y'all picked up their spirits, took it into your own energy field like some psychic sponge, and made their frequency your own. That's why you gotta guard your mind."

He glanced over at Nephew, his expression serious. "You gotta learn not to let your emotions play you. Average dudes out here these days, more emotional than their women, letting anger cloud their logic and judgment till they can't see straight—blind to what's ahead—caught up in trivial debates and shyt. Don't fall for that trap. End up doing something stupid, something irreversible."

"That dude you mentioned? Blinded by rage, crashed out over something trivial, I bet." Probably won't even remember what it was this time next year, but his record will. Uncle shook his head as they drove, the city lights blurring past. "Don't ever let yourself get so caught up in nonsense that you forget the real stakes. A real boss wouldn't waste a second on fights that don't pay, fights that could cost him everything over nothing." Loosin it like a damn 8th grader or something.

The car hummed softly as they continued, Uncle's words cutting through the night, a reminder of the higher standards he expected Nephew to maintain.

He glanced over at Nephew, ensuring his words sank in. "Don't be like those fools ready to die over nonsense. You know why they call'em crash-outs, right? That's short for crash dummy; it sounds cooler, but it's the stupidest shyt I've ever heard. Have you ever seen those crash dummy commercials? You do know what happens to the dummy, right?"

As they cruised past the bustling streets, Nephew took in Uncle's advice, feeling the weight of his words and the truth they carried. The ride became a mobile classroom, a sanctuary from the chaos, where real lessons were imparted away from the noise of the world. If anybody knows Unc they know once he gets going, he's off to the races. The conversation that evening went a little something like:

Alright now, let's chop this up real slick, nephew. So you say you was slick petty with ya old lady and started a screaming match like some damn kid's having a temper tantrum. That's what chirren do. To that I say, don't be like Mookie and Pookie 'cause "Mookie and Pookie will die over the Coochie," it's not just about the rhymes; it's about the life lines. It's about understanding how deep the pit of desire can pull you down if you ain't careful.

See, a fool, he trades his freedom for a fantasy, gets caught up chasing skirts till he's buried under the dirt—now that's no way to hustle, nephew. Cats out here gettin' lost in the sauce, trading solid gold for glitter, chasing temporary thrills that lead straight to permanent chills. They lay it all down for a fleeting pleasure, not realizing the real cost until the bill comes due—freedom, fortune, and future all forfeit for a fantasy.

Now, let's get into the real meat of it. Desire and attraction, those some powerful drugs—they pull stronger than gravity and twice as addictive. Let me lace you up with something tight, something right. This ain't just street talk; it's real-life strategy. Desire, my boy, is a double-edged sword. It can cut a path to victory or slice down your chances before you even start.

But here's where the real players set themselves apart: '**Risk Analysis.**' It's about measuring what's at stake, about knowing when the juice is worth the squeeze and when it's just fool's gold. Gotta choose yuh battles. Real hustlers, real moguls—they play for keeps, not just kicks. Ain't tryin' to get tricked out of their fortunes and their freedom. They value themselves, which is more than I can say for someone willing to be a crash dummy. Crashouts feel worthless—like trash. They feel like they don't have any value so they'll throw themselves away for cheap.

Real bosses ain't out here chasing every thrill, either because they know that every foolish fling could cost them a real fortune and their future. They look at the long game, see the big picture. Learn about desire, attachment, and risk analysis—because I know you'd rather dwell in palaces than on the chain gang with hands bruised by calluses, yuh feel me?

Some peoples personal life aint no different, they'll hit anything raw. It's because they don't value themselves—they don't think they're worth anything better. think about it, if somebody give it up to you in under twenty-four hours, they probably gave it up to a hundred others in under twenty-four hours—and you want to hit that raw? Yeah, you dont love yo-self! Be honest with yuh-self, you don't value your body. You don't think your worth anything. You think of yourself as trash, so you risk throwing your future away.

Look here, when you get wrapped up in what feels good now, even if it's that cathartic release of emotions where you just lose control, you risking what could be great later. It's like playing poker with your life's work on the table—you don't go all in on a weak hand just because it's thrilling. Nah, you play smart, hold your cards tight, and bet on sure things. This about being a visionary, not a daydreamer. You gotta detach from them wild desires that lead nowhere but down. Lock in on what truly matters—where the real value lies. Let the peons make life decisions that keep'em squabbling in the dirt with the worms.

Think about it like this: every choice has a cost, every gamble has its ghosts. You gotta ask yourself, is this move gonna lock me up or set me free? Is it gonna build my empire or crumble my castle? That's the kind of thinking that separates the legends from the lost. You gotta strategize like a general in the game of life. Position your pieces with precision, because every misstep on the minefield of desire can blow your whole hustle to high heaven.

Remember, nephew, the game is as much about the thrill as it is about the throne. So while you out there, **calculating risks** and cutting losses, don't forget to savor the sweet spots. The game's got its perks, but only the wise get to taste the true treasures without falling trap to the trifles.

And here's the twist, the real spit: it's about **attachment**, or better yet, the lack thereof. Get too hooked on anything—be it the fast life, easy money, or forbidden fruits—and you'll find yourself a slave to a master that don't care about your well-being. Freedom, true freedom, comes from knowing when to engage and when to walk away. It's about having the wisdom to see beyond the smoke and mirrors, to value what's genuinely worth your time and energy versus being triggered at every lil turn and letting your emotions flood your brain chemistry to blackout then crash out.

See yuh potnuh who you told me about, that tried to off his broad because she was kind to the server at the restaurant and almost had a gun-fight with twelve—now he sittin in jail and the server could be servin his gal well. He was trying to save her, when they she didn't ask to be saved and at the end of the day he was the only one played. He played his-self. See, Mookie and Pookie will die over some coochie, but a real boss? He lives for the legacy, like his wife carrying a pregnancy.

So, keep your head when everybody around you is losing theirs. Play for the prize that promises progress, not just a momentary please. That's how you stay flying high without falling hard. When you find yourself getting in your feels, and letting some emotional shyt get under your skin—walk away, like you did today. Some fools trade the crown for a cocktail and a cheap smile—and wonder why they wake up broke in both pocket and purpose.

Let me drop something heavy on you real quick. I had a lil' sno-bunny back in the day who put me on to this group, Red Hot Chili Peppers. Now before you ask, let me just say, ain't no money like sno money, cause ho' money from a snow-bunny is fa'sho money. I started rockin' with their music heavy. Anyway, the lead singer, Anthony Kiedis, wrote a memoir called **Scar Tissue**—and after reading it, I respected the man even more. He tells his story of fame, fortune, and the deep personal cost of addiction and thrill-chasing. I could liken his journey to so many folks I knew who let the lack of self-control and impulse drive 'em right off the road. But see, Anthony? He was a survivor. He stumbled, yeah—but he fought to see another day.

Now, while we on the subject of books, that low-key changed my life regarding self control, **Anger: Wisdom for Cooling the Flames** by Thich Nhat Hanh—one of my stomp-down gurus—breaks down anger as something to be understood, not feared. He teaches you how to transform rage into clarity, and that, my boy, is power.

And to put the icing on the cake? **No More Mr. Nice Guy** by Dr. Robert Glover. That one's a mirror. It unpacks how all that repressed anger and people-pleasing don't just sit quietly—it builds up, explodes, and can sabotage everything. I've seen bosses on the brink of wild success lose it all behind what they couldn't say out loud, what they couldn't let go, or what they kept swallowing down.

I could go on and on naming celebrities who threw it all away for lack of control—some caught up in murder, others swallowed by drugs and crime. The world was their oyster, and they had it all... until they lost it all, like a forest swallowed overnight by a California wildfire.

Remember, young blood, every move is concentrated prep and a calculated step down the path of your choosing. On some real spit—the book, **'The Twin Elemental Effect'** goes hard into life and timeline trajectories as well as divergent timelines based on decisions made and the people around you who subtly influence some of those choices. Now that book is on some deep 5th dimensional cosmic thinking—I'm talkin' some psychic training where you see all your alternate realities simutaneously in yuh minds eye type shyt, by default.

Look here, don't be like Mookie and Pookie, nephew, lost to the game like a lame, cause they can't see past the now. Fallin' in love like a scrub—puttin' their lives at risk for what they thought was love but really just an attachment to gettin' they stick rubbed. Play for keeps, not kicks and grow in that shyt. Aim for those real deals that make life truly rich, not the cheap thrills that leave you empty without a pot to piss in just three hots and a cot and a cell to shyt in.

Right on cue, Nephew's phone lit up with a text—it was bae, dropping an apology wrapped in a heart and sunshine emoji, like she was tryna send light through the screen. "Brighter days," it read.

"Things are looking up already," said Uncle.

"Indeed," Nephew replied, a small grin creeping in.

Nine

A Player With No Discipline Is Just A Clown With Charisma

Discipline over Disaster cause
Charisma without Control is Classified
as Comedy. That how yuh
life becomes a Dramady—where
punchlines sometimes punch back.

*U*ncle and Nephew stood in front of the old foreclosed building, its facade weathered from years of neglect and the echoes of failed enterprises. This structure wasn't just any property; it carried a history, once owned by an old player from Unc's early day's, who had inherited it from his father way back when. Over the years, it had morphed from a tire shop to a bar, then a restaurant, and other failed ventures.

Each business fizzling out under the weight of mismanagement. The last owner's penchant for trickin' and gambling and his general *lack of commitment to the business essentials—like securing proper financing and understanding credit—had eventually led to its fore-closure.* Imagine that... land passed down through generations, lost to a tax sale, up for grabs by strangers, while the bloodline drifts like dust in the wind.

As they surveyed the property, Uncle turned to Nephew, his expression serious but edged with a hint of opportunity. "See this place?" he began, his hand sweeping over the view of the dilapidated structure. "It's a lesson in what not to do—a testament to the cost of neglect and poor discipline. But it's also a potential gold mine, and that's why I brought you here.

I was thinking about partnering up with you on this venture if we both decide it's a solid move. I value your opinion, and I'm considering whether we should bid on it. You've got a sharp eye for real estate, and you understand the grind.

He paused, allowing the gravity of his proposal to sink in. "Say less," *said nephew. Uncle continued. "This building could be a money pit or a major payoff, depending on how it's handled. The previous owner tricked off and gambled away his chance, distracted by everything but his business—yep, full of potential but lacking the discipline to harness it.*

He gambled away more than just money; he gambled away opportunity." Uncle's voice held a mix of disdain and sympathy as he continued, "We here because I want you to learn from his mistakes.

As Nephew listened, he pondered the weight of the building's history and Uncle's words grounding him in the reality of what it took to succeed in business. As they prepared to delve deeper into the building, exploring its potential and its pitfalls, the lesson was clear: success wasn't just about seizing opportunity; it was about maintaining discipline and focus, avoiding the distractions that had doomed its previous owner because as L. Boog once said, it ain't bout what you cop—it's about what you keep.

Nephew processed intently, understanding the dual nature of the opportunity in front of him. It wasn't just a chance to invest; it was a potential turning point in his relationship with Uncle—a partnership that could define their future endeavors.

Staring at dust piles, peeling paint, and scorch marks where fires had clearly raged, the two of them stood in quiet thought, imagining the potential this place still held. As Uncle continued lacing the air with game, he circled back to one of his favorite themes: how lack of discipline'll rob a man blind, even when the opportunity's right in front of him. Uncle went on.

I remember that fool was tryna be a player back when he was attemptin' to run an after-hours players joint. Not gon' cap, it was actually a nice lil spot—how y'all say—lit, yeah, it was lit. I peeled plenty-o-pussycat and beat plenty playa's out they trap right at a pool table that sat right where you standin'. I tell yuh the truth, A player with no discipline is just a clown with charisma.

See, in my line of work, you had to have your emotions in check and your business tight. If you was wildin' out, not keeping a cool head, things get messy fast. That's losing control, and that's when the whole operation can flip on you. Discipline keeps you in charge, keeps the game smooth.

When you ain't disciplined, you just askin' for trouble. You make one bad call, and it's like leaving your door unlocked in a shady neighborhood. Other players, the cops, anyone looking to take what's yours, they see that weakness. If you aint sharp and alert, you get played. You want to last in this game, you gotta think long term. Discipline is what makes sure you ain't just a flash in the pan, here today and gone tomorrow. Ruled by your lowerself and the worse version of you. It's about managing your money, your people, and your moves with strategies on top of strategies. No discipline means no plan, and no plan means no future.

You'll phuk around and find out the hard way. Once the game turn on you, you shyt outta luck 'cause your reputation is everything out here. It's your currency. If the streets see you can't control your setup, can't keep your team in line, yuh story strait, and your brand consistent, they won't respect you. Discipline earns you your respect, and respect is what keeps you in play. Lose that, and you're just another wannabe. End up looking like a pimp named nature boy—and you got to say the whole thing like a tribe called quest.

Lastly, nephew, this ain't no game for the foolhardy. Every step you take, every move you make, got potential risks. Discipline's what helps you weigh those risks, decide when to hold back and when to strike. Without it, you're just gambling with your life, your money, and your freedom.

As far as charisma, that's that spark—that shine, that makes you the cat everyone wants a piece of—that It factor. But charisma alone, without the solid backbone of discipline, is just a flashy car with no engine—it looks good sitting there but ain't going nowhere like a wig wit' no hair. Discipline is what keeps you on the straight path when temptations are throwing block parties on every corner. It's the **mastery of self**.

Real talk. It's like watching a high-wire act with no net, all dazzle and flair, but one slip and the whole show comes crashing down. Discipline, that's the chain that links the charm. It's the grind behind the glamour from Compton to Alabama—it's the power behind the throne. You got dreams of hitting it big, playing with high stakes? Well, discipline is your ticket to the big leagues. Without it, you're just another wanna-be with wishful thinking.

Don't be like most young men outcheah today nephew, they more emotional than disciplined by far. They more emotional than woman, letting anger, and jealousy and envy rule their path. A man with no self control is a man that can be manipulated and enslaved as easy as takin' candy from a baby. You can trick him out of his freedom quicker than you can pull yuh pecker out and take a piss nephew. Trick him out of his property, his money, even his ole lady. Have his kids callin' you daddy.

As they stepped inside the dimly lit hallway at the back of the old building, the echo of their footsteps and discourse blended with the creak of floorboards, creating a poignant soundtrack to their inspection. Rays of sunlight pierced through cracked windows, casting shadows across the faded tiles—a stark reminder of the building's former glory and the dormant potential waiting to be awakened. every part of the building brought up thoughts and themes of the conversation at hand.

Lookin' round this place I can't help but think about ole charlie behind the bar grinnin, full of life, in it to win it. "Now, picture this," said Uncle: "You're in the game, heavy, playing to win big. Charisma might get you in the door, get you noticed by the big players, the shot callers, but what then? If all you got is a smile and a smooth talk, you find yourself playing in the minor leagues forever. But strap on discipline? Suddenly, you not just playing; you're dominating."

"You might even find your self on the verge of a deal, the kind that could set you up nice, but then comes the temptation—fast cars, fast company, faster falls. That's when discipline steps in, pulls you back from the edge, keeps your eyes focused like a lazer beam. Charisma plus Discipline means showing up every day, ready to hustle, ready to conquer. It means having a plan and the persistence to stick to it, no matter the noise around you. It's what it is when the motivation tank on empty.

Here's the formula nephew. Listen closely! Motivation will get you started but then you got to tap into your discipline after the motivation is gone long enough to turn it into a habit. Then you won't need discipline or motivation as much, because it becomes second nature. It becomes crystalized as a lifestyle, what ever it is—workin' out, eatin right, spittin game like a beast. You remember those three steps—motivation, discipline, and habit, you got a foundation for manifestation.

Discipline is that middle point, that hill you got to get over aint about dodging disaster; it's about designing destiny. It's the daily decisions that dictate direction—do you fold under fire or fortify your future? It's the anchor that turns flashy into formidable—that turns potential into power. Oh-Noo, It ain't about killing fun at all, nephew; it's about keeping focus. Cause in this game, **the distracted get detracted, and the calculated get elevated.** Do I need to repeat that?

Think of it like this, nephew: every boss and every mogul you respect—they got that ironclad discipline. It's waking up with purpose, controlling those impulses that lead to chaos, and focusing on long-term goals over instant gratification. It's about being a master of self, not a slave to the moment.

But here's the real game—when you combine discipline with charisma, you become unstoppable. Your hustle turns ice-cold, and your game's razor-sharp, player. You're not just slidin' in the room—you're steppin' up, takin' charge, and makin' it known exactly who runs the show. You're the type who doesn't just make moves; you make history. That's the key difference, understand? Charisma draws 'em in, but discipline holds 'em tight, makes 'em stay, makes 'em pay, and keeps 'em wantin' to play.

In the back room, remnants of a tire shop still lingered in the air, thick with the scent of dust, rubber and oil, tangible reminders of past enterprises. Nephew ran his hand along the dusty workbench, its gritty texture sparking staining his fingers with dust and oil—still visualizing the space transformed, bustling with new life and purpose.

"I stay on point. Got to, said Uncle," I keep my mind sharp and reading is one of the tools I use to do it—thats why I'm always suggesting books for you nephew. In fact, regarding this pit here, one of my favorite books is **Can't Hurt Me** by David Goggins—he preaches that lack of discipline is the fast lane to regret. It's a mindset war manual, plain and simple. And **Atomic Habits** by James Clear? That's the number one go-to when you need a mental tune-up on the subject. Solid game, no fluff.

Always remember, it ain't just about havin' charm; it's about having the chart to navigate the stormy waters. It's **discipline or disaster,** nephew. Charisma without control? That's just comedy, and the last thing you want is to be a joke. Discipline is your secret weapon—use it to sharpen your charisma, turn your sparkle into a steady flame. Let it not be said that a player like you ever played himself by lacking the grip to hold onto the game.

Keep your game tight and your plans tighter. A real boss moves with purpose and precision; they know that while the crowd loves a joker, the bank respects the calculated. So set your sights, line up your shots, and remember, a player with no discipline is just a clown with charisma, and nobody's paying top dollar to see a clown run the circus. Keep it classy, keep it controlled—discipline, that's your true show of force.

Ten

Hook Up or Get Shook Up. Can't be Scurrd.

You can Link with this Game or Sink in Shame—Align or decline; the Choice is Always Yours.

The ballroom shimmered under an ornate chandelier, golden light reflecting off polished floors and velvet drapes. It was an elegant space, but tonight, it served as an audition hall where ambition clashed with entitlement. Nephew sat with Uncle, surveying the dancers—some dazzling, some lackluster, and some acting like they were doing him a favor by showing up.

Perfume, heated stage lights, and anticipation thickened the air. This was no casual gig. Nephew envisioned a bachelor party that felt cinematic—recreating moments from his closest friend's life with dancers who could blend movement with performance. But instead of professionals, he was getting lateness, attitudes, and distractions. This bachelor party was being filmed as a pilot to a docuseries and being entered into a film festival. On top of that, whoever was chosen would get paid top dollar and have consistent work.

At the break, he made his way to the refreshment table, where coffee steamed beside a tray of untouched pastries. Uncle was already there, sipping his cup with effortless calm. Nearby, some of the dancers giggled and snapped selfies, oblivious to the business at hand. Nephew set his cup down, arms crossed. "Let's be clear. Y'all here to work, or to waste my time? He asked. 'Cause if it's the second one, grab a muffin and bounce."

Uncle chuckled, shaking his head. "Now that's what I like to hear," he said, his deep voice carrying authority. "See, a lot of y'all think looking good is enough. That's like a rapper thinking a chain makes him hot. Or a hustler thinking a pack makes him a boss. Nah, baby. You gotta bring more than expectation—you gotta bring yuh A-game."

He gestured around the grand room. "This ain't amateur hour. This is a business. And y'all showing up like customers instead of competitors. I'm trying to put you on. But what y'all doing? Acting like you already made it. Let me tell you something—made women don't act entitled, they act valuable."

Nephew nodded. "Value ain't in being the loudest, showing up late, or rolling your eyes. This is an opportunity. A chance to be in front of real people, on real footage, with real potential. But instead of seeing the bigger picture, y'all caught up in petty nonsense."

Uncle chimed in, "And that's how you get shook up instead of hooked up. The game favors those who know how to move in it. You wanna be chosen, but you ain't positioning yourself to be a choice. The bag don't chase you—you chase the bag."

He smirked, watching their faces shift. "Ever notice how the ones who really got it together don't do all that extra talking? They come in, handle business, and leave an impression. Meanwhile, the loudest ones be the first to go when they realize looks ain't enough."

Nephew leaned in. "Y'all wanna be professionals? Start moving like it. I can fill this roster with women who see the vision. And if I gotta replace folks, I won't lose no sleep." Uncle set his cup down, brushing off his blazer. "Now, y'all got a choice—hook up, meaning lock in and act like you want this. Or get shook up, meaning stay in your feelings and get left. 'Cause one thing I can promise you—this train is moving. Whether or not you on it? That's up to you."

The silence that followed wasn't uncomfortable—it was clarity. Nephew scanned the room, already knowing who got it and who was stuck in ego. This wasn't about the best dancer—it was about who was serious, and after this break, that's exactly what he'd be watching for.

Later, after the spectacle wrapped up and the choice talent was selected, Unc and Neph took their time organizing the space—sweeping, putting tables back, and chopping it up about the day's events. One of the chosen talents decided to hang back and help reorganize the space. You could tell she was sharp—probably looking to gain an advantage over the rest by sticking around to soak up some extra game.

She looked over at Unc and asked, "What did you mean by that little talk earlier?" Nephew chimed in with a smirk, "Yeah, Unc—what was you talkin' 'bout?

I told them, "Hook up or get shook up," because they needed to know it ain't just about making connections; it's about making the right ones. It's about linking arms with the game, or watching your dreams wash down the drain. It's your play, your call. You either roll with the winners or you stall with the sinners.

When I was out in them streets, nephew, I'd ride beside the baddest trade on the blade and say: *Look here, baby, you either hook up with a winner or get shook up by a beginner—'cause this game don't wait for no late learners. You can ride first class with a boss or get lost and tossed in the sauce with these lames, but understand one thang: elevation ain't free, and hesitation ain't cheap. Choose wisely, cause in this life, you don't get no second chance to make a first-class life. Then I'd yell—You betta Hook up or get Shook up,* and peel off with nothing but my dust in the rearview.

In this grand hustle, it's all about alignment. Like gears in a luxury watch, you gotta mesh smooth or you grind to a halt. Think about it—every big player who ever set the streets on fire didn't just slide in by chance. They chose their shots, picked their partners like a master chef picks herbs—carefully, deliberately, perfectly. The gods in the game, I'm talkin strait up deity status run compatibility plays from a whole other level—I mean everything from human design to astrology and then some.

Truth be told, it's really all about **'strategic alliances.'** This game, this dance of destiny we're all stepping to—it's played best when you're in sync with those who can enhance your rhythm and reach. Think about it, nephew: strategic alliances are the power plays that transform good hustlers into great ones. They are the master moves that make kings out of knights, elevating every endeavor from mere motions to monumental milestones.

You got to invest in relationships that return more than they take—connections that compound your capital, both social and economic. Sometimes you gotta put ya pride aside and know when to ride—knowin' when to lead and when to follow. Being part of something bigger, badder, and better than you could ever be on your lonesome is the key. It's about finding your tribe, your crew, the squad that complements your strengths and compensates for your weaknesses.

When you align strategically, you're not just adding names to your Rolodex; you're crafting a coalition, a united front where every member brings something unique to the table. This ain't about collecting contacts; it's about curating comrades who bring competence, courage, and capital to your cause—the power network, yuh dig.

That's the difference, nephew. Are you networking up, reaching out to those who can elevate your game? Aligning with the architects of industry, the princes of powerplays. Or, watching yourself decline with the do-nothings, the dream-talkers who never walk the walk. It's about synergy, not just sitting pretty in someone's shadow—or in a place where there ain't enough light to even cast shadows at all.

Now, I ain't just spitting game for the thrill of it. This is survival of the fittest, and you gotta be fit to fight. This is the fast track, the world blade nephew, and if you ain't sprinting, you're sinking. Aligning yourself with the movers and shakers, the legit bread-makers, means you're setting up for the high stakes. See, in this game, your network is your net worth. If you the fifth fool in line, behind four fools who ain't got a pot to piss in, guess who else ain't got a pot to piss in. Who you linked up with dictates how you level up—or whether you do at all. You betta get out that line and find a line with some bosses in it so you can be the fifth.

Now on the real, peep game. Mentors, nephew, are your GPS through the maze of success. They are the seasoned captains who's charted and sailed these turbulent rough seas before, mapping out the currents and the cliffs so you can steer clear of shipwreck. Having a mentor is like having a treasure map in a world where most are digging blindfolded. They lend you their hindsight, foresight, and insight, so your sight doesn't come at the high price of blind trial and error. Sometimes the right mentor is worth more than twenty stacks.

Their role is crucial. Mentors infuse your hustle with wisdom, guiding you through the clutter with seasoned advice. More than just educators, they ignite your ambition and mold your resolve into something formidable. They push you to surpass your limits and tackle your flaws head-on. They possess the cheat code to the game. With a mentor, you access a wealth of knowledge that shields you from costly blunders and needless wanderings. They simplify the complexities of the game, offering shortcuts and tactics that speed your progress. They're more than teachers—they're agents of change, turning potential into prowess.

Cherish these mentorships, young king, with the dedication of a scholar and the devotion of a warrior. In this strategic game of life, a mentor's wisdom is your prime asset. Let their teachings elevate you and their insights embolden you. With their guidance, you're not just on a path—you're constructing a superhighway to greatness. The right mentor and the right network is like rocket fuel to the cosmos. They have the key's to open the floodgates to opportunity. Just make sure your situation is filled with integrity 'cause you don't want to end up in one of them after the after party type mentorships if you catch my drift. End up with a missing organ or missing virgin hole.

If you been paying attention, every choice to connect is a chance to construct your castle or your cage. Choose wisely who holds the keys. You gotta vet your allies like you vet your strategies. It's about discernment, about seeing beyond the bling to the brains, beyond the swag to the substance. And here's the raw, uncut truth: sometimes you gotta walk alone rather than run with the wrong crowd. It's better to build your empire solo than to lay foundations on quicksand with the shady or the shaky. Align or decline, that's the mantra. Hook up with the solid, the sure, the steady. Ditch the dodgy, the dicey, the dubious.

Hooking up in this game is crucial, but only if it's the right hook-up. The streets are littered with tales of those who got shook up 'cause they got hooked up wrong. Choose your allies like you choose your battles—strategically, selectively, successfully.

If you're lookin' for a blueprint, crack open The Third Door by Alex Banayan, then slide into one of my personal favorites, Never Eat Alone by Keith Ferrazzi—two powerhouse plays for any youngsta ready to climb from the curb to the penthouse. These pages break down how access, alignment, and authentic connection can put jet fuel in your hustle. Stack that with Your Network Is Your Net Worth by Porter Gale, then lace it up with the timeless OG How to Win Friends and Influence

People by Dale Carnegie. That's a four-card spread to have you suited, booted, and steppin' through doors like you own the building.

Remember this: Your choices are your chains or your wings. Hook up right, rise high. Make the wrong choice and that's on you. You might get shook up. The game waits for no one, and neither should you. Link with the best and phuk the rest. You'll soon learn that, It's always a treat when real players meet. So always align with the aces in sanctified spaces, rise with the rulers, and let the suckas sink in the shadows. That's how a real boss plays it, not just to survive the game, but to own it, win it, and run it.

Eleven

Pimpin' ain't a Position, It's a Disposition.

Ain't no timecards to punch and no middle management; we self-made, self-paid, and self-sustained—this ain't no nine-to-five; it's a 24/7 grind and state of mind.

T he upscale high-rise condo downtown buzzed with a casual kind of luxury, the kind that felt almost... normal now. Nephew leaned against the kitchen island, posted up with his lady, both of them half-heartedly digging through the fridge—looking for something that probably wasn't even there. Meanwhile, Unc was kicked back in the recliner, a foreign beer sweating in his hand, soaking in the whole scene like he owned the view.

The thing is, Nephew thought he had cracked the code—left the rat race but kept one foot in, running his businesses while holding down his corporate gig. Security from the check, power from the hustle. But what he really built? A prison with two sets of keys.

At first, it felt like the perfect setup—money flowing, stability meeting ambition. But that security came at a price: late nights, early mornings, deadlines clashing with business demands. Two worlds pulling him apart, and the only thing slipping through the cracks? His peace, his family, his time. Some evenings, he drags in, exhausted. His kid holds a basketball, eyes hopeful. His woman scrolling, tired of eating dinner alone. But Nephew? He ain't got nothing left to give. Drowning in his own success—burnt out, missing moments money can't buy.

Unc pours up a drink and lays it down plain: "You ain't built a business, you built a job with no clock-out button." Nephew looks up, confused. "You thought you bought freedom, but you just switched masters. Used to be the company—now it's your clients, your deadlines, your own damn expectations. You ain't running your business, your business running you. That ain't bossin', that's bondage."

Relying on a job for security is an illusion. People stay trapped in the "Rat Race" because they chase a paycheck thinking it's safety, not knowing that real security comes from owning assets—things that make you money whether you clock in or not. A job can vanish overnight—companies fold, restructure, or cut you loose without warning. Employers pay you just enough to keep you showin' up, but never enough to set you free.

The room goes quiet.

*"You wanna get free? You gotta do what real bosses do—**automate, delegate, elevate.** 'Cause money that don't move without you ain't wealth, it's weight. And right now, nephew, you carrying too much.*

Wifey grabs her purse. "On that note, I'mma head to the store."
Nephew leans back, nodding slow. He knows Uncle's right. And
that's when an old pimp starts to lace the brain with some real game.

You ever seen a lion clock into work—lil nukka? At 6'2,
nephew looked over at Unc's five foot seven frame and chuckled. Unc continued. Ever seen a shark ask permission before it
swims? Nah, 'cause nature don't punch no timecard. Predators
don't wait for a green light to go get what's theirs—they just
move. That's the difference between the ones who lead and the
ones who follow. You don't do this; you are this. Pimpin'—and
I don't just mean street game, I mean the mentality of independence, power, and control—isn't about what you do, it's about
how you move, think, and operate.

Ain't no supervisor watching over your shoulder, no quar-
terly review to tell you if you doing good or bad. This ain't
no nine-to-five, nephew. This is 24/7, 365, rain or shine. You
either self-made, self-paid, and self-sustained, or you another
cog in somebody else's machine, waiting for them to decide
when you eat. And the ones who truly understand this? They
ain't just out here working the game—they are the game.

Now, let me bust it down for you. Workers need structure,
rules, a schedule. They wait for payday like it's the finish line,
not realizing the real race is for ownership, not wages. But
when you built like this, you don't wait to get paid—you make
sure the money chases you. You're not surviving off a check;
you're thriving off what you create, control, and collect.

This ain't about a title or position; it's a disposition—a state
of mind that don't shut off just 'cause the sun go down. If you
gotta be told to grind, if you need somebody to light a fire

under you, then you already behind. The real players don't need motivation 'cause the hunger lives in 'em. A man with a job who recognize he wasn't born to pay bills and die; who leverages that job for a higher purpose whether to take care of his family, or as a means to an end or maybe his job is his first investor to a master plan is a wise man.

Employees follow, but entrepreneurs lead. If somebody else cutting your checks, they also deciding your ceiling. Bosses don't wait; they create. No disrespect to workers because you got to follow in order to learn the game of how to lead. That's the only place it's taught. You'd be out of touch if you couldn't relate from a genuine place.

Game recognize game, but it also recognize gaps. I had this young 'P', thought he had everything figured out. Had some charisma, had a mouthpiece, but he still moved like an employee. See, he got into a situation where he let somebody else dictate the terms of his hustle—was waiting on another man to put him on, give him the ame and the green light to shine. And what happened? Soon as that opportunity dried up, so did his money, his confidence, and his so-called "business."

That's why I had to sit him down and let him know—if your whole game depends on another man's structure, you ain't a boss, you a pawn. That ain't no independence. That's waiting on permission to be great. Before you know it, yo ho's will be on payroll or knocked until you end up ho'less and doughless.

Let's flip it into some real-world game. Say you slangin' on the blade—whatever your product is, whether it's street or store-bought, you gotta control your supply, set your price, and make sure demand never dies. If you ain't running it, if you just working for another plug, you're just another hustler with a middleman problem. That's not sustainable.

Now take that same mindset to business. You wanna be the owner, not the operator. Owning the team and playing on the field are two different jobs. If you running a clothing brand, a restaurant, a consulting firm—it don't matter. If you still clocking into your own business, still handling every small detail like a worker instead of delegating, automating, and expanding, you're still in a position instead of a disposition. If you ain't controlling your time, then your time is controlling you. Kiyosaki calls it the cash flow quadrant.

Bosses don't build businesses just to have another job. They build systems. The ones who don't? They end up burnt out, wondering why their so-called empire feel more like a never-ending shift. Take note when I tell you young man, **systems and models** is where it's at.

A real boss ain't outcheah **micromanaging** every little move—he's setting up the play so it runs without him. Hustling ain't about being busy; it's about being efficient. The difference between grinding and growing is simple: automation. If you gotta be present for every dollar that comes in, you ain't running a business—you just built yourself another job.

I had another young hustler come to me, frustrated. Said he was making money but felt trapped—couldn't step away without everything falling apart. I told him straight: "If your business crumbles when you step away, you didn't build a business, you built a burden." That's when I put him up on game—systems and models, mane. The sharpest players in the world don't just work hard, they work smart. And if you really on some mastermind shyt, you let the system do the work while you focus on the next move. It's like having a gang of robotic bottom Bee's keeping everything running smooth.

Tim Ferriss touched on this in *The 4-Hour Workweek*, but the game been preaching this long before the bookstores caught up. The real winners got businesses running like a self-cleaning oven—tight, efficient, and automatic. That means delegation, automation, and replication. "A proper model runs like a well-laced track—every piece in place, every step smooth, no stumbles."

Think of your operation like a trap house versus a Fortune 500 company. A trap is always hands-on, always needing someone there to manage it. But a corporation? The CEO might be on a yacht while his system is making money in every time zone. "Smart hustlers don't chase checks, they create machines that print them on autopilot." That's the difference between playing the game and designing the game.

You build a model so every move is repeatable. If you selling something, don't just sell it—systematize it. Set up the blueprint so the next play runs smoother than the last. A well-built model makes every play repeatable—turn one win into ten without breaking a sweat. We call that **10X.**

Whether it's real estate, e-commerce, consulting, or whatever lane you moving in, you got two choices: build a business that owns your time, or build a business that gives you time. One keeps you on the block and on the clock, the other keeps you in control—and control? That's the real flex.

Pimpin' Ain't Just Money, It's Mastery. I'm talking power moves nephew. See, when you truly living by this mindset, you ain't chasing short wins—you playing for long-term control. You ain't just flipping money; you building something that pays you even when you ain't working. Investments, ownership, licensing deals—real wealth comes when your money works harder than you do—even when you're asleep.

A smart man ain't just trying to own a product; he's trying to own a market. He ain't just trying to sell a service; he's trying to own the lane that service operates in. If you still thinking like a worker, you thinking small. Real bosses don't ask for a piece of the pie—they figure out how to own the bakery.

When you move like that, it's a lifestyle. A pimp, a hustler, hell even a celebrity don't stop being what they is when the clock strikes five. Ain't no breaks, you own all day every day. You don't get no days off from being who you are. Ain't no vacation from dominance. This mindset ain't a switch you flip when it's convenient; it's a rhythm you move with, a code you live by. When you really in the game, you ain't thinking day-to-day, you thinking legacy. You eat, sleep and breathe this shyt. When you love it, it's not even work no more, it's just your life.

And the ones who understand that? They ain't just players, they ain't just hustlers—they're architects of their own destiny. While everybody else punching clocks, waiting for somebody to tell them when they can live, you already out here setting the price on your own time. And that's the difference between being in the game and owning the game. It aint on yuh, it's in yuh.

Twelve

Stay Three Steps Ahead or get Played Instead

Pimping is chess, not checkers. From anticipation to congratulations, majesty gone trump tragedy every time.

Nephew slumped into the chair across from Uncle, frustration written all over his face. He ran a hand over his sweaty head, let out a sharp breath, and shook his head like he was trying to shake off the lesson he already knew was coming.

"Man, Unc, I thought I had it lined up perfectly. This was supposed to be a super come-up, my first big move of the year. Dude came through talking big money, big promises—said he had connections, said he could put me in position. Everything sounded right, the numbers made sense, and I ain't wanna miss out. So I jumped."

He exhaled, looking down at his hands like the whole situation was sitting there, slipping through his fingers.

"Next thing I know, the paperwork don't match the pitch. He got what he wanted, but I'm the one left scrambling. My name on the contract, my money locked up, and I ain't even got full control of what's supposed to be my own damn business. Now I gotta figure out how to untangle myself from this mess before it gets worse."

He leaned forward, rubbing his temples, and his voice dropped lower, like he wasn't sure he even wanted to admit the next part.

"And it ain't just that, Unc. My boy? The one who brought me in? He knew. He knew dude was on some slick shyt and still pushed me into it. Probably got his cut and dipped, 'cause now he ain't answering my calls. I ain't see it coming. Thought we was solid, thought I could trust him. Now I see I ain't been playin' the game—I been getting played. Imagine that, this ain't like me."

He looked up at Unc then, searching for something, maybe a way out, maybe just a little wisdom to make sense of how he ended up in the position he was in. Unc let the silence sit for a second, let the weight of his words settle. Then nodded, leaned back in his chair, and laced his fingers together.

"Alright, nephew. Let's talk about chess."

This chess, not checkers, son. You gotta be a visionary in this game, seein' moves before they're made, anticipating the play before the players even get their pieces in place. It's about making moves that set you up for the win while everybody else still figuring out their openin' play.

In the game of life, especially in the streets, it's all about staying three steps ahead, or you might as well consider yourself played. This ain't just about surviving; it's about thriving, about making sure every move you make is calculated, like a grandmaster in chess who already knows his win before the pieces touch the board. You gotta be like that—anticipating moves, predicting counters, and settin traps where others think there's an opportunity.

Here's where it gets real. If you react, you late. If you anticipate, you'll be great. The same way a chess master anticipates his opponent's moves, a true hustler anticipates market trends, whether it's the blade, the block, or the warehouse shop. Changes in consumer behavior and economic shifts gone always hit, and that's a fact, Jack. He who aligns his business strategy to not just survive but thrive is a man who's hella wise. He's not reacting; he's anticipating, adjusting, advancing, with moves so calculated, it's like playing chess with time itself.

A real boss sees five years ahead while lames can't even see tomorrow. And when all the pieces move according to plan, when the permits clear, the credit lines open up, and the foundation is solid—then comes the sweet payoff. You transition from the grind to the growth, from beans and rice to steak, from survival to success.

Anticipating the win aint just a skill, it's a survival tool, especially when the streets are your office. In this high-stakes game, if you ain't three steps ahead, you're falling behind—simple as that—if you ain't early, you late. Some call it 'Productive Paranoia.' There's even a book called Only the Paranoid Survive, by Andy Grove. See, nephew, a certain level of paranoia can be advantageous, promoting preparedness and resilience in both personal and professional contexts.

But I know you're wondering—how do you anticipate in a world where loyalty is always in question, and the game is perpetually shifting? You observe, you learn, and you strategize.

Every interaction is a lesson, every outcome a textbook to be read and studied. Not just the play, but the players, not just the hustle, but the hustlers.

Picture this, nephew. Back in '84 on them neon-lit nights in the city, I was in Manhattan and thought I was the king of the concrete jungle. Every step I took was calculated, like a grandmaster plotting his way through a championship match. See, in the game, just like in chess, you gotta think long-term—anticipation is your best ally, and foresight, your fiercest weapon.

Let me paint you a scene to show you the street smarts behind the strategy. Imagine hustling on the blade, where every move could mean profit or peril. There was this one night when the whole vibe was crisp and charged like the air before a storm. I had my eye on expanding my situation like every good P should, bringing more assets under my guidance, turning small-time operations into an empire that spanned the globe.

Now, here's where chess comes in. I wasn't just looking to make a quick turnout; nah, I was setting up a dynasty. For that, you need a strategy—three moves ahead, always. My first move was to scout the landscape, identify the key players and the potential allies and threats—ya know, clockin' for the knockin' so I sent my best broads out there to preach the gospel of my program. This is like your pawns moving forward, creating a structure, protecting the king, and controlling the center of the board. I had so many on one blade all pettling the same stories twenty 24/7.

The second move—developing relationships with local businesses, greasing palms where needed, and ensuring the streets respected my name and my game. Like a real promotional giveaway. This was my bishop slicing diagonally across the board, cutting through barriers, opening lines.

The third move, that's where the real magic happened. I orchestrated a merger between two factions, gangstas and police—turning enemies into allies. This wasn't just shaking hands; it was aligning interests so tightly that betrayal was off the table. That's your queen, powerful and pivotal, turning the tide of the game.

Each of these steps was a layer of strategy, building towards a bigger picture. But here's the kicker—the payoff wasn't just in cash; it was in credibility, stability, and longevity. That's the majesty that trumps tragedy, the sort of move that turns a street hustler and mack into a street legend. You got to always plan your next step. Plan your next move. Plan your next win.

But let's break it down even further, get into the nuts and bolts of business beyond the blade because business is chess—not dice—it's strategy over luck every time. When you're plotting to set up a legit business, something above board, you're dealing with permits, building codes, business loans—boring? Sure, but necessary—for damn sure. Each of these steps is like setting up your pieces in a chess game. You're securing your king, plotting your strategy, ensuring your defense is ironclad while preparing to go on the offensive. If you don't make the right moves, the game gone make a move on you.

The waiting game, like waiting on permits or business credit to come through, teaches you patience, young hustler. It's like playing a long chess game where each move is deliberated, each decision calculated. Majesty moves with patience and tragedy moves in desperation. Just like in chess, where you set traps and plan escapes—in business, you prepare for audits, market shifts, and competition—it's all apart of the game.

In this grand game—from anticipation to congratulations, your moves gotta be precise, your strategy sound, and your execution exemplary. Every risk managed, every opportunity optimized, every threat neutralized. It's about building something that lasts, something that makes the street tales turn into lessons of legend—yeah, even in the corporate world.

Majesty in the streets comes from mastering your craft to the extent that your moves aren't just reactions—they're well-thought-out strategies leading to inevitable success. You don't just dodge tragedy; you orchestrate triumph. Every maneuver you plot is a step towards an empirical outcome, ya dig—building your kingdom one calculated risk at a time. This ain't just about avoiding pitfalls; it's about creating legacies.

You elevate your game so high above the standard hustle that what would be a setback for others is just another stepping stone for you. Turning anticipation into action and action into accolade is the quintessence of playing the game at its highest level. Every congratulation you receive is a nod to your ability to foresee, outsmart, and outplay the chaos that throws others off course.

Even when you three steps ahead, you keep that playbook tucked away under lock and key. In the streets, the loudest one in the room is often the first to falter. Your moves should be felt before they're heard.

In this campaign for street supremacy, selling yourself ain't about loud pitches or brash promotions; it's about **strategic visibility**. You make them see what you want them to see, when you want them to see it like a magician. And when they finally realize what you've been doing, you're already at the finish line, turning back with a grin. The hated became the most motivated because you either lead or bleed, scheme or dream, take what's yours or get lost in the stream, ya dig.

To keep it all the way one hundred, Im'ma put you up on some fire books that directly focus on not gettin' played by snakes, anticipating market shifts, navigating uncertainty, and staying several moves ahead—just like a grandmaster playing chess.

First, one of my favorites is **Blue Ocean Strategy** by W. Chan Kim and Renée Mauborgne, because it focuses on how to anticipate crowded markets and shift toward uncontested "blue oceans" where competition is irrelevant. Imagine that, you so different that you the only king lion or gorilla in the jungle. Then there's always **The 33 Strategies of War** by Robert Greene, which is essentially "chess with life." I always liked the way he explained the art of preempting threats, creating momentum, and thinking offensively and defensively in business and beyond. You got to see the whole forrest, not just the trees in front of you, you feel me?

Then of course you gotta check for this one called **'Seeing Around Corners'** by Rita McGrath, which is specifically about how to predict and act on **inflection points** before they disrupt your business. It's all about developing **strategic agility**. And don't forget **'Your Next Five Moves'** by Patrick Bet-David, 'cause like I always say, may yuh next move be yuh best move. See this one is tailor-made for entrepreneurs and hustlers alike thinking multiple steps ahead—combining chess-style foresight with real business-building tactics.

And what kind of person would I be if I didn't mention **Good Strategy Bad Strategy** by Richard Rumelt and **The Art of Strategy** by Avinash K. Dixit and Barry J. Nalebuff—both breaking down game theory and decision-making, showing how winners stay steps ahead through strategic thinking. They teach you how to recognize weak strategies early and build strong ones that adapt to changing conditions—critical for moving ahead before the market forces you to. Man if you get them uploaded in yuh mental frame, how can you not win. Automatic boss status yuh dig. Without access, don't count on ever seeing success. Get the knowledge and stay three steps ahead, or get swayed, played, and filleted instead—it's your choice, you can starve or get fed.

Thirteen

No Shame in your Game

A King Never Explains; He Just Reigns—So Own Your Lane & Claim your Name while you're deciding to be a Leader or a Lame.

*T*he deep purr of the G-Wagon's engine hummed beneath them as they coasted through the city's golden hour. The skyline, a jagged silhouette of power and ambition, stretched out before them. Neon signs flickered to life, reflecting in the slick asphalt as they rolled past high-end boutiques, upscale bistros, and looming glass towers that housed the kind of deals that didn't make the news but moved the city's undercurrents.

Inside the plush cabin, the scent of fine leather mixed with the faint trace of Uncle's expensive cigar from earlier, still lingering in the fibers of his tailored overcoat. Nephew gripped the wheel, his jaw clenched, thoughts rattling around in his head like loose change in the cupholder. His voice carried a mix of frustration and disbelief as he recounted the real estate deal he let slip through his fingers.

"So, she practically laid the red carpet out for me, Unc," Nephew admitted, shaking his head as they hit a stoplight. "She kept throwing hints, letting me know she had the power to stall the other buyer's paperwork. Even slowed her speech like she was waiting on me to say the magic words—but I didn't. I just sat there, overthinking, talking about, 'Well, I wouldn't wanna interfere with the process'. He exhaled sharply, drumming his fingers on the steering wheel. "Man, soon as I left, I knew I fumbled it."

Uncle, reclined in the passenger seat with one hand draped over his knee, let out a long, knowing chuckle. He had heard enough. Adjusting the brim of his hat, he turned his sharp, seasoned eyes on Nephew with that mix of amusement and disappointment only elders could perfect.

"let me make sure I'm hearing you right. So you say you was about to close a deal, and the woman who held all the cards, all the leverage, was sweet on you," he mused, his voice carrying the rich timbre of someone who had seen the game play out a thousand times before. "Sounds like you had the cat in the bag—no puns intended." He shook his head, pausing for effect before landing the punchline. "But you was acting like you wasn't good enough? Like she was outta yo' league?" He smacked his lips and gave Nephew a sidelong look. "And dollars was involved?" A slow smirk crept across his face. "Boy, is you sure we blood? 'Cause that was kinda simpish there, Nephew."

The light turned green, and as Nephew pressed the gas, the tension in the cabin cracked. They both laughed—Uncle's deep and hearty, Nephew's a little begrudging. He knew he deserved that.

"I hear you, Unc, I hear you," Nephew conceded, shaking his head. "But it ain't like I meant to drop the ball. I just wasn't sure how hard to press; didn't want to overshoot and brick it."

Uncle waved a hand, dismissing the excuse before it even landed. "You wasn't sure? She gave you the lane, handed you the ball, and you still ain't wanna take the shot?" He scoffed. "You better learn to recognize when the universe is nudging you toward a win."

The G-Wagon glided through the next intersection, past a construction site where men in hard hats labored under floodlights, stacking bricks toward someone else's dream. The scent of sawdust and fresh pavement drifted through the cracked window, mingling with the crisp night air.

Uncle leaned forward, adjusting his cuffs as he continued. "See, Nephew, there's a difference between patience and hesitation. Patience is calculated—it's waiting for the right moment with full confidence you gon' execute without a doubt. Hesitation? That's fear wrapped in an excuse. And what did hesitation just cost you?"

Nephew exhaled, gripping the wheel tighter. "A multi unit commercial investment property. A fat commission check. And a real shot at making a major play." Uncle nodded, satisfied with the self-awareness. "Exactly. And now? Now you got work to do." Nephew glanced over. "You think I still got a shot?" Uncle grinned, smoothing his jacket. "That depends, young blood. You finally bringing your A-game this time?"

The streetlights overhead cast streaks of gold across the hood of the G-Wagon as they pulled into the parking lot of the property they came to see. this was a strategy session and walk around. The opportunity might've slipped once—but the game? The game never closed its doors.

Whatever generational curses got you feeling shameful, you gon' have to let that go nephew, said Uncle. You can't have

"No shame in your game," youngin. I'm pouring out pure, undiluted truth—like a shot of the finest cognac—strait no chaser. It's meant to warm you up to the power of 'Authenticity.' A King? He don't waste no breath justifying his crown; he wears it, and that's statement enough. Stand in your power and glow on dat ho'.

See, it takes real king shyt to be genuine—I'm talkin' real pimpin to stand firm in who you are and what you believe, even when it's tempting to blend in or bow down. That authenticity? That's your signature, your seal, your mark that says, 'This is me, take it or leave it. You can cum or you can go, it don't make me no nevermind.

See, stepping into your truth ain't about fitting into someone else's frame; it's about crafting the frame yourself, custom-fit and color-matched to your own style. **Authenticity**, that's your greatest asset, your sharpest weapon. It's what sets you apart in a game flooded with fakes and wannabes—the whole damn scene is cluttered with clones. You gotta be the real deal, the 100% no-fillers-added kind of real. Dive deep into what drives you, what defines you. Then, bring that to the forefront of everything you do, 'cause what's meant for you is yours, and what's not is a waste of your damn time.

Now, let's dive deeper, nephew. Authenticity ain't just about keeping it real with others; it's about being real with yourself first. It's about knowing your strengths, your flaws, and rocking them both with equal confidence. You can't lie to yuh'self; you can lie to a trick but it takes a special kind of fool to lie to themselves.

It's like this—imagine you a brand, your own unique flavor in this vast game called life. Whether you're selling a product, pitching a service, or just presenting yourself, if you're genuine and authentic, you're golden.

Now hear this, young blood, valuing yourself is the core of any real hustle. You gotta recognize your own worth before you can expect anyone else to. It's like setting the price tag on your skills, your time, your presence—not just in the hustle, but in every room you step into. You're a premium brand, not some clearance rack deal. When you know your value, you don't settle for less; you command top dollar. You make sure every deal, every move, every relationship pays you what you're worth, in respect and in revenue.

See, the game respects those who respect themselves. It's about charging what you're worth and refusing to discount your value for anyone. Whether you're closing deals, choosing circles, or charting new paths, your price is set by the highest bidder: yourself. When you value yourself, you create a standard—a benchmark that tells the world, 'This is what I'm worth.' You don't chase opportunities; opportunities start chasing you.

Authenticity comes with its tests. You definitely gonna face doubters, haters, those who'll try to dim your shine. But that's when you gotta be firmest, gotta show that a king never explains; he just displays his power by how he plays the game. John Henric Clark said, A Lion don't give no phux bout the lamb's opinions"—I'm paraphrasing, of course nephew.

Look at legends in any field—artists like Basquiat, entrepreneurs like Steve Jobs, or big time music moguls. They all shared one thing: an unshakeable sense of self that came through in everything they did. They owned their stories, their struggles and turned them into strokes of genius on the vast canvas of their fields.

Let me kick game real quick—authenticity also means **resilience**. It's easy to follow the crowd, play safe, blend in. But to stand alone, to stick out? That takes big gut's. It's about being the same dude in the street as you are in the suite. It's about your words matching your actions so tightly that people can't help but give you respect. That respect? That's currency, nephew, more valuable than any dollar bill. And remember, owning your authenticity means never having to say you're sorry for being yourself. It means navigating the noise with your head held high and your steps sure. It's not just about resistance; it's about **resonance**—creating a vibe that others can't help but feel, can't help but follow.

You gotta step into each day like you're walking into a bank to negotiate a million-dollar deal. Dress like it, talk like it, walk like it—because you ain't just selling something, you're selling someone: yourself. Let the confidence marinate in every word you speak and every move you make. Remember, if you don't know your worth, somebody else will define it for you—and they'll penny-pinch. So set your standards, wear your worth like a gold chain around your neck, visible and undeniable.

That's not just confidence; that's economy, nephew. You're the CEO of a corporation called 'Me Inc.,' and business is booming. Own it, flaunt it, bank it. No shame in your game means every step you take is a deposit in your legacy bank. Keep it classy, keep it lucrative—play for keeps, and the market will always respect your stock.

So as we round this corner, remember: throw out that fake facade, that costume you think you gotta wear to get ahead.

Strip it down to the real you, the best you. Because when you're genuine, you ain't just playing the game, you changing it. You become not just a player but a pioneer, not just a hustler but a trailblazer. **Unfu*k Yourself:** Get Out of Your Head and into Your Life" by Gary John Bishop and **The Gifts of Imperfection**" by Brené Brown are the perfect reads for leveling up that inner game—look 'em up and you'll see exactly what I'm talkin' about.

Essentially, young playa, no shame in your game means you need to shine your light so bright that the haters gotta wear shades. You walk your path so sure that others can't help but follow your steps. Own it, nephew. Reclaim your name, reign in your lane, and let the kingdom come. That's how you play it—not just with skill, but with soul. Let them know—a real boss plays for keeps, and he keeps it real, from the street to the elite. That's not just playing the game; that's running it, powerfully and unapologetically, ya dig.

Fourteen

Get the Bag, Don't let the Bag Get You

Ya Gotta Have Principles with your Prosperity. Don't lose yourself when you chase the wealth, or else you're bound for the lost and found.

*T*he scent of burnt rubber still lingered in the air, thick with the heat of revving engines and the faint metallic hum of high-performance machines cooling down. The set of the music video was alive with energy—cameramen adjusting lenses, directors barking orders, models strutting in impossible heels, and the relentless pulse of the bass rattling everything from the pavement to the bones in a man's chest. Neph stood near the lineup of exotic cars he and Uncle had brought out for the shoot, the afternoon sun bouncing off the chrome so bright it forced squinted eyes.

His homie, fresh off a new feature that nephew finessed with a rising rapper, was standing near the monitors, nodding his head to the playback while chain-smoking between takes. The whole production was a spectacle—drone cameras soaring, fire-lit barrels casting flickering shadows against graffiti-splashed warehouse walls, *and stacks of cash getting tossed for slow-motion shots like confetti at a championship parade. The budget was bigger than expected, and Neph had an inkling that the rapper's pockets or his production company weren't the ones footing the bill.*

Uncle was posted up a few steps back, leaning against the hood of his classic convertible, taking it all in. Unlike the younger crowd, he wasn't easily dazzled. He'd seen money move—real money, old money, quiet money. And he knew the difference between ownership and obligation just by the way a man carried himself. The rapper in question? He was shining, sure. But it was the kind of shine that came from borrowed light, ya know, from *labels, investors, execs—and when you got borrowed light, eventually, they want it back—with interest.*

Neph had been too busy managing his artist to really dig into the details, but something about the way Uncle watched the scene told him there was a lesson brewing. Just as another take wrapped and the director called for a break, Uncle exhaled slow, like a man about to unload some wisdom.

"Boy, this look good—real good," Uncle started, shaking his head as he glanced around, eyes trailing the movement of handlers adjusting costume jewelry, stylists fixing collars, and someone off to the side literally fanning the rapper between shots. "Real good. But the question is—who own it?"

Neph and his homie exchanged a look. Uncle wasn't talking about the cars or the chains. He was talking about the bag and everything in it, including the people appearing to shine the brightest. The homie chuckled and said beneath his breath, " well everyone here knows who's bars are the hottest on this track and who the real talent is, so you got one thing right, my man shining off of my light, but he

the one with the contract." Nephew followed with, you betta not let
nobody hear you talkin like that, with a chuckle.

"You ever been so hungry for a plate," Uncle continued, cracking
his knuckles like a preacher about to deliver a sermon, "that you ain't
even check what they was feeding you?" After catching wind of the
rapper's 360 deal and the whispers about what he might've done for
this budget, Uncle cut straight to it—'Don't ever chase the bag so
hard you put a price on your soul.

That was all it took. Neph knew what was coming next—the kind
of game that separated the players from the played.

Listen here, young blood, it's all about keeping your cool
when the cash starts calling. "Get the bag, don't let the bag
get you." It's more than just a slick saying; it's the golden
rule. This game of green can glisten like gold or gunk up like
grease—depends on how you handle it.

You see, the chase for cheddar can be a thrilling hunt, but
lose your head, and that hunt can haunt, like a haunted house.
Money's a masterful magician; it can disappear as fast as it
appears if you ain't mindful. It makes a great servant but a
terrible master. That's why you gotta have **principles with
your prosperity.** It ain't just about stacking stacks; it's about
staying solid while you do it.

Now, I'm gon' lay it down straight—money should be a tool,
not a tyrant. Use it to build, to boost, not to blind or bind.
It's easy to get twisted up when the dollars start adding up,
thinking more is better, always reaching for the next zero. But
remember, nephew, every figure in your bank account adds

another link to the chains if you let it control you—then you stuck in the illusion of a golden castle.

Hold on to who you are, the real you, the grounded you. Don't let that money morph you into something you ain't, or you'll find yourself rich in cash but bankrupt in spirit. You chasing the wealth, but if you lose yourself along the way, you'll end up in the lost and found, soul sold for a few extra fast zeros. But here's how you play it smooth: Make that money, don't let it make you—and make a lot of it. Draw a line between your needs and your greeds. Sure, upgrade your lifestyle, but never downgrade your **integrity.** Keep yuh principles polished like the platinum in your pocket.

And always remember why you started. Was it just for the luxury and labels, or was it to change the game, to elevate, to innovate? Keep your purpose clear, your vision sharp. That way, when the storms come—and they will—you're the captain of your ship, not a castaway lost at sea because your compass was cash, not character. Now I know that might sound unfamiliar comin' from an old pimp, but thats just it, Imma Old Pimp, super seasoned in this game. I done seen it all. I aint new tho this, I'm true to this. A young P' wet behind the ears ain't got enough experience to wipe his ass clean enough to keep his drawers crispy white. This here is pure unadulterated Game. Take my money, take my honey, but please, just dont take my game.

Listen to me when I tell you; In this game, learn, earn and let your wealth amplify your worth, not replace it—cause a worthless millionaire is the laughing stock of the billionaires boys club. Stack that paper, but stack your values higher. You wanna be the boss that commands respect, not just because you can buy a sit down but because you've earned the conversation.

So, as you young men go out there and grab that bag, clutch onto your roots with the other hand. That **balance**—that's what keeps you from getting lost in the sauce. Let the dollars dance, but you lead the dance. Don't just get the bag—own yuh bank, and make sure it never owns you. That's how you win this game—rich in pocket, rich in soul.

Now, some of my playa potnuhs will tell you that money is their god. You got some out here so desperate they'll give up their virgin hole along with their soul just for the promise of a fat bankroll. They want you to sock it to they pocket, they'll show you they soul and beg you to knock it. Remember, to be greedy is to be needy, and you never wanna be needy. Keep your dignity as rich as your pockets, and never trade your worth for wealth. Money comes and goes just like you cop and blow hoes.

Once you realize that you are the capital, you can choose it, lose it, sometimes abuse it, and like a boomerang, you can get it right back because you are the value that you're leveraging for that energy they call money. When you're rich in spirit, creativity, and imagination, it's like you are a printing press. When your game is so extremely laced, you can talk a dime out of dirt, compound and multiply that dime into a dollar, and make it holler till it's a million more—again and again, whenever you want to win.

The young men listened intently while the production around them prepared for the next shot.

"Truth be told, every now and then, a book don't just land in your lap—it lands in your life. That's why I make sure to drop the direct path on you. They ain't just reads, they're keys—dropped between the lines for those sharp enough to catch 'em, said Uncle."

Now picture this: you sit with **The Psychology of Money** *by Morgan Housel*, and soak up the quiet wealth and wisdom in classics like **The Millionaire Next Door** *by Thomas J. Stanley & William D. Danko*, or revisit the timeless truths of **The Richest Man in Babylon** *by George S. Clason*, and crack open the psychological dynamite that is **The Laws of Human Nature** *by Robert Greene*. That ain't just financial literacy—that's a full-blown mindset upgrade G'.

These books don't just teach you how to make money—they teach you how to move with it. From how your mind handles money, to how discipline builds silent wealth, to ancient principles still ringin' through time, and on to the deep truths behind why we do what we do—it's all game -baby. And when you absorb it right, you're not just learnin' the game—you're changin' your position in it, and lockin' in the blueprint for who you're meant to become.

What it all boils down to is the principle of **financial discipline** and becoming the version of yourself that's a money magnet—as a default character setting. This ain't just 'bout making money; it's about managing it wisely. Financial discipline means setting limits, following a budget, and making calculated decisions that align with yuh long-term goals. It aint about what you cop, it's about what you keep—and that's scripture my Negus. It's the art of controlling your cash flow instead of letting it control you. Master this, and you master the game—church!

Fifteen

You Can't Flex First-Class With Coach Cash

Luxury costs, so level up because Big Tastes need Big Bucks. You trying ta sip champagne with a Kool-Aid budget cousin.

*T*he low hum of conversation filled the terminal, a blend of business chatter, the occasional boarding announcement, and the rhythmic shuffle of designer luggage against polished tile floors. The scent of fresh coffee lingered in the air, mingling with the faint musk of recycled airport oxygen.

Uncle and Nephew had settled into the lounge, a quiet sanctuary away from the general boarding chaos. They weren't just flying out for leisure—this trip to Vegas was a mix of business and play. Their eyes were on a few promising properties, potential investments that could turn into government-subsidized halfway houses. But, of course, no trip to Sin City was complete without a little dice rolling.

As Nephew scrolled through emails, a voice cut through the ambient murmur like a bad saxophone solo—loud, off-key, and trying too hard to be noticed. Across the terminal, a stocky man in a too-tight designer tracksuit was holding court, phone pressed against his ear like he was negotiating a million-dollar deal.

"Nah, nah, I told him—don't even hit my line unless it's at least six figures," he barked, adjusting his oversized Versace shades, the gold plating reflecting the overhead lights. His wrists clanked with jewelry, but even from a distance, the dull shimmer betrayed its truth—costume gold masquerading as the real thing.

Uncle glanced over the rim of his whiskey glass, smirking. "Boy talkin' big, but them jewels ain't sayin' much," he murmured to Nephew. Nephew just shook his head, entertained but unimpressed. "Soundin' rich don't pay the bills."

Soon enough, their first-class boarding was called, and they made their way down the jet bridge. Settling into their leather seats, Nephew leaned back, already envisioning the properties they'd be inspecting later. The boarding was shaping up to be smooth—until the unmistakable voice from the terminal resurfaced.

It was Gym Bag Man. He waddled down the aisle, his oversized duffel bouncing off seats as he made his way to the back of the plane. His sunglasses were still on, despite the dimmed cabin lights. It wasn't long before the murmurs started. A commotion broke out near the rear of the plane—Gym Bag was getting loud again.

"The hell you mean I ain't got no space? Y'all trippin'—I PAID for this damn flight!" A flight attendant tried to pacify him, but his voice carried forward.

Uncle, sipping his pre-flight bourbon, let out a quiet chuckle. He turned to Nephew with that signature look—the one that meant a lesson was coming. "You see, this right here," he said, motioning

toward the commotion, "is exactly why you can't flex first-class with
coach cash."

He cracked a grin, sat back, and started storytelling the way only
he could.

You know who he remind me of said Unc, Bernice boy
Marlo. Nephew, what's up with ya cousin Marlo anyway? I
see he in that G-Wagon, but his pockets laggin, and the boy
stay flashin, but the landlord always harassin'—and the crib
look tragic. Him and ole gym bag back there ah prolly get
along real good, huh. Here's the lesson, young blood: don't
be out there driving a Land Rover if you're still runnin from a
landlord. Ridin' a benz, but the brokest, most dusty and highest
ninjas on the block is yuh only friends. It's about keeping your
foundations as fly as your facade.

Now, let me drop some heavy game on you. Remember how
Grandma used to check us at the dinner table, saying, "Your
eyes are bigger than your stomach"? She wasn't just talking
'bout food; she was schooling us on life. Greed, nephew, is the
first cousin of need. When you grab more than you can handle,
you set yourself up for a fall—life's way of serving indigestion
on a platter.

Looks like the lifestyle aint aligned with the reality. Let's
chop it up about this thing called **'lifestyle alignment.'** It
ain't just a fancy term; it's your financial game plan. It means
lining up your bankroll with your life goals. You dreaming
of champagne breakfasts and silk sheets? That's cool and all,
but you gotta make sure your budget ain't screaming ramen
noodles at midnight. Sync your spendin' with your vision,

make every dollar push you closer to those dreams. What's the purpose of even crankin' up if you know you ain't got the gas to make it to the destination.

You see, it's like this: you gotta match your cash to your class. Stepping into the spotlight with just pennies? Nah, that ain't gon' work. You wanna roll high, live large? Then you better be hustling hard. High rollers know this: your flow gotta match your show. So, elevate your hustle to meet those goals, boost your grind to align with that fine life you envision.

Financial discipline, that's the real MVP here. It's about controlling your coin so it don't start controllin' you. Don't let your desires for high life drain your life's worth. It's about making smart moves, not just making money moves. Budgeting ain't just for the broke; it's for the bosses too, those who know how to make their money work for them without slipping into debt's deadly grip. You don't wanna owe the plug if you can't afford an army.

And let's get real—being greedy is just another way of being needy. And in this game, showing need is a weakness. Needin' attention, needin' validation, needin' to feel some since of importance to people who can care less about you is some derelict shyt. It's like telling the world you're ripe for the taking. So, you gotta stay sharp, keep your needs in check and your wants even tighter. Don't let that lust for luxury turn into a leash around your neck.

A fool and his money ain't even gotta break up, 'cause they was never really together.

The low murmur of conversation blended with the soft clinking of glasses as flight attendants moved through the cabin with effortless grace. A subtle chime signaled that the plane had reached cruising

altitude, its smooth ascent leaving the cabin feeling weightless—an
island of quiet luxury above the clouds. The rich scent of aged leather
mingled with the aroma of dark-roasted coffee, the kind that tasted
like it belonged to a different tax bracket. Warm, buttered croissants
and freshly brewed espresso added to the indulgence in the air.
Unc stretched slightly in his seat, adjusting the crease in his slacks
before giving a passing flight attendant an easy nod.
"Go 'head and top me off, sweetheart," he said smoothly, motioning
to his glass. As she leaned in to pour, he turned back to Nephew, his
tone casual but weighted.

Let's talk about money moves versus money illusions—'cause too many folks out here dressing like a boss while living like an employee. See, real wealth don't gotta announce itself. If you got it, you got it. But if your pockets light and your bills heavy, you ain't hustlin', you hemorrhagin'. You on yo' fake it till you make it type time.

See, you different from ya cousin nephew, but the Broke Boy Ballet is real. You ever see a cat like Marlo pull up in a G-Wagon, drippin' designer, talkin' big… but then you peep his reality? Rent late, phone off, food stamp card sittin' right next to that Gucci belt. That's burnin' money for the illusion of success. If more goin' out than comin' in, you got the game ass backwards.

See, the rich don't where they money on they chest and they for damn sure don't work for money—they make money work for them. Money is the new slave and you got to be a damn good overseer. The game ain't about how much you spend, it's about how much you generate, recycle, keep and flip. Money should circulate, not evaporate. If you livin' check to check but drippin' head to toe, you got the game twisted. Real bosses don't spend every dollar—they stack 'til they can't see over it. Ain't nothin' but a lil sacrifice, the time gon' pass anyway, might as well lock in and get it over with—otherwise you in the red till grey hairs coverin yuh head.

You got negative cash flow? That's like ridin' a flat tire—gon' leave you stranded. If your outflow is bigger than your income, you ain't progressing—you stressin' and guessin'. You paying the cost to flex for folks who don't care. That's not winning, that's wasting. Stop fundin' a lifestyle you ain't financed for. Yuh money should multiply, not disappear like a magic trick. Big bank take lil' bank. If you don't learn to control your money, your money will control you. If you stay in a cycle of stunting for status instead of stacking for stability, you gon' wake up one day and realize that half the folks you was flexin' for can't even remember your name, and the other half don't even remember your face.

The real flex ain't the car, the clothes, or the clubs. The real flex is freedom—the ability to move how you want, when you want, with who you want, and never stress a bill. If you gotta finance the flex, it ain't a flex—it's a liability. You wanna play the game right? Start stacking instead of stunting. Let your money work, let your assets grow, and most importantly, let your financial habits reflect your long-term vision, not your short-term ego.

All I'm tryin'ta tell you is align your spend-game with your endgame. Don't be caught flashing a gold chain when your wallet's filled with copper change. Be the master of your money, not a slave to it. You gotta walk like a boss, talk like a boss, and most importantly, spend like a boss who knows his empire isn't just about the glitter—it's about the gold that backs it up.

Remember, a real boss knows the game. It ain't just about looking rich; it's about being rich—in your spirit, in your mind, and yes, in your bank account too. So next time you think about stepping up your lifestyle, make sure your finances are stepping up right there with you. Don't be like Mr. gym bag and cousin Marlo.

'Matta–fact' Type these three titles in your phone real quick, nephew. Imma put you up on some solid game your mind gon' need to maintain so you aint neva got to explain. You seem to do pretty good with the recommendations I shoot ya, so you'll prolly knock these out in under a week. Trust me, this ain't just reading—this is a mindset shift, a realignment of how you move with your money.

First up, *"The Psychology of Money: Timeless Lessons on Wealth, Greed, and Happiness" by Morgan Housel.* Listen, the biggest mistakes folks make with money ain't about numbers, it's about emotions. Ego, impatience, greed—they all got a price tag. This book breaks down how your mindset shapes your pockets, and how real wealth ain't about what you flaunt but what you *keep*. The ones who win long–term? They move with discipline, not desperation.

Next, type in *"I Will Teach You to Be Rich" by Ramit Sethi.* Now, this one ain't about pinching pennies or living like a monk. It's about putting systems in place that let your money grow on autopilot while still enjoying life. You ever notice how the real wealthy don't stress over money? It's 'cause they got a plan. This book lays out the steps—automating your bills, investing early, and spending on what truly matters while cutting out the waste.

And last but definitely necessary— "**The Index Card: Why Personal Finance Doesn't Have to Be Complicated**" *by Helaine Olen and Harold Pollack.* See, that loudmouth on the phone? Flexing hard but flying coach? That's what happens when you put on for the gram instead of putting on for your future. This book simplifies everything—live below your means, invest in what lasts, and stop trying to impress people who don't even care. Ain't no shame in stacking quietly until you can step out loudly, *for real.*

Get on these, nephew. 'Cause the real flex? That's knowing your bag is solid, even when nobody's watching.

Nephew nodded, tapping his phone. "Say less Unc. On it. I'm 'bout to download this audiobook now, kick back, and let it ride with me. If I knock out, wake me up when we touch down at Harry Reid International Airport."

Sixteen

I Need Money Like a Rat Need Cheese

No dough, No dinner—Aint no feast without finance and he who does not eat perishes.

*I*n the dimly lit parking lot of an underground gambling spot, the palpable buzz of excitement hung thickly in the air, and the charged energy of hustlers spinning narratives painted a mean scene comparable to the Last Poets's mean machine. Nephew stood shoulder to shoulder with Uncle, surrounded by a circle of seasoned players, each trying to outdo the other with tales dripping with bravado. Uncle, ever the charismatic storyteller, delivered what could only be described as pimp poetry, his voice smooth and assured, the words rolling off his tongue with the ease of long practice.

As he wrapped up his vivid narrative with the punchline, "negus please—I need money like a rat need cheese," the group erupted into hearty laughter, slapping backs and nodding in respect for the artful delivery. They lingered for a moment, basking in the camaraderie of the player's circle, before dispersing into the night, each man disappearing into the shadowed corners of the lot.

Walking back to the Maybach, Uncle turned to Nephew, his expression shifting to one of contemplation. "That's more than just spitting game, boy," he said as they slid into the plush leather seats. "It's a true story, it's real life." As he started the engine, the soft purr of the Maybach cut through the night's silence, Uncle began to peel back the layers of his statement. The car rolled smoothly out of the parking lot, and as the city lights blurred past, Uncle delved into the realities of their hustle, explaining the necessity of their grind and the relentless pursuit of money—a pursuit as instinctual and necessary as a rat's quest for cheese. Cue the music, and dim the lights—because that's when the real story started.

Alright, listen up, nephew—this is key. When I talk about "needin' money like a rat need cheese," I'm getting into the real grind, the essence of what separates the movers from the shakers, the rich from the poor. It's all about the habits that define our relationship with that dough. Truth be told, at this poirn't in my life, the way I look at it, is the more I have, the more I can help. I can't trust that anybody else can cover the estate, trust and legacy for me and mine like me. After I'm gone, who knows? The whole family could go into poverty, so im'ma do my part to make sure that don't happen. Not on my watch.

You see, money, it's like the blood flow of life; it's a current that moves, circulating, touching every aspect of our being. From the hood to the high rises currency is what keeps the heart of commerce pumping. In olden times, like them old editions of Black's Law Dictionary would tell you, money wasn't just paper and metal. Nah, it was anything people agreed had value—cowrie shells, livestock, grains, or metals like gold and silver. These items held intrinsic value and served as the backbone for bartering and trade. They were the real MVPs of their day, making sure folks could handle their business, securing goods and services vital for survival. Essentially, money is jus **Assets**. Billionaires don't spend paper money and swim in big towers of gold coins like Scrooge McDuck.

Just like them shells and grains, today's bread—whether it's that paper, plastic, or digital dough—fuels our everyday hustle and can just as easily be stocks, land, or equity in a company. Billion-dollar deals ain't always paid in cash—they're traded in value, assets, credit, and influence across countless forms of exchange. It's what buys the supplies, pays the rent, and keeps the lights on. But here's where the game comes in, nephew: understanding and respecting the flow of money is crucial. You gotta be wise, can't be no fool with your funds because money ain't just about spending; it's about sustaining, growing, and securing a future. You gotta keep that currency flowing, because stagnation is the first sign of decay.

Money is a tool, nephew, use it wisely. Leverage it, don't let it leverage you. Make it work so hard for you that even when you're asleep, your money's out there hustling on the streets like a real street stalker—and compounding. Mack math simple: let it percolate and circulate round and round till the shine get thick and all the stacks compound. I dont't know about you, but Im'ma always let it bubble and double and marinate in my hustle. I had to learn the hard way—a money spread ain't no real bread. I can't buy no private plane with paper money. I can buy a bunch of depreciating material shit, though, that's worthless as soon as I walk away with it, but that's a whole other lesson.

Now, here's the deal: like I was sayin' earlier, the rich, they don't just spend money; they circulate it. They send it out on missions, making sure each dollar brings back a few of its friends. The ism taught me to send ho's out to knock for moh' hoe's. They was my best wingmen. A ho' that could bring me another ho was sometimes more valuable than one bringing me a Rolex or a bag, especially if it was a good hoe'. I call that an appreciating asset. A hoe can be anything from a dollar bill to a tractor-trailer, as long as it circulate and bring me back more of my favorite kinda hoe—Wealth.

That's the difference, you see. While the average Joe might blow his paycheck on the latest trends, the savvy ones invest theirs in assets that appreciate—stocks, real estate, businesses that expand their wealth exponentially. They understand a crucial rule in the game: your money must multiply. It's not about having cash; it's about leveraging it to create more. You gotta make your money work for you and hustle hard now so you dont have to later.

Never buy stuff with your money, create money servant's to buy it for you. If you like cars, don't buy them, create a turo account and let that LLC buy them for you. The people that trick off with your cars, let them pay for your whips. You just control the assets and jump in and out of them when you want to. You like to travel to vacation spots and stay in nice vacation rentals. Let your BnB pay for that shyt. You like to jump on planes and fly first class, let both those LLCs pay for it, rackin' up frequent flyer miles and points so you can go anywhere you want for free. An LLC is the most money gettin hoe you will ever meet and I like to have me a stable of a hundred of them if I can help it.

We ain't just talking spending here; we're talking circulating, ya dig. Like blood pumps through your veins to keep you alive, money needs to flow through investments to keep the flood gates open wide. It's a cycle, nephew. Stagnant money is swamp money. I need that movement money—flowing like the Nile River. You invest, it grows, you reinvest. This cycle, it's what builds empires. You send dollars out to scout the terrain, find opportunities, and drag back more dollars. That's how wealth is built. That's how you keep the feast going without ever hitting famine.

This idea that money shouldn't die; it must multiply—take that to heart. The rich get this. They don't stash cash under mattresses. They use it as seed money, planting it where it can sprout profits. Each dollar is a soldier in the field, capturing more territory, securing more resources. The poor? They often see money as a means to an immediate end—something to be spent, not invested. It comes, and just as quickly, it goes, leaving nothing but memories and missed opportunities. They shortsighted on the terrain and not peeping the long game. Can't see the forest for the trees.

You gotta shift that mindset. Think of money like a tool—a key that unlocks doors to the future. When you start seeing your money as an agent of growth, not just a means to satisfy immediate desires, you align yourself with the tactics of the truly wealthy. It's about creating a system where your money cycles through growth avenues, continuously expanding, never stagnating. That's like the difference between a pimp and a trick.

When it comes right down to it, the bottom line is all about concentrated **profit focus**. See, having a sharp eye on profit is key in both business and personal finance—it ensures sustainability and growth by strategically directing resources towards generating and maximizing financial returns. I ain't going over yuh head or talkin' to fast, now am I? If you can't keep up, let me know.

Bottom line, nephew, it's not just about making money; it's about making your money make more money. This is the art of financial hustle. Better known as **financial intelligence—get you some.** So, let your dollars go out there, hustle, and bring back some friends. That's how you play this game smart. In this world, the money you manage wisely today decides the freedoms and fortunes of your tomorrow. Ain't no feast without finance, and famine certainly ain't for me.

With only a minute or two left before dropping Nephew off at his rest, the city lights slid across the windshield like liquid gold as they cruised through the quiet streets, the hum of the engine filling the space between them. Neph leaned back in the passenger seat, the kind of tired that comes with more thinking than drinking.

Unc had one hand on the wheel, the other draped lazy out the window, eyes fixed on the road but thoughts miles ahead. A toothpick danced on his bottom lip as he glanced over at Neph, watching how the youngin' was soaking it all in. He gave a slow nod, then dropped the kind of knowledge that don't come with a price tag.

"Look, money ain't just power—it's potential, nephew. It's a tool. It buys you time, buys you options, lets you move how you need to move. But don't get it twisted—real wealth ain't about flexin', it's about what you build, what you protect, and what you leave behind."

He let that breathe for a second, letting the weight settle in the cabin like thick smoke.

"Y'know," he continued, his voice calm but cutting sharp through the silence,

"folks think money gon' solve everything. And it can solve a lot, no doubt. But money? Money ain't the destination. It's the vehicle. Neph glanced over, but stayed quiet. He knew when Unc was building to something deeper.

"The real ones don't just chase the bag—they learn how to move with it. Flip it. Stretch it. Let it breathe and bless. Not just flex. 'Cause the bag heavy if you ain't built to carry it with purpose."

The car slowed at a red light. Neon signs flickered outside a closed barbershop. Unc tapped the wheel and leaned in a little, his tone more deliberate now.

"You get hip to that book **Happy Money** by Elizabeth Dunn and Michael Norton? They break it down—money can buy happiness, but only if you spend it right. Not on stuff, but on time, on people, on memories. That's what makes it hit different."

Neph nodded slowly, the night air creeping in through the cracked window, both of them exhausted from the day.

"And then there's **Thou Shall Prosper** by Rabbi Daniel Lapin. That one's heavy. Talks about makin' money with integrity. Through service. Through value. Turnin' profits into purpose. 'Cause it ain't just about what you earn—it's how you earn it, and who eats off your overflow."

Green light. The car rolled forward, and Unc eased back into the rhythm of the road.

"So don't just stack—build. Don't just grind—align. Make your money mean somethin'. 'Cause when you get it right, the bag don't own you. You own the bag, which puts you in the position to make astonomical impact."

The streetlights blurred like dreams half remembered. And Neph? He didn't say much. But he heard everything.

Seventeen

Never Let a Slow Dime PhukUp a Fast Dollar

If she's solid with a little, she's golden with a lot. Can't always judge a book by It's cover, so don't trip on the shine—Check The Spine,

*T*he ballroom shimmered under the glow of opulent chandeliers, each crystal reflecting the elegance of the evening. A jazz band played soft, sultry notes in the background while a sea of well-dressed entrepreneurs, investors, and philanthropists moved through the space while sipping champagne and exchanging business cards. The event, a charity gala for female entrepreneurs, was hosted by none other than **her**—the woman Nephew had been courting.

Tonight wasn't about business. At least, not the usual kind.

A woman was in the picture. Not just any woman, though. A super-goddess, a boss chick, one of those rare finds who seemed to have her whole world locked in. Beauty? Check. Brains? Heavy. Bag? Secured. She carried herself like a woman who wasn't waiting to be *chosen—she was the choice. And for the first time in a long time, Nephew was considering playing his polyamory card.*

Though he hardly played that card—seeing as most potential partners weren't on the level to build with him, or they were stuck in romance consciousness. Nephew's old lady had long accepted him and his choice to practice ethical polyamory when it made sense. She was always super secure, being the beneficiary of his trust, part owner in several of his businesses, and the mother of his three children. They were actually best friends and shared a partnership and love deeper than mere romance.

Every now and then, however, he'd meet a dope mind and heart in a woman, but rarely did it escalate beyond close friendship. This time, though… this time felt different. He saw potential, the kind that made a man stop and consider. The kind that made him rethink his usual approach.

Nephew stood near the black velvet-draped entrance, dressed in a sleek black suit that spoke quiet power. Unc, never one to underdress, leaned on his cane—more for style than support—his gold cufflinks catching the light as he surveyed the room with that ever-watchful gaze, possibly hoping to come up on a rich, PYT to keep him company from time to time. The scent of money, ambition, and imported perfume filled the air.

Then she appeared.

Draped in a shimmering rose gold Versache gown that fit like it was made for her and only her, she moved with an effortless grace, commanding attention without demanding it. When she reached Nephew, she pressed a slow, deliberate kiss to his cheek, her manicured hand lingering on his chest just a second longer than necessary.

Perfect. Everything about her was perfect. But Unc just watched, swirling the ice in his bourbon, expression unreadable. Nephew picked up on it immediately. "What?" he asked, half-amused, half-curious. Unc took a slow sip before answering. "She sharp, no doubt. But nephew... something ain't floatin' right in the water."

Nephew smirked but glanced back toward her as she effortlessly worked the room, shaking hands, exchanging pleasantries, navigating the crowd like she had been born to it. "What you mean, Unc?" Uncle set his glass down on a passing waiter's tray. "She move like she already own stock in your life." Nephew let out a short laugh but couldn't deny there was something there. She was stunning, brilliant, successful in her own right, a real ten out of ten to the naked aye—a dime-piece no doubt. But she also had a way of challenging nephew—not in the iron-sharpens-iron way, but in a way that made simple things feel unnecessarily complicated.

"She just a lil slow with the instructions sometimes," Nephew admitted, adjusting the cuffs on his suit jacket. "Like, I ask her to do something, she don't say 'no,' but she push back—almost outta reflex, like there's a disdain for leadership, you feel me. Then later, she'll come around and be like, 'Oh, that was a good idea.' But it's like... why the pushback at all? Almost like she got some deep-embedded trauma or somethin'."

Unc nodded slowly, watching her across the room as she laughed with some city officials, effortlessly working their egos. "A woman like that," Unc said, voice low but steady, can be dangerous, she ain't used to following a lead." She used to negotiating one. And if she questions every instruction, she don't trust the program and she definitely aint got no real faith in you. She misguided and undecided. Obviously, she ain't got the vision to make the right decision.

Nephew exhaled through his nose, rubbing his chin in thought. Unc straightened up, adjusting the diamond pin on his lapel. "Ain't sayin' she ain't a queen with the potential to be a top earner within *your organization, but nephew, if a woman moves like a buyer before the auction even starts, you might not be the one making the final bid, yuh dig." The weight of Unc's words lingered between them as another round of champagne was passed. Nephew took a glass but didn't sip—just lifted it in a casual toast and shot her a quick wink. She had glanced over at that exact moment, as if sensing she was the topic of conversation. He was starting to see what Unc saw. And just like that, the lesson had already begun.*

I see that she definitely got aura bright as the stars in the cosmo's, nephew. I ain't trying to knock you, but I do want to shock you. She seems to argue with you every time you try to make a move. She seems real jealous and insecure too. Wanting to parade you 'round like a show piece or trophy. I think she think she the prize with all the value as if she helping you come up. Just like a trojan horse, you let something like that in the gates, she'll throw a monkey wrench in your whole operation the first chance she get in her feelings. Mess up the good thing you already got goin.

Yeah, she's fine as wine and got a butt big as a truck, but hear me when I tell you, nephew, never let a slow dime mess up a fast dollar. I'm gonna school you to the rules and break down the game of distinguishing the genuine gold from the fool's gold.

The bottom line is value over vanity and **assets over liabilities,** all day, everyday, ya dig. This game is all about speed and strategy. It's chess, not checkers, how many times I gotta tell you that. You gotta move with purpose, with precision. In this shiny world, not all that glitters is gold. Sometimes, it's just a shiny wrap over a rusty trap. So check the spine before you sign. Dig beneath the surface to discover the purpose and maybe you'll strike the real gold. Remember, nephew, in the grand market of life, like I said before, it's value over vanity when It come to recruiting your other half. Don't just look at the bling; look for the blessing.

In this game called life, every player and every play got its own weight. Some are gonna beef up your stack, keep feeding your roll long after the dice have stopped tumbling. Others? They're like those shiny plastic rims on a beat-up ride—sparkle plenty but ain't pushing you forward. We're talking about the difference between what truly fills your pocket versus what just burns a hole through it.

This lesson is straightforward—shine can blind, if you ain't careful, especially if it's artificial. True value's buried deeper than the surface; it's not flashing for attention. It's quiet, steady, and sure, like that old-school ride that runs long and strong way past the finish line. Don't let the outer swag fool you into missing the core swag—that's where your gold's at—at the nucleus and in the soul.

She might be fine as wine and shine like a dime but don't get hustled by appearances; that dime might look sweet but is it slow on the feet. It's about those smart moves, and wins that build to big gains even in social situations. We're playing a long game in a short game's clothing—swift, smart, and always ahead of the game. Trained like a soldier to follow the order of the play—sticking to the script like a true thespian on broadway.

Keep this in your playbook, young king: aim for what adds value to your stack, cuts the flack, and packs more than it peels back. We're talking assets over liabilities always—the real deals that keep your treasury tight and right. Don't let the dazzle of a slow dime dull your sense of gettin' at a dollar. Remember, it's all about keeping your game tight and your gains right. Look for value that lasts, not just a fadin' flash.

Check it, youngin, game ain't just played on the streets or in the suites, it's played in your wallet too. It's played in your heart and even your spirit. It ain't just flesh and blood, It's principalities out hear. Now, here's how a real player rolls: If it's a link up that's gonna stack more green in your pocket over time, that's an asset, and that's what you wanna cop. But if it's gonna bleed you dry, siphoning off your energy and your currency stash as it sinks in value, that's a liability—leave that noise for the next man.

You see, it's like this: if it appreciates, if it's gonna fatten up your bankroll and your over all lifestyle, you buy that; lock it down. But if it depreciates, if it's gonna be worth less the minute you walk out the door, you rent that—ain't no shame in keeping your cash and your emotions fluid. That's the game, young blood. Invest wise—buy the breeders, rent the bleeders, 'cause who you lay with is the biggest investment you'll ever make.

The low hum of jazz had paused, giving a young pianist the floor. His melody drifted effortlessly through the room, weaving itself between the soft clink of champagne flutes and hushed conversations. Beyond the towering glass windows, the city skyline shimmered like a promise—distant yet magnetic, a silent witness to the quiet power plays unfolding in every corner. The air carried the scent of fresh-cut orchids, mingling with the warm spice of top-shelf cognac. Unc leaned

back slightly, adjusting his tie, his gaze steady as he took in the scene
before him. Nephew listened intently but never took his eye off his
potential chérie amour.

Whether material things or social flings, you gotta stay mindful of what you stand to lose or gain. Some folks, they look like the real deal—dressed to the nines, flashing smiles that could light up the dark side of the moon—but deep down, they're just liabilities wearing a fine suit. They'll drain your energy, your time, your pockets, and leave you with nothing but a bunch of receipts for things you never really needed. You gotta be slick, you gotta peep game. Check the core, not just the coat.

A pretty face can hide an empty space, and that's the kind of deficit no bank account can cover. Always remember, if they ain't adding value, they're hanging around to make a withdrawal. Choose your circle like you choose your investments—wisely, with an eye for what they bring to the table, not just what they look like when they arrive.

What we're talking about here ain't just nickels and dimes—it's about understanding the real from the fake in a world brimming with fakes. We diving into what it really means to have an asset, not just some flashy trinket—arm candy type—model face, with a slim waste and bad taste—masquerading as a prize in the center of ya eyes. Hell nawl, c'mon, nephew—stay wise.

I'm here to school you on recognizing real value, making sure you're building a stack of true assets, not just piling up liabilities that glitter like gold but turn to dust when tested. Now, is you pickin' up what I'm laying down.

"Damn Unc, you seem real passionate'bout this here. I'd think you was hatin' if I didn't know you, but I would't disrespect you," said nephew. I feel like you must have some first hand experience and there's some PTSD lingerin'. who was she and what did she do?

Let's just say I've been around this block a few times—and it ain't no fun when a Trojan horse or two (or three) leverages your ignorance to trick you outta your stable, your money, your sanity, or your freedom. I've seen it happen time and time again in the game. Some cats got knocked for their whole squad, some dyin' slow from that monster, and some doin' fed time for messin' with what they thought was a dime.

Ill tell you what, if you ain't gon' study up on yuh astrology and get readings on the people you involved with, then you need to cop these on audiobook or drop'em in ya tablet when you get a chance, 'cause you need to know what these folk's out here really be on—so first make sure you get: **The Laws of Human Nature** by Robert Greene. That one'll have you seeing past the surface, past the charm and the looks, straight to the core of who somebody really is. 'Cause if you can't read a person right, you might end up investing in a liability disguised as an asset."

He tapped the table lightly, as if emphasizing the next point.

"And this one—**Ego is the Enemy** by Ryan Holiday. See, some folks ain't in it to build, they just in it to be seen. Sometimes, being surrounded by the wrong influences—those obsessed with status, image, or personal validation—can blind you to real opportunities. This book helps differentiate between what truly matters and what is merely surface-level distraction.

This one'll teach you how to separate real players from the ones just playing themselves."

Unc leaned back, taking a slow sip from his glass before dropping the last gem.

"And **Who Not How,** by Dan Sullivan & Dr. Benjamin Hardy—this one's major. It's about aligning with the right people. 'Cause a dime piece might look like a ten, but if she ain't built for the mission, she'll have you moving like a zero. The right people multiply your progress—the wrong ones drain it. Read up, apply it, and watch how much further you go."

Just then, ole girl snuck up from behind, pinched nephew's bottom with a smile and whispered in his ear, "what you boys up to?"

Eighteen

You on the Right Track, But the Wrong Train

Redirection on yuh destination 'cause course correction is key on the road to riches—when they got the right idea but with the wrong pimpin.

*T*he new office still had that fresh-start smell—polished floors, crisp whiteboards untouched by the scrawled chaos of late-night strategy sessions, and furniture that hadn't yet settled into the weight of long hours. Nephew had built this from the ground up after going through Y Combinator, a powerhouse **start-up accelerator** known for turning startups into giants. He soaked up every lesson, every gem, and now, with a fully incorporated tech company under his belt, the real work was beginning.

But something was missing.

While he had the vision, the foundation, and the initial funding—thanks to his own bankroll and Unc stepping in as an **angel investor**—he still hadn't found the right partners to share the found-

ing process. He had carried the weight solo, but if he was going to land some heavy investors to put real fuel behind his vehicle, it wasn't too late to recruit some top-tier talent and break off a little **equity** *to make it worthwhile. Nephew knew that big wig VC investors didn't even get out the bed for start-up's that didnt have at least a minimum of two or three founders.*

That's where the problem came in, Nephew was the only one with the vision to make decisions.

Sitting in the office's glass-walled conference room, Nephew flipped through résumés, stacks of them, spread out across the polished table like playing cards. The city pulsed outside, the skyline flickering through the panoramic windows, but inside, there was only quiet deliberation. Unc sat across from him, one leg crossed over the other, his hat tilted slightly forward as he watched his nephew wrestle with indecision.

"So, you got your team yet, or you still shufflin' the deck?" Unc finally asked, breaking the silence.

Nephew exhaled, shaking his head. "Man… I met Rene Monae, through either the Shiny.com or CEO Worldwide sites for head hunting executives, and I ain't gon' lie—her mind is different. Sharp, driven, got a real fire for what I'm building—and an A+ and AI Programmer, But she locked in on another project already. And then, just like that, after meeting her, more talent started falling in my lap. And then there's this dude name Ceaser. That Bo'w eat sleep and breath this corporate hustle life.

He like a self taught walkin' MBA—got himself a few courses teaching corporate law, contract law, trust law—I wouldn't be surprised if the ninja got a law of the jungle course comming out soon. I'm like I don't need your courses homie, I need you to jump aboard and come get this shmoney with me, ya diiig. It's like the floodgates of talent finally opened, but now I got too many options and no clear choice. I need partners, Unc, not just employees. Renae and Ceasar my top picks but, with all these others, who do I roll with?"

Unc smirked, rubbing his chin. "it's like the game chose you. Now, it's just about playin' it right." Nephew sighed, scrolling through résumés he already knew by heart. "I just don't wanna fumble this, man. The right team could make or break everything."

Unc let the words hang in the air before shifting slightly in his chair. "See, here's the thing, young blood—you looking for the best partner, but that ain't just about résumés and talent. That's about **alignment**. *You can have all the right pieces, but if they don't fit together, you just got a box full of potential with no puzzle. Yuh dig?"*

Nephew nodded, but his mind was still tangled. "Yeah, but that don't tell me who to pick."

Unc chuckled, shaking his head. "That's on you. But if you vibin' with Rene like that, then campaign for her commitment. Let her know she got the right idea—but she doin' it with the wrong pimpin'." Nephew cracked a small grin. "So, you telling me to recruit and campaign like I'm running for office?"

Unc leaned forward, adjusting his hat. "Like a real candidate, nephew. 'Cause if she really got that fire, then she need to know that what she's buildin' would hit different with you in the picture. Now, if her loyalty to that other project too deep, then you step back like a boss and make another move. But if there's room to work, you let her see the vision through your eyes."

Nephew sat back, letting the words settle. The decision was still his, but now the path felt clearer. Some doors didn't open unless after knocking, you opened them yourself and a closed mouth don't get fed—type shyt. Like the needle dropping on a record, the lesson played from track one.

"Young blood, let me chop it up real quick with-ya about how this game spins," Uncle said. "Sit tight—let's decode the street's creed into corporate deed. Y'all all on the right blade and know how to run the fade, yeah—right track fuh' sho'. Your vision's locked, you hustle hard, yuh heart fiercer than furnace fire. But your'e worried about if you can link up with a team that can execute the dream. You prolly hold trauma from past situation-ships that didn't know whether they was comin' or going. Couldn't run a play if they owned the day.

Sounds like you had a problem with picking grinner's, beginner's, and chicken dinners instead of world class winners. You had potnuhs that could've made life easy but kicking it with'em made you feel sleezy. In your future endeavors you definitely don't wanna let amateurs and fools handle your funds, payroll, taxes or what ever positions you need them on to ensure a smooth sailing of the ship; 'cause negligence could wreak havoc and be disastrous.

I think I get where you coming from. See, back in my day on the track, I saw some pimpin' running their game all wrong, but not me. I played it like chess, reading folks better than they could read themselves. I was pulling the best out the game, choosing who to move with, who to school, and who to leave behind. It's like headhunting in those corporate high rises—pick the best, forget the rest.

The way I saw it—a mack might peep game and see a good earner, a real down chick on the blade working her magic. But if she's with a 'P' who ain't maximizing her potential, who ain't steering her right, she in the right place being led by the wrong face. My job was to show her, "You on the right track, but you riding with the wrong conductor? Time to **reassess and redirect**. Baby, you need to **course correct**. I was on my **'One Minute Manager'** type time.

It's like telling one of your soldiers they lined up perfect, but rollin' with the wrong leadership. Ain't nothing personal, it's all business—it's about finding that right fit, that glove that matches the hand.

When I was out there making moves, I wasn't just another player. I was the playmaker, the game-changer, the strategic mastermind that could spot potential a mile away. My reputation? Built on knowing how to maneuver, how to position myself not just on the street but in any field demanding respect and yielding power.

My bravado ain't just confidence; it's assurance—proof that with me on your side, we ain't just going places, we're setting the destinations. See, when you choppin' it up with these angel investors, VCs, and anyone who you need to get on board with your activity, you got to make them feel like you're the only deal that's real. They'd be foolish not to roll with you. You're the jewel they can't afford 'cause you own the whole jewelry store. You not just playing the game; you're dictating the terms. You the dealer, the player, and the house—and the house always wins.

Peep this: My rep wasn't just built on bravado alone but on a keen eye for the keenest allies. My name echoed not just on street corners but in the hallowed halls where power plays were plotted. I was the kingmaker, the silent partner in the dance of dollars and sense.

And as you move forward, brand this on your brain: Your hustle isn't limited to the lanes you started in. It should stretch to the horizons you're heading toward. From the streets to the boardrooms, from concrete jungles to corporate towers, your hustle should always be about climbing higher, pushing further, living smarter. Your **directional focus** should always be in the direction of ascension, blocking all other noise out.

This ain't just about pulling hoes, crews, employees or investors into your circle; it's about pulling winners. It's about assembling a team so solid, so savvy, that the game itself bends to your will. Even when you're hiring temps to run your day-to-day, you gotta' vet your circle like I vetted mine: no stow-away's, only down by law crew. Only the best.

Now, bring that into today's world—your world. It ain't just about the corners and the concrete anymore. It's about those corporate streets, too. It's about choosing who you ride with very wisely. The team, the partners, the squad, those are the passengers and you're the train. If they become an extension of you then they're the train. The industry, the grind, the hustle—that's your track. Getting all this aligned? That's where you find success.

And here's the game-changer: You ain't gathering no ordinary crowd; you're crafting a conglomerate. You're building a brigade so bulletproof, the game morphs to meet you. You're not anyone's underling; you're the underboss, the capo, stepping up to be the Godfather. You might find yourself on the right track—yeah, that path where your hustle feels right at home, where the grind makes sense. But sometimes, even on that right track, you might be stepping onto the wrong train your damn self. You know what I'm saying? This ain't about turning you into anyone's subordinate; it's about showing you how to captain your ship, right through those real world seas, navigating past sharks and straight to the treasure.

Here's where we link the old with the new, the gritty with the strategic. Pimping taught me about more than just control and cash—it taught me about insight and influence. Choosing your partners with the same precision a seasoned pimp picks his lineup. You need cats who aren't just in your world but are part of your plan. People who add, not just ride along. People who push the whole damn train forward, not just punch tickets. I'm talkin 'bout the kind of people where it ain't on'em, it's in'em.

So here's how it plays: Assess your circle like you would vet your hoes or colleagues in your case. Ask yourself, are they just there for the ride, or are they pumping coal into the furnace, making that engine roar? If they ain't adding to the hustle, they're just dead weight. Send'um to the caboose and cut'em loose. Get with folks who got that same fire under their ass, that same hunger in their belly.

The conductor, whoever it is, gotta stay sharp, hungry for success, and slick with strategy. Picking a partner ain't just about who got the flashiest resume or the smoothest talk. Nah, it's about aligning with those who match your hustle, mirror your ambition, and manage the rails you ride with the precision of a Swiss watch. In this game—be it streets or suits—it's all about who you roll with because yuh network is yuh networth.

Here's the play: Redirect if you must. If the conductor of your trains can't see your vision, it's time to pull that emergency brake. Course correct, nephew. Find those who not only ride but accelerate your journey. This ain't just about riding together; it's about rising together. Assess your alliance. In the relentless pursuit of riches, the right partners are your best leverage.

Look here, young church, let me lace your boots real quick—'cause game ain't just about talkin', it's about knowing how to pick the right players for your squad. There's a couple dynamite books you need to check out that break all this down that I'm tryin' to explain: *The Talent Fix* by Tim Sackett and *Topgrading* by Bradford D. Smart. I'm talkin' game on top of game? Man, they gon' teach you how to sift through the suckers and separate the A-1 steppers from the sideline watchers, ya dig.

See, you ain't just lookin' for warm bodies—you lookin' for cold executioners. *The Talent Fix* gon' show you how to modernize your approach, make sure you pull the top-tier hitters in this competitive jungle. And *Topgrading*? That's your blueprint for upgrading your roster—putting prospects through the wringer so you don't end up investing in liabilities when you need certified assets.

A real boss don't just choose—he *selects*. And if you ain't pickin' with precision, you just throwin' dice, hopin' for a seven. Get them books, apply the knowledge, and make sure your team ain't just runnin' plays, but winnin' rings. You feel me?

Nineteen

Light as a Feather in Any Type of Weather

Soft on the landing, strong on the standing. A real Player bends and never breaks. If the game switches up you pivot because smooth seas don't make seasoned sailors.

*T*he scent of sweat, leather, and old canvas filled the air, blending with the rhythmic thwack of gloves hitting mitts and the steady bounce of jump ropes smacking the floor. The gym was alive with movement—fighters slipping, ducking, weaving, each man sharpening himself like a blade against resistance. Watching fighters train had become a more familiar scene for both Unc and Nephew lately. They'd been finding themselves in the gym more often, both on their own paths to level up physically, seeing that discipline in the body sharpened discipline in the mind.

But today, it wasn't just about their personal fitness grind. Unc had been toying with the idea of expanding his horizons, stepping into the *fight management and promotion game. Boxing had always been one of his favorite pastimes, but now he was looking at it as more than just entertainment—he saw an opportunity. And the young fighter in the ring? He wasn't just some up-and-comer—they were watching a future contender, a real problem in the making, and Unc had already agreed to invest into his pursuits and sign him to a management contract.*

Leaning against the ropes, arms crossed, Unc observed his new fighter with a keen eye, nodding in approval as the young man moved through his sparring session. Nephew stood beside him, absently stretching his shoulder, half-watching, half-reflecting. Lately, life had been swinging heavy, and he'd been feeling like he wasn't slipping punches the way he used to—whether in business, personal relationships, or just the unexpected hits life throws.

"You see that youngin' right there?" Unc finally said, nodding toward the fighter dancing in the ring, slipping past every wild swing with ease, tapping his opponent with sharp, calculated strikes. "That boy ain't fighting the air, ain't wasting a lick of energy. He move light as a feather, but every shot he throw got weight on it. You know why? 'Cause he ain't letting nothin' shake his composure. Soft on the landing, strong on the standing."

Nephew exhaled, watching as the boxer ducked a sloppy overhand and countered with a body shot that made the whole gym wince.

"You was just tellin' me the other day how you been feeling hit harder than usual—like you takin' losses you don't recover from the same way," Unc continued, eyes still locked on the action in the ring. "That's 'cause you swinging too wild, reacting instead of responding. Makin' plays you hadn't fully assessed or prepared for. You know you got to have a plan A, plan B, and a plan C, in this game—thinking ten steps ahead and prepared for whatever cause if you stay ready,

you ain't got to get ready nephew. A real player bends, never breaks. If the game switches up, you pivot. You keep moving, keep finessing, and most important—you never let 'em see you stumble."

The young fighter in the ring sidestepped another hook, landed a clean shot to the chin, and the whole gym murmured in approval. Nephew watched him closely now, hearing the lesson before Unc even had to say it.

"Life gon' throw them punches," Unc said, finally glancing at Nephew. "Question is, you gon' swing blind? Or you gon' learn how to slip, dip, and make 'em count?"

The lecture had already began, but nephew knew to buckle up because more was on the way, Uncle continued.

A real player moves like the wind—unseen but always felt, shapeless yet always shifting, adapting to every environment like a master of the elements. See, nephew, the game don't sit still, and neither do those who win in it. You gotta be light on your feet, heavy in your impact. That means knowing when to float and when to land, when to drift and when to dig in. Stiff trees crack in the storm, but bamboo bends and bounces back. A real player? He ain't out here getting uprooted—he sways, he adjusts, but he never falls.

Now, a fool? A fool gon' stand rigid, stubborn in his ways, chest puffed out like he's immune to change. But when that hard wind blows, he gets knocked clean over, flat on his back, wondering what the hell happened. That's because he ain't built for endurance, only for appearance. He built for show, not for survival—now how many negus you know like that.

See a real boss? He ain't afraid to adjust his crown when the wind shifts. He knows the secret to longevity is **fluidity**—you move when the game moves, you flex when the streets flex, you float when the tides rise, and you drop anchor when the waters get rough. That's the difference between playing to last and playing to impress—now, go learn 'bout dat.

Let me tell you something, nephew—pimpin' ain't just about the gab, the glow, and the get-down. It's about adaptability, about seeing the turns before the road curves. The ones who make it, they ain't the hardest; they the smartest. They the ones who know when to reinvent, when to recalibrate, when to rebrand. A cat who can only operate in one lane? He dead before he even realizes it. The streets, the boardroom, the whole damn world—it rewards the nimble, the versatile, the ones who can flip the script and still stay in control of the story.

See, when I was on the track, I wasn't just watching the weather—I was reading the sky, feeling the air change before the first drop hit. If the blade got hot, I had my next move ready before the cops even knew they was looking for me. If a ho's rhythm started shifting, I already knew if she was getting restless or ready to level up. I wasn't out here waiting to react; I was dictating the flow. That's the difference between surviving and thriving. You either master the pivot or you get spun out the game.

It's the same way in business, in life, in any game you play—success don't belong to the ones who stand still, it belongs to the ones who adjust before they're forced to. Look at the legends, the moguls, the ones whose names ring bells across industries—they ain't just one-trick ponies. They shifted lanes when the lane they was in got too crowded. They went from flipping hustles on the street to flipping properties, from running their mouth to running million-dollar negotiations. They ain't get stuck in one identity, one hustle, one bag—they expanded, adapted, evolved. That's the only way to keep stacking and keep standing.

So look, nephew, lemme run it down to you real clean—'cause what we talkin' about right now? This is the split between them that rise and them that rust. See, the **teachable** ones? They the ones that stay winnin'. They soak up game like a sponge in a rainstorm, takin' knowledge, flippin' it, stackin' it, and usin' it to finesse their next level. But them other ones? The ones who get stuck in their ways, too proud to pivot, too stiff to shift? They the ones that get left behind—watchin' the train pull off while they still arguin' 'bout whether to pack a bag.

A real player understands that knowledge ain't just power—it's propulsion, ya dig. Every new gem you pick up? That's fuel in the tank, pushin' you further down the road. But the stubborn ones? They see a bump in the road and think it's the end of the journey. They hit a little friction and fold like a lawn chair. You ever tried to teach a fool somethin', and he argue with you like he know better—only to turn around and trip over the same damn rock you tried to warn him about? That's what I call a **broke mindset**. Not just in the pockets—but in the spirit. Stagnant. Rusted. Hollow. A fool too stiff to adjust gon' snap when the pressure hit, 'cause he never learned how to bend.

See, **teachability** ain't just about listenin', it's about application. A sucka could sit in the same room as a boss, hear the same wisdom, and still walk out dumber than when he walked in—'cause he refuse to humble himself to the lesson. And that right there? That's the real reason some stay stuck. It ain't the world holdin' 'em back—it's their own resistance to the game that could set 'em free. They'd rather argue their limitations than accept the blueprint to elevation. They'd rather be right than be rich. Rather be comfortable than be capable—is you pickin' up, what I'm layin' down, church?

But let me lace you with this: in this game, the only constant is change. The hustlers that last? They the ones that evolve. They the ones who take feedback and flip it into finesse. But the ones who refuse to learn? They walk themselves right into obsolescence, outdated, unused, like an old flip phone or last decade's computer. And computers? They're notorious for how fast they go from cutting-edge to collecting dust—a prime example of obsolescence.

Players on that path get passed up by the sharp, outpaced by the swift, and outplayed by the ones who ain't afraid to recalibrate. Life don't care how long you been in the game, if you can't keep up and get right, you get left. A tree that refuses to bend gon' break when the storm comes. A player that refuses to pivot gon' perish when the game shifts.

So the question ain't just, "Are you learning?" It's, "Are you adaptable? Are you willing to unlearn what don't serve you and rewire for what does?" 'Cause in this world, nephew, the choice is simple—you either level up, or you get leveled out. They say it ain't the strongest who survive, nor the smartest—it's the ones who can adapt. The ones who can evolve without losin' themselves. That's real survival. That's power. Everything else? Just potential waitin' to be replaced.

Unc grabbed his sweat towel as him and Nephew began to step down from the side of the ring. Another set of boxers and their trainers were stepping in to the ring on the adjacent side as Uncs potential new client greeted them and climbed through the ropes on the other side. Nephew and Uncle started heading in the direction of the locker rooms as uncle continued his monologue.

Now, let's bring it home. You out here trying to build, trying to grow, but are you light enough to move when the game calls for it? Are you too weighed down by your own pride, your own stubbornness, your fear of change? Because let me tell you, pride is the heaviest weight you can carry, and it will drown you faster than any failure ever could. If the business needs to pivot, you hit a 180. If the investment dries up, you **reposition**. If the market shifts, you shift with it. It ain't about holding your ground—it's about knowing which ground is worth holding, and when it's time to plant new roots.

And in your personal life? Same rules apply. People change, circumstances change, even your own damn dreams change—so what you gonna do? Get bitter because the world ain't moving the way you thought it should? Or you gonna be light on your feet, heavy in the street? Because that's what separates the bosses from the bystanders.

Some can't get past the **learning curve**—the stretch between struggle and mastery—where the game weeds out the weak. Some climb quick, others trip at the first step and sit down, mistaking difficulty for defeat. Then there are those who stay lost in the fog, lacking the guidance to recognize their **points of resistance**—those mental roadblocks where ego, fear, or comfort keep a player frozen in place while the game moves on without them. The greats move with the flow, but they never lose control. They adjust without losing essence, they shift without losing strength. Figure out what your point's of resistance are and what it takes for you to blow past any learning curve if you want to stomp down in this game of life.

Look here, **The 4-Hour Workweek** by Tim Ferriss and **The Lean Startup** by Eric Ries come to mind when you talk about moving light through the money game—like a soldier on a mission. You can't be carrying all that baggage when you're trying to get to the bag. Both books preach efficiency, agility, and trimming the fat—whether it's about your schedule or your startup.

That's what being light as a feather in any type of weather really means, nephew. It ain't about being weak; it's about being untouchable. It's about being too fluid to break, too smooth to shake, too smart to stumble. Because in this game—whether it's pimpin', business, or life itself—the only ones who truly fall are the ones who refuse to move. Now listen young church, I dropped some good game, some heavy easter eggs for you to marinate on. Pray-tell Im not wasting my time trying to uplift yo mind—if not, then let the congregation say Amin.

Twenty

If You Ain't Moving, You Losing

Slow feet don't eat and momentum makes money so make a move or miss the meal cause if the wheels aint turning you aint earning.

*U*nder the last strokes of a molten sun, the world seemed to pause at the horizon, bleeding gold across the sky and reflecting off the gentle surf. The tide whispered against the shore, a rhythmic hush that matched the slow drift of Nephew's thoughts. The sky burned in hues of amber and indigo as the sun made its final descent, casting its majesty across the pristine sand. A salty breeze carried the faint scent of charcoal and ocean mist, mingling with the crisp bite of imported beers resting in the arms of their chairs.

Nephew leaned back, exhaling slow, watching the waves roll in. This was what he liked to call his private beach, one of his first rental properties—acquired before he even knew how to properly finesse a lick in the house-flipping game. Now, however, it was a thriving Airbnb. He'd come to check on the renovations his older uncle had overseen, a man with three decades of construction game under his *belt. The work had been solid, but the property had stirred something else in him. A reminder. A whisper of the grind that got him here.*

Lately, he had been coasting. Business was good. His ventures were stacking wins. But something inside him felt stagnant. The hunger wasn't gone—just dulled, like a blade that had seen too many battles without being sharpened. He glanced over at Unc, then at his other uncle—the man who had given this place a fresh face with a craftsman's touch. The three of them sat in weathered beach chairs, the waves licking at the sand just feet away, their bottles sweating in the thick evening heat.

"Man, I ain't gon' lie... I feel like I been out the game too long," Nephew admitted, rolling the bottle between his palms. "Back in the day, I'd make moves like it was nothing—now, I don't know. Feels like I lost my touch." Unc let out a deep chuckle, shaking his head—him and his older brother, both lookin' like Nephew'a grand daddy. He stretched his legs, digging his heels into the cooling sand. "Man, please. That's like saying you forgot how to ride a bike or swim. Once you got it, you don't ever lose it," he said, lifting his bottle in a casual salute. Older Unc, chiming in with a, " Yep—it ain't on you, it's in you."

Nephew smirked, but the weight of it still sat heavy. He knew Unc was right, but knowing and feeling it were two different things.

"You just sittin' still too long, young blood," Unc continued, his voice smooth but firm. "Momentum makes money. Slow feet don't eat. Ain't no playmakers get paid sittin' on the sidelines. You either movin' or you losin'—so what's it gon' be?"

The waves crashed a little harder against the shore, as if echoing the question. And with that, the lesson began.

Young blood, let me lace you with something solid—game that's been tried, tested, and true from the streets to the boardrooms and suites. If you ain't moving, you losing. That's the law of the land, the creed of the conquerors, the unbreakable truth of the game. Motion is money, momentum is mastery, and standing still? That's just waiting to get swallowed whole by the next hungry hustler who got the nerve to move when you hesitated. See, this ain't just about running the track; it's about keeping your pace, keeping your presence felt, and keeping your paper circulating. If I said it once, I said it a thousand times, slow feet don't eat, nephew, and if your wheels ain't turning, then your pockets ain't either.

Back when I was out there, ten toes down, making my name ring bells in every city and town worth touching down, I saw it first-hand—cats who thought they could coast off reputation alone, sitting back while the game evolved around them. Thought they had it all figured out until they woke up one day and realized their stable dried up, their money stopped calling, and their name wasn't worth the spit it took to say it. Why? Because they stopped moving. Got too comfortable, got too **complacent**, got too damn slow. But a real player? A real boss? He stays ahead of the current, riding the wave before it drowns him.

You ever seen a shark stop swimming? Nah, and you never will, because the second it does, it sinks. That's how you gotta be in this game. You ain't just floating, nephew—you hunting. Whether you out there on the blade, in the boardroom, or running your own enterprise, the same law applies. Make a move or miss the meal. See, a lot of these folks get caught up in the illusion of busyness, mistaking motion for movement, spinning their wheels but never getting nowhere. But when you really in it, when you locked in on your bag, your vision, your purpose, you know the difference. You ain't just out here running in circles—you setting direction, dictating pace, steering your hustle with precision.

What it boils down to is **'Proactivity.'** A real boss moves before the moment demands it, nephew—that's what separates the ones making power plays from the ones playing catch-up. Proactivity ain't just about staying ahead; it's about controlling the current before the tide turns against you. See, the game ain't won by the reactors—it's won by the architects, the orchestrators, the visionary **tacticians** who sculpt the landscape before the rest of the world even sees the blueprint.

You anticipate trends like a stock trader on a hot streak, pivot like a grandmaster in chess, and execute like a war general in the thick of battle. The weak wait for permission, the wise create momentum. The broke wait on a blessing, the rich engineer their own elevation. That's the law of the heavy hitters, the cerebral strategists, the ones who shape reality rather than let reality shape them. Proactive means preemptive, and preemptive means unstoppable—when you make your move before the opposition even sees the play forming, you don't just win, nephew. You dominate.

It's like this, nephew: In my day, the best in the game weren't just the ones who had the prettiest players, the most money, or the flashiest cars. It was the ones who knew how to move—strategically, relentlessly, without hesitation. The ones who knew when to switch lanes, when to switch hands, when to make a new plan. It's the same reason why some cats in corporate America stay stuck in middle management while others break through ceilings like they paper-thin. It ain't about being the smartest, the strongest, or the luckiest—it's about having the guts to move when others freeze.

The tide brushed against seaweed and sand as the last traces of sunlight cleared the horizon, casting a soft pinkish glow from the clouds to the seashells. The breeze carried the scent of ocean salt and fading charcoal from a distant bonfire as the brothers, Nephew's uncles, rose from their chairs, stretching off the evening. Gathering their things, they started the slow walk back to the bungalow, the boards creaking beneath their steps. Uncle kept the conversation rolling, his brother chiming in here and there, passing down the kind of wisdom that didn't come from books—only from years in the game of life.

Ain't no room for hesitation when opportunity knocks, nephew. See, that hesitation is the difference between the one who secures the deal and the one who spends the rest of his life wondering what could've been. You think the big dogs in business, in tech, in investment, sit around waiting for the perfect moment? Hell nah. They move fast, they strike first, they capitalize on the momentum before somebody else snatches it out their hands. When a market shifts, they don't sit around complaining—they bust a move. When a deal looks promising, they don't spend months debating—they execute—trying to be **'first to market'.** That's the difference between playing for keeps and playing for maybe.

Same rules apply to life, nephew. You want to climb the social ladder? Expand your network? Build real connections that can open doors money can't buy? Then you better be in motion. Can't expect to make power moves when you stuck in the same circles, talking to the same folks, going through the same routines like life ain't meant to evolve. You gotta put yourself in the rooms where the conversations are happening, where the deals are being made, where the influence is circulating. That don't happen by luck—that happens by movement.

And let's talk family, because even there, the same rules apply. Ain't no progress in a household where everybody stagnant. You wanna be the man your people can depend on? You wanna set the tone for your household, make sure your loved ones ain't just surviving but thriving? Then you gotta lead by example. A man in motion inspires movement in others. When they see you grinding, leveling up, making things happen, it creates a ripple effect. It shows them what's possible. But if you just sitting still, waiting on some magical breakthrough to come save you, all you teaching them is how to watch life pass them by.

See, youngin, a lot of folk get comfortable, <u>lost in a comfort zone they never recover from</u>—stuck. Playin' video games, watching TV, talkin' 'bout hustlin' and startin' a business, but they get caught in the labor trap—just paying bills, just getting by. They let life slip through their fingers like sand, thinking they got time, thinking they'll make moves 'tomorrow.' Then one day, they look in the mirror and see a gray-haired individual starin' back at 'em, wonderin' where the years went. 'Talkn-bout—when I went to sleep, I was 21; when I woke up, I was 51. Time don't wait on nobody, so if you ain't moving, you losing. You either stacking or slacking, making strides or making excuses. So tell me, which type time you on?

See, nephew, the game is the game no matter when, where or how you apply it. If you moving, you winning. If you sitting, you slipping. Life don't wait for nobody, and neither does success. The opportunities don't wait, the bag don't wait, the time don't wait. You either catching flights or catching L's, the choice is yours. So stay sharp, stay swift, and stay in motion. Because the second you stop moving? The game moves on without you—And trust me—you don't want to be the one left standing still.

Personally, I like the message in **The Startup Way** by Eric Ries, the same guy who wrote **The Lean Startup**. That's square talk for what I'm trying to say right now. He applies these same principles to established companies, showing how entrepreneurial management keeps momentum strong and drives continuous innovation. It's similar to **Built to Last** by Jim Collins and Jerry Porras, where they study visionary companies to reveal the key to lasting success—consistent improvement and innovation, basically, if you ain't movin' you losing.

Unc took a slow sip from his bottle, letting the lesson settle in before hitting Nephew with the final gem. "See, Nephew, if you can get you a system going—one that keeps the wheels turning, and the assets earning—you'll streamline your process, for continual progress—you'll never stress and stay blessed with success so you can multiply the checks. The pressure gon' minimize, and all you gotta do is keep the momentum alive---ya dig?

Big Unc finally chimed in, "Neph, let me tell you somethin'. You tryin' to build somethin' solid? Something that don't fall apart soon as you blink?"

Nephew nodded, waiting for the drop.

"Then you gotta actually start thinkin' in systems—not just tasks. I ain't talkin' checklists. I'm talkin' structure. Pick up that book **Work the System** by Sam Carpenter. That one'll show you how to build something that runs smooth—without runnin' *you* into the ground."

He paused, then added, "And while you at it, get into **Thinking in Systems** by Donella Meadows. That one right there? Game changer. It breaks down how everything's connected. Stuff you think is luck or talent? Nah… it's structure. Feedback loops. Patterns. Real invisible gears type stuff."

Systems and models, Nephew, systems and models.

Twenty-One

Hoe Up to Blow Up

Priests need nuns, doctors need nurses. Ho's need pimps. No Team, No Dream—Get a team and get this cream, cause It takes a village to raise a Hustle—Naw'Mean

*T*he hum of Nephew's espresso machine echoed through the open-concept loft, where tall windows let in slices of sunlight that danced across concrete floors and exposed brick. Floor plans, tax folders, and blueprints were sprawled across the marble island like a game of capitalist Jenga. A wall-mounted flat screen flashed between Zoom dashboards and real-time analytics from several ventures.

Nephew paced slowly, AirPods in, half-listening to his virtual assistant list off weekly reports from his various LLCs.

Stacks of manila folders lined the edge of the kitchen counter like troops ready for battle—S-corps, holding companies, real estate projects, a new app in beta, and even an online clothing brand that just crossed into five figures and projected to go even harder. It was the kind of portfolio most folks dreamed about. But the more it grew, the heavier it felt.

Unc sat posted in a leather swivel chair near the balcony, sipping coffee from a "Boss of Bosses" mug, watching his nephew like a hawk eyeing a young lion still learning how to manage his pride.

"Looks like you collectin' more corporations than your homeboys collectin' sneakers," Unc said with a chuckle, nodding toward the stack of legal docs. "That's cute. But you gon' burn out tryna quarterback every play yourself."

Nephew rubbed his temples, laughing. "I just don't trust folks with too many hands in the pot. One false move and a whole empire gone."

Unc leaned forward, elbows on knees, his tone shifting from playful to purposeful.

"Let me put you up on something real. You need a team, fam—mo—a squad. Hell, even an interim CEO to run that holdings company while you focus on the big plays. You trying to juggle all this solo, and that's why the game wearing you thin." I see you finally managed to get a couple partners for your start-up, but that's just one business. What about the trust and holdings company that manages all the businesses.

He paused, a glint of mischief dancing behind his seasoned eyes. "Back in the day, my potnuh's in the life used to say: Hoe up and blow up. Now back then, it meant blowin' up in all the wrong ways, sometimes slick and sloppy."

He smirked, then leaned back in his chair. "But today? I'm flippin' the script. I'm tellin' you: It's like gettin yuh bread up. Gettin yuh hoe's up simply means gettin yuh assets up. Build you a stable. Not of women, but of warriors. Solid players. Specialists. Experts, Hustlers who can hold weight. Folks who ain't just lookin' for a check—they looking to check boxes and build empires."

He pointed toward the window like he was drawing up a vision.

"If you get your hoes up—your assets, your alliances, your aces—you can blow up like the Goodyear Blimp, filled with money from here to the moon. But right now? You hoe-less, doughless and tryin' to control-shyt—by yourself that is. And if you don't get you a stable, you gon' be hopeless and homeless. 'Cause no man's an island—and your ship will sink just as quick as you set sail."

Nephew shook his head, grinning. "Man, I'm just sayin'—trust ain't easy to come by."

Unc cracked his neck, set the mug down like it was the gavel in a courtroom, and leaned in. "That's exactly why I'm talkin'. Trust ain't given—it's built. And if you don't start layin' bricks, you gon' be stuck stirrin' the pot with no kitchen left to cook in."

And just like that, the lecture began.

With all these haters and negativity instigators, I feel you, nephew—it make you wanna say "funk-it" and go dolo. But peep game—ain't never been no such thing as a self-made millionaire. That's a fairy tale for fools who wanna look like gods but move like mortals. See, every king got a court, every general got an army, and every real player got a team. A pimp without a stable is just a dusty dude with a limp wrist and a loud mouth—ain't no power in that. You can talk slick all day, but if ain't nobody riding with you, you just another fool talking to himself.

That's the problem with cats who think they can do it all alone. They wanna make all the money, take all the credit, but they don't realize the real paper comes when you got an in house squad making moves in every lane. It's like running a company with no employees—who answering the phones?

Who handling the paperwork? Who bringing in the business while you busy trying to do everything yourself? The only thing a one-man show guarantees is exhaustion, not elevation. Now don't get me wrong, that's all changing with AI, but that's another story, and even then the apps and software you purchase are assets and an artificial team.

Peep game—back in the day, a pimp with no ho's was just a trick with delusions of grandeur. He can't hit the blade and try to pull his own licks, that's just a criminal, not a pimp. Let's be real—one man can only do so much. He ain't scaling, he ain't growing, and he damn sure ain't running no empire. That's why the real players focused on management. They built a stable, structured their game, and made sure the revenue was flowing from every direction.

Fast forward to today, and it's the same principle—different playing field. You ain't gotta be out there recruiting a stable full of women, but you do need a team that can make your business boom. Every real boss needs a **CPA** to keep the books right, a lawyer to make sure he ain't slippin' legally, a receptionist or assistant to keep the operations smooth, even if they're virtual. And a marketing team to make sure the brand stay visible—and that's just the tip of the iceberg, slim.

But let's not stop there—what about a social media strategist to keep the people engaged? A business coach to keep your vision sharp? A sales team to close deals while you focus on expansion? A gang of mentors to keep you in line when you start to run crooked. Did I mention already that you can even hire an interim CEO to ensure you get that dough?

The truth is, if you ain't **delegating**, you ain't elevating. A CEO don't waste time filing paperwork—he got people for that, and you got him, if you bossin' on that level. A general don't fight on the frontlines—he got soldiers for that, and a king got a general. A real boss moves like a conductor, orchestrating every piece of the puzzle while making sure the money keeps flowing—a mutha phunkin ring master. You can either be the worker or the one signing the worker's checks—or the bank issuing the checks to be signed, the choice is yours.

Now let's get to the real sauce—how do you build a team that works? First, you gotta know your own weaknesses. Ain't no shame in admitting you ain't the best at everything—that's why you find people who are. If you trash with numbers, get a bookkeeper. If you don't know contracts, get a lawyer. If you can't market yourself, hire someone who can. A lot of fools let ego keep them broke because they too proud to ask for help. But real bosses? They hire their gaps for perpetual traps and make sure every part of the machine is working.

Second, you gotta define the roles. You wouldn't put a hoe in charge of handling investments, just like you wouldn't put your accountant in charge of creative direction. You gotta structure your squad so everybody plays their position like a got-damn football team. Every successful company got key departments—finance, marketing, operations, legal, sales, customer service—and whether you're running a Fortune 500 company or a corner sto' hustle, you need those same pillars holding up your empire.

Third, and this the most important—you gotta invest in your team. Ain't no such thing as free game, nephew. If you want quality, you gotta pay for it. Ain't no business ever grown by being cheap on talent. That's like mackin on suzie screw who ain't never knew what to do. The same way a pimp invests in keeping his stable laced and motivated, you gotta make sure your team got what they need to stay sharp, stay loyal, and stay on top of their game. If you build right, the returns gonna be tenfold.

Let me give it to you straight—money don't move on its own. It takes people, processes, and precision. If you want to get rich, you gotta think bigger than just yourself. You gotta build an engine that runs whether you're there or not. That's how the rich stay rich—they build systems, not just stacks. You got to get on your **Cashflow Quadrant** mentality.

So remember this: a one-man hustle is just a job, but a well-run team is an empire in motion. You can keep playing small, trying to do everything yourself, or you can step into the big leagues, put the right pieces in place, and let the money make money. That's the difference between a player and a pawn. Question, nephew. Would you rather have 1% of a billion, or 100% of nothing?

The book, **Good to Great** by Jim Collins shows you how to get the right people on the track and the wrong ones off, so y'all can figure out how to set that track on fire together. And, **Who: The A Method for Hiring**, by Geoff Smart & Randy Street? That's the one that breaks down how to vet, campaign, and mack the best pros for the right roles. It's a whole tactical blueprint for building high-performing teams from the ground up—I'm talkin' super strategies. Get your mind on that wave, and you'll be a'ight.

Let ya math get to mathin on that because at the end of the day, nephew—you gone have to ho up to blow up. When you ho-less and dough-less, you out here like a general with no soldiers—war plan tight, but ain't no troops to execute the fight. Get your team right, structure your game, and watch the empire rise—like a mothership in the muthaphunkin skies.

Twenty-Two

If You Ain't Stackin, You Slackin

Broke habits make rich dreams impossible and rich dreams require multiple streams.

*T*he engine of the blacked-out Hog purred steady at the curb, chrome gleaming under the soft slap of late-afternoon sun. Nephew was at the wheel, dressed casual but crisp, sipping on a protein shake while glancing at the time—determined to keep his word to make it to his son's middle school game. Unc rode shotgun, his window cracked just enough to let in the cool breeze and the faint smell of fresh-cut grass.

Nephew pulled up, gave two quick honks, and seconds later, Junior came sprinting from the driveway where he'd been hoopin' with a couple neighborhood kids. Ball under one arm, sneakers scuffed just right, he slapped hands with his boys and called out, "Gotta go play a real game—y'all stay trash!" before chucking the deuce with a grin.

He hopped into the back seat without missing a beat, tossed his gym bag carelessly over the center console like it owed him money, and immediately locked in on his phone screen. "What up, Pop?

What up, Unc," he muttered, thumbs already scrolling, eyes glued to the glow.

Nephew smirked and shook his head as he pulled away from the curb, easing the Hog back into the street. "Man, this boy ain't even look up. You'd think he got stock in that screen."

Unc adjusted his cazelle shades and let out a knowing laugh, "Lil dude actin' like he just filed taxes and got motion."

A few minutes into the ride, Junior piped up, eyes still on his device. "Aye Pop, I was thinkin'... I need some extra bread for them new J's. Oh—and that Supreme jacket everybody at school be rockin'. I gotta stay fresh."

Nephew side-eyed the rearview mirror. "What happened to all that money you get for good grades? Allowance? Birthday drops? Shouldn't you be sittin' on a bankroll by now?"

"I spent it," Junior mumbled, not missing a scroll. "Stuff came up..."

That's when Unc twisted halfway in his seat with a slow grin, already warming up the lesson. "You tryna be like them other kids that flex but can't cut a check, huh?" let me find out you given all your money to that lil red girl with them sister locks—lookin like the lil mermaid.

Nephew laughed, "This boy get more allowance than some grown folks get on their weekly checks. He oughta have more money than me by now."

Unc leaned back, cracked his neck, and looked over at Jr. "Lemme ask you this, lil man—why you ain't got the fattest bankroll in the whole school? You supposed to be the one floatin' lunch loans, not beggin' for Jordans. See... this where it all starts."

And just like that, the real game began.

Lil nephew, let me lace you with some game that separates the kings from the court jesters, the bosses from the bums. Money ain't just made—it's multiplied, magnified, and managed. It's a tool, a seed, a soldier in the battlefield of wealth. Throwin' it away at the wind is asinine and if you ain't stacking it, then you slacking with it. See, in the game of life, it ain't about how much you make—it's about how much you circulate. What I keep, flip, and grow is all a ninja know. You ever see a fool with a fist full of cash but no plan? A player with pockets fat today but flat tomorrow? That's because they treat money like a moment, not a movement. And let me tell you something, young blood: wealth ain't about moments—it's about momentum.

I call them fools 'a monkey with a million'. You can dress a monkey up even train it how to drive a lil bedazzled go-cart and call it a Cadillac. You can give that same monkey a briefcase with a million dollars cash and guess what that monkey gone do? Look for bananas! Don't know the value of what they have like the untrained eye when looking at a piece of dusty coal that's really got a diamond inside. Same thing with a lot of pimps, simps, gangstas and rappers—they just monkeys with millions.

Give'um a million dollars cash, they liable to go crazy like a ninja who just won the lottery but broke a week later. A monkey wit a million aint where it's at lil nephew. Don't be no monkey with a million. Them people's will give a monkey on TV a million dollars real quick cause they know that the monkeys dribblin, shuckin' and jivin, ain't got the intelligence to make real moves. They'll tell'um to shut up and dribble cause that's how they view them—as monkey's.

A real hustler understands that money loves direction. It follows the wise and flees the foolish. Even the bible say a fool and his money will soon part. That's why broke habits make rich dreams impossible—and you showin' sign's of some real broke habits, lil nephew. You can fantasize all you want about Bentleys, beachfront villas, and offshore accounts, but if you ain't got the discipline to stack, you're just dreaming with your eyes open. And a dream without a plan is just a wish, nephew. Wishes don't pay bills.

See, money got a language, a rhythm, a flow. It ain't meant to be hoarded under mattresses or flexed on the 'Gram for likes and then thrown away on material, valueless trash—it's meant to work—ten toes down certified on the town. That's what the real ones do. They let their money move, circulate, and **compound** like a snowball rolling downhill, getting bigger with every turn. That's **'The Compound Effect'**, nephew—small, consistent wins stacking up into an empire. Every dollar you invest, every asset you acquire, every **revenue stream** you create is another brick in the fortress of your financial kingdom. You ever see a dripping faucet in a plugged up tub or bucket, leave for a while and come back the drip turned to drops and the drops need mops. That's the power of **compounded interest.**

But let's talk about them **multiple streams** because a one-trick pony don't last long in a high-stakes race. You put all your eggs in one basket, and one bad move got you scraping pennies. That's why the wealthy don't just rely on one hustle—they **diversify**. Stocks, real estate, businesses, digital assets—hell, even side hustles that make money while they sleep. You ever wonder why the richest men own pieces of everything?

Because ownership, nephew, is how you graduate from making money to making moves. That's how a ninja stay holdin something and when I say holding, I'm talking about **holdings companies** holding multiple LLC's. See, some collect shoes and some collect jewelry, but you nephew, If you soak up this game I'm drenching you in right now, something proper, you'll be collecting LLC's—while yo potnuh's them collect shoe's, tee's, and fees.

You ain't to young to soak up this game I'm giving you, especially if you can recite every lyric of your favorite rappers last three albums. There are several 14 year old millionaires bussin' moves right now as we speak. Farrah Gray, the author of Realionaire, was fourteen years old when he made his first million dollars.

You got to think of yourself as a bank, and banks don't operate off one deposit. They keep that paper moving—loans, investments, interest. That's why banks stay rich and most folks stay broke—because banks understand the game of flow. You let your money stack, collect, reinvest. You build streams so strong that even if one dries up, you still got rivers feeding the ocean of your motion.

Now let me tell you where fools fall off—spending like the money gon' last forever. They get caught up in that feeling, that first high like a bass head riding that first blast off. They treat cash like it's infinite when really, it's fragile without a foundation. You get a check and blow it on liabilities instead of assets, and before you know it, you're back to square one.

That's why stacking is about more than just putting money away—it's about making sure that every dollar you touch has a purpose. See, real bosses don't spend money, they allocate it, ya dig.

Peep game: you ever heard of **the 50/30/20 rule**? Fifty percent goes to needs, thirty to wants, and twenty to investments and savings. That's a basic formula, but the real ones? They flip it. They make sure investments and assets come first because they know money begets money. Every dollar put to work is a seed planted for future wealth. And LIL nephew, if you plant nothing, you harvest nothing. I want you to download a book called **The Richest Man in Babylon** nephew, and I promise you'll thank me for that. If I aint never did nothing for you, you gone tell ya grandchildren, I did that.

But real talk, the problem ain't that people don't make money—it's that they don't know how to keep it. You can't just make a bag, you gotta protect that bag. You gotta learn how to build a moat around your money, make it bulletproof, make it recession-proof. And that means stacking with a strategy. What's the move? Assets over liabilities. Land over luxury. **Equity** over expenses. Do you know how to protect yo' bag youngin.

"Yep," said Junior. "Stop lie-in' "said Unc. "I call cap on that," said Nephew.

You ever see how the real players move? They ain't worried about quick cash, they're focused on ownership. They own real estate, stocks, intellectual property. They making money in their sleep while the average man trading hours for dollars. Nephew, if your money ain't working harder than you, you're doing it wrong. You suppose to have so much money, you can borrow against the money you got, and never have to spend yo own money.

Nephew added, " when I was your age son, my money was selling candy and clothes.

By the time the Hog rolled into the lot at Paul B. West Middle School, the energy was already electric. The parking lot buzzed with motion—parents, teachers, and students weaving between cars, all funneling toward the west entrance and into the glow of the gymnasium lights. Jr. grabbed his bag, slung it over his shoulder, and stepped out with swagger. He spotted a familiar face across the lot and lit up. "Oh yeah, my man gon' get this work tonight. Imma Steph Curry and Allen Iverson him in one move—might even twist his ankle if I can!" Unc and Nephew both laughed from inside the truck. "Quite the confidence, young player," Unc said, shaking his head with a grin, then leaned back in his seat and slid right back into the game he was lacing.

Bottom line youngsta, If you ain't stacking, you slacking. Ain't no way around it. Broke habits keep you broke, and wealth is a byproduct of discipline. It's a long game, a patient grind, a marathon, not a sprint. You got to let your money mature, let it compound, let it grow into something that lasts generations. Because true wealth ain't just about what you got—it's about what you can pass down. That Insured Trust money won't ever treat you funny.

So, Im'ma leave you with this—every dollar you touch, give it a mission. Stack like your future depends on it—because it does. Move smart, invest wise, and remember: Rich dreams require multiple streams, and if your money ain't multiplying, you're just playing at the table, not running the casino.

"Look here, son," how's this for motivation, Unc said, turning in his seat to glance back at Jr. "The first book I ever gave your pops was **The Richest Man in Babylon.** Nephew, make sure you gift that to the boy soon as y'all get back home."

Then he smirked. "Now my personal favorite? **The Compound Effect** by Darren Hardy. Jr., if you read that book from front to back, I'll drop a stack on you—swear ta God."

Nephew chuckled. "C'mon, Unc..."

"Nah, for real," Unc continued. "And if he wins this game today? I'll throw in another three hundred for them shoes and that jacket. If he win, he earned it. And that book? You already know."

Nephew nodded. "Alright then, here's the play—finish that book in under a week son, I'll match Unc's stack. That's two racks just to flip some pages, you feel me? But you definitely got to present what you learned and it betta make sense"

Jr. sat up straight, eyes wide. "*Bet. Say less.* I'm 'bout to have $2,300 in under 72 hours—double or nothin' though," said Jr.

Unc laughed, leaning back with a grin. "Slow down, young playa'. Crawl before you walk."

Twenty-Three

The Glow-Up Is Heavy, When the Hustle Is Steady

Water your game daily, and your paper gon' bloom in season because consistency is King. Sow right, and the Harvest gon' be Bountiful. The Gow-Up don't require no co-sign.

*H*ints of barrel-aged brandy mingled with the musky sweetness of a Cuban leaf burning slow, clung to the air like legacy, heavy and familiar. City lights glittered in the distance, winking through floor-to-ceiling windows that framed the rooftop penthouse like a portrait of everything they'd survived—and everything they were about to conquer. Laughter echoed beneath the soft hum of Gen Z, R&B spilling from hidden ceiling speakers, while the heat lamps cut through the November chill, casting a warm orange glow over leather seats and linen suits.

Nephew leaned back, Cuban cigar in hand, the weight of accomplishment pressed gently on his chest like a tailored overcoat. A final *round of toasts had just settled into the marble-top bar, and for a moment—just a short moment—he felt untouchable.*

A true November Sagittarius, he was celebrating more than just another turn around the sun. It was real birthday vibes, Thanksgiving energy, and the sweet afterglow of the biggest play of his entrepreneurial career. That morning, he'd closed on a wholesale deal that offloaded what had become a cluttered mess of low-yielding businesses: a barbershop, three laundromats, eight rental properties, a catering company, and one of his restaurants—all sold in one fell swoop to a childhood friend from the old block.

His friend, a former street king and heavyweight now looking for a cleaner way to scale, was smiling like a man who just bought back his freedom. And Nephew? He felt like a king. He'd moved a money pit off his plate and leveled up—stepping into higher-stakes ventures that moved fast, earned faster, and stacked real value in his portfolio. It was the kind of pivot seasoned players live for. The homie had the time and the motivation to nurture all of the assets offloaded to turn profits. Nephew just wanted the bag and a headache-free business plan for leveled-up living.

Now, surrounded by select guests, fine drinks, and panoramic views, the night had shifted from celebration to reflection. Nephew, his old friend, and Unc finally peeled away from the noise and tucked into the velvet-lined VIP section. Cigars lit. Glasses refilled. Time slowed. Unc swirled his drink, his "Boss of Bosses" ring catching the dim light, and leaned in with a knowing grin.

"So... how it feel to finally enjoy the fruits of your labor, Nephew?" And just like that, the wind shifted. Nephew exhaled a smooth puff of smoke, and before the cloud had a chance to fade, Unc leaned forward—ready to drop that heavy game, the kind that don't come in books.

Look here, nephew, you a real inspiration, even to people that you'll never know is watchin', including yuh haters. Everybody wanna glow, but don't nobody wanna grow, and that's fuh-sho'. Everybody wanna flex, but don't nobody wanna build cause of what come's next. See, this here game is like a garden—you can't just throw seeds in the dirt and expect a feast overnight. You gotta water that soil, tend to them roots, and stay on it daily, 'cause the bloom don't come from staring at the moon with wishful thinking—it come from the work. The ones who shine the brightest? They the ones who grinded the longest, stayed diligent while the rest dipped out. The glow-up don't come from sudden sparks, it come from steady embers that never burn out. It might look like it happened over night, but we know the truth.

You ever seen a dude hit a quick lick, come into some fast money, and six months later, he back down bad? That's 'cause he ain't have no foundation, no steady drip. Money ain't magic, it's mathematics—you suppose to stack it slow, stack it right, and let it multiply, ya dig. The fool blows his first bag like it's his last, but a real player treats every dollar like a thoroughbred, sending it on a mission to bring back more. Consistency is the glue between ambition and achievement—it's the middleman. Without it, you just running in place, sweating but never stepping forward, like a hamster on a hamster wheel.

And that's where **commitment** comes in. Yes sir, baby boy, consistency and commitment. where them things like super powers id you can help it. See, most folks think success come from talent, luck, or even just hard work alone. But real power? Real wealth? That come from dedication to the long game. Think about it like this: if you improve by just 1% a day, in a year, you ain't just 365% better. Nah, because of the way compounding work, you'd be about 3,778% better—that's 38 times the person you started as. But if you quit every time the progress slow, if you take breaks 'cause you ain't seeing big moves overnight, you resetting yourself back to zero every time. It's called **'Consistent Growth'** and without it some folks never get ahead—they keep stopping and starting instead of stacking their wins. How you gone establish anything if you keep breakin up and startin over. Most people ain't got the vision to make the right decision, and as a result, they misrepresent the pimpin'.

It's like building a brick wall, one brick at a time. You don't see the full picture on day one, or even day fifty. But you keep stacking, keep layering, and by the time a year pass? You sitting behind a fortress while everybody else still standing outside wonderin' why they lil' pile of bricks never turned into some-thin' solid. Commitment is stackin'—consistently, relentlessly, with precision—'til what you build is too strong to be knocked down. In the P-game, that's when you considered verified and bonafied.

Now, check this, nephew. There's two types of people in this game: the ones who dabble and the ones who dedicate. The dabblers work when they feel like it, push when it's convenient, and wonder why they pockets stay light. Lazy, if yuh ask me—and ripe for the knockin. The dedicated? They work when they tired, grind when they uninspired, and push through the droughts 'cause they know the rain gon' come.

And when it do? They eating. Heavy. 'Cause they ain't just hustle in the sunshine—they built in the shadows, they stayed down 'til they came up, yuh dig.

And that's the key right there—**momentum.** You ever seen a snowball roll down a hill? At first, it's small, slow, almost unimpressive. But let it keep rollin', let it keep building, and before long, it's an avalanche. That's what consistency do for your hustle—it take something minor and turn it major. One deal turns into two. Two turn into ten. Ten turn into a legacy. But if you keep stoppin', keep resettin', keep hesitatin', you gon' forever be at square one, watching everybody else eat while you trying to plant new seeds every season. Same rule's apply to relationships. That's how a person get multiple baby mommas and baby daddies. Can't lock in long enough past the mistakes and lessons to get to the blessin's. It take time—and within that time you gon' have to jump over endless hurdles, but if you want to actually get to the finish line, you already know what you gotta do.

You see, the streets and the suites ain't much different. A broad don't get chose off one night of good action—there's a grace period. She get chose off consistent results. Same with business—investors, clients, customers, they don't just look at your highs, they look at your track record–ya credentials. Can you deliver every time? Can you stay solid when the pressure on? Can you show up and show out, not just once, but always? You got 90 days to show and prove. That's what make folks put their trust in you. The man who moves right once is lucky. The man who moves right always is legendary.

That's why I tell you, nephew, don't get caught up chasing the illusion of overnight success. The glow-up come with the work, not the wish. Social media got folks thinking you can just wake up one day, drop a product, and be rich by noon. But they don't see the years of preparation, the failures, the lessons, the daily deposits that built the overnight "miracle." Real wealth—real power—come from putting in that work on a steady basis, not just when the cameras rolling. Aint no pimp ever stabled up to ten bad bitches in one night, he had to hit that blade and campaign like a runaway train. He had to stack'em one by one—like Wing Lee Chun–who ever the phuk that is.

You want the real sauce? Here it is: **compounding effort.** Write that down. It's like compounding interest in a bank account. You put in work today, it builds on what you did yesterday, and tomorrow? It builds even more. Every day you skip? You losing momentum. Every time you quit and start over? You resetting the clock. But when you stay at it, stay building, keep watering that game, one day you wake up and realize—you ain't just surviving no more, you thriving.

They say money talk—bullshyt walk, so let's get at it. If you saved just $5 a day, that's $150 a month. Sounds small, right? But after 10 years, that's $18,000, and if you investin' it smart? That could easily flip to $50,000 or more. Now, imagine if you stacking $50 a day instead. You see how big them numbers get? That's why slow and steady gon' always beat quick and careless. The glow-up ain't about luck, it's about consistent, strategic moves that build over time. Utilizing model's and systems.

So peep game, nephew: You ain't gotta move fast, but you gotta move daily. One step a day still get you further than standing still for months—and that's pullpit-shyt. Every boss, every mogul, every king started with small moves that turned into big empires. Imagine startin' out sleepin' in your car producing plays, then flipping that into a billion dollar empire with your name on more TV shows and movie's than Disney. Ain't nobody out here planting a seed today and eating tonight. But stay steady, keep that water flowing, and best believe—when the season hit, your harvest gon' be so heavy, you might just need help carrying all them blessings.

Unc leaned back in the velvet booth, smoke curling from his cigar, and said, "Y'all ridin' high now, but the real ones don't just toast the moment—they build legacies." He glanced between Nephew and his childhood friend. Hope you takin' notes adn writing down every jewel I pass to yo' crown.

"You ever read **Grit** by Angela Duckworth? She breaks it down—talent counts, but effort counts twice. She tells real stories that prove when you put in that long-haul grind, there's real payoff at the end. Success don't come from luck or shortcuts—it's about staying in the game and learning how to enjoy your wins when they finally come. And if you want to understand what it takes to level up beyond good, pick up **Relentless** by Tim Grover. That man coached legends like Jordan and Kobe. His take on hard work, obsession, and the payoff of staying relentless is unmatched. Y'all winning today, but don't just taste the fruit—learn how to plant orchards so you can eat forever."

"Aye—Keep sowing, keep growing, and watch how the glow-up do you justice—ya feel me?" Said Uncle, before standing back up, grabbing his drink and ending it with, "now I'm bout to get back to this celebratin' thang and go figure out why this pretty young thang keep staring over her at me like I'm a piece of rotiserie gold with rosemary sprinkled on top."

Twenty-Four

A Real Boss Moves in Silence—But His Impact is Loud.

Quiet hands can stack loud bands—real power don't need a microphone.

*T*he venue was something out of a high-society dream—crimson velvet drapes, chandelier halos kissing the ceilings, and the rich undertone of aged merlot mingling with candle wax and polished mahogany. Uncle stood posted near the rear terrace, his blazer sharp, his charm sharper. One of his new friends—a high-society widower he'd met at an art auction weeks prior, the Clair Huxtable type—had invited him to accompany her to the private wine tasting. She was elegant, affluent, and refreshingly generous, having inherited her late husband's multi-millions and the confidence to spend freely.

When her phone buzzed with news of her ailing mother's emergency, she clasped Uncle's hand and apologized, urging him to stay and enjoy the evening. "My driver will return for you whenever you're ready," she promised. Uncle, calm as ever, waved it off with a smile.

"Don't worry, darlin'—I'll have my nephew scoop me. You go check on Momma."

By the time Nephew arrived, the tasting was in full swing, soft jazz floating through the air like a fine mist. Waitstaff moved like whispers, refilling flutes and clearing canapés with practiced ease. Uncle spotted him right away, raising a glass in greeting and motioning him over with a slow grin.

"Mane, you missed the caviar station," he teased, clapping Nephew on the shoulder before turning back toward the crowd. *"But come on—let me give you the tour without even walking."*

As Nephew swirled a glass of Bordeaux and let notes of oak and dark cherry settle on his tongue, Uncle leaned in with that low, knowing tone. He nodded toward three men mingling near the gallery wall. *"That one owns half of downtown. That one sold his tech startup for eight figures. And that one? Inherited multiple billions."* Let's not forget about the lil crowd over there.

He let it hang in the air before adding, *"Logistics, infrastructure, real estate… these the kinda cats who could be behind you in line buying bagels in a coffee shop and you wouldn't even know it."* Basically, **The Millionaire Next Door** type—which, by the way, is a solid read. Written by Thomas J. Stanley and William D. Danko, it breaks down how most real wealth moves in silence—modest lifestyles, smart investments, and zero interest in flashing for attention and validation.

Nephew blinked, giving them another glance. *"They the most unassuming people in here,"* he said, swirling his wine. *"They don't even look like billionaires."* Uncle cracked a smile as they made their way toward the valet. *"Well then,"* he said, sliding a hand in his pocket, eyes fixed on the night, *"what does a billionaire look like to you?"*

And just like that, the lesson began—on perception, presence, and the kind of power that don't need to raise its voice to be felt.

"Real G's move in silence like lasagna," said Nephew.

Yeah, Young Tune-chi wasn't just rhyming when he dropped that line; he was giving you the whole blueprint in one slick slice of good game, said Unc. Apparently, his *chi* was *tuned* to a higher frequency with that bar—no pun intended. People makin' plays, stackin' wealth, and solidifying power without making a damn sound—that's real G' shyt. That's next-level game, 'cause in this world, the loudest one in the room is always the easiest target.

Think about the Walton family—the minds behind Walmart. Collectively, they sitting on a fortune worth over $400 billion—that's damn near half a trillion—a mountain of money so high, you could put a mansion on the moon with it. I wouldn't be surprised if they had one up there now, and you just didn't know about it. But let me ask you, nephew—can you name any of those siblings' names? Their kids? Their grandkids—the ones running the company now? Probably not. Yet, chances are, something in your fridge, something in your closet, or something in your stomach right now came from their empire. They are literally inside you and on you. Talk about, it ain't on yuh, it's in yuh—well they on ya and in you. Hey mane, they wealth whisper and they business shouts.

The name of the game is **'Strategic Silence.'** They don't need to stunt for attention because their power speaks for itself. In fact, nephew, do you know the names of any of the world's top richest families? Probably not. That's the game. True and living game—and more than enough to knock the lining out the frame.

Im'ma break it down further, 'cause too many ninjas out here think bossin' up means broadcasting they every move. Broadcastin' they signals like they Cox cable or Comcast every time they log on. Nah, nephew, it's the opposite. You ever see a lioness announce she bout to hunt? Nah, that beast stay low in the grass, moving in silence, waiting for the right moment to strike. It's the ones making all the noise that get spotted first—the flashy peacock, the barking dog, the loudmouth in the club talking about how much he got. But the real heavy-weights? The silent killers? They don't need to say a damn thing. They let the results do the talkin', like a virus from the Wuhan lab.

Now, let's chop up why this matters. When you loud, you expose yourself. You put a target on your back. Whether it's the streets or the boardroom, the more you talk, the more people know how to move against you. You stunt too hard, the jackers start plotting. You brag too much, the feds start watching. You let folks in on your next move, suddenly they running the same play before you even get off the bench. That's why the real bosses keep their mouths shut and their minds sharp.

They move with precision, like a chess master thinking five moves ahead, never tipping their hand until checkmate is already in motion. The Harlem OG's taught us all a hard lesson back in the 70's when they was wearin' chinchilla fur's to fights and gracin' the cover of The New York Times magazine. Unless you got Blackrock backin' you—keep the stuntin' private.

Let's take it to business, 'cause I know you trying to build something major. When you running a brand, starting a company, making investments—you don't tell the whole world your playbook. If Amazon told folks in the '90s that they planned to dominate every industry from retail to cloud computing, you think folks would've just sat back and let it happen? Hell nah. If Tesla revealed every innovation they working on, other companies would be racing to drop their version first to the market. See, the best moves are the ones people don't see coming until it's too late. That's why patents exist. That's why NDAs exist. That's why silence is one of the most valuable currencies in the game. That's why silence is golden.

And look, I know the world we in makes it hard to move like this. Social media got everybody broadcasting their wins, flexing for likes, showing off every play they making like the game is some damn reality show. Just folks seekin validation and attention—probably didn't get no lap time on daddies knee when they was babies but nephew, trust me—real money don't need an audience. The loudest voices online? Half of 'em ain't got a dime to their name. They want validation more than they want success. They want clout more than they want cash flow. And that's why they stay losing while the silent movers stay winning.

Let me hip you to a real example. Look at Jay-Z. Early in his career, he was loud—had to be, 'cause he was coming from nothing, trying to force his way into an industry that ain't want him. But once he got established? The moves got quiet. He went from rapping about selling dope to quietly buying up art that appreciates by the millions. From flashing chains to owning liquor brands and making strategic investments in companies folks ain't even know he had stakes in. He learned the truth—when you got real power, you don't have to announce it. Unfortunately everybody already know his name. Imagine he was born into the wealth, trained and now all he had to do was maintain. He could be a ghost—making billion dollar toast.

Man, let me put you up on some high-level game, right? It's this cold book called **Only the Paranoid Survive** by Andrew Grove—the big homie who ran Intel. He breakin' down what he calls **Strategic Inflection Points**—that's when the whole game change, silently, slick, and if you ain't payin' attention, you outta position before you even realize you slippin'. Homie said bein' paranoid ain't weakness—it's wisdom. Paranoia ain't fear, it's foresight. It's how you protect the paper, the power, and the position. See, squares get comfortable—kings stay cautious. That's why I always say, don't just move... maneuver."

Nephew, I know you got dreams of building something big—something that's gonna feed you, your family, and your legacy for generations. But if you wanna make it happen, you gotta stop thinking like a showman and start thinking like a strategist. Every move don't need an audience. Every dollar you stack don't need to be posted. Every play you make don't need to be a spectacle. You need to move like a whisper but hit like a hammer.

Silence is power, and discipline is the tool that wields it. The world don't need to know your every step—just let 'em see the results when you reach the top. When you talk too much, you give folks a chance to counter your plans. But when you move with quiet strength? You stay ten steps ahead, untouchable, undeniable. Man, is you listenin'.

Lock this in, nephew:

- **Move like a ghost, but hit like a heavyweight.**

- **Let your presence be felt, not heard.**

- **Stack quiet, play smart, and make 'em wonder how you did it.**

Because at the end of the day, a real boss don't need a microphone—his empire speaks for itself. I'll leave you with this nephew. Why do you think when you going through it, it helps to talk to someone? Because you get to release the energy. The same rules apply when you talk to someone about your plans—you release the energy instead of letting it fester within and bubble up till it pop and make the money drop. That's why when you tell everybody your master plan, you eventually lose steam—and yo' reality remains a dream. **WAKE UP NEGUS!**

And I mean that in a most ethopic way.

Twenty-Five

BOSS UP

Elevate your game, establish your authority, and seize the throne. But first ask yourself, do you deserve to be followed or just left alone. A real boss delegates, not dominates.

*T*he smell of garlic, basil and oregano, seared into grilled lamb filled the air as servers glided between tables, balancing trays and whispering wine pairings. It was a full house at the flagship spot—linen crisp, jazz soft, and the dim golden lighting casting halos over steaming entrées. But beneath the surface of polished silverware and polite laughter, something sharp buzzed in the air—like the prickle of static before a storm.

Cee was behind the line, apron dusted with flour, wrist flicking over a sizzling pan like a symphony conductor. This was his domain. He'd earned it—after five years upstate and a rebirth that started behind a steel kitchen door in a prison cafeteria. Now, he was respected, clean, and cheffin' like a man with something to prove. And he was proving it. Every plate that left his kitchen had a piece of his soul on it. You'd think Ancestor Mamie was whispering recipes in his ear.

But even reformed soldiers got triggers.

Cecil was Nephew's older brother. Always had been the protector, the enforcer, the first one to throw hands when things got sideways. Back in the day, the hood called him "Cee' Merkah"—half joke, half warning. He was good with his hands and even better with pressure—you just might get merked if you played with him.

Did a five-year stretch in the pen in his early twenties, came out sharp and hungry. But he wasn't trying to live on survival mode anymore. After his release, he hit up culinary school, turned his heat into hustle. Flame, flavor, and focus became his new weapons. He started a family, leaned into fatherhood, and found peace in the kitchen.

Nephew saw his brother's vision and backed it with capital—Cee handled the kitchen, Nephew handled the numbers. That was the arrangement. But no matter how far Cee came, he still had that switch. That part of him that never fully turned off.

These boys was raised on a creed: **Am I my brother's keeper?** *Always. Even when your brother's slipping back into shadows you thought he left behind.*

The tension had begun with a server breaking protocol—hooking up one of their people with extra plates and a table they hadn't earned. That kind of thing slid sometimes, if done right. Quiet. Respectfully. But this dude's people? Loud, sloppy, and talking greasy. Real belligerent. Real disrespectful. Word around the staff was the guest had said something slick—something that turned Cee's eyes cold. He'd already taken the apron off. Hands twitching. Neck flexed. Cee was about to merk the bol. That old Cee-Merkah energy resurfacing from the depths.

The energy in the dining room shifted sharp—like silverware scraping porcelain. A few patrons froze mid-bite. One of the new hostesses slipped quietly into the back, reaching for her phone with the police queued up on speed dial. Cee was just about to open-hand slap the man where he stood—right there in the middle of the restaurant like it was D-Block chow hall—yet a place where anyone from the mayor to a millionaire could've been dining. Right on cue, like a god send, the front doors chimed open.

Nephew walked in—fresh from a morning meeting, cheesin', blazer open, gold Rolex catching light. But he wasn't alone. Unc was right behind him, looking like trouble's older cousin in a felt-brimmed hat and that long trench that always smelled faintly of leather, cologne, and legacy. Unc clocked the situation before Nephew could even blink. He didn't raise his voice. Didn't rush. Just stepped in like gravity itself had entered the room, dispersing chaos like fog in sunlight. The guests kept eating. The staff exhaled. Cee just stood there, fuming.

"Let's take this out back," Unc said, hand resting on Cee's shoulder like a gentle clamp. He walked both his nephews out back like it was a family matter. Because it was. Out in the alley, the sounds of the city returned—muffled horns, an air vent humming. Unc reached into his coat and pulled out that long green and white pack of 'pote-wanhunnits', Tapped two out. Handed one to Cee, lit it for him, then lit his own.

The silence hung like smoke. Nephew stood between them, a bit flustered himself and unsure if he was about to witness a breakdown or a breakthrough. Nephew smiled at Cee and said, Damn Cee, I thought you was a finesser, not an aggressor—man, I would've hated to see that boy face had you went through him. "Man down, I repeat, man down, send for back up.'

They both chuckled and then Unc exhaled slowly, looked Cee in the eye, and said, "Now, we all got pressure points. But if you ain't

careful, pride'll cost you more than prison ever did." He leaned in,
voice low, and the gospel of experience began.

My nephews, listen close, and get ya note pad out 'cause
I ain't got time to babysit no grown-ass boys still throwing
tantrums in the sandbox of life. There comes a time when every
player has to put away his childish ways and grow da phuk
up. Not just in age, but in mind, in spirit, and in movement.
You wanna be a boss? Then act like one. I know both of y'all
wanted to hit ole boy but all that means is you slippin on
ya pimpin. The moment you revert back into a gorilla, you
runnin' out of pimpin'. Ya 'P' tank runnin' on E. See, a king
that moves off impulse is a king that loses his kingdom. This
game don't reward temper tantrums and reckless reactions. It
rewards composure, foresight, and calculated execution. Read
The 48 Laws of Power to learn how you deal with a chump
like that.

Nephew and Cee both looked at each other and silently
mouthed, 'Chump' ? then smirked as uncle continued.

Ain't no real leadership without self-mastery. You can't expect to run an empire when you can't even run your emotions.
Gorrila-pimpin' is to close to killa-simpin' for me—remind
me of gang member pimpin. Just to much anger, chaos and
emotion for my taste, but to each his own. If you like it, I love
it for you.

Regarding those emotions though, you ever see a general
cry on the battlefield? A beloved CEO throwing a fit in the
boardroom? Not hardly. Power moves in silence, discipline
walks with dignity, and real bosses make decisions, not excuses.

Emotional intelligence, nephew, is the ability to control the beast within, not let it run wild. That's the difference between a man that commands respect and a boy that demands attention. I'd advise both of y'all to look up a hundred videos online about emotional intelligence before sun-up tomorrow. You cant kill emotion, but you can control it and harness it like a weapon, otherwise it'll be weaponized—against you. When that happens, it'll then be all types of criticism and evangelism against yo' good name and reputation. It takes a whole season to build it, and a split second to burn it down.

Now, let's chop it up about **social intelligence**, 'cause a fool with no foresight will lose to a man with a plan every time. It ain't just about what you say—it's about how you move. The way you carry yourself, the way you engage with people, the way you finesse situations without forcing 'em. **'Power vs. Force,'** It's knowing when to speak and when to stay silent, when to press forward and when to fall back. The loudest one in the room? That's the easiest one to finesse. But the one who observes, who calculates, who keeps his emotions in check? That's the one who wins. The self controlled man vs. the unhinged man. The cash out, vs. the crash out.

Let me put it in perspective—you ever seen a seasoned pimp beg a hoe to stay? Hell nah. A real one keeps his emotions under control cause' often times, she look betta going than she did coming. She wanna go? Then let the door be her chauffeur. Why? Because a boss don't chase—he attracts. He don't force—he persuades. And he don't crumble under pressure—he applies it. You can't lead if you're out here acting like a crash dummy, making reckless moves off emotion instead of strategy. That's the job of a killa or a gorilla, not a peeler and a thriller.

A real boss **delegates**, not dominates, 'cause power ain't about doing everything—it's about making sure everything gets done without you breaking a sweat. See, a fool thinks control means micromanaging every move, barking orders, and keeping a tight grip on every little detail. But a true boss? He moves like an architect—he lays the blueprint, puts the right pieces in place, and lets the machine run smoothly. He don't need to flex authority 'cause his system speaks for itself. There are some bosses out their, they don't have to say a word, it might incriminate'em. They just give a look and we got actions and activity. The system already pre selected and set up is automated and activated.

Domination is insecurity disguised as leadership. Delegation is real power—it means you trust your team, your vision, and the foundation you built. The difference between someone who get's this and who doesn't? One runs an empire, the other runs himself into the ground. It takes real mental control to move like that, nephew. Pimpin' been a non-contact sport from day one—all mind, no muscle. You got to make a choice on which one you plan to be because if you misguided and undecided oh how the pimpin' gone show up in yo' game 'of life', then you already lost at being a boss.

That's why only the sharpest players thrive. This game is by choice not force; it's about finesse. It takes a steel mind to lead without lifting a hand, to command without chaos, to win without war. And that's why I can lace you with this wisdom—I ain't just talking, I'm speaking from experience. I know the game 'cause I mastered the game.

Ego is the Enemy by Ryan Holiday breaks down how cool heads build empires, hot heads lose them. Unchecked ego and reactive emotion will destroy everything you building. You got to observe your emotions, don't become them. Michael A. Singer teach you that in **'The Untethered Soul'**. All of'em scroll's to get you on a roll.

Forethought, nephew. That's what separates a peasant from a king. It's the ability to see ten steps ahead while everybody else is focused on the step they on. *Sun Tzu,* the master of war, said "The greatest victory is that which requires no battle." Meaning, if you gotta' fight every time to win, you already lost. If you ain't Money 'mutha-phunkin' Mayweather then you a got-damn clown is what you is, fightin' all the gotdamn time. The best players finesse their way to the top without breaking a sweat.

Now, let's talk **mindfulness**, because that's another pillar of real leadership. A weak mind is like a broke pocket—it ain't got nothing to offer but struggle—and that's realer than real deal Holyfield. A real boss don't just react—he processes. He moves with intention, not impulse. You ever seen a cat playing chess, sweating over his next move? No. He already seen the checkmate before the other fool even grabbed his first pawn. That's the kind of patience and presence you need in this game.

And don't get it twisted—bossing up ain't just about stacking money, it's about stacking wisdom. You can hand a fool a million dollars, and he'll be broke in a month. But hand a real boss a dollar, and he'll turn it into a dynasty. Why? Because wealth is 80% mentality and 20% currency. A weak mind will fumble a fortune, but a sharp one can manifest an empire.

So ask yourself—do you move with purpose, or do you just exist? Do you react, or do you anticipate? Are you controlled, or are you chaotic? 'Cause in this life, you can be the storm or the shipwreck—either way, the ocean don't stop moving.

As they lit up another cigarette, the assistant manager peeked out the back door, hesitant. "Y'all good?" *Nephew gave a nod without turning his head.* "Yeah, we'll be back in a minute."

A real boss ain't just somebody with money—he's somebody with presence, with poise, with the ability to make folks want to follow him. He got knowledge, wisdom, and magnetism. The only way to hold on to that starts with discipline. You master yourself, you master the world. You control your emotions, you control your outcomes. You refine your **social and emotional intelligence**, you'll never be on the losing side of a deal.

Boss up, nephew. Ain't nobody gone crown you if you still thinking like a pawn. It's time to move like a king.

Twenty-Six

Every King Was Once a Rook

A King with a weak kingdom is just a clown with a crown. Always play your position and remember, foundations first cause reign requires real estate and beans and rice eventually deserve steak.

*T*he soft hum of the Tesla Cybertruck barely registered over the quiet tension riding shotgun. Its matte finish caught the amber glint of streetlights as it glided through the city like a whisper in motion—futuristic, smooth, and silent as powerful game being laced under the breath. Unc rested one hand on the wheel, the other cradling a pair of designer shades he hadn't bothered to put on since the sun dipped.

Nephew sat in the passenger seat, still buzzing from the heat of what almost went down at the restaurant. The scene played on loop in his head—the disrespect, the chaos, the edge in his brother's voice that meant things were a split second from spiraling. He tapped the passenger window twice with his knuckle, thinking.

"This whip crazy, Unc," he muttered, nodding at the quiet engine. "Feel like we floatin'." I might have to get me one.

Unc cracked a half-smile. "Gift from ole girl from the art auction," he said casually. "The one with the silk gloves and dead husband's millions."

Nephew chuckled but quickly shook it off, his mood darkening again. "Man, I love my brother, but he be wildin' sometimes. I handed him the keys to a whole kingdom—got him in the kitchen doin' what he love, makin' bread and building a name. But he still be one trigger away from turnin' the dining room into a damn boxing ring."

The city lights flicked across Unc's face as he turned down a quieter road. Nephew went on.

"You can lead a horse to water, Unc, but you can't make him drink. Sometimes I feel like I'm throwin' lifelines and he tryna swim with bricks in his pockets." Unc eased up on the accelerator and looked over. "Ease up, Nephew," he said, voice calm but rooted like oak. You aint to far removed from when you was about to body slam an executive like Rick Flair at the downtown spot. You forget? Every King was once a rook!"

And just like that, the lecture began—in the hush of a high-tech cockpit, riding through the night, one generation pouring game into the next like aged wine into a crystal glass. Unc leaned over the wheel, city lights sliding across the windshield like chessboard squares. The silence didn't last long—Unc had a parable on standby.

"See, everybody wanna be the King, Neph. They want the crown, the throne, the respect. But what they forget is—every king was once a rook. A piece that moved in straight lines... No flash... Just execution."

"The rook don't move like the knight, jumpin' all over the place, or the bishop, slicin' through on angles. Nah. The rook moves deliberate—up, down, side to side. It clears the board. It holds the line. It protects the king. And when the time comes? It castles with the king and shifts the balance of the whole game."

"The rook represents structure, movement, and strategic execution. No nonsense.
A King don't get there by chance—he was once a piece on the board grindin', defendin', advancin'.
To be a King, you first gotta master the fundamentals—just like a rook."

"You start out as a rook—movin' steady, buildin' systems, learnin' the layout, protectin' your position. That's how you earn the right to sit still and be the piece the whole board revolves around. That's King behavior... but it starts with rook mentality."

In this game of thrones, haste makes waste. A wise ruler plots his path with the precision of a grand chess master, mindful that each move sets the stage for the next. Build your base with the diligence of a craftsman, ensuring that every brick is laid with intention and recognize that slow and steady crafts the crown. Without the foresight to develop strong roots a King's just a jester with jewels and a pawn on another man's board. Foundations first, yuh dig. Patience ain't just a virtue; it's the blueprint for empire-building. Ultimately, the climb from the gutter to the gilded gates is a marathon, not a sprint.

See, big boss game dictates you keep your eye on the endgame, where beans turn to banquets, and patience pays off in power. That's how you transform today's hustle into tomorrow's dynasty. Consider this young blood: the streets don't hand out favors; they test the tenacity of every player pitching for a palace. You gotta navigate the alleys of adversity with the agility of a street-savvy fox, turning traps into stepping stones. Every mistake, a lesson learned; every loss, a map to a hidden treasure.

Your reputation in this realm is the currency that can neither be counterfeited or contested. Cultivate it with the craft of a goldsmith, cause a king without credibility is a commander without a command. Let your word be your bond, stronger than the strongest steel, and let your deeds be the drums that announce your approach.

Let me paint you a picture real quick, 'cause I see you getting tangled up in that red tape, zoning permits, and all that bureaucratic shyt. It's like this: back when I was mastering the game on the streets, handling business wasn't no different from playing chess. It's all about **foundational success**—that's what we're really talkin about, laying down each piece with precision, patience, building up to that powerful position where you run things without a hitch.

Back in the day, when I was the new face on the scene—fresh off the porch, thinking I could run before my shoes were tied, I had this little operation with a couple of real loyal ones. Thought I was the King, right? Nah, I was just a rook, moving straight, no fancy tricks. But here's where it gets real: each move I made, even the ones that seemed minor, were setting up my future plays. Every flex, built on to what was next.

How you handle those small moments, those first steps—that's what builds your empire from the ground up. That's **'foundational focus,'** the kind you can't skip if you wanna reign supreme later. I remember hearin' the actor Denzel talk once—said Sidney Poitier laced him up early, told him, 'The first few roles you pick gon' shape how the whole world sees you.' That conversation set the tone for his whole career—made him the juggernaut you see on the screen now. Same rules apply to us, Neph. How you move in the beginning? That's the blueprint the streets, the suits, and the squares all gonna read you by. You lay it sloppy now, you spend your life patchin' holes. You lay it solid? Man, you just keep stackin' floors till you sittin' in the clouds.

Now, translating that to the legit business world, it's the same hustle, just different tools. You start slow, lay down each piece with a strategy. Ain't about rushing to the top; it's about building so solid that when you get there, no one can knock you down. And yeah, this part of the game involves all that boring stuff you dread—permits, licenses, building codes. But think of it like this: each permit is like choosing the right hoe for the track—pick wrong, and it's trouble; pick right, and you ah'ite.

You see, securing a permit, waiting on those zoning approvals, building that business credit—it's all part of laying down your kingdom's foundation. Just like how I had to coach my girls on the rules and regulations of the blade, you gotta coach your business through these early hoops. It's tedious, yeah, setting up the moves for that checkmate, but when the play comes together? That payoff is sweet, nephew, sweet like the first big score after a dry spell.

And remeber, when you settin' that foundation, run as fast as you can from them 'quick flip-real fast folk,' that's slick talk for, "I'm about to scam you sucka." Anything worth having got to be done with precision, like a surgeon operating on your heart.

If you hear the doctor say, lemme cut this man open real quick and get him off my table real fast, chances are, you aint gone make it. So take your time when ever you building foundations and don't skip none of the steps for gettin to them checks.

I know I'm preachin' to the choir but let me give you one example of how following the script to the letter—meaning crossing your T's and dotting your I's without deviating from the plan no matter how long it takes can get you to the super bag. Somethin' like business credit for instance, hits ten times harder than personal credit, but it's a script you gotta follow out the hustler's playbook, just like the rules to any game. In this case, first, you start with the basics—**secured lines**—to show you're serious, then level up to unsecured. Set up your **vendor credits** next, stacking them like a seasoned player arranging his chips.

Register with **Dun and Bradstreet**; keep those accounts flawless. Make payments from 3 to 6 months and beyond, unlocking doors to bigger plays, until you have access to the assets. But you've got to patiently set that foundation up first on some methodical shyt. Follow the rules step-by-step to run it up. There's more than enough coaches out here to put you in the game and mentor you strait to the bag. Some people ain't got the mind and ain't cut out for this though—lacking the discipline to learn and follow through. But for those who do, the payoff ain't just access to assets—it's an oppurtunity to build a legacy of power and respect.

All it is—is simple instruction's to avoid self destruction, but you'd be surprised how many people misguided and undecided with the nerve to offer criticisms when they ain't got the visions to make boss decisions. It's no different than this game of pimpin and distributin' this ism. A quick bytch gone experience gettin rich and a slow hoe gone remain po'. Don't let **learning curves**, growing pains, or **points of resistance** slow your hustle. Keep pushing to the finish line so you can shine and sip champaign and wine.

Now check game, youngin'—that **'Outliers: The Story of Success'** joint by Malcolm Gladwell? Straight up breaks down the **10,000-hour rule** and reminds you that even the greats had to crawl before they balled—and put in real time before the shine for the mastery to be divine. And since we on mastery, can't forget **Mastery** by Robert Greene—dude goes deep on how to level up your craft 'til it's second nature. I'm gone keep reiterating certain books untill you get them. But what I was really wanting to put yuh brotha, Cee on to back at the restaurant was, **'The Obstacle Is the Way'** by Ryan Holiday. That boy need that. It's a cold reminder that setbacks? Just setups in disguise. Every emperor got tested before he got crowned, feel me?

And look—my personal favorite, the one I feel every man need to read at least once? **'The Alchemist'** by Paulo Coelho. That one hit different. Not just on the surface, but deep. It's about becoming. Trustin' the process, even when the road don't make sense yet. That book don't just talk to you—it speaks through you. Believe it or not, this whole game is about alchemy.

Remember, just like on the streets, every delay, every obstacle, you turn 'em into stepping stones. Use each setback as a setup for your next big win. That's how you build something that lasts, something solid that'll hold up your empire when you start to really build high. Just like we did on the track, way back, moving from rook to King, slow and steady, making sure every piece is right and ready—and exactly where it needs to be.

So don't rush his process, young blood. Embrace it, learn from it. 'Cause when it's time to feast, when it's time to sit back and slice into that steak, both of y'all will savor it more knowing the grind it took to get there. That's **foundational success**—the type that turns beans and rice into steak dinners. That's the King's way, the only way if you wanna rule long and strong.

Just then, a slick-haired young Italian-American–looking cat—like a Temu Tony Robbins with a Rolex—pulled up beside them at a four-way stop in a black-on-black Tesla truck dipped in **Vantablack**, the kind of paint that absorbs 99.965% of visible light like a black hole. He looked over, flashed a grin, and threw a smooth two-finger salute—like *"Welcome to the club,"* before skrrting off damn near before the light even turned green. "That triple blackness hard, ain't it Unc? "Menacing" said Unc!" —Nephew then continued, "But yeah, I already got them titles in the notes. On it—like a hornet!"

Twenty-Seven

If They Gotta' Guess, You Already Failed The Test

Keep your moves and intentions authentic; transparency in the game leaves no room for shame and blame. Get chose with ya mouth closed, that's how you campaign.

One summer afternoon in Chicago, the heat clung to the pavement like it had a point to prove. The air buzzed with the kind of humidity that made linen stick to your back and time felt like it was moving in slow motion—a stark contrast to the ice-cold, windy winters. Uncle happened to be riding through the city in a navy blue Cadillac rental—something smooth but understated. Nephew riding shotgun, soaking up the skyline as it passed by in glimmers of mirrored glass and rusted brick was relaxed and suave per usual.

They were headed to one of Unc's old stomping grounds—a shadowy little watering hole tucked behind an alley where pool tables leaned like crooked teeth and the scent of brown liquor and cue chalk *hung thick in the air. If the walls could talk, that place would tell stories the average man couldn't fathom. But before they pulled up, Unc made a quick detour to scoop an old pimp potnuh from the North Side.*

*The man, uncle's homie, had long since traded silk suits and gators for quiet mornings, a mortgage, and a marriage to the world's finest bottom chick—one who could pick a stock just as well as she picked a mark, a pocket, or a trick. After doing a dime in the pen, the big homie pretty much went off grid to get that slow yet long money nice and quietly—albeit, more than he ever made in the game—*which says a lot considerin' that he ran up a real bag when he was outside—and *with a sixteen broad squad that looked like, 'dreaming of a white christmas.'*

As soon as we pulled up, he climbed in the backseat with a grin and that same old twinkle in his eye, while hollerin', "still sharp beneath the crow's feet, I see."

"Well, if it ain't Dr. Phil Huxtable—where yuh sweater at negus." Unc responded with a smirk.

"Well, If it ain't Uncle Phil—face ass," his old pimp potnuh fired back, grinning. "How's Bell Aire, negus?"

They both laughed, and then the potnuh turned to Nephew, squinting. "And look here—Nephew lookin' like Isaac from The Love Boat. What kinda slim young negus grows a full mustache, no beard, and rock a short Kobe afro?" " Got Jokes, I see," said Nephew. "Yall some real comedians today huh?" Unc let out a deep, belly-shaking laugh and said with that signature growl, "Aye—It's always a treat—" And they both finished in unison, "—when real players meet." Yuh diiiigg…

Laughter filled the cabin as the rental glided back into traffic. And just like that, the wheels were in motion—on the road and in the game.

As they rode, the two old lions made a friendly wager—who'd get recognized first once they stepped into the spot. "Bet you I still got more weight in this joint," Unc said, tapping the steering wheel with that trademark smirk. "New or old, my name still echo off them walls."

His potnuh chuckled, adjusting his cufflinks. "Man, please. I had 'em sweatin' like pastors at confession back in the day." Besides, we in MY city.

When they walked in, the smell of brown liquor, cheap cigars, fried food, and old money hit 'em all at once. A shadow of it's glory days, yet you could still catch a few underground millionaires in here sittin' right beside you and you wouldn't even know it. Unc didn't make it past the second pool table before a crowd gathered—new faces and old heads alike nodding in recognition. His name still rang bells like Sunday mass. But his friend? He caught a few curious glances and whispers.

One fine waitress leaned over and asked, "Who's Unc's silver fox friend?" One of the OGs chuckled and replied, "Used to be one of the coldest to ever do it." She smiled, then disappeared into the back. Though not as dramatic as they were with Unc, his potnuh still was able to get a lil fan fare as well. They were both still stars.

Unc leaned toward his potnuh with a coy grin and said, "If they gotta guess, you already lost the test." He held out his hand like a pastor passing the plate. The old player shook his head and laughed, peeling back five clean stacks and slapping it into Unc's palm. Aint nuthin to a boss ya dig, thats my lunch money. "Game recognize game... but sometimes the mirror get foggy."

Nephew laughed, clapping his hands. "Drinks on Unc—he got it!"

And just like that, with the swagger of a man who never forgot the rules of engagement, Unc leaned back against the bar, threw back four quick shots back to back, lit a black and mild, and began holding court, like tithe time, after the song and before the sermon. Nephew could tell, Unc was on one today.

Alright young church, we gone dive deep into the craft today. Gonna learn ya how to sell—not just in these streets but in any arena you step into. Now, hear me clearly when I say this: If they gotta guess what you're packin', you already lost and primed for jackin. Lost before you even got your shoes on the pavement. Remember when I tell you—first impressions last, so make 'em vast.

Listen here, Neph—your name? That's like your cologne and your credit. It walks in the room before you do, and it lingers long after you bounce. "See, a player can lose a chain, a ride, or even a chick—but if he lose his reputation? Game over. Ain't no comebacks once the whispers turn into headlines. You gotta keep your name clean like your kicks. 'Cause once it get dirty, everybody start steppin' on you like a welcome mat. And trust—they watchin'. They ain't always listenin', but they always watchin'."

He gave that sideways grin, like he knew something Neph didn't.

"Keep your rep polished like chrome on a Sunday—'cause even if the engine ain't runnin', folks still respect the shine."

Then he capped it with a proverb only Unc could pull off:

A real one ain't just known—he's remembered. And that memory? That's currency, youngblood." In this world, your clarity—how you present and carry yourself—gotta be as crystal as the ice on a rolli that glints and glistens in the moonlight. But here's the real, the beautiful contradiction of our game: you gotta move in silence too. It's like being a ghost with footprints. Visible when you wanna be, but invisible when it counts. A muthaphukin phantom. That's not just moving; that's moving with purpose. It ain't what you do, it's how you do it—if the sauce is right, they bound to pursue it.

Integrity and **Transparency**, is what sets real players apart from the pretenders—can't be no fake. Your actions, they gotta echo your core, resonate with the same frequency as your soul. 'Cause let me tell you something, in the hustle and bustle of life, integrity ain't just nice-to-have; it's your must-have. It's what keeps you from being just another jester with jewels, thinking they're a king.

We talking top tier **branding** but not the kind that they teach in those fancy marketing classes. Nah, this is street branding. It's every look you give, every word you spit, every promise you keep. It's how the streets whisper your name when you ain't even there. You gotta be your brand, live it, breathe it, be it. It's not about showing off; it's about showing up, the right way, every damn time—'cause that reputation gotta be gold and spend like money. Yo' brand is literally your currency, it's the original credit card. The credential of all credentials.

When you step into the world of reputable branding, it's like stepping onto the main stage. You gotta look sharp, talk slick, and move with purpose. First thing's first, your visuals gotta match your vibe. Think about it like your threads—your logo, your colors, they gotta be fly enough to turn heads. It's not just about looking good; it's about feeling right. When folks see your brand, they should feel like they know what you're about without you sayin' a word—you don't want them to have to guess.

Standin' out ain't just about bein' seen; it's about bein' distinct. What's your story? What makes you—You? That's what you gotta push, heavy. If you blend in, you might as well be invisible. Carve out your own space. Make 'em remember you. Be that brand that folks flock to 'cause they can't get what you offer nowhere else. Remember, brandin' ain't just about sellin'; it's about tellin' a story that resonates. It's building trust, making connections, creating a legacy. Make sure every move you make, every piece you put out there, tells the world exactly who you are. Make it count, 'cause in this game, it's all about how slick you play it.

What they say about you after you've left the room—that's your marketing doing its whispering. You wan't to have permanent real estate in people's heads up under all the perms, fades, braids and dreads. Think of it like this: every step you take is a commercial, every gesture an advertisement, selling the most important product on the market—You. Why? People aint buying your product, they buying You—the experience you give them, the way you make them feel. And if you do it right, you can do it without ever saying a word. Your brand will be so tight, they'll see it in the night—like a beacon of light.

But check this out. Here's where we flip it. If your pitch is off, and your stick is soft—if your vibe ain't hitting—then you're not just failing to sell; you're actively unselling every bit of potential you got. Some got the gift of gab and others talk themselves right out of a good deal.

So, keep your strategy tight, your game face on right, but let every step you take, every word you drop, be part of a larger plan and one that's on brand. Something so seamless, they can't can't figure out what happened until you're making your victory lap. Pack a punch but don't telegraph it. The only thing they should see is the knockout from a mile away.

Now listen, back in the day, the streets was my classroom. I had this young blood shadowing me, but flashy like a neon sign. His game was all surface, no depth. Kid was out there playing big, talking a storm, but his moves were as clear as mud. He confused every player in the game and when the real test came? He folded, 'cause his hustle couldn't stand up to the clarity it needed. That's why you gotta be like an open book—easy to read but hard to put down. He wasn't keeping it real, he was keepin it wrong.

Uncles playa potnuh chimed in, I know exactly who you talkin' bout too. What ever happened to that boy. Not sure, said Unc. Last I heard his ship was sinkin real fast. Haelth problems—he liked to get high off his own supply with know protections, and I aint talking narcotics. What I do know though is, Uncle
continued:

If they got to guess and unsure about that feeling in the pit of they stomachs, then there aint gonna be no support for your movement. People will pay more for a trusted brand because they value it versus some knock off. Once you build that name and stack that fame—stay consistent, and don't switch up on the game.

Unc took a slow drag from his Black & Mild, eyes tracking the room like he was reading the energy in braille.

"See nephew, this right here—this *ain't* just nostalgia. This branding," he said, tapping his chest with two fingers. "It's how your presence speak before your mouth ever do."

His old potnuh nodded, "Facts. That's that **Brand Within** type game. Daymond John wrote a book with that title. Real spit on how your image, your story, your vibe—all of it—is your first and last impression. It's chess, not checkers."

Unc cracked a smile, "And since we talkin' inner and outer game, you might as well lace yourself with **The Way of the Superior Man** too. David Deida break it down cold—emotional control, purpose, discipline. All the real ammo a man need in this world."

Nephew took a sip of his drink and grinned, "Y'all giving me a whole syllabus today."

Unc winked. "We giving you survival tools, youngin'. The world don't hand out passes—it respond to presence."

This ain't just about looking the part, it's about being the part. You gotta make every move speak volumes about who you are and what you're gunning for. Let your actions do the talking, and let 'em talk loud cause it aint no need to yell, just show and tell and let the work ring bells. If you got to explain, you already lost. From how you dress to how you address the mess, it should all scream your status, your taste, your savvy and your intelligence—and be the strongest hook point there is. In fact, the book: **Hook Point: How to Stand Out in a 3-Second World** by Brendan Kane? Man, that's a dope testament to exactly what I'm talkin' about right now, for real. Cop that one right there, Nephew—game all through it.

Right there on the line between visible and invisible, between mystery and history, between being a ghost and leaving footprints. That's your pimp Campaign, that's the art of selling yourself. Everytime you get chose is a chance for the legend to unfold. "After this? You got no choice but to step out and make 'em believe in the legend of you nephew.

Twenty-Eight

A Real Player Never Runs Out of Plays

Run plays for days, stack game in waves, and finesse every phase—'cause the game's about positionin', not just ambition.

*T*he player weekend is what they called it. Big cuz was always telling the fam about the game Unc dropped constantly. On this particular weekend, all the boys were over and kickin' back on the deck of Unc's lake cabin, steaks and fresh caught fish on the grill, smoke in the air, cognac swirling slowly in heavy glasses. This weekend was about all the other nephews. The vibe was easy, but Malik? Malik was sittin' there with that look. That "I just took a major L" look.

"Man, Big Cousin already tried to school him," one of the others said, shaking his head. "Told him he was moving reckless, but you know how 'lil cuz' Malik is." Unc looked over, already knowing what was up before a word was spoken. "Tell me what happened, lil nephew," Unc said, slow and steady.

Malik sighed, rubbed his hands together, staring at the firepit like it held the answer. "Had a good thing going. Plug was solid, money was coming in smooth. Then one day—poof. Gone. No warning, no backup plan. Now I'm just... stuck."

Unc chuckled, took a pull from his cigar. "A real player never runs out of plays, nephew. You had one lane, and when it closed, you ain't have nowhere to pivot. That ain't hustlin'. That's hopin'.—and hope don't run nothin'." *The game rewards the resourceful and If you stay ready, you aint got to get ready.* He let that settle before leaning in, his voice cutting through the night air like a blade.

"You bet your whole hand on one move, and now you empty. Next time? Multiple plays. Multiple lanes. Multiple exits. The game ain't about holding one card—it's about having a full deck, ready to play whatever hand gets dealt."

Malik nodded slow. Lesson learned.

Before the conversation could shift, Darius cleared his throat, still staring into his glass. The sunset threw gold across the lake, but the weight on his shoulders had him staring straight through it.

"Same thing happened to me, Unc," *Darius finally said. Unc raised an eyebrow, waiting.* "Man, Big Cuz already told him what was up too," *one of the others cut in.* "Tried to lace him about stacking another bag, but he ain't listen." *Unc smirked, swirling his glass.* "That so?"

Darius exhaled, shaking his head. "I thought I was good, Unc. Job was paying nice, benefits was sweet. Then outta nowhere—gone. Just like that. I got a lil savings, but..." *He sighed, rubbing his face.* "I ain't got nothing else lined up."

Unc knocked the ash off his cigar, shaking his head.

Like I just said, "A real player never runs out of plays, nephew. You was living off somebody else's clock, thinking that check was *yours. But if another man can decide when you stop eating, then it was never really your plate, was it?"*

Darius looked down, jaw tight.

"Next time, make sure you got a play running before the job play you. Side investments. Hustles that don't need permission. Because when one door closes, a real player already got two more cracked open. You see what I'm saying?" Darius nodded, the weight of the words sinking in.

Unc lifted his glass. "Then drink to that, and get back in motion."

A few more moments passed before Unc finally tore off into they ass. He couldnt help himself.

Nephew, you ever seen a coach with a playbook that only got one or two plays in it? Nah, 'cause that coach get ate up quick—the game too unpredictable for that.

Now, on a whole other note—but still the same truth—you ever seen a big jungle cat hesitate before it pounces? Not at all. Predators don't freeze up when the landscape shifts—they adapt, they adjust, they keep huntin'. And real ones? They move the same way. 'Cause if you ain't flexible in this game, you stiff—and when you stiff, you break.

A real player never runs out of plays. I don't care if he in the streets, the suites, or running game somewhere in between. If one lane closes, he already got two more open. And if there ain't no doors, he builds his own entrance. That's the difference between a boss and a buster—one creates opportunities, the other waits on them. And waiting? That's for the weak.

Those without that lion heart gon' freeze in the face of pressure, fold when the heat rise, and hesitate when it's time to strike. See, it ain't just about strength—it's about spirit. When the jungle gets loud and the ground starts shakin', the real ones step forward while the weak ones break rank. The ones who pivot and adapt always end up running shyt, while the ones who sit still get left behind. If you don't have a plan B and a plan C, then you might as well see yourself out of the game.

Nephew, I done seen too many dudes bet the house on one play, thinking they set for life, only to get caught slippin' when the tide turned. They'll lose a hundred stacks in vegas and have to call they poor lil' ole momma for a bus ticket home. They thought they had it all figured out—until the streets dried up, the plug changed numbers, or the hustle they built got snatched right from under 'em. They went out like Marlon and his potnuh in that movie **Requiem for a Dream.**

My playa potnuh once thought he was on top 'cause he had a steady re-up coming along with his pussy pedlin'. Every week, he moved weight, flipped it quick, and stacked his paper. Problem was? He only had one plug. One stream. One move. So when that pipeline got shut off—boom—his empire crumbled overnight. No backup plan, no new lane to switch to, just a broke fool trying to figure out where he went wrong. He was double-breasted and mispimpin', so naturally, I knocked him for his remaining stable. But he wasn't dedicated to the game anyway, so he eventually became management material at UPS.

What did I tell him when I served him? "A real player never runs out of plays."

Because in this game, if you ain't got options, you ain't got power. You gotta think like a chess master, not a dice roller—'cause dice is luck, but chess is strategy. And a real boss? He got five different moves lined up before he even agrees to play the game with you. In fact, I once heard a man say the true definition of wealth is having options—and I couldn't agree more."

Now, let's bring it home for you youngins who think game stops at the curb. Take a player like me—always ten toes down, always moving with purpose. When I saw the street game shifting, I didn't just sit there and cry about it—I flipped my knowledge into books, speaking engagements, podcasts, business investments, real estate—and I could go on. The game didn't stop; I just changed how I played it.

Same thing with them rappers turned moguls—Jay-Z, 50, Nipsey, all them. They ain't just sell music; they sold brands, liquor, clothing, real estate. When the CD game slowed, they already had other streams cooking, so they never drowned when the tide turned. Hell, even them Wall Street hustlers move the same way. You think Amazon makes money just off books? Nah, they got cloud services, delivery networks, AI, a whole damn empire. They knew from day one—one play is never enough.

So tell me, cousin, why is you still relying on just one hustle? Look, I ain't saying you gotta be in ten different lanes at once—spread too thin and you stretch yourself out. But what I *am* saying? You gotta **stay fluid**. You gotta always be in a position to pivot, yuh dig. It's like that book **The Obstacle Is the Way** by Ryan Holiday, Neph. Old school Stoic game—basically sayin', when something blocks your path, you don't quit, you reroute and conquer.

That's why I tell every young hustler—get multiple streams. If you in the streets? Stack that money and invest in something legal. If you got a business? **Diversify** your income—don't just rely on one type of customer, one platform, one product. If you working a 9-to-5? Use that paycheck to buy back your freedom, not just sell it to pay bills—and that's church on a hundred. Me personally, I practice polymoney, that means I'm polymoneyous, which means I'm married to multiple streams of income.

Hell, look at real estate—cats buying up cribs, renting them out, flipping 'em, turning a liability into an asset. That's what I call playing the long game. Some even renting the spots and still turning'em into an Airbnb's. But here's the real deal, like Holyfield, nephew. It ain't just about stacking plays—it's about staying ahead. Because a real player don't wait for the storm to hit before he grab an umbrella. He got one tucked before the first drop falls.

You know why some businesses folded when the pandemic hit, but others came up crazy? Because the smart ones adapted before the problem came. They already had online stores, delivery setups, digital options before the world forced them to. The unprepared? They were scrambling, reacting too late, getting swept up. And the ones that didn't prepare for when the wave the pandemic brought was over, also learned a valuable lesson about anticipating setbacks so they could stay in a position to serve multiple plays.

Same with the stock market—when recessions hit, the ones who anticipated the dip cashed out big, while everybody else panicked. You see the pattern here? The ones who move first, the ones who stay ready, are the ones who eat forever.

The playa potnuh Fillmore Slim once said, "They took 15 of my hoes, so I flew in 15 more the next day." That right there is the epitome of staying ahead of the game. No panic, no hesitation—just immediate adjustment. It speaks to deep-rooted resourcefulness and the power of preparation. He understood that setbacks are just setups for stronger comebacks. The game rewards those who can adapt and pivot without missing a beat.

He also said, "I went to the penitentiary for five years. They took five of my best hoes... but when I got out, I had ten more." Whether it's jail, losing your girl, or business drying up—he kept the game moving. He adapted, rebuilt, and came back stronger. That's the essence of resourcefulness, resilience, and staying ahead of the game.

Like I said before, If you stay ready, you ain't gotta get ready.

That's exactly what "A real player never runs out of plays" is about. When you move with unlimited flexibility, obstacles turn into opportunities. If you got a deep roster, a tight system, and a mind built for the long game, you ain't ever scrambling. You just making the next move, like it was part of the plan all along. At the end of the day, nephew, it don't matter how much money you got, how much clout you built—if you ain't resourceful, you just one bad move away from losing it all.

In that book **Shoe Dog** by Phil Knight, he rappin' about how he had to scramble, adapt, and move money creatively just to keep Nike alive in its early days. Had to hustle smart—of course till Jordan came through and blew up the spot. Now his lineage? Man, way out in 2254 and beyond, they gon' be straight.

Money don't make you smart. Resourcefulness does. Success don't keep you on top. Adaptability does. The game don't respect wealth alone. It respects hustle. A real boss ain't never out the game 'cause he always got another move ready by default. So I'ma ask you one last time—Is you playing to win? Or just playing until the game plays you?

Remember, money ain't loyal to no man—it moves where momentum moves. If you stiff, you lose it. If you fluid, you grow it—so stay liquid and lethal my boy—yuh heard?

Cop & Blow—Fast or Slow

Options baby, master the art of acquisition and application so you can streamline your rotations with automation. (Dare I say, all across the nation.)

Game Recognize Game

If I don't know nothing else, I know that real recognize real—and you lookin' mighty unfamiliar.

*T*he midday sun hung high over the golf course, casting long shadows across the manicured fairway. Nephew and his trading buddy, Marcus, were riding high off of a couple of recent wins and feeling like they had the markets figured out. Uncle had invited them out to the course, not just for the game but for the real lesson that was about to unfold.

Marcus, feeling himself a little too much, leaned on his club and started running his mouth to an older, well-dressed investor they had been paired with. "Yeah, I been killing it lately," Marcus said, flashing his phone screen like a badge of honor. "Made ten racks in a week trading options. Quick flips, fast gains—that's the real money."

The older man let him talk, nodding along like he was entertained. Then, with the smooth patience of a man who had seen it all, he said, "That's cute. I've held Apple stock since '98, and bought my first bitcoin in December of 2010—just experimenting, and it wasn't *the last. You can't even imagine what that look like. My dividends alone make more in a quarter than you, your daddy, and your grand daddy made throughout your entire lifetimes and that's assuming all of y'all are rich. Aint braggin, just wanted to bring you into focus. " He lined up his shot, took a slow, effortless swing, and sent the ball flying straight down the fairway. And all this is coming from a man who use to be homeless and grew up in a trap house, said the gentleman as he began to walk towards the golf cart.*

Marcus's grin faded. Nephew caught the look on Uncle's face before he even said a word.

"Game recognize game," Uncle finally said while smerking, grabbing his tee and walking over to tee off. And right now? That old man just let you know—you ain't in the club yet." He took a step closer, lowering his voice just enough for only the two of them to hear.

You out here talkin' loud, flexin' quick money, but you ain't listening. See, Marcus, real wealth ain't in the flash, it's in the foundation. That man didn't have to stunt, didn't have to prove nothin'—his portfolio been working while he been sleepin'. Meanwhile, you out here braggin' about playin' checkers when the real players been playin' chess. If you just shut up and listen sometimes, you'll realize that a player can grow into a real mack just by being around some real game.

Marcus shifted uncomfortably, gripping his putter like it might save him. Uncle shook his head, chuckling. He nodded toward the old investor while lining up his next shot. Take notes, young-blood. 'Cause when the game really recognize you? You won't have to say a damn thing." The old man with his silver goatee and Caesar cut sat on the plush seat of the golf cart, settling in like he owned the course.

A gentle breeze swayed the trees over the green as the two young men listened closely when Unc began to school them.

Imagine being in a room where the air shifts soon as somebody walk in? Not because their loud, not because they flashy, but because their presence carry weight? If your presence carries weight as well, that's game recognizing game—real ones sensing each other without a single word being spoken. You ain't gotta announce yourself when your energy already loud. A wolf don't need a business card in a room full of sheep. But the flip side? If you ain't real, the real ones can smell it on you like cheap cologne. And If real don't recognize you, you either invisible or you fraudin'.

This principle runs through every lane—whether you moving through the streets, navigatin' business, or climbing corporate ladders. If you solid, your reputation introduces you before you even step through the door. But if your game ain't together? If you fakin', frontin', or movin' out of desperation? Then you're gonna stick out like a sore thumb, and the game will expose you faster than you can cover it up. Character and value show up in fruit, not flash. Matthew 7:16 tell yuh, Ye shall know them by their fruits. You gonna know the real by they results.

When I first got into the game, there was this young pimp from Miami who thought highly of himself, thought him was movin' right, but he ain't understand this principle. He had a little money, had a lil mouthpiece, so he thought he was untouchable. But confidence without credibility is just noise.

He stepped on the scene trying to stunt, thinking his new money could buy him a seat at the table. Problem was, he didn't realize the table was invite-only.

See, in this game, you don't just declare yourself a boss. Your presence, yuh proof, and yuh power pave the path to prosperity. Yuh moves, yuh history, your consistency, ain't no mystery—all that speaks for you before you even open yuh mouth. Hard to get chose when you've been exposed. This young'un thought he could fake his way into the inner circle, but the OGs peeped his flaws instantly. His lingo was off. His patience was low. His spirit was desperate, like he was trying to prove something instead of just 'being' something. And the ones who really had it? They ain't recognize him, 'cause he wasn't one of them.

And that's where he played himself. See, when real players don't recognize your energy, you ain't just invisible—you a target. If you begging to be seen, you ain't ready to be recognized. He wanted to be part of the game, but the game studied him, tested him, and ultimately cut him out. His money might've been real, but his essence wasn't. And when real ones don't recognize you, they either ignore you or use you. Either way, you lose fool. Me? I always got claimed without a campaign because it was in me, not on me. Your best campaign ain't the car, the clothes, or the cash—it's you.

The same principles apply in every room where power moves are made. You ever see a young executive trying too hard? Ninja walking into a boardroom, wearing an expensive suit but talking like a rookie? The veterans peep it immediately. His handshake weak. His words don't hold weight. He quoting books instead of speaking from experience. He trying to fake his way into respect, but respect don't work like that. If the room don't respect you, the streets gon' neglect you. I know they say fake it til' you make it, but you got to pick and chose yuh battles.

Now compare that to the real power players—the ones who don't gotta talk too much, flex too hard, or sell themselves. You either carry credibility, or you get carried out the conversation. Their resume do that for them. Their past wins, their presence, their certainty—it tells the room everything they need to know. And that's why they get listened to, respected, and trusted. They ain't chasing credibility; they carry credibility.

That's why in business, your name gotta mean something. The biggest brands in the world? Nike, Apple, Louis Vuitton—they don't introduce themselves. They don't beg for recognition. Their reputation walks into the room before their representatives do. That's the power of good game. If people gotta question whether you solid, then you already failed the test. This don't take away the fact that everybody got to crawl before they walk, even the big companies, so never count yourself out.

But here's where it all ties into anticipation and strategy. If game recognizes game, then it also exposes weakness. And that's a dangerous place to be if you're not moving right. If the real ones don't acknowledge you, best believe the frauds and vultures will. That's when you become food and easy picking's.

You ever notice how scammers, fake gurus, and hustlers with weak hands always target desperate people? That's 'cause they recognize someone hungry for **validation**, someone willing to pay for a shortcut, someone trying to force their way into a level they ain't ready for. That's why I always tell young players: move with patience, move with power, move with proof. A real boss ain't out here begging to be seen. He builds so much **value**, they can't ignore him. You develop your craft, sharpen your skill, master your lane—so by the time you step into the big rooms, they ain't asking, "Who is this?" They already know.

One thing about this game, nephew—it see through the smoke and mirrors. Some of these youngsta's out here think they running plays, but best believe—I done ran 'em, refined 'em, and sold the blueprint with a bow on it. Wrote the rulebook, and sold copies worldwide. This is another example of game recognizing game, see.

You ain't finessing no finesse master. They out here thinking they slick, throwing up lil' scams like alley-oops, but game recognize game. I probably created them same plays while they was still at KinderCare, sippin sippy cups. You out here runnin' a scam—like a hot Atlanta ham, thinking you cookin', but I done already ate, licked the plate, and left the restaurant with the pretty chef on a gotdamn date.

Here's the bottom line, lil bruh: like I said, if real don't recognize you, you either invisible or you fraudin'. Either way, you ain't winning. This game? It's built on respect, credibility, and presence. And that's something you gotta earn—brick by brick.

A real player don't need to prove himself. He just is. He don't force the room to see him, the room acknowledges him on sight. His energy do the talking. And if you moving right? If you carry yourself with **authenticity**, confidence, and mastery? Then game will always recognize game. And that's when you start winning for real. Even the Word say it: the wise roll with the wise, game been speakin' on this since scrolls was still scrollin'. Proverbs 27:17 say Iron sharpeneth iron; so a man sharpeneth the countenance of his friend." See, Strong minds refine each other. Game builds game. Power recognizes power, and wealth moves with wealth. That's why I brought y'all out here today.

High-level minds attract other high-level minds and leverage those **strategic associations**. If you want a masterclass in strategic relationships both of y'all need to pick up the book **Never Eat Alone** by Keith Ferrazzi so you can learn how the powerful build with the powerful, and real success comes from mutual recognition of value, yuh dig.

And while you at it, go'on and cop that Your **Network Is Your Net Worth** book by Porter Gale so he can explain how aligning with power moves you into power and how proximity builds prosperity. Oh, and one mo' before I stop bumpin' my gum's, one that shine some light on social proof and whatnot and how like-minded, like-valued individuals attract each other is **Tribes** by Seth Godin. All *'tree-uh-dem'* gon' get yuh mind right on sight and I promise, you gon' take flight.

Thirty-One

If They Can't Keep Up, They Can't Come Up

A sharp mind gon' cut through the mediocrity everytime—and separate the stagnant from the stellar, so keep up or keep out.

*T**he Coliseum** pulsed with energy—music blasting, sneakers squeaking, the scent of buttered popcorn and stadium food hanging in the air. Uncle and Neph were courtside, soaking in the game while their ladies had just stepped away for snacks and the restroom, leaving them to talk business uninterrupted.*

Neph snapped a quick pic for the Gram, barely putting effort into the caption before shaking his head. "Man, I need to get serious about this social media thing. Feels like a young person's game, though. Algorithms, content, all that tech stuff—it's overwhelming." Uncle smirked, sipping his drink slow. "Ain't no young person's game—it's a sharp person's game. You think these billion-dollar execs running they own pages? Nah, but they sure as hell understand how the game moves."

Right before halftime hit. The whistle blew, and the coach called a timeout, pulling his players into a huddle, drawing up a fresh play. On the other end of the court, an old-school vet, once dominant, took a slow walk to the bench, wiping sweat from his brow. He had the experience, the name, but the younger, faster rookies were running circles around him. The game wasn't waiting on him—it was moving past him.

Uncle nodded toward the court. "See that, nephew? Used to be his game, but now? He just trying to stay in it. Ain't no retirement plan for the unprepared. If you can't evolve, you dissolve. That's life, that's business, that's the game." Neph leaned forward, watching the coach adjust the strategy on the fly, his mind clicking into place. "Sounds like you're saying I gotta treat this social media like a new playbook? Adapt or get left behind?"

Uncle leaned back, grinning. "Now you catching on. Let me sprinkle a little knowledge on yuh dome piece nephew."

—This life? It ain't for slow movers or the easily distracted. See, this game don't wait for nobody. And the ones who fall behind? They get left behind.

In a relay race, ain't nobody waiting on the weak link to catch up. You either in stride with the motion, or you getting lapped on. That's how the game works, in the streets, in business, on the internet, and in every corner where power circulates. If you can't keep pace, you get erased—slow feet don't eat, and slow minds don't shine. Motion is money, and hesitation is starvation—yuh dig?

Real ones move fast—not recklessly, but strategically. They don't just see the play; they stay ahead of it. The problem with most people? They *think* time is on their side when in reality, the clock is always ticking. The game don't slow down so you can catch up. Either you keep up, or you fall off. Ain't no room for slowness in the fast lane. Imagine being on the freeway doing 80, and some fool in the slow lane trying to merge? He either speed up, or he get ran down. That's how the game moves—no sympathy for hesitation. If you can't keep up, you can't come up. Period.

Fluid intelligence, nephew, is the ability to think on your feet, adapt, and problem-solve in real time. It's what separates the ones who stay ahead from the ones who get left behind. See, book smarts can only take you so far, 'cause memorized knowledge is static—but fluid intelligence? That's dynamic. That's the ability to walk into any situation, read the room, and adjust accordingly. That's when you can identify 'points of resistance' on the fly and smoke'um.

That's why a real player don't freeze up when the game switch—he pivots. A sharp mind ain't just about what you know, it's about how fast you can process and apply what you learn in the moment. You ever seen a cat who memorized every business book in the world but can't negotiate his way out of a paper bag? That's 'cause knowledge without agility ain't power—it's just storage. The ones who truly make moves? They got the ability to see patterns, anticipate shifts, and move before the wave even forms. That's fluid intelligence. That's what keeps a hustler eating while everybody else still reading the menu. The game is gladiator school for this mindstate, everyday you get practice just trying to survive.

Now, let me tell you something about **learning curves** and **teachability,** nephew. The ones who make it in this game ain't the ones who think they already know everything. That's a surefire way to stay broke and confused. The real movers and shakers? They know there's always more to learn. They soak up knowledge like a sponge, whether it's from the old heads who been in the game for decades or from the young hustlers who see things through a new lens.

They call it a learning curve for a reason—if you ain't learning, you getting curved. You ain't gotta be the smartest, but you gotta be **coachable.** If you ain't teachable, you ain't reachable, and if you ain't reachable, then you sure as hell ain't climbin' nowhere worth going. As far as I'm concerned, if you aint coachable, you aint even approachable. Dead weight, in fact.

I remember when I was just stepping into the game, barely out my teenage years but already seeing the moves being made around me. Most young players? They was out here thinking small—fresh threads, some fly jewelry, maybe a clean hog, if they was really getting to it, but me? I wasn't just watching what my peers was doing—I was watching what the OGs was doing. I never ran with people my age—they couldn't teach me nothing.

There was this old-school player, name was Golden. He was cut from a different cloth, one of them smooth, sharp-dressed, always-thinking-many-moves-ahead types. He had his hand in everything—women, cars, business, and most importantly,

real estate—like hotels and coner stores. Now, at the time, I wasn't thinking about property. I was thinking about stacking, flipping, and staying fresh. But Golden? He sat me down one night and told me something that changed my whole trajectory.

"You got the mouthpiece, youngin', and you got the discipline, but you thinking too small. These cats out here wanna lease a Benz, but the real money is in owning the car lot the Benz is sittin' at. They wanna' buy from the store, but I'm telling you to buy the store it self. Think bigger.

That stuck with me. So instead of blowing my money on every new toy, I started making moves. I bought the toy store's—asset's that bought the toys for me. I found rooming houses all over the city that was going for cheap. Started leasing them, flipping the rent, stacking my bread until I could buy the property. While other young players were fighting over who had the coldest ride, I was quietly building up a real foundation.

By 20, I had properties bringing me **passive income** while other players was still scrambling for their next move. The pimpin bug had already bit me and was in me somethin serious. I wanted the property so I could pimp even colder than the next P. That's why it was so easy for me to knock a next negus broad so hard.

That's called **competitive edge**, nephew. That's what separate the top dogs from the lap dogs. See, everybody wanna shine, but most don't wanna do the work to stay shining. And that's where they mess up. You gotta always be leveling up, always sharpening the blade, always putting yourself in a position where the game don't control you—you control it.

Let me tell you something—the game don't wait. Ain't no pause button, ain't no "lemme think about it" when the moment's at your feet. Opportunities ain't loyal to the hesitant. The second you flinch, someone sharper, someone quicker, someone hungrier done already moved on what you was contemplating. Like Bob Marley say in his song, "You got to strike the hammer while the iron is hot."

Opportunities multiply when you seize them. The ones who make power moves don't just capitalize on what's in front of them—they turn one win into two—two into four, until the whole board is moving in their favor. That's why the first-movers in any game—whether it's the streets, business, or tech—end up controlling the landscape. The ones still waiting? They playing catch-up. It's about 'first to market' in this game no matter what you thought you was doing.

A fool will sit around overanalyzing every angle, overthinking himself into paralysis while another man already made the play. Overthinking breeds hesitation, and hesitation gets you eaten alive. The smartest in the game don't hesitate—they move. But they don't move reckless, they move with intention, clarity, and strategy.

This same principle applies whether you're flipping cribs, stocks, businesses, or influence. The corporate world is the same jungle as the streets. You step into that boardroom without knowing the game, without being ahead of the curve? You getting chewed up and spit out before you even realize what happened.

Look at most of the succesful **start up's**—they ain't staying on top because they sitting still. They constantly innovating, evolving, and anticipating. They ain't just reacting to trends;

they creating them. The minute they see the market shifting, they already three steps ahead, making sure they the ones dictating how the money moves. That's the mindset you gotta have. You need to get up on that **"Fund me If You Can"** Journal for real if you trying to be one of the top start ups, cause' that one will teach you how to win like a championship contender.

You gotta have competitive adaptability, baby. Stay sharp, stay fluid—or fall off. That's the truth. The book **Who Moved My Cheese?** by Spencer Johnson breaks it down plain: if you don't adapt, you get left behind—simple as that. And **Mindset: The New Psychology of Success** by Carol S. Dweck? That one's all about teachability. Folks who stop learning stop leading. They fall off not because they ain't capable—but because they believe they can't grow.

If you stagnant, if you still relying on yesterday's game to win today's battles? You already lost. The world moves too fast. And let me tell you something else. Just because you in the room don't mean you got a seat at the table. And just because you got a seat at the table don't mean you eating like the bosses. If you can't keep up with the conversation, if you can't add value to the room, you getting phased out faster than a broke trick at a high-stakes poker table.

The real game is in being able to see where things are headed before they happen. You gotta be watching the patterns, studying the trends, seeing the opportunities before the rest of the crowd even know they exist. That's what separate the wolves from the sheep.

A thinking man don't react—he predicts, prepares, and prevails so he can respond correctly. You gotta stay learning, stay sharp, and stay ahead to keep your mind moving faster than the crowd and keep your hustle one step ahead of the competition. Most of all, never get comfortable. Because the second you stop growing, you already rotting. Procrastination, ain't patience. When it boils right down to it, nephew, the ones who over think too much end up watching the ones who act too fast. If you can't keep up, you can't come up. And if you can't come up, you gon' stay down. And that? That's a slow death. Simple and plain.

The impromptu lesson took about as long as halftime—and hit just as hard. While fans rushed back to their seats with fresh nachos and cold drinks, Unc leaned back like a man who'd just dropped a full semester of game in under fifteen minutes.

The arena lights dimmed again, the bass of the music thumped back to life, and the second half tipped off like nothing happened—but everything had.

Nephew sat a little different now, shoulders squared, mind sharper. The game on the court was back in motion, but his mental scoreboard had already shifted. His lady leaned in, whispering something playful, but he was still replaying Unc's words like a highlight reel—staying fluid, moving smart, learning fast, or getting left—Church on the court.

Thirty-Two

Keep Your Mind On Your Money And Your Money On Your Mind

When yuh mind on the money, the game stays sunny, and when you concentrate on the cheddar, yuh life get's betta. See, when you aim for the riches, life fulfills all yuh wishes, and if your attention's on the coin, you invite greatness to join. All Im saying youngsta is focus on the dough and watch your kingdom grow—ya dig.

*T*he winter wind rattled against the coffee shop window, but inside, the air was thick with the scent of fresh-ground espresso and cinnamon. The rich aroma of coffee and warm scones made the cold feel like a distant problem. Nephew sat across from his uncle, his pumpkin spice latte cooling untouched. While an exceptionally gorgeous young woman Nephew was vetting to take on some respon-

sibility for him, stepped away to take a call, leaving the two of them alone at the table. I bet you ain't never been to a business meeting like this, have you, Unc.

Uncle took a slow sip of his black coffee—no sugar, no cream—watching Nephew's restless energy. "Can't say that I have nephew, can't say that I have, Unc repeated. Something on your mind, young King?"

Nephew sighed, leaned back while rubbing his hands together. "Man, I just feel like... life be life-ing. I got a gang of women I'm trying to vet to see who can manage my social media. My kids doing the most these days, I need a buyer for this property like yesterday. I'm still fighting this lil' case, and I'm trying to cop this G-Wagon from the auction on Monday.

One day, everything's flowing, and the next, I'm scrambling. My business only runs smooth when I'm locked in, but the second I get distracted—things seem to grind to a halt. It's like if I ain't moving, the money ain't either. I gotta figure out how to automate my operation and keep it tight. Still too many moving pieces, I feel like I'm juggling instead of bubblin'. I'm trying to be on my four hour work week type shyt, yuh dig?"

Uncle nodded, setting his cup down. "Mmm-hmm." He reached for his napkin, dabbing the corner of his mouth before adjusting his Cazals and fur. "That's real," he said, leaning back. "But see, that right there? That's exactly what I been tryin' to tell ya." He stretched his arms, cracking his knuckles as he prepared to lace his nephew with something real—something that wasn't just about today, but about every play he'd ever make moving forward. Something he called laser focused pimpin'.

Nephew, let me get you right: a mind divided is a bag declined. You ever see a poker player worried about what's happening at the other table? Hell nah. They locked in, eyes sharp, focus unshakable—because one slip up, one moment of looking left when they should've been looking forward, and it's game over. Same goes for this money game. You either focus on the bag, or you fumble it. Simple as that.

See, when your mind on the money, the game stays sunny. And when you concentrate on the cheddar, life gets better. This ain't about being greedy—it's about being intentional, mane. Money is a tool, a weapon, a security blanket, and a passport all in one. It moves how you move. If you treat it like an afterthought, it'll treat you like a stranger. If you court it, study it, respect it, and flip it properly? Then you and wealth gon' have a long, fruitful marriage, ya dig?

But the moment you take your eyes off it? The moment you start letting **distractions** and emotions dictate your plays? You'll be sitting in the backseat while somebody else drives your life. Now, you already on the right track gettin' this lil brown-sugah lookin thang to manage yuh socials, cause, Lord knows, those little notifications can distract years off you and your millions—and you got to get to the money come hell or highwater.

Don't get me wrong, 1st Timothy 6:10 in the Kang James Bible say "the love of money is the root of all evil"—but I ain't tell you to love the shyt, I told you to use it and not abuse it, or else you'll lose it. A trucker don't love his rig, but he damn sure ain't gon' treat it like a lemon—he keep that oil changed and stay in the trucker's lane. A builder don't romance his tools, but if a junkey try to snatch his hammer, tell me what you think he gon' do?

Listen, Let me tell you about a player I once served notice to. Had a strong stable, money flowing nice. But he got lazy. Started cupcakin' too much, started indulging instead of reinvesting and game testin'. The game was calling, but he wasn't picking up. Looked like he had his girl's on payroll too. Next thing you know, one ho gone. Then another. Then the trick with the biggest pockets moved on. His security flipped into uncertainty. His confidence turned into desperation. And desperation, nephew, is the stink that attracts the wolves like flies on a garbage can.

By the time he realized that money don't wait on no man, it was too late. His rep was bruised, his bankroll light, and the game? The game had moved on without him. Lesson? **Stay locked in.** Don't let comfort fool you into thinking the flow can't stop. Money loves motion. The moment you get too comfortable, you already slippin'. If you spread to thin and got to much on your plate, naturally the gears ain't oiled and your machine gonna grind to a holt. Gotta' pull maintenance son if you want it to move smooth.

If I knew then what I know now, I would have at least told the man to invest in some annuities or somethin—know what im sayin'. But his mind wasn't on the money, it was focused on the honey. The business of the blade ain't know different than the business of the boardroom blood. This game right here ain't just about the streets. You think them billionaires play different? The Jeff Bezos's, the Elon Musk's, the ones flipping billions like we flip a stack? They wake up thinking about the bag. They go to sleep strategizing about the next one.

You think Nike just lucked into being a household name? Naah-mane, they keep the flow in motion. When sneaker sales slow down, they drop apparel. When apparel gets stale, they push something else. When one lane dries up, they got five more already in the pipeline. Same way a pimp don't just rely on one ho. That's foolish. The strongest game is a diversified game. Multiple streams. Multiple options. Multiple plays in motion.

And that's exactly where most folks mess up. They treat money like a moment instead of a mission. They think one win means they set. But the real ones? The ones who keep stacking, keep flipping, keep maneuvering? They never let one win be their last win. The next move is always the best move, and so on while moves just get better and better. The Next Move Always Matters and that's where the real players separate from the spectators. Some folks focus on the bag in front of them; and can't see the bag's for the bag. The bag in front of them causes a blind spot. Real ones focus on the bags behind the bag and those behind that one too. That's church!

Think about it like real estate. The smart investor don't just buy a house and stop. Nah, he flippin', renting, leveraging equity and setting up credit lines, making sure he ain't just making money—he making money move. Same way the best hustlers don't just sit on a bankroll; they keep the rotation tight.

Ever wonder why the rich stay rich and the broke stay broke? Because the broke spend their money and on frivolous valueless trinkets, while the rich circulate theirs on more assets. When energy is spent, it's gone. When it's circulated, it returns. Addition and subtraction, simple math. When I want something, I don't buy it with my money—I buy something that's going to buy it for me. If I want a mansion, I buy a mansion party company to buy the mansion for me, If I want a fancy car, I buy a car rental company to buy several fancy cars for me. That way I have access to all of it when ever I want, in fact it's giving me money, not taking my money. Most folks wanna flex for validation from people that don't care nothin' bout'em, and lack the patients it takes to let the strategy unfold and put the asset right in yuh hands like clockwork.

Naw, you ain't got to fall in love with the money at all but the facts remain, you either master the money, or It masters 'You'. And if you didn't know, It makes a great servant but a terrible master. It'll have you looking like Kunta but instead of Toby it'll force your name to be Donald Debt, yuh feel me. You heard about them celebs who had it all then lost it overnight? See 'em flexing in the Maybach one year, filing for bankruptcy the next? That ain't by accident. That's the consequence of treating money like a guest instead of a Biyitch—I mean a tenant.

When you focused on the wrong things—keeping up appearances, chasing the next high instead of the next investment—you setting yourself up to lose. A fool with money is just a fool with temporary power—a monkey with a million. A player, though? A player keep his mind on his money so he can build something that lasts. Secure the bag, but more importantly, secure the mindset. Look, nephew, it all comes down to one thing: is your money spent leaving you with lent, or is you stacking your wealth and securing your financial health—for generations to come?

Money is easy to make, but wealth that lasts? That's a whole different game. See, every dollar you touch is a soldier in your army, and if you play this game right, them soldiers don't just march—they build empires. But real game will tell you, an army without a fortress is an army waiting to be wiped out. And when you talking about securing wealth for generations, the strongest fortress you can build, I'm talkin' bout one you can trust, is something so simple they put the truth right in the name—it's called a **Trust**.

Now, let's take it even further—what good is an army if you don't **insure** the troops are safe? That's where life **insurance** come in, another layer of fortification making sure them soldiers live longer than you do. Because here's the reality—we all gotta die, but our dollars don't have to. They can stay alive, working, flipping, stacking, and soldiering for generations to come. When you and every member of your bloodline head on over to the upper room, them soldiers don't get buried with you—oh no—they stay locked in the trusting fortress, standing guard for the next generation still moving in this here lower room. Death benefits don't play, they pay.

When the new generations time come? The process repeats, the payouts stack, and the legacy compounds until your bloodline eating for the next thousand years. If a hundred of us goes to the upper room, that's a hundred payouts, soldiers secured in an insured and trusting fortress—the fact is, death? That's a destination you already got a ticket to, paid in full. Might as well let the bloodline benefit from it. That's pimpin' money on a whole other level, nephew. And if this flying over your head, ask around—because those that know, know.

Imagine all the seeds after you being born into privilege for countless generations because they born into a family trust and a personal family bank with distributions that cover basic necessities of the luxurious type, enough to get you the best of everything as a spring board into your own wealth building lifestyles and careers. That's family pimpin' you see, on a whole other level of keeping your mind on your money and your money on your mind.

Some people see a bag and think "What can I buy?" Real ones see a bag and think "How can I multiply?" So ask yourself—is you chasing money, or is money chasing you? Because when you got your mind right, when you focused on the flow, when you treating money like the tool that it is? Then the game stays sunny, and your kingdom keeps growing. And that, nephew, is how you really come up.

Just then, Nephew looked up and caught eyes with the young lady he'd met earlier that day at a quaint coffee shop. She held up one finger as if to say, "Give me one more minute." She looked a bit concerned as she spoke, and Nephew thought to himself, "I hope she's alright… but I don't have all day, either."
Turning back to his uncle, he said, "Unc, what was that you said earlier about annuities? I been meaning to look into it, just hadn't gotten around to it yet." Unc leaned back with that knowing smirk and said, "Take your pen out and get to scribblin', 'cause I'm only gon' run it down once. And besides, your friend over there look like she about wrapped up." Nephew pulled out a blue pen, opened his tablet, and got ready to catch game.

Now first off, imagine this: You out here grindin', stackin' your paper, but you tired of playin' financial hopscotch—feast one year, famine the next. So what do you do? You slide some of that cheddar into a long-term hustle that pays you back later.

That's what an annuity is—it's like puttin' your money on the track and lettin' it run laps 'til it come back to you with interest.

Step 1: What It Is

An annuity is a contract—usually with an insurance company. You either drop a lump sum or make payments over time, and in return, they guarantee to pay you a check later on, either for a set number of years or for the rest of your life. It's like turnin' a big bag into a stream of income that keeps on drippin'.

Step 2: The Types

Immediate Annuity – You drop the money now, and the checks start comin' right away. That's for the folks ready to eat now.

Deferred Annuity – You stash the money, let it marinate, and the checks come later. That's long-term hustle. Stack now, shine later.

Then you got flavors:

Fixed Annuity – Steady and predictable. Like clockwork. You know exactly what you gettin'. Variable Annuity – Riskier. Your money's in the market. If it grow, your checks grow. If it crash... well, so might your payout. It's like bettin' on a dice game with insurance on the back end.

Indexed Annuity – Hybrid style. It's tied to a stock index like the S&P 500, but you got a safety net. You might not get all the gains, but you won't take a hard L either.

Step 3: Why Use It

Let's say you tired of countin' on Social Security or worried your 401(k) won't stretch long enough. An annuity is peace of mind. It's a pension you buy yourself. You buy it young, let it grow, then when you older and greyer than a raincloud, you still gettin' paid like it's Friday.

Step 4: The Catch (Cuz You Know There's Always One)

Don't get it twisted, nephew—not all annuities is created equal. Some got high fees, some lock your money up tighter than Fort Knox, and if you try to dip early? They hit you with a surrender charge that feel like a breakup with child support. That's why you gotta read the terms like you read the room—carefully.

Step 5: Real Game Application

If you stackin' and want a piece of your future secured no matter what's goin' on in the world, an annuity can be a solid piece of your retirement puzzle. But don't throw your whole bag at it. Balance it out—stocks for growth, annuities for security, cash for flexibility.

Bottom Line, an annuity is like buyin' your future self a paycheck. But like any play, you gotta know the rules before you jump. Don't let slick talkers sell you a dream—know what you signin', how long it locks your bread up, and how much it's really gon' pay back. 'Cause in this game? It ain't just about makin' money—it's about managin' money so it don't manage you—Yuh dig?

A simple search will show you that there's countless books and videos out there that'll teach you how to plan your estate, set up a strategic living trust, and even initiate family banking systems usin' insurance and funding instruments to get that financial compounding in motion. The game ain't just about makin' money—it's about positionin' it but you got to focus like you on that hocus-pocus.

Just then, the cute little chica returned from the restroom, flashing a smile as she rejoined the group.

"Sorry, I had to take that," she said, sliding back into her seat. "So, where were we? What were y'all talkin' about lookin' all serious?"

Unc leaned back, cool and composed.

"Just breakin' down how to be the executor of your own trust—and secure your bag in the process."

Nephew jumped in with a grin.

"Yeah, we on that 'focus and finance' type time. Gotta keep our minds on the money."

He looked her way.

"And that's where you come in—helpin' manage this social media so I can lock in on the bigger plays."

He leaned forward, voice just a touch more curious.

"So you say you a highly sought-after virtual assistant, huh? Tell me more about that…"

Thirty-Three

The Mouthpiece is Mightier than the Muscle.

Dialogue dominates, so learn how to articulate, because like casting spells, if you master your words---you'll master your world.

*T*he energy in the arena was electric, you could smell sweat, musk, cologne and ass in the air. That fever spilled into the frenzied crowd, who erupted in a roar as the ref waved it off. *One fighter lay flat on the canvas—all muscle, no plan. The homie who accompanied Nephew, Unc and one of Unc's playa potnuhs let out a loud laugh.*

"Damn, he got slept quick! said Nephew's homie."

Uncle shook his head, watching the replay on the big screen. See that? Strength with no strategy. He thought brawn alone would win the night. But the man in the other corner? He ain't just throw hands—he studied. Smart ones know the mind moves faster than the fist. Unc's playa potnuh, shrugged and said, I can only imagine his internal dialogue.

As the next fight was getting set up, Uncle shifted his gaze two rows up to ringside, nodding toward a man in a tailored suit, cool and unbothered, sipping from a crystal glass while everybody else was caught up in the spectacle. Just at that moment, the man turned to view his surroundings and caught Uncle looking in his direction. He smiled and held up his glass with a knowing look. Uncle threw up a cool deuce.

Unc turned and said, "You see that man over there? The one you can't quite tell if he's Mexican, Arabic, Italian, or Black? Y'all watching the fists, but that man right there? He the one making the real moves. Ain't never threw a punch in his life, but every fighter in this building answers to him. That's the power of the mouthpiece."

Nephew's homie leaned in, eyes curious. "What you mean, Unc?" Uncle smirked, adjusted his cufflinks, and leaned back in his seat. "Let me put you up on some certified 'G'... And right there at ringside, with the stadium lights flashing and the crowd still buzzing, Uncle broke it down.

The pen gonna always be mightier than the sword. Tell me somethin'—You ever hear of a king raising his sword before his scribe put the plan in writing? Ever seen a general charge into battle before the war strategy was mapped? Of course not. Because power ain't in the brawn—it's in the living word. And a man who truly masters his words? He controls the whole game.

I wonder if you ever thought about why they call it spelling when they writing? Because words cast spells, nephew. Every sentence you speak is a blueprint for your reality. This whole world runs on language—verbal language, computer language, body language, and so on. Bond's and contracts are created through these spellings, which is another word for spell-craft or spell-cast. Now you know why they call crafting spell's and casting spell's—spelling.

It's important that you always crossin' your T's and dottin' your I's, so that your contracts and spellings ain't saying one thing and meaning another—end up losing all your assets on a technicality like that. That's like puttin' one wrong ingredient in a witch's brew or chemical cocktail that blow the whole building. Spell casted all crooked. Imagine a voodoo priest puttin a monkey paw in the pot when it called for a fish bone. When you don't cross yuh T's and dot yuh I's, you might not be writing your future—you might be signing away your freedom, so say what you mean and mean what you say.

Even your signature is casting a spelling that seals deals. I bet you didn't know that, did you, nephew? Yeah, your name is a contract, and when your mouthpiece proclaims it, you do it with the strength of ten muscle-bound men. A family name can carry a lot of weight and so can a family seal or crest. A family crest is a sidual and that's basically a logo which is also a spell. At the end of the day, a spell is just a contract.

The city you live in? Built by contracts. The money you chase? Governed by contracts. That job you work, that lease you signed and sealed with your spelling, that business deal you negotiating—it's all contracts. Hell, even that lady you lacing, it's verbal contracts that you callin good game. If you can't master the language that controls the contracts, then you ain't in control at all. Whether on the streets or in the municipalities, all rule of law is contract, and contract law is the game of rulership—whether you know it or not. Yep, mouthpiece magic. My spells gone forever hypnotize and magnitize till stars in they eyes.

The courtroom? That's where the sharpest mouthpiece's play the biggest game of wizardry. Not a muscle in sight, but the strongest gangstas get served life. The judge ain't moving the gavel until the lawyers lay down the words. Deals ain't done till the ink dry, and that ink? It don't move until the conversation creates the deal, and the spell-craft gets real. Contract law rules the world.

Proverbs 18:21 tell yuh straight up—death and life live in the power of the tongue. And over in Matthew 12:36-37, it say that on judgment day, everybody gon' have to answer for every idle word they done spoke. By your words you'll be justified, and by your words you'll be condemned. Why you think they call it The Word? The Bible been leadin', guidin', and controllin' whole populations for millennia. That's how powerful words really are. One book. One message. Whole empires shifted off the strength of what's written and spoken. So don't ever play small with your tongue—'cause even a whisper can move mountains when the message got weight behind it.

Keep this in mind—it ain't just about what you say; it's how you frame it. That's called **psychological framing**, nephew, and King James did a hell of a job casting his frame. The power of conversation ain't just in the words—it's in the setup. The way you present an idea determines how it's perceived. It's the reason why a pimp don't ask—he assumes. It's why a CEO don't negotiate from a place of need, but from a position of authority. If you let the other side dictate the frame of the conversation, you already lost leverage before you even opened your mouth. You walk into a deal talking like a beggar, you gon' leave like one. You walk in like you the one with the solution, the power shifts before a contract is even charged with a signature.

Now let me put you on to something deep—**Neuro-Lin-guistic Programming (NLP).** That's the game within the game, nephew. NLP is the science of how words shape the mind. It's about embedding commands, reframing narratives, and using language to influence without resistance. You ever hear how salesmen can make a client think it was their idea to buy? That's NLP. You ever watch how a courtroom lawyer sets up a witness, leading them to a specific answer? That's NLP. You'll never have power if you don't study what I'm telling you right now. Even in the game, the best pimps use NLP naturally—repeating key phrases, controlling tonality, pacing their words to match the energy of who they speaking to. It's an art, nephew, a science, and a weapon all in one. Study it, and you won't just talk to people—you'll talk through them.

I remember a time I could talk whoever I wanted to date into an orgasm over the phone a thousand miles away just by using words and guiding their thoughts to where I wanted them to be. Body sensations concentrated on heavily by the sound of my voice and the guidance of thoughts. That's the power of language, nephew. When the gift of gab meet the art of finesse, every 'no' turn into a 'yes'. That's how deep the game goes. You can't lose with the stuff I use—when the game is in you, it's always a win.

Same thing on the track, nephew. The blade ain't just about beauty—it's about belief. That's where subliminal influence comes into play. See, the sharpest game ain't just what you say—it's what you leave unsaid. The best pimps don't just talk; they lace the subconscious. They plant ideas that sprout later, making the listener think it was their own thought all along. This is why a trick ain't gotta be convinced—he gotta be led. A ho ain't forced to believe—she gotta feel like she chose to believe. The best manipulators don't impose—they embed. That's game on a hundred.

I done seen plenty of so-called tough guys—gorilla ninjas—get wiped off the board because they thought muscle ran the game. The real ones? They know the power of patience, of calculated conversation, of playing mental chess when everybody else still playing checkers. They stay on that Bumpy Johnson type time. A weak man tries to buy or bully loyalty. A strong man builds it with words and follows up with actions because a slick tongue can get more done than a quick gun.

I had a young potnah once—strong as a damn ox. Thought he was running things just 'cause he could outfight the next man. But when the game flipped, and it wasn't about throwing hands, but about negotiating weight? He was lost. Couldn't talk his way out of a paper bag. So what happened? The ones with the gift of gab got him wrapped up, used him for his brawn, then left him in the dirt. He went from a boss to a do boy.

Can't bring muscle to a mouthpiece fight. Because in this world? A sharp tongue slices deeper than any cutlass. The game is bigger than pimping—this is life philosophy and a fool who don't understand that is just another pawn in a pimp's play. That's why some of these broads drive these brothas crazy—they can't out-talk they lady.

Let's get deeper—you ever wonder why symbols, logos, and 'coded language' control society? That's 'esoteric symbolism,' nephew. Language. Contract. Mouthpiece vibrations. Every major power structure—from governments to corporations—has used symbols and hidden language to shape perception. Every great empire had its own coded language, every religion has its sacred texts, and every street operation got its own coded slang. I remember being out here feeling like I was lost when I first heard the youngsters talkin' bout slidin' on an op. I say slidin' on a what?

Words ain't just wordslatters, and symbols—they carry weight. That's why corporations don't just sell products; they sell identity. That's why governments don't just pass laws; they weave narratives. And that's why every major contract in history got loopholes buried in the fine print. If you don't understand the layers, you playing checkers while the real bosses are playing Chinese chess with invisible pieces.

That's the game, nephew. Knowing how to move people without touching them. A weak man lets the world put words in his mouth. A strong man chooses his words wisely and makes the world move accordingly. He knows when to let his silence do the talking as well. The sharper the speech, the deeper the reach. Whether it's the Emancipation Proclamation, the fall of the Berlin Wall, or Malcolm X lacin' Oxford with uncut game—when the mouthpiece move right, a well-placed word can do what an army never could.

Communication—whether through speech, networks, or systems—is the true metric of an intelligent and civilized entity. Without the ability to communicate, there can be no coordination, no progress, no power. Even the wisest mind ain't worth much if it can't make itself understood. Real power speaks—clearly, and with purpose.

Unc leaned forward, resting his forearms on his knees like he was about to lay out the blueprint.

"See, Neph, real power don't always come with a loud voice or a heavy hand. It come from knowin' how to speak so that people lean in, not lean away. Communication—that's the currency of Kings, companies and Nations. Without it, ain't no order, ain't no empire."

He tapped his temple twice.

"You need to peep that book **Crucial Conversations** by Kerry Patterson and them. It teach you how to talk when the stakes high, emotions flarin', and the wrong word could cost you the deal, the relationship, or the bag. That's pressure talk—you gotta know how to handle it without foldin'. Then there's **Nonviolent Communication** by Marshall Rosenberg. That one? That's grown man talk. It's about choosin' your words to connect, not control. Speak with clarity, not ego. That's how advanced folks move—through mutual respect and sharp intention, not noise and nonsense."

Neph nodded, soaking it in.

"And as always," Unc added with a knowing smile, "you can't go wrong with **How to Win Friends and Influence People** by Dale Carnegie. That one been schoolin' players since before your granddaddy was wearin' gators. Learn how to make folks feel seen, heard, and valued, and you'll never lack influence in any room."

He leaned back, letting the silence land heavy for a moment.

"Master communication, Neph, and you master access. And once you got access? You can shape worlds with just your words. In the end? The mouthpiece don't just run the game. It is the game."

Thirty-Four

Rules Regulated, Respect Generated then Demonstrated

Establish clear standards; without that, you risk tolerating anything—even disrespect.

*T*he steakhouse had that old-money ambiance—dark wood, crisp white tablecloths, the kind of place where the sound of a well-aged whiskey being poured held more weight than raised voices. The air was thick with the scent of prime steak sizzling on an open flame, the clink of crystal glasses, and the low hum of hushed conversations.

The restaurant was upscale—dim lighting, deep mahogany—somewhere you'd go when every bite cost a bill and every table had power sitting at it. You didn't come here for the meal alone—it was the atmosphere, a spot where the movers and shakers broke bread while making the kind of deals that never got written down.

Unc, Nephew, and Momma—Nephew's grandma—were seated at a corner booth, enjoying a rare evening out together–fresh from the casino. Mama didn't get the nickname 'Lucky' at seven years old for nothing. On this evening, after a pretty prosperous day and w*hile sipping wine and cutting into a $300 dry-aged ribeye that melted under the weight of a knife, they recanted the evenings events. Momma had her pearls on, looking sharp, carrying herself with the quiet grace of a woman who'd seen everything and survived it. She had that old-school wisdom in her eyes, the kind that didn't need to be loud to be felt.*

Then, across the room, a scene started unfolding. A woman at a nearby table leaned in close to her man, her voice just above a whisper at first—but that whisper turned sharp real quick.

"So you just gon' sit there like you don't hear me?!" she snapped, her voice cutting through the low hum of polite conversation.

"I know damn well you ain't bring me to no steakhouse just to tell me 'be grateful'—you got it, so spend it! My friend just got a Birkin, and I'm sitting here with a damn filet?! You should be embarrassed!"

Her man, uncomfortably shifting in his seat, clearly not built for this kind of pressure. He glanced around, avoiding eye contact with the nearby tables, his posture caving under her words. He rubbed his forehead, let out a sigh, and pulled out his phone like he was debating whether to make a last-minute transfer or just disappear into thin air.

Momma, cutting her steak with the patience of a woman who'd seen a million different shades of foolishness in her time, shook her head. "Ain't no sense in a man letting a woman talk to him like that," *she said, her voice smooth but firm, and quite unbothered, seeing as she had just come off a winning streak on the slot's.*

Nephew, still caught up in the spectacle, chuckled, leaning back in his seat. "Yeah, but you know how it is, Grandma. He probably just tryna keep the peace. Ain't tryna argue in a place like this."

"Mmm-mmm. That boy lost already." said grandma.

Nephew glanced over at the couple, frowning. "What you mean, Grandma?"

She took a sip of her wine, then gave Nephew a knowing look. "He sittin' there negotiatin' his worth when he shoulda set the standard."

Unc, who had been watching the whole thing like a slow-moving car wreck, finally set his fork down and wiped biscuit crumbs from his mouth with his napkin. He leaned forward, elbows on the table, eyes sharp as ever. <u>"See, that's where y'all got it twisted,</u>" he said, motioning toward the scene unfolding across the way with his steak knife. "<u>Ain't about keeping the peace, Nephew. It's about setting the tone. 'Cause if you don't establish it, how you expect to be treated, you might as well be out here passing out free disrespect tokens to all the players in the game.</u>"

Unc picked up his glass, took a slow sip, then set it down with intention.

<u>"Respect ain't requested—it's required. And right now? That boy over there's showin' you exactly what happens when a man don't lay down no law. She don't respect him—she runnin' him. And why wouldn't she? He ain't put nothin' in place to stop it, and now she makin' him look like easy profits. People treat you how you let 'em treat you. They take their cue from you. Now, let me put you up on somethin' certified…"</u>

And right there, under the warm glow of chandeliers, while a man across the room debated between his pride and his pockets, Unc laced Nephew with a lesson he wouldn't ever forget.

Let me bless your brain with some game, nephew. Respect? That's a currency, just like money. And just like money, if you give it away for free, folks gon' treat it like it ain't worth a damn thing. Imagine somebody thank they gone walk into a high-stakes poker game with some pennies? They'de get laughed right out the room. That's how it is with respect—if you don't establish your value, people gon' shortchange you every time. The Unwritten Rule of the Jungle says, "The Game Don't Reward the Weak."

See, the problem with a lot of players today? They think just 'cause they breathing, they entitled to respect. Like it come packaged with birth certificates and first names. Nah, nephew. It should be—common decency and basic respect, right? But In this game, in business, in life—you get what you enforce. If you let folks talk crazy to you, if you let 'em step outta line without correction, then don't be surprised when they start treating you like you ain't worth checking in with at all. If they don't like it? They can kick rocks after lettin' the door hit'em where the dog shoulda' bit'em.

I remember back when I was just coming up in the game, barely wet behind the ears but already thinking I had it all figured out. I had my stable tight, had my foot on the pavement, but I was too green to understand the most important thing—a man without standards is a man waiting to be played. I figured quick, When the Streets Don't Respect You, *They Run Over You*, and I wasnt trying to ride that train.

I had this one chick, smooth talker, real sharp, but she was testing my pimpin from day one. Disappearing for hours, always had some excuse, bringing in half of what I knew she could pull. And instead of nipping that in the bud, I let it slide. Thought I was being cool, thought I was giving her space. But what I was really doing? I was giving her permission to play with me. And once you let a hoe play with you, it's only a matter of time before you looking stupid and others feel as if they can get away with it to.

Next thing I know, she done ran off to some other cat—one who had his foot down firm from the start. It was my first knock, And I couldn't even be mad at her, nephew, 'cause I taught her how to treat me. I was waiting on the phone call, cause I knew it was comin'. That was the day I learned: *respect ain't requested—it's required.* And if I expect it, I need to see it demonstrated, 'cause actions always speak louder than words.

I realized first and foremost, I had to set the tone. Respect starts with self-respect. Do I need to say that again so the negus in the kitchen here me? If I don't carry myself with a certain standard, how can I expect anyone else to see me how I should see me? People watch how you move before they decide how to treat you. They'll treat me exactly how I allow them to. That's why I make it crystal clear—there ain't no room for misinterpretation when it comes to the level of respect I require.

I refuse to let anyone move in ignorance regarding my standards. If you in my presence, you gon' be properly educated. And understand this—*every* moment of disrespect is a teachable moment, but you only get one of them. After that? You either moving right, or you moving on. Business Ain't No Different.

Think about them big CEOs, the ones pulling the real money. You think they out here begging for respect? You think they walking in rooms waiting on folks to validate 'em? Hell nah. They set the standard from the jump.

A strong leader don't tolerate incompetence and don't let his employees dictate the terms. Ever notice how the most respected brands got the highest standards? Gucci don't let just anybody slap their logo on some trash. Rolls-Royce don't cut corners just to make an extra buck. The brands that command top dollar do so 'cause they demonstrate their worth—they don't ask for it.

Same thing applies to you. Whether you running a business, leading a team, or just moving through life—if you don't set the standard, people gon' assume there ain't one. And when there ain't no standard? You inviting disrespect. A fool thinks respect comes from being the loudest in the room, barking orders and demanding attention. But real bosses move different. The sharpest players don't beg for respect—they command it just by how they carry themselves. The silent power of **'Boundaries'** is the culprit.

You ever been around a man whose energy alone made people sit up straighter and choose their words more carefully? That's 'cause his presence alone enforces boundaries. He don't have to tell you he ain't one to play with—you feel it. And that, nephew, is the kind of respect you want. Respect ain't about making people fear you—it's about making 'em consider you. Before they act, before they speak reckless, before they try you—they hesitate. And that hesitation? That's the moment they recognize they gotta move different with you. This chuuch shyt im talkin', real scripture.

Look at Elon or Jobs—love'em or hate'em, they got standards. They don't tolerate mediocrity, and if you can't keep up? You out of there. Ain't no "I tried my best boss" speeches in they boardrooms. Most high level execs the same way—perfection or nothing. And because of that? People move different when they walk in the room.

You gotta train people how to treat you, whether you in the streets or in corporate meetings. If you tolerate lateness, sloppy work, disrespect—guess what? You just gave 'em permission to keep doing it. But if you demand excellence? If you cut off weak links? You attract the kind of people who operate at a higher level.

Moguls might not be the nicest, might be down right evil and other worldly but I bet you gone respect them in they presence. As far as yuh man over there gettin his rights read to him by that dusty broad, I wish his daddy would have taught him that pimping is instruction—when you stop instructin', she starts self-destructing—case and point.

See, a weak man waits for disrespect before he react. A strong man? He anticipates it. He know human nature, he know how people test boundaries, and he shut it down before it even start. That's why the coldest players in any game got a sixth sense for nonsense. They can see a slick talker coming a mile away, can feel the energy shift before it even happens. If you don't anticipate, you always gon' be reacting. And the man who always reacting? He already lost control. I personally have a zero tolerance policy my self and you should too—shiiiid, look at who taught me, she sittin right here.

Self-respect, boundaries, and personal standards teach people how to treat you—whether in relationships, social settings, or business. And if you don't believe me, and need to hear it from a psychologist or one of them ol' doctor Negus to make it hit different, check out **Boundaries: When to Say Yes, How to Say No** by Dr. Henry Cloud and Dr. John Townsend. That one breaks it down clear—your lack of boundaries teaches people exactly what they can get away with.

And if you want to go deeper—**The Six Pillars of Self-Esteem** by Nathaniel Branden is a heavy one. A foundational piece on how your self-respect sets the tone for your whole life. That book'll show you how internal standards shape external treatment. Yuh dig?" that's the kind of stuff the average man ain't even up on.

Let me leave you with this lesson in the lesson, nephew—what you tolerate is what you invite. You set the bar, or you let the world set it for you. And trust me, if you don't enforce your standards, somebody else gon' enforce theirs on you. And theirs? Ain't never gon' be in your favor. Disrespect is like vampire law, it can't get you if you don't invite it in first. Same goes for thought's, spirit's and shady opportunities. And that's a Message!

So whether you in the game, in business, or just living life—establish your rules early, make'em clear, and enforce'um with precision. 'Cause if you don't? You ain't runnin' nothing. And nephew, if you ain't running nothing… you just waiting to get run over.

Just then, without warning, ole boy stood up and slapped the fiye out ole girl. It made an echo and the only thing that pierced the following gasp and silence was grandma saying loudly, oh lordt—it'ssa fire! …

(The last line was for slap-stick comedy. We don't condone violence)

Never Chase, Always Attract. Desperation Repels.

Chasing what don't wanna be caught is a lesson learned in fool school. It's charm over chase and calm plus pace, always. Attract—never lack.

The Best Ho's Bake the Best Bread

Quality over quantity because a Pimp is only as good as his product and the finest dough make the sweetest ho-cakes.

*N*ephew had recently escalated his business ambitions by leasing a spacious warehouse on the outskirts of town, aiming to establish a thriving import enterprise. As they entered the sprawling space, the distant murmur of city traffic mingled with the serene concentration enveloping the area. The timing was impeccable, coinciding with a major conference nearby, presenting an excellent opportunity to showcase his venture and secure lucrative wholesale deals. Nephew, recognizing the potential, enlisted Uncle's seasoned perspective for guidance.

The warehouse, laden with towering stacks of boxes, mirrored Nephew's aspirations. However, a closer inspection revealed cracks in the facade. Nephew had trusted the management of his operations to a few friends, whose inexperience in logistics was now painfully evident as they idly focused more on their smartphones and crackin jokes than *on the quality of goods. Uncle, observing the lax atmosphere, realized it was an opportune moment to impart a vital lesson in business discipline.*

"Look here, young blood," Uncle began, his voice reverberating off the concrete, "this operation is like a finely tuned machine—every part gotta sync perfectly. You can't afford half-ass'ed efforts when your reputation's at stake. It's all about the people you choose to steer your ship. Only the best ho's get the best bread, ya heard. Choose dog faced slackers, and you bleeding efficiency." As they moved deeper into the warehouse, Uncle's critiques became more pointed, highlighting damaged shipments and mishandled products. "This," he said, gesturing towards a marred item, "represents your brand. First impressions are lasting. Send out subpar goods, and you tarnish your reputation."

Their inspection was interrupted by an urgent call from another friend, also gearing up for the conference, who relayed that major competitors were floundering due to logistical mishaps. Seizing the moment, Uncle's tone grew intense. "Boy, this is your chance to outshine them, but you got to act fast. Elevate your standards, resolve these quality issues, and you could dominate the conference. Remember, nephew, always be ready so you ain't gotta get ready."

Motivated by Uncle's urgency, Nephew quickly mobilized his team, addressing the issues with a newfound resolve.

"If you don't wanna be here, bus' a move—early! those who rock with me gon' get a bag, simple and plain." said Nephew. "the tightest crew is the one who win the championship and take home the ring.

Uncle watched with a proud smirk tugging at the corner of his lips, Nephew's words still hangin' in the air, ridin' the echoes of the warehouse—the steady hum of machinery, the occasional clang of a forklift, all underscoring the need for a serious reset. Nephew had set the tone, no question. His leadership showed in every command, every expectation laid clear. Then Unc stepped in—not to take over, but to reinforce. His voice, weathered and wise, cut through the ambient noise like a scalpel, slicing right to the core of what needed to be said. Nephew gave 'em the blueprint—Unc brought it home with the gospel. He started by saying...

Quality, mane, that's that top-notch show-up that pulls 'em in. Ain't no need to holla when your movement speaks volumes, that's realism, like magnetism. Everybody can win, but you have to have a winners mentality. A mogul **mindset** makes money multiply. Peep how them high-rollers like Rolex or Louis Vuitton operate—they ain't pleading; their name alone does the heavy lifting, their reputation speaks volumes. While flexin the shine, Unc continued. They ain't just selling you a watch or a bag; they granting you entry into a rare club.

That's playin' on another level of the game, where primo quality builds a rep that pays off big and top-tier quality fortifies a solid reputation. Me, a mogul in my own right, I invest in my squad, treating'em right, and in turn, as a boss in this game, I keep the quality of my inner circle A1. My game plan's bulletproof. I make sure the quality of my connections is nothing less than stellar. Even with all that, I don't give as much as my nephew is givin' y'all, yet this how you treatin his time and his money.

When I was just a young hustler first gettin my feet wet in the game barely off the porch, I remember me and my potnuh stepped into this ism at the same time, he thought he could fly slick though, running them junkies in his stable like it was all about quantity over quality. For every dime I had, my man was hustling three pennies—now, if you got any sense, you know that math don't stack up and our pockets was the proof. That was the first real lesson I peeped out there in the wild, seeing for myself how quality reigns supreme, every time.

Look here, nephew, you gotta recruit them highsteppers, them thoroughbreds with the smart and the heart to match. The type of team that's sharp as a tack and heavy on the track—real top-drawer, high-grade players that push the game to the next level. The best team ain't just a team, they family, ya dig? I don't know what you got goin' on right here. Look like they tryin' to play witcha. In my world, a real ho don't need convincing—she already knows what time it is—we focused and tryin to get to it.

The shuffle and bustle of the warehouse paused momentarily as Nephew and his team absorbed Uncle's words, with the importance of their next moves settling in under the stark warehouse lights.

See, yuh team plays into the whole eco system of success. I know my business model is bulletproof cause' the way I look out for my squad, I treat 'em royal, and watch 'em go the extra mile so that respect and money keep stackin'. They push through boundaries to keep my cash flowing and respect growing. But even more than that, I make sure whatever kind of product I'm pushin is better than the next mans. If it's got my name on it, it's practically gonna sell itself. Your street rep, just like them high-end labels, grows when folks only know you for top-shelf dealings. I stand by my brand.

When they know you all about that elite business, it cements your legacy, ensuring your brand gone always be about that quality life. It make it easy to chose me—and folk gon' work hard to run me that choosing fee. Them solid relationships, connections, and brand loyalty, ain't just important; they the bedrock of personal and professional growth—opening doors to solid progress plus more leverage and more money.

Look here gang, **sustainability** in any hustle, means your moves got to be clean and your game, good. Anything otherwise is unsustainable and what's the purpose of jumpin in if you gettin pushed right out. It's about strategizing to sustain your influence and ensuring you can last In this game. Sustainability means your plays are poppin' and your strategy sharp to ensure you not just a one-hit wonder but you got more hit's than a pot got grits. Whether you pushing products or servin' up services, shoot for the top 'cause sustainability is the anchor that keeps the ship steady in turbulent waters. Y'all don't want to be on no sinkin' ship, do you?

By now, other's from around the warehouse had began gathering around and taking an interest in the lesson plan at hand. Clearly this was Pimpin' they was listening to by the way the Ism shifted the prizm.

Seeing the shift in movements, uncle continued, talking mostly to his nephew now, but hinting at certain things to communicate subconsciously and indirectly to the crew.

"Excellence pulls in the crowd and locks down their loyalty. Stick to that high-grade hustle to keep 'em coming back for more. Invest good game in top-notch people because that's like selecting the finest garment or ingredients for a gourmet meal. The quality of your team can define your success, turning good results into great ones. Whether you selling hoe cakes or snowflakes—the best ho's bake the best bread. Investing in the best folks is like picking the choicest cuts for a feast."

This real rap here—you grow by who you know and how you treat'em. Surround yourself with top-notch people. It's about building a network of solid, reliable folks. That's true in life and in hustle. Strengthen your circle, with that kind. Invest in them people like they blue-chip stocks. The better they feel about their role in your world, the harder they work to keep the empire strong. And those that don't—fire'em, on the spot. Never waste your time with people who don't respect your time.

The caliber of your team can make or break your hustle. Boosting skills in your squad and keepin everybody up on game means everyone's top-notch, making sure the whole business runs smooth as silk. **Competence** on the squad means every player is peak, and in the **flow-zone** so the whole operation keeps runnin' like a well-oiled machine. I look out for my stable like a guardian angel. And that's yo job captain. So be good at it.

Remember this gang: better quality means a better hustle period-point-blank. The mo' money we get, the more we can spread. This ain't just chatter; it's straight fact, Jack. Top-level work and worker turn into top-dollar pay. It's been proven, time and time again superior output naturally translates into superior earnings and if you ain't earnin', yuh lifestyle burnin'. Stand out by being the best. In a sea of hustlers, be the big fish boss who shifts the game with unmatched quality, making sure you get the respect you deserve. Keep your eyes on building a legacy, not just quick scores.

A vision for enduring success forges legacies that outlast momentary wins. How you handle your business reflects directly on you as leaders in yuh industry. Push them high standards and watch your stable rise to meet'em. First-class hustling and top-notch pimpin' of whatever it is you pimpin' breeds loyalty and loyalty is royalty. When yuh clientele know you the cream of the crop and they can expect the best, they don't phuk wit the rest—they become evangelists for your brand.

Consistently doing things right, ensuring every deal is clean, every product top-notch, keeping it 100, and making sure every move is premium, lays down a trust foundation that elevates your whole game. **Superior offerings** my man, I'm talkin top shelf, high-end trap will boost your brand's value and worth til the end of time. Our moves are so clean, they shine brighter than the sun, making competitors blink and they heart skip a beat.

A high quality hustle pulls the right eyes and sets you apart from the pack. Its the difference between blue magic and red tragic. You wanna keep ahead of the game by always stepping up and innovating.

Quality management ain't just about upkeep; it's about shaping strategies that change the whole scene. It's the difference between that pure and that trash. It's mobilizing organization that can influence the nation. When you lay down high standards, you don't chase trends—you make 'em. Lead with quality and watch the whole game line up behind you. I'm tellin' yuh. Listen to me, I know what I'm talkin' bout. How you handle your business reflects directly on you.

Always remember dedication to quality is what sets the gold standard everywhere. Stick to this belief, and you not just playing the game—you writing the rules. I don't care what it is you're doing, do it to the best of your ability because **how you do anything is how you do everything.** If you subpar and slackin' with a little, that tells me exactly who you are and that you'll be subpar and slackin' with a lot. If you lazy with a lil bit, you gon' be lazy with a lot. It's a character thang yuh dig.

At that moment, in the midst of warehouse ambience, Nephew jumped back in to wrap up the lecture.

"I hope y'all really lockin' in on what Unc just laid down," he said, scanning the room. "Look here, gang—bottom line? This ain't just game, it's guidance. What you do with it? That's on you. If you really wanna eat with me, you gon' need more than appetite—you gotta bring alignment. Everybody want the perks up top, but not everybody ready to pay in discipline, teamwork, and character.

You can't force the game on nobody—it's by choice, not by force or coercion. So here's what I'ma do—put y'all on some required reading. These two books? They'll separate the players from the placeholders. I'll know who's really ridin', and who just undecided. First one: **Leading Through Quality Questioning: Creating Capacity, Commitment, and Community.** That book teaches you how to think sharp, listen deep, and lead with intention—straight essentials if you tryna perform at a high level.

Second? **The Ideal Team Player: How to Recognize and Cultivate The Three Essential Virtues** by Patrick Lencioni. It breaks down what makes somebody truly valuable on a winning team—humility, hunger, and people smarts. Study 'em. Apply 'em. 'Cause by the time the next conference comes around, I'll know who's really built to run this bag up with me… and who just taggin' along."

Thirty-Seven

Control The Mind And The Body Will Follow

Mind over matter guarantees your pockets get fatter and yuh game go deeper than submarine secrets.

*I*n the heart of Aspen, surrounded by landscapes blanketed in flawless snow, the family had come together for a reunion, generously hosted by Uncle. The setting was postcard-perfect, but beneath the surface, there was a simmering tension. Children, fueled by the excitement of the slopes, were ignoring instructions, while the adults found themselves embroiled in petty squabbles over who should take to the ski lift first.

Nephew, observing the scene with a mix of amusement and exasperation, decided it was time to step in like the young elder he was becoming. He pulled out a bag of candy, offering it as a sweet incentive for the kids to form an orderly line. The effect was immediate—the young ones' eyes lit up, and their antics settled as they queued up for their treats. Redirect for maximum effect," he said with a smirk, tossing a knowing glance up at his aunt while Unc stood beside her, arms crossed, clearly approving.

Seeing this tactic work wonders, Uncle decided to raise the stakes to restore peace among the adults. His voice, both firm and enticing, cut through the cold air, <u>*"Let's all get it together. If we can enjoy this day without any more fuss, I'll treat us all to dinner at one of Aspen's finest dining spots tonight. Otherwise, we'll be heading back to that drab hotel we stayed at before this cabin."*</u> *The adults exchanged glances, their earlier frustrations replaced by the prospect of a gourmet meal, and quickly came to an agreement.*

As they approached the ski lift, Uncle gave his nephew a knowing chuckle and said, "If you can control the mood, you control the mind." The two of them then ascended on the ski lift, leaving the squabbles behind. As the lift carried them higher, the noise of the crowd faded into the background, and Uncle began to share deeper insights into the subtle art of influence.

<u>*"See, it's not just about keeping everyone happy,"*</u> *he explained,* <u>*"it's about steering the energy in the right direction. That's true control."*</u> *The mountain's tranquility offered the perfect backdrop for Uncle's lessons on leadership and persuasion, turning a family outing into an impromptu masterclass in psychology.*

Nephew, listen up, you gotta understand this: controlling the mind is where the real game's played. That's the core of every P's playbook, right? You control the mind, the body's gonna line up right behind it. I ain't no Krishnamurti, but I'll teach you a thing or two about how the mind runs most folk's show—get the mind right, the body falls in line. Without that mastery, the whole machine just jams. But this ain't just street knowledge, it ain't some shadowy corner wisdom. Nah, the big guns—the suits in those shiny high-rises, them marketing moguls, and population management types—they been playin' this game long before it hit our blocks.

They call it **'Dark Psychology,'** and trust, it's deep in everything from how they sling products to how they spin the world. It's all about wielding mental tactics like a maestro to dominate both your personal arena and the larger social game. Let me lay it down for you, school you on how this power play rolls out from Wall Street to your streets and trust and believe, it's big league, high-stakes knowledge. Let me take you down into the depths of this mind control, schooling you on how it ain't just for the streetwise or the boardroom bosses—it's a universal play for power.

Even in the game with this here Ism, a lotta young men think with they little head instead of they big head and get tricked out of they energy, be it financial, emotional or psychological energy. That's why we call'em tricks. A woman can get sex anywhere—what she can't get anywhere is a man who makes her think. A lot of these men will do anything short of selling they soul to get a little bit of her gold—damn near go on a forty-day fast for a big-head bihh to give him some ass.

If she can play on your lust, she can play you out of your pockets. See you got to reside and abide in her mind, not just her behind. Every other man is running after her—be the one she has to chase. Procrastination builds the anticipation for the fornication—make her wait, and she'll value the moment more. It's all psychology, son.

Look here nephew, from the tricky strategies of ancient emperors to silent battles waged with Cold War espionage, the art of psychological manipulation ain't nothing new—yuh heard. It's about using your brain to control the flow, dictating the pace and direction of your interactions with precision and stealth. The congregation of international players has been studying it for damn near a century now, and this is that game that's passed down for a fee, but nephew, you good because you rollin' with me.

As the crisp mountain air nipped at their cheeks, Uncle paused to adjust his scarf, his eyes twinkling with a mischievous glint. 'You see,' he continued, as a group of skiers swooshed by, their laughter echoing off the mountainside, 'it's all about understanding the terrain, both in the real world, in boardrooms and even courtrooms.

On these funky streets, where every day's a battle, knowing how to twist psychology to your favor is key to holding down a stable and commanding respect. It's like peeping into a crystal ball, Knowledge is power, right? See nephew, digging into dark psychology, as they call it, can boost your personal game to new heights. It can lay out ways to sharpen your relationships and spot your own weak spots before someone else does. You gotta stay sharp, learning non-stop, and reflecting on your own moves. Elevate yourself by mastering the mind games, and behavior patterns for turnin' those insights into a tool for growth.

Ain't no one gon' play you if you sharp on the signs, ya dig? Take it like this—when somebodies lien' between they teeth', they might flick their eyes to the right, 'cause that's where they're whippin' up fantasies, using that right hemisphere, the home of creativity and making stuff up. But when they're digging for the truth, they'll glance to the left, tapping into that logical left brain, where all the facts are kept neat and tidy.

Those are examples of telltale signs you might spot. But keep it one hundred—this ain't a one-size-fits-all deal. Different folks got different tells, all depending on how they wired up, so you gotta stay observant and decode their blueprint. If they start twitchin', sweatin', and stutterin', you know somethin's off.

Pay attention to the war stories from the old heads who've been around the block and dodged the bullets of manipulation. They hand out the tools you need to build up your defenses, with good game to keep your emotional constitution strong and protect yourself from these smooth operators and tricky manipulators—so you don't become an incubator for the scheme of a finessin' ass, boss player.

In the hustle of the streets, knowing how to manipulate mental levers is crucial for keeping your family loyal and your operations moving without a glitch. Legends of the game have turned psychological warfare into an art form, using their minds to secure their reigns and command respect without ever needing to flex physically. Finesse Gods of the game is what they call'em.

And in the corporate jungle, where the stakes are high and the plays even higher, this game of mind control is critical. It ain't just about skill sets; it's about mindsets. The big dogs in the skyscrapers play chess with live pieces, orchestrating moves that manipulate competitors and colleagues alike to climb to the top. CEO's is what they call them. This game right here peels back the layers on how these high rollers use their brains to play chess in them corporate halls.

We got stories of the slickest moves and the dirtiest scandals. And yo, it's all about knowing the game to spot and dodge these tricks in the office battlegrounds. Plus, we keep it real about where you gotta draw the line, 'cause even in the game, there are rules. From civilized to savage, there's always gonna be rules. the purpose of keepin your mind sharp and staying on top of your psychology is to stay ready for those who like to break the rules.

If you've been paying attention—you'll know that ultimately, we're talking social engineering from the lowest to the highest levels and how it's used to play on people's minds, making use of their mental shortcuts and blind spots. Look, when you start messin' with folks' heads using them dark psychological plays, you steppin' into some murky waters, feel me? The game of mind tricks ain't played the same everywhere—different spots on the map got different rules. Check how this dark psychology is turning up in ads and media across the globe. Now, gettin' wise to these plays, no matter where you at in life is key, 'cause understanding the flavor of manipulation helps you guard against it.

Look here, it's all about knowing how to hit those switches and yank on them emotional strings to swing things your way. Mastering this game? It's deep—understanding the hustle behind manipulation, why it ticks, how it rolls, and all that brain game behind it. I been telling you, nephew, you gotta study **NLP** like you're a hungry rat on a cheese mission.

This ain't just about putting other folks under your spell; it's about shielding yourself from those trying to play you. You gotta peep the game, arm yourself with that know-how, 'cause that's your best shield right there. You gotta be sharp, mane—knowing when you influencing or just straight up manipulating, that's the real key because you can lose social credibility if you out here livin' foul.

When it comes to your inner circle, dark psychology can be a double-edged sword. You got to maintain balance—knowing when to influence and when to back off, ensuring that your relationships remain genuine and your integrity intact. Manipulation for personal gain is a slippery slope, and playing it right means playing it ethical because that same rat chasin cheese can end up in a rat trap—ya dig.

Look here, nephew, if you lookin' to delve into the complexities of social interactions and psychological strategies for real? Consider books like **'Games People Play: The Basic Handbook of Transactional Analysis'** by Eric Berne and **'How to Analyze People with Dark Psychology: Secrets to Influence Anyone Using Mind Control, Manipulation and Deception'** by R.J. Anderson. These scriptures provide insights into the subtle games played in everyday life and offer techniques for understanding the shyt beneath surface interactions.

Now for a deeper exploration into the darker aspects of the human psyche, consider Richard Campbell's **'Dark Psychology or Manipulation'** and **'Manipulation Secrets'**. Both these jawns are crucial for learning how to defend against and understand manipulative behaviors. Along with those you got, **'Dark Psychology: The Ultimate Guide to Learn How to Analyze People, Read Body Language and Stop Being Manipulated'** by Abraham Lee is indispensable for anyone eager to master body language, detect deceit, and comprehend the psychological triggers in people's behavior because if you give it, you need to know how to take it.

Now of course, there's always 'The 48 Laws of Power,' 'The Art of Seduction,' and 'The Laws of Human Nature' by Robert Greene, and 'Dark Psychology 101: Learn The Secrets Of Covert Emotional Manipulation, Dark Persuasion, Undetected Mind Control, Mind Games, Deception, Hypnotism, Brainwashing And Other Tricks Of The Trade' by Michael Pace.

I'd put all of them in my Amazon wishlist and slowly bring'em on home if I were you. Basically, each set of books has its own flavor, diggin into different layers of how people tick and how you can navigate that landscape without getting played yourself.

But let's keep it one hundred, this aint nothing new, **Machiavelli and Sun Tzu,** aint just nick names for tupac and rap song titles, and they wasn't just droppin' game about battles and thrones, nah—they were teachin' us about the chess moves of life, where every piece plays a part in the big picture of power and control—namely that mind control. I'm dropping some bonus game on you now.

Check it—Machiavelli, he was the type to tell it like it is, no sugarcoating. My man was all about keeping your hands clean while letting your shadow do the dirty work. He said you gotta be both the fox and the lion; the fox to recognize the traps and the lion to scare off the wolves. Real talk, that's about being smart and strong, knowing when to hit hard and when to step back and strategize. Machiavelli's teaching us to be loved when you can, but feared when you must. It's like keeping your squad tight and loyal, but also having that rep that commands respect without you even saying a word.

Mach V. was all about that respect through power, but not by being dirty or ruthless. It's about showing you the boss who makes the calls, and those calls? They sharp, they smart, and they stick. You lay down the law in your house, make sure everyone knows the deal, and that your word ain't just heavy, it's the law. This way, folks know where they stand and they respect the throne, not because they fear you, but because they know you ain't playing games—you gon' stand on business everytime.

On the other hand, you got Sun Tzu, the master of war tactics who knew **the battlefield is everywhere**—from the streets to the boardroom. His motto? **"All warfare is based on deception."** That's real game right there. He's saying keep your moves stealthy, let your enemies sleep on you while you're setting up the win. Sun Tzu was all about knowing your enemy better than they know themselves.

Sun Tzu, the grandmaster of the chessboard, was teaching us that to win the war, sometimes you gotta be the shadow. It's all about keeping your moves slick and letting folks underestimate what you're packing. You give just enough to make 'em think they got you figured, but behind the scenes, you holdin' the aces.

This means when you step into that negotiation room, you're two steps ahead, having done your homework, knowing their weak spots, and ready to steer things your way without them even seeing you coming. That's how you control the game, by anticipating the next move. It's about manipulation, but the kind that's strategic and slick, keeping your intentions hidden while you're smiling in the board meeting or nodding in the negotiation.

Both these cats, Machiavelli and Sun Tzu, they was speaking on the same truth—control the minds, and the bodies will follow. It's about that psychological dominance, making sure you the puppet master, not the puppet. Whether you're running a business, leading a team, or just trying to climb to the top, it's about using what these legends taught to manipulate the circumstances to your favor without anyone even peeping your game.

This game keeps you on yuh toes and understandin' the players and the haters because that's crucial. Both them guys stressed knowing your field—I mean like, really knowing who you up against. What gets them ticking, what shakes them, and how they move so you can manipulate the mental realities your dealing with for an advantage. This ain't just good for keeping enemies close, it's perfect for making sure your allies are tight and right with you. Use what you know to keep everyone in check and pull them into your game plan, making them part of your winning team.

Run yuh game like one of them wise general's as the strategic prince of the streets. Tell 'em, "We ain't just playing checkers; this is multidimensional chess, where every move is calculated, and every player has a role. We building empires based on the blueprint the OGs laid down, using wisdom to win wars without ever drawing a sword."

A gust of cold wind rushed past them, causing Nephew to pull his hat down a bit tighter. Uncle chuckled, his breath visible in the frosty air. 'And in the concrete jungle,' he resumed as they neared the top of the lift, 'it's about being as observant and adaptable as that mountain pine over there bending but never breaking under the weight of snow.

The ski lift creaked slightly as it ascended further into the cloud-dotted sky. Uncle leaned forward, lowering his voice as if to keep it from being carried away by the wind. '

If you wanna outmaneuver your competition without burning bridges while keeping it solid—first off, like Sun Tzu, know your competition like the back of your hand. This ain't just about watching their moves; it's about understanding their goals, their strengths, and their pressures. But here's the key: you do it with respect. You learn to anticipate their moves so you can stay one step ahead, not to knock them down, but to position yourself where you need to be. This way, you're not making enemies; you're just making smart plays like a boxer in the ring.

Now, Machiavelli had some tough talk about power, but here's how you finesse it: wield your power with a light touch. Be decisive, be clear, and show that you're a leader who makes moves that others can respect and rely on. When you make those big decisions, you explain your why. You let people see the reason behind the move, making it easier for them to get behind you rather than feel sidelined.

In negotiations, use that art of deception subtly. I'm talking about keeping your cards close and playing your information strategically. Share enough to keep the game fair but hold back just enough so you're not giving away your playbook. This way, you keep the trust, but you also keep some aces up your sleeve for when the game gets tight.

Build alliances, nephew. This is crucial. **Networking** ain't just for show—it's your support system, your early warning, and sometimes, your cavalry. When you connect with others, do it genuinely. Help out where you can, share opportunities, and build a give-and-take relationship. This turns potential competitors into collaborators who might just share their moves with you, allowing for a joint front where everyone wins more.

The business game changes quick, and flexibility is your best defense. When you adapt in response to the market or to what your competitors are doing, do it openly, yet strategically. Let your network know why changes are happening. This transparency shows strength and foresight, not weakness. It keeps everyone in the loop, making'em feel part of the process rather than just spectators or pawns. It make'em more loyal to the gang.

And last but not least, always be ready to pivot, pivot, pivot. When you treat emotional detachment like a survival tactic—kinda like De Niro's character, Neil McCauley, in that movie Heat, where he lived by the code, "*Don't let yourself get attached to anything you can't walk out on in 30 seconds flat if you feel the heat around the corner*"—thinking like that, pivoting becomes second nature.

So there you have it. Outmaneuvering the competition ain't always bout cutting no throats; it's about being the smartest player on the board. It's about using knowledge, power, and connections wisely to keep you ahead without leaving a trail of wreckage behind. Influencing all the mind's present so that their bodies will be in alignment with what you got going on is the move. Play it right, and you keep all those bridges intact and sturdy, maybe even build a few more on your way up.

"That's how a wise player and an intelligent hustler, flips ancient wisdom into street-smart strategies. It's about leveraging that knowledge to not just survive the game, but to rewrite the rules and run the table. Now let's take these lessons, these mental maneuvers, and make 'em work for us in this game of life,"

Uncle said as the lift finally reached the top.

Thirty-Eight

Keep Your Pimp Hand Strong—Never Let'em See You Sweat.

Stand firm, and never let 'em catch you slippin' cause the moment you fumble, the game gone crumble.

*A*t the annual Player's Ball, the air was thick with anticipation as Uncle and Nephew rolled up in a spectacle that turned every head—a candy-painted 24K gold Tesla truck, gold window tint, and datons, with under-glow lighting and the sparkle of metallic flakes in the paint enhancing the glimmer as they pulled up with the butterfly doors rising slowly like wings of a mechanical phoenix.

The electric hum of the Tesla was drowned out by the bass thumping inside the grand venue, where the city's finest hustlers and players gathered, each dressed more extravagantly than the last. This made the truck feel like a UFO as they hovered in front of the space.

ll you heard was the host at the front door say in the mic, Gyaawd Dayumn! Da phuk is dat.

Inside, the grand ballroom was a dazzling spectacle of lights and luxury, every surface gleaming, reflecting the glitter of the night's attire. The famous faces of the game's elite were all in attendance. Unk and Neph lit by chandeliers, casting prismatic light over their jewel-encrusted outfits made of golden sequence. Uncle, lookin' like King Jaffe Joffer himself, was draped in a golden-auburn chinchilla that flowed over his shoulders like molten lava.

On his head sat a matching Fila Zanna cap from Nigeria—tall, creased, lion-skin textured, and trimmed with intricate gold embroidery—lookin' like the head of state while *moving through the crowd with an air of undisputed authority. Not far behind, nephew adorned in some of the same golden bedazzled sequenced material added a stark contrast in a black mink coat and matching top hat adorned with a striking gold feather, jewelry game stupid—symbols of his emerging status in this gilded arena. Next to him, on each arm, his soulmate, an Yvonne Orji looking goddess and his twin flame, a Willow Smith looking Empress with mesmerizing eyes and a hypnotic aura.*

As they navigated the room, a ripple of murmurs followed them like a wave. Two women, in particular, couldn't keep their eyes off of them. One player's companion, draped in a slinky dress that clung to her like a second skin, kept casting reckless glances at Uncle, her eyes sparkling with mischief and maybe something more. Nearby, another lady, her gown shimmering under the lights, eyed nephew with an intrigued smile, clearly captivated by his youthful charisma and the different glow about him.

Uncle leaned in, his voice a smooth whisper over the swell of the records and chatter, schooling his nephew right there amid the revelry.

"You see, nephew, it's not just our threads that got 'em looking. It's the aura, the way we carry ourselves—like kings of an urban jungle. We don't just step into a room; we own it. And that, my boy, is why they can't keep their eyes off us. Looks like you might get chose with yuh mouth closed if you keep up yuh pose.

Uncle's keen gaze followed the glances of the two women, his sharp instincts picking up on more than just casual interest. With a wry smile and a nudge to his nephew, he murmured, "See that, nephew? Those ladies are just a breath away from being peeled off of whoever they came with. They man ain't keeping a strong hand. He paused to let the lesson sink in, his eyes scanning the room with the confidence of a king surveying his kingdom. "Go ahead, put 'em under pimp arrest," nephew joked with a chuckle, but Unc's voice soon dipped into the serious timbre of a seasoned mentor. "listen close, this is crucial."

Uncle straightened, his presence commanding silence around them despite the records spinnin' and chatter. "It's all about maintaining that pimp hand, young blood. Not just about flaunting what you got or keeping your threads flashy—it's deeper. You gotta be firm, show you in control at all times. It ain't about tyranny; it's about assurance. Make 'em feel secure, respected, but never doubt who's leading."

He leaned closer, his voice dropping to ensure only his nephew caught every word. "When you hold your ground with that kind of certainty, when you manage your affairs with that level of precision, nobody in your circle ever has a reason to look elsewhere. They know what they got is solid, unmatched. You see, Uncle continued, sweeping his hand to encompass the grandeur around them, "in these halls, we play more than just a game of dazzle; we play a game of dominion.

He patted his nephew's shoulder, a firm grip that conveyed years of wisdom hard-earned on the streets and polished in gatherings like these. You've learned a lot recently and that's probably why you felt confident enough to bring your secret weapon's out to a party like this amongst all these wolves. I personally know you got this here on lock, plus they got your kid's and are beneficiaries in your trust.

Honestly nephew, I think you'd probably go crazy and try to off one of these P's if they got to close to your gold—only cause you aint the pimpin. The pimpin is a gentlemen's sport. You run out of game and start making decisions from yuh pain. All jokes aside though, remember, it's not about the gold on your coat or the feather in your hat—it's about the steel in your spine and the silk in your approach—and with that, as nephews ladies danced with each other right there by his side, Unc began his sermon.

Keep that pimp hand strong—fair and firm, always ready. This ain't about wielding no iron fist; it's about commanding respect, like a veteran captain guiding his fleet of ships through the roughest waters. The game ain't changed—it's all about dominating the play, controlling the board and every piece on it. Each move is precise, mixing old-school street savvy with cutting-edge strategies.

Every hustler's mantra should be: anticipate, adapt, and overcome without attachment to the outcome either way. Glide through challenges with the smoothness of a graffiti artist, transforming the dusty into the dynamic. The streets don't just challenge; they educate those willing to learn. They teach resilience, strategic thinking, and, most importantly, how to earn lasting respect.

The heart of the matter is this: 'Steady and firm is how leaders lead and rulers rule.' This ain't just some slick talk; it's the blueprint, the secret sauce, the unwritten rule that runs the streets and the executive suites boss. You got to have a hustler's heart and an entrepreneur's mind, when you chasing down them dreams that others can't find.

Now, let's break it down and see how this principle of steadiness plays out. **Consistency** is key—you can't be flipping scripts every day and expect folks to rally behind you. And being firm? That's about standing your ground, not just when the going's smooth, but especially when the chips are down. That's the time the gang gotta' trust and believe in yo' word like it's the gospel with no doubt in they minds that your power is almighty.

Whether you're running a crew or managing teams, your folks need to see that steady hand guiding them—decisions firm, no second-guessing. If you shaky, they shaky, and then the whole empire's at risk of tumbling down. Sometimes you got to be the referee, the judge and jury—but when you gotta ease the tension, conflict shouldn't be no match for yuh intervention—not if you keepin' a strong hand. Your whole movement got to be built on **decisiveness** and swift **execution.**

Now, shift gears to the business world—or even the social scene—it's the same rule but a different playground. Business tycoons, they playing the same game. Steady leadership is what builds Fortune 500 empires; firm decisions cut through market noise like a sharp blade slices through butter. You execute each move with precision. I personally keep a gang of possibilities and options with all types of characters and my network is woven with golden threads, 'cause even in professional circles, I'm the head.

Here's how it breaks down: Steady and firm. Echo that—steady and firm. It's a mantra, it's a battle cry, it's what carves legends out of pretenders. This principle ain't just about climbing to the peak; it's about mastering it, reigning supreme with a grip that's tight yet fair. Initiate and situate to set the record straight. Then dictate and illustrate let the wisdom radiate.

Watch how this unfolds in the alleys under flickering streetlights—every successful hustler who dominates their scene knows this rule. It's about control, not chaos. Swing that up to the skyscrapers scraping the sky, and you spot CEOs who pilot their companies like well-tuned engines. They're steady, unflappable. They're firm, earning respect with every decision they stamp. Steady and firm, my G'—that's how leaders command and rulers reign, both in the gritty game of the streets and the high-stakes world of boardrooms."

Back when I was young and runnin' through traffic downtown, it wasn't just about holding my real estate on the blade—it was about how I held it. Everyone who worked with me watched my every move, learning the ropes. I kept a tight ship, ensuring that everything and everyone operated like clockwork. Discipline was key, but so was respect. I led by example: always calm, always strategic, never letting the pressure show. I might break a bihh, but you'd never see me break a sweat. As for as anyone was concerned, all I did was talk shyt and swallow spit while servin' the finest game the world had ever witnessed on a bish. But like slight of hand people only saw what I allowed them to see.

I made it a point to be seen doing the right things—paying the right respect, making smart deals, and walking away from bad ones. This wasn't about fear; it was about setting a standard. My crew knew that to work with me meant a certain level of conduct, a certain level of expectation, and in return, they got stability and a leader who'd have their backs. Everybody ate and everybody was happy. We traveled the globe, puttin' on a show everywhere we went like we was the UniverSoul circus.

By keeping everything tight and moving smoothly, I built a system that ran well, even when I wasn't looking. This wasn't just about control; it was about creating a culture. The outcome? We not only survived but thrived. We avoided major heat, kept the peace, and more importantly, everyone knew the deal. They knew that working under my watch meant being part of something larger and more lasting than just a street hustle—it was about building a legacy of smart, respected leadership.

Transitioning from the gritty street hustle to the polished corridors of corporate strategy might seem like a leap, but the core principles remain strikingly similar. In the business world, just as on the streets, it's all about leadership, respect, and strategic foresight.

Just then, a small crowd began to gather, drawn by the gravitational pull of Uncle's presence. Their shadows cast long and curious across the gilded floor, lit intermittently by the flicker of the chandeliers above, as they hung on every word, the lesson turning into a spectacle as mesmerizing as the event itself. Soon more ears was tuned in to Unc than the host and DJ passing out awards and trophies.

Unc looked over to his Pimp Potnuh King Tony, smiled and said, "
gotta teach the young with game to pass, mentoring minds from class
to class." And then continued.

See, I innovate, then I renovate; with silver-tongued deals you can feel. Man it's like breaking chains when my influence reigns. The same tight ship I ran on the streets? It's mirrored in how effective business leaders manage their teams and operations in the corporate realm, these principles transform into corporate governance and executive leadership. They maintain order, enforce discipline, and push a culture of mutual respect and **accountability**—essentials for driving any successful enterprise.

Big business lead with a vision, just like I led my crew with clear rules and goals. First, get the paper and deal with that other mess later. This strategic approach ensures that every member of my team knows what is expected and that they work towards a common objective, enhancing efficiency and output on any stroll in America.

These principles of disciplined leadership and strategic management are universal; no matter if you're running a street crew, you're a silverback in the jungle, or running a multi-national corporation. The context may change—the stakes, the terminology, the scale—but the essence of effectively keeping that hand strong remains the same: steady and firm, guiding with precision, and setting the standard for excellence.

See, the real magic of leadership, the kind that lasts, comes from understanding and maneuvering the inner workings of your squad, your team, your family. Leading ain't about just giving orders or flashing bling—it's about inspiring trust and loyalty from the heart. It's like being the conductor of a grand orchestra. Every player has got their part, but they're looking to you to set the rhythm, the pace, and to bring out the music that they didn't even know they had in 'em.

First off, you're the rock, the whole foundation—steady, reliable, and unshakable. Your crew needs to see that you don't crumble under pressure; you thrive on it. They need to feel that you've got the vision to see through the fog, the kind of foresight that can spot opportunities and pitfalls long before they appear on the radar. You've always got a plan A, plan B and plan C. That's how you build real respect and trust. When I'm on my kingpin groove, I orchestrate, dominate and and I set the rates. I ride through storms and never drift; I can navigate any challenge—that's my gift. My people get to see they rollin' with a real boss playa. I got the answer before they even processed the question.

This ain't about being hard; it's about being smart. You set clear expectations and you hold everyone to 'em, including yourself. It's about **accountability.** When folks know exactly where they stand, when they know the leader applies the same rules to everyone, including himself, that's when you get real loyalty, real effort. You cant tell them not to be a buster and they turn around and see you being a buster. That's some sucka shyt.

From the gutter to the glam, a true leader stays fluid, adjusts to the situation like water—flowing when you can, crashing when you need to. It's about knowing your people, their strengths and weaknesses, too, and fitting them into the right slots on the team. But here's the real deal—it ain't just about what you build today; it's about teaching your folks to fish, not just feedin'em for a day. You're investing in them, showing them how to think, how to lead themselves. That's the ultimate mark of a leader: creating more leaders, not just followers.

If you want a real world example, picture this: Back in the day, Apple tried to fire Steve Jobs from the company he founded. But when Apple was down and out, right on the brink, about to bust. They had to go retrieve Steve, the original hustler, back at the helm of the ship he built.

Now he coulda' been mad from before but, he was cool as a breeze with the composure of a King, keepin' his head when he stepped back in the ring. First thing he did? He cuts the fat—slashes down all them confusing products they was messing with and zeroes in on a few that could really shine. Simple, clean, just how the game should be played.

Then, my man Steve, he wasn't just about cleaning house; he was about pushing the envelope. He rolls out the iMac, iPod, iPhone—gear that wasn't just cool, it was revolutionary. And with every drop, Apple wasn't just climbing back up—they were setting the bar sky-high.

But Steve, he knew the look was as crucial as the tech. He revamped their whole vibe with that "Think Different" campaign, making Apple not just a brand, but a badge of honor. He turned Apple from nearly broke to no joke, all with that steady hand and a vision so clear you'd think it was written in neon lights. Under his lead, Apple wasn't just back in the game; they was the game. And that, folks, is how you play it. Not just bouncing back, but doing it with such style and swagger that you change the whole playing field.

As Uncle's words sliced through the ambient noise, the scents of expensive perfumes mingled with the robust aroma of cigars, weaving through the crowd. The luxurious textures of silk and velvet brushed

against one another as the attendees shifted closer, the room's atmos-
phere thickening with intrigue and admiration for Uncle's command
over his audience.

See, disciplining those under your fellowship ain't just about laying down the law; it's about doing it with such swagger that they still want to follow you, not out of fear, but respect. It's like this: you gotta be the kind of leader who can tell someone they messed up without messing up the vibe. You keep it smooth, direct, and when needed, you sprinkle a little charm on it so the medicine goes down easier. But not so easy that they take you for a joke.

Now, maintaining magnetism while you discipline? That's an art form, baby. It's like being that cool cat at the party who can tell folks to keep it down without killing the groove. You let your crew know the boundaries clearly and firmly, but you do it with finesse and a smile, maybe even a joke. You're not just a boss; you're a leader they admire and want to emulate.

You gotta remember, every interaction is a chance to re-inforce your influence. You're not just correcting behavior; you're shaping it. Use your charisma like a brush on a canvas, painting the picture of what your team could be, of what they aspire to become under your guidance. This ain't about breaking spirits; it's about building them up, keeping everyone aligned with the vision while making sure they feel valued, not just used. If you use all yuh energy on breakin' spirits, ain't gone be none left to break the bank.

It all boils down to one truth: lead with a vision and hold your ground with integrity, yuh dig. Whether you a street-savvy hustler, a mackadocious pimp or a high-flying executive: Keep your game tight, your strategy tighter, and remember, the way you lead not only sets the pace but sets the standard. When you step out onto your own battlefield I wan't you to remember these tales, remember these strategies, and craft your legacy with the precision of a master and the wisdom of a sage.

Essentially, keep your discipline steady but keep your hand light, not heavy, yet strong and always ready. When you master this, you ain't just running a tight ship; you're captaining a loyal crew ready to ride the waves with you, no matter how choppy they get. That's how you maintain order without losing love. This way, you'll be able to lead a squad, a fleet, and a whole damn armada—spicin' up the game like a hot enchilada from the presidential suite at the Ramada while dressed down in Prada.

Now listen, first I want you to remember to dig into **"Leadership"** *by Doris Kearns Goodwin.* This gem takes you on a journey across various epochs, showcasing leaders who've steered through storms in their careers. It's a masterclass in resilience, persistence, and empathy—key ingredients for any leader worth their salt. It's a blueprint to how to keep that pimp hand strong and that game long for the street savy.

Next, there's **"Winning Through Intimidation"** *by Robert Ringer.* This one flips the script on intimidation, breaking down how a bold approach can bring in the big wins, though it's sure to stir up some debate. It can put you on to some certified ism from another prism but only if you can handle that kinda mysticism. How you think them boy's in blue keep the biggest gangstas in check.

And last, don't sleep on **"Power: Why Some People Have It and Others Don't"** *by Jeffrey Pfeffer.* It's a real-deal look at the power plays that shape modern organizations. Jeffrey lay's down some savvy advice for navigating the murky waters of office politics and climbing that influence ladder. No matter the playin' field, if you can't play nice with others, you aint gone make it. Once you understand human behavior and the social politics that drive that shyt, you can position yourself to develop the strongest hand out of the whole deck.

Each one of these books packs a punch, offering you the tools you need to boost your leadership game and turn you into a powerhouse in your own right. Integrating this game into your plays keeps you runnin' all boards like you run the block, keeping yuh governance solid as a rock.

After listenin' to what felt like Sunday service drippin' in silk and sermons, the velvet-lit ballroom of the Players Ball shimmered like a jewel box dipped in honey and ambition—thick with cigar smoke, some pimp-hop spinnin', and the scent of imported cologne mixed with powdered egos. Gold-plated goblets clinked against diamonds, and the bass from the DJ booth made the marble floors hum like a low purr. Every corner of the room dripped with style and bravado—minks dragged the floor, gators gripped the tile, and custom-tailored silk whispered behind every calculated step.

Up near the chandelier-lit stage, a velvet-robed MC gripped the mic like a scepter and leaned in with a grin too slick to trust. "And now, ladies and gentlemen—players and playette's, shot callers and boss ballers—the moment you've been waitin' for... the Player of the Year award!"

The crowd stirred. Chains settled. Conversations paused. Unc, perched cool on a leather bar stool with a Cuban smolderin' and a drink barely touched, wasn't expectin' more than a good show. He'd been out the game for years—retired with receipts, soaked in wisdom, and a legacy that still echoed through alleyways and executive rooms alike. But then—clear as a champagne flute on a glass countertop—it rang out: "And this year's Player of the Year goes to... the man they still whisper about in barber shops and boardrooms alike... "

The spotlight hit him like a memory. Necklaces swiveled. Heads turned. Even the new school froze mid-toast. Nephew's eyes went wide, jaw halfway to the floor. "Damn, Unc," he muttered, grinnin'. "You ain't even active and still cleanin' house." Unc rose smooth—buttoned his blazer, adjusted his cufflinks like it was just another Tuesday, and gave a slow nod to the room. The crowd erupted—some outta respect, some outta disbelief—but all in recognition. They knew what time it was. And as he made his way to the stage, every step echoed like the close of a chapter... and the beginning of a legend retold.

Thirty-Nine

Dread or Fed—Faker or Shaker

Stamped in history or lost in mystery, you can't fake foundation—either you built for it, or you break from it because If it ain't real, it don't resonate.

*T*he chilling echo of the metal gates closing behind them resonated as Uncle and Nephew navigated through the stark corridors of the county jail, a place as cold and unforgiving as the business betrayal that led them here. They were immersed in the oppressive sounds of confinement—the clinking of chains, the shuffle of inmates, the stern commands of guards—each step a stark reminder of the consequences that awaited treachery.

Beneath the shadow of towering, grim walls, they found themselves in a sterile waiting area, a sharp departure from their usual environments. To think—just 48 hours ago, the two of them, along with a few close associates, family even, were posted up in St. Barths, French-Caribbean breeze in their faces, sittin' in a cliff side infinity pool that spilled into the sky. Paradise, no doubt—cut short by the reckless moves of someone they thought they could trust. *The air buzzed with a low hum of tension and despair as they sat on hard metal chairs, the scent of industrial cleaner and stale air mingling uncomfortably.*

As they awaited the guards' call, Uncle leaned in, his voice low and steady, "This place is where bad choices come to roost, nephew." *They were there to see Mike, the brother-in-law who had crossed the line—his ambition had led him straight into the clutches of the competition, and ultimately, into these walls.*

"Mike got greedy, dipped his hands where he shouldn't have. He played with the competition, thinking he could outsmart everyone, ultimately playing himself," *Uncle explained. The fluorescent lights flickered overhead, casting a harsh light on his stern expression.* "Today, we get him to sign over his shares and clean up the mess he left behind. Remember, it's not just about the hustle—it's about knowing who truly rides with you."

Uncle's voice cut through the ambient noise, sharp and clear, "This, nephew, is the price of betrayal. Mike chose to side with our rivals, thinking he could cut side deals and outplay the game. They over there livin' crooked with rats and C.I.'s in they midst, while we doing square business. He underestimated their ruthlessness and overestimated his cunning. Now his dumb-ass got pegged as a fall guy. I'll tell ya what, He ain't taken us with'em.

" *As they approached the visiting room, the smell of despair thickened in the sterile air, a potent reminder of the unforgiving nature of misplaced trust.*

"Today's visit is about securing our future, ensuring he can't do more damage," *Uncle continued, his gaze unwavering.* "It's a hard lesson about the weight of loyalty and the cost of greed." *Mike, with his long dreadlocks and gold teeth—yet a double agent in this case—was once a trusted family member and business partner, now*

a cautionary tale draped in an orange jumpsuit. He was the perfect
example of the critical question: is this a dread or fed, faker or shaker?
As they waited they deliberated over identifying true friends versus
false ones in their inner circle.

Back when I was just carving out my name in the game, I
had this competitor, Rico, try to play me. He thought he was
slick, sending over one of his new girls, Jasmine, to spy on
my operations and steal my secrets. Now, Jas wasn't just any
girl; she was playing a double game, working undercover for
the law while pretending to be green in the streets. Guess she
figured she could knock off two birds with one stone—she was
a triple-double agent.

Rico was to stupid to see though I commend his efforts. The
night she walked into my world and chose up, I could tell
something was off. I've always had a way of reading people,
you know, a kind of sixth sense for sniffing out trouble before
it hits my doorstep. So, I ran her through my usual line of
questioning, the kind that digs deep. It didn't take long for the
cracks to show. Her answers were too rehearsed, too polished
for a newbie.

By the end of our talk and a good smashin' she broke down
and spilled everything—how Rico sent her so he could knock
me for everything and her real gig with the cops. Now, instead
of turning her away or worse, I saw an opportunity. After
convincing her that I was a legit talent manager, I talked to her
about her real dreams, which turned out to be singing, not this
life or the lies she was living.

She wanted to experience true freedom, so I helped her quit the undercover job and start fresh. I managed her career in entertainment, kept it clean, and made sure she never got close to my other interests in the game. That's how I turned a potential disaster into a win. It taught me early on the importance of keeping your eyes open and never taking things at face value. That's the kind of sharpness you gotta have in this game. You met her before, nephew, at the family reunion. It's my son Dante's momma.

You gotta' understand, nephew, trust, authenticity, and integrity, they ain't just big words, they the foundation of your rep in the streets and in business. Without 'em, you just another hustler with shaky ground beneath your feet. These three, they like the holy trinity of the game; mess with one, and your whole domain could tumble. Keep 'em solid, and you're golden, whether you're closing deals or running the block.

In both the boardroom and the back alleys, if folks don't trust you, they won't do business with you. Period. And if they think you're fake, you might as well pack up and head home. Authenticity and trust, that's what draws the line between a true hustler and a con. You maintain those, and you command respect in any arena.

See, my boy, being genuine might open doors, and being manipulative might get you in the room, but only one will keep you at the table without looking over your shoulder. I'm talking about the difference between straight shooters and schemers. Watch how the real players move and learn—you gotta' spot the difference to play the game to the highest level.

Authenticity though, is about being the real you, not just the version you think the world wants to see. In the streets or in business, this realness is what sets the legends apart from the liars. Being authentic means your word is your bond. You say it, you live it. Anything else is just cheap talk, and cheap talk don't last in this game.

I'm gonna tell you the benefits of being genuine in low-trust environments. In a world where everyone's wearing a mask, being the one with nothing to hide makes you a luminary. That's power, especially when trust is more valuable than cash. Hell, it beats cash and gets you the right kinda credit when folks know you good for it. Like I say, your word is your bond and as good as cash money. If I say it—BLEEVITT!

When trust is rare, being the one person who's real can turn you into the go-to guy. It's like being a diamond in a pile of fakes—a diamond always stands out. Take any big player who's lasted in this game, and you'll see a trail of genuine moves. They build empires not just on cash flows but on trust flows, too.

Look at stand up cats like Malcolm X or Muhammad Ali—or even old-school hustlers like Bumpy Johnson or Iceberg Slim; their authenticity in vision and action drew people to them, built empires, and kept their legacies tight and right. Once folks smell that inauthentic stench on you, it's like a mark you can't wash off. They'll doubt every move you make and every word you say.

Being tagged as fake? That's a quick way to see your dynasty crumble. You lose respect, you lose credibility, and worst of all, you lose power. Keep it real, or keep it moving, 'cause the streets and the boardroom—they both got no room for fakes. *As Unc dropped the game on loyalty, A big cornfed lookin' guard's footsteps approached, and the sharp clink of keys briefly interrupted,*

his voice echoing coldly, "It'll be a few more minutes," amplifying the
oppressive atmosphere of the waiting room.

Man, truth be told, on the street or in the suite, cats often wear two faces—one where they shine with smiles and another where they scheme in shadows. In the limelight, they're the picture of respect and charm, but when the cameras roll out, the knives roll out too, cutting down anyone in their way.

Everyone's playing a role, nephew. Out here, they toast with you by day and ghost you by night. You gotta' watch who claps for you and who just claps back when you turn around. Folks tend to keep their true selves locked down like a safe; in public, they wear a mask so perfect, you'd think it's their real face.

It's all about keeping up appearances with these folk, maintaining that mask so tight that even they forget who's behind it. It's survival, playing the part that gets them ahead. This mask game ain't just for show; it's a calculated move—show the world what it wants to see, while the real hustle happens behind closed doors. In the game, you learn quick: the face they show is just the bait; what's behind it is the hook. Real recognizes real, but fake? It takes a keen eye. A real hustler plays it like poker—showing one hand, playing another. You gotta' know who's legit and who's just out for a quick score.

On these streets, you meet two kinds of people: those who front hard but got your back, and those who smile to your face but stab you in the back. Knowing the difference? That's your lifeline. Up in those high-rise offices, execs parade around like sheep, all mild and meek, but underneath, they're scheming wolves, ready to pounce for power. It's a game of facades, where the sharpest suits hide the sharpest claws. They smile, shake hands, and silently calculate your worth—and their next move.

Don't be fooled by the corporate smooth talk and polite nods; beneath that sheepskin, there's often a strategist plotting their rise and your fall. Influence is guiding without forcing, leading folks to water and all the while feedin' them salt, makin'em thirsty to drink. See, Manipulation? That's makin'em drink whether they thirsty or not.

Influence is earned, nephew, built on trust and respect. Manipulation? It's taking and grabbing power by any means necessary. The line between influence and manipulation is thin and blurred. Walk it carefully, or you might find yourself on the wrong side, where trust is burned and bridges are broken.

In the boardrooms, code switching is the dance; you gotta' talk one way to the suits upstairs and another to the team downstairs. It's strategic, playing to your audience to maximize your sway. This switch-up ain't just about fitting in; it's about standing out, knowing when to switch your tone to close the deal or inspire your crew. The real game in business is knowing which mask to wear and when. It's a survival skill, flipping between who you need to be and who you truly are without losing your core. The thing is, it's a thin line. You still got to remain authentic.

People react different when they feel played versus when they feel led. Manipulate'em, and they might follow today but they'll flee tomorrow. Influence 'em right, and they'll ride with you till the wheels fall off. I had a couple girls ride with me for over 15 years straight. Ya aunty been with me for 25 years. Couldn't get rid of her if I tried. Wouldn't want to.

But check it out, out here in this cold world, though, watch for the switch-up, it tells you everything. Someone who's true stays steady; a faker flips the script when it suits them. Then you looking at 'em like, muthaphukin dread or fed. Like yuh brotha-n-law back there behind this wall.

See, Influence builds loyalty; manipulation breeds resentment. Keep it real, and your circle stays tight. Play puppet master, and watch your puppets cut the strings. Survival ain't about being the strongest; it's about being the most adaptable. Read the room, change your colors, blend or stand out—whatever keeps you ahead.

You gotta' be like water, nephew—flowing or crashing as needed. Adaptation is about knowing when to shift and how to survive the change. In this game, the quick and the flexible devour the slow and the stiff. Keep your senses sharp, your mind open, and your strategies flexible. When the game turns dirty or the market shifts, be it the hoe market, the blow market, the dough or the show market, it's your ability to pivot that keeps you playin. Adapt or die—it's that simple, that brutal.

Preparation meets opportunity, but adaptability meets survival. Be ready to switch gears at a moment's notice—your survival in the hustle depends on it. Adaptability is your best tool in both the street and the suite. It's about anticipating the curveballs and swinging before they're even pitched. Unfortunately, most negus couldn't adapt and switch up they thinkin' to save they life, which is exactly where we at now. The ignorance done crystalized in they neural exchange. They hardwired to be fools, like yuh brotha-in-law back there.

In the streets, reading someone right can mean the difference between profit and loss, or worse, freedom and captivity. You learn to pick up on the slightest cues—a look, a twitch, a hesitation. The street teaches you to read the unspoken—fear, bluff, or honesty—it's all written there if you know how to look. Use that in business, and you're always a step ahead.

I use to love watchin the first 48. I had a lil friend I use to knock off who use to be a homicide detective. I remember her telling me how every detective got to work them streets for a minimum of five years before they can be a detective. They got to learn how to read people like a book. Every glance, and every word has weight. We use to watch the show together and she'd say read 'em like you read the street signs—cause they'll tell you what's ahead and how to navigate. Those street lessons? They translate straight into the boardroom. Reading an opponent, a partner, a market—it's all the same hustle, just different stakes. *Just then, A female guard with uniformed pants tighter than a* secret between two snitches with way to much body spillin' out, *happened to pass by, her intrigued glance lingering briefly on Unc as he checked his Rolex, the cold, oppressive ambiance of the visiting room was palpable, echoing with the distant clanks of chains and the muffled conversations of other visitors and inmates. Gaht-damn slave farm, Unc mumbled before continuing.*

Business ain't nothing but a big old hustle. The cues, the reads, the moves—it's street smarts scaled up. You got to use what you learned on the corner in the corner office these days. Take that street savvy into the corporate world and watch how you navigate negotiations, partnerships, and competitions. It's the same dance, nephew, just a bigger floor.

My man Mos Def, excuse me Yasiin Bey said it best in Respiration when he said, *"No Batman and Robin, Can't tell between the cops and the robbers*

They both partners, they all heartless, with no conscience. Back streets stay darkened, Where unbeliever hearts stay hardened. Whoo, that man snapped on that one, but you don't nothin about that nephew. You grew up on that Soulja boy, Bow Wow and Playboi Carti. All young playas no doubt.

Back in the day, those slick street moves were all under the table, but now? They just part of the game, taught in business schools as strategic genius. Shiiih, what used to be called sneaky is now seen as savvy—those street tactics have dressed up and gone corporate, turning cutthroat moves into boardroom maneuvers. These plays, they've come out the shadows; what was once frowned upon is now celebrated as disruptive innovation in the boardroom. The streets keep teaching, and the suits keep learning. Watch, soon enough, every sneaky trick will be a case study on how to win at the game of business at Harvard—taught by confidential informants.

Every big play in the streets eventually got its polish and hit the mainstream, turning old tricks into new respect. Cons and scams in the alleys have evolved, now they're textbook examples in **MBA classes**, showing how to win in the market. It's wild, man. Yesterday's back-alley deal is today's next big app in the market, I can gamble and play slot's right on my smart phone—what was once deceitful and frowned upon is now just damn clever business acumen. I mean it kinda make sense, take the biggest criminal and give'em a job. soon you won't even be able to tell who's a real dread or a phukin fed.

We headin' to a future where the line between street smart and book smart is just a blur. Wearing two faces is taxing, man. Drains you in ways you don't see coming—it's like battling yourself in the mirror every day. This duality, it's a double-edged sword. Saves your skin one day, slices your soul the next—it's all about managing the mask without losing the man.

Best strategy? Know when to wear the mask and when to take it off. Balance, nephew, balance—that's how you manage not to lose yourself. Keep a tight circle, ones who know the real you. This way, you can navigate the duality without getting lost in your own disguise. Some rappers and athletes, once they make it, they blend in so much to the new people around them, you can't tell the difference no more, people start calling them clones.

Code-switching ain't just survival; it's about thriving too, using the right identity at the right time to unlock doors and break down barriers. Without getting lost in the sauce that is. When you balance those identities right, you ain't just surviving, you're leading. It's like having the right key for every lock, opening opportunities others can't see.

Trust, it's like money, nephew—hard to earn, easy to lose. You build it up, stack it high by being solid, by being someone people can count on. A trust deficit? It's like a debt that keeps on taking—leaves you isolated, vulnerable. In the hustle, that can mean your downfall. In business, like on the street, a lack of trust can crumble empires. It breeds suspicion, sabotage—poisons the well everyone drinks from.

If you slipped up? Start with the truth. It's tough, but it's the first step back to rebuilding what's broken. Be transparent, be consistent. Rebuilding trust is like healing a wound—it takes time and care. Show up, show integrity, and slowly, watch the trust return, stronger for the scars. If you don't get got that is, depending on who you dealing with.

Look, manipulation can be a tool in the game—some cats argue it's about survival, about making moves when the chips are down. But remember, every move got consequences. Using manipulation can turn on you fast, burn bridges you didn't know you'd needed to cross again. It's a risky play, might get you a quick win but loses you long-term respect, especially when you sittin in that little room with a DT, eatin' popeyes chicken, gettin' ready to sing like lil Michael Jackson after Joe got to'em.

Long-term, manipulation damages more than just your rep—it messes with your own head too. You start losing sight of where the line is, and that's when you start losing yourself. Seen hustlers try to balance the scales—use a little manipulation and keep their integrity. It's like walking a tightrope, and not many pull it off without a fall. Like a fed who's in to deep that eventually becomes the gangsta he's pretendin' to be, can't turn back. Or the dread that can't do the time so he'll do what ever it takes to get back to freedom.

What about the blue boys that got into it to do some good but everybody around them crooked and if they don't get down they might be laid down, or the business mogul who used slick tactics but never crossed the line into fraud. The one who managed to build an empire without losing his soul, showing it's possible, but stressed because it's damn hard. From a societal level, rampant manipulation breeds distrust, makes every deal a potential double-cross. It's a toxic cycle that's hard to break mane.

Personally? It isolates you. Leaves you looking over your shoulder, wondering who's gonna come at you with the same tricks you used. Maintaining your integrity when the heat's on? That's the real test of character. It's easy to keep it clean when everything's smooth, but the pressure reveals the real from the fake and the shake from the Jake. If you solid, It's about holding your ground, even when every fiber's telling you to bend. Those who do, they're the ones who last and turn respect into legacy. Ain't to many left.

Keep it 100, and you'll find doors open for you—people trust people who are true, and that trust turns into opportunities you can't even imagine. Authenticity is your brand, trust is your currency, and your integrity is the flag you wave in both the battles of the streets and the corporate battle. Lose any of these, and you fightin' barehanded in a world where everyone else is armored up. Keep'em, and you command armies. These principles ain't old news; they more relevant than ever. As the world spins faster, holding tight to what makes you real is what's gonna keep you grounded.

If you tryna really get the game on this, peep these two heavy hitters: **"The Speed of Trust"** by Stephen M.R. Covey, where he lays down how trust ain't just some feel-good word—it speeds up the whole business game, cuts down costs, and pumps up the profits and satisfaction. Then you got **"Daring Greatly"** by Brené Brown, she's all about keeping it 'one-hunnid' with vulnerability and transparency, showing that's the real deal for building solid, trust-filled connections that hold up both in your personal life and your money moves.

You already know, your uncles a reader and if nothing else I'm definitely gone recommend some books to back up what im sayin.

Just then, the door creaked open and the officer with the tight pants stepped back in, nodding toward the exit—voice still too polite.

"If you're ready, we can proceed." Unc stood up slow, cracked his neck.

"Been ready," he muttered. "Yeah... let's go collect what's owed." And just like that, they stepped into the belly of betrayal.

Forty

Phoney Tony The One Trick Pony

A little shine don't mean you got the glow—I mean, even a broken clock is right two times a day.

*B*athed in the vibrant neon lights of the city's electric nightlife, *The Velvet Diamond stood as a beacon of indulgence—an upscale gentleman's club famed for its exotic charm and the discretion it offered its elite patrons. Eager for a night of revelry, Nephew invited Uncle to join the festivities at a friend's bachelor party, promising an evening rich with celebration and unforgettable moments. As they approached the club's grand entrance, the air thick with the musk of cologne and the distant throb of bass, they were greeted not by an anonymous bouncer but by a familiar face—Tony.*

Tony, once a young hustler in the game, known for his flashy style and a golden girl who was the envy of the block, now donned a different uniform. The Eagle laden security badge pinned to his chest glimmered under the neon lights as he performed methodical pat-downs at the door. His presence there was a stark symbol of how fortunes can turn; from a promising young pimp to a night guard keeping watch over other men's fantasies.

As Tony recognized Uncle, a wry smile broke across his face, the kind that knew the depth of the streets and the height of falls. "Never thought I'd see you at one of these joints again," Tony quipped, his voice heavy with a mix of respect and resignation. Uncle clapped him on the shoulder, the thud of old camaraderie echoing softly. "Times change, Tony. We play the cards we're dealt," Uncle responded, his eyes briefly meeting Tony's, sharing an unspoken understanding of the highs and lows of their chosen paths.

Inside, as the pulsating lights swept across the sea of faces and the air filled with the perfume of excitement and excess, Uncle leaned in towards Nephew. Over the din, he began to weave the tale of Tony's rise and fall—a cautionary tale about the perils of betting it all on one hand and the critical importance of diversifying one's hustle. This, Uncle explained, was not just a rule for the street but a fundamental principle of any successful enterprise.

Whether in the shimmering allure of velvet-draped rooms with diamond life atmospheres or the cutthroat clarity of corporate boardrooms, one must remain, poly-money-ous, that is, practicing having multiple streams of income. Multiple offerings was not just wise; it was essential for survival.

Man I tell ya Nephew, once upon a time, I thought ole Tone might have the potential to be player of the year. Fortunes can flip faster than a hustler's hand and Tony's tale tells all. He had this one bad thoroughbred, could run circles round them broads on the track, put'em to shame. He had a couple others too but this one, whew—turn a pimp into a trick.

He was checkin' so much money out that trap—a pimp had no choice but to give him dap. He musta thought she came to stay though. When she left his ass, as they all do, he was out of plays. I guess she was on her—you made me, ok, make another me—type time. He tried to hold on, but eventually fell off. Riding high without a net? That's a circus act doomed to fall.

See, being the real deal goes way deeper than just looking the part, 'cause a facade might dazzle 'em today but it won't stand the test of time. Facades are like cheap paint, looking good when it's fresh but it peels off fast, leaving you exposed when the storms hit. Wear that mask too long, and soon enough, you won't recognize the face staring back at you in the mirror. You might fool 'em at the jump, but time tells all truths, and when that facade crumbles, so does your credibility. It's like building a house with no foundation; it looks good until the first storm rolls through.

Keeping up a front is draining, man—it eats at you, 'cause you're always playing a part instead of being yourself. The more you fake, the harder it gets to keep your stories straight, leading to slips and falls you can't afford. Then you find yuh'self broke as a joke. Cash or crash, multiple streams keep your dreams afloat. Flash without cash is just smoke—without the fire, you just blowing cold.

I've seen hustlers flash big stacks and talk a big game, only to disappear when it's time to show and prove. In that corporate world you like to moonlight in nephew, companies pump up their value with big talk all the time, but crash when they can't deliver on those promises. In that same corporate jungle, look at the firms with the best track records—they not the ones with just a single big win, but those delivering quarter after quarter, those the ones to study.

Consistency is the name of the game and it's all about being the same dude—steady and true, no matter the heat or the high. It's your rock, your steady hand in a shake-up, showing folks you're the same cat day in, day out. A flash might catch the eye, but only steady hands build empires. It's about long runs, not just quick sprints. True power lies in being able to deliver, time and time again, not just shining once and then fading out. No body would know who Jordan was if he only brought home one ring or slammed that ball one time no matter how fly he looked while slammin' it.

Whether you're moving units in the projects or pushing projects in the office, being consistent means they can count on you to deliver. Consistency ain't just a good trait—it's a must-have, setting the platinum players apart from the one-hit wonders. You gotta move like clockwork, reliable, predictable with the quality, not just in timing but in maintaining high standards. You gotta keep your emotions in check, your plans tight, and your performance top-notch no matter the pressure—I'm talking that Frank Lucas quality.

The biggest challenge is complacency for most—getting comfortable at a certain level and losing the drive to push harder. To stay on top yuh gotta keep setting new goals, keep challenging yourself and your team, and never settle for 'good enough.' Start with small promises and keep 'em, build a routine that supports your goals, and stick to it like glue. It's about discipline, about doing the work even when you ain't feeling it—especially then. Otherwise you just lying to yourself.

Look, nephew, gettin' twisted up in misconceptions, it's like steppin' on landmines in both your personal life and your business dealings—missteps based on bad intel can blow up your whole spot. Misconceptions, they cloud your judgment, lead you to make moves that ain't aligned with the real deal, costing you more than just money—it can cost you respect and relationships.

Real talk, It's about asking the right questions, listening more than you talk, and watching actions, not just taking in words—people reveal their true selves through their moves, not just their mouthpiece. When reality hits hard, grit keeps you glued to your path, turning every no into a not yet, you feel me?

In the game of life my man, you gotta roll with a strategy, and part of that big ole game plan is keeping multiple moves up your sleeve. Plan A, that's your front line, where you're putting all that heart and hustle, aiming for the dream. But even dreams hit some bumps, right? That's when Plan B slides in—think of it as your safety net, your just-in-case scenario, some insurance.

Ain't about doubting your moves; it's about playing it smart, staying ready. When one door starts giving you that creaky noise or slams shut, you've got another cracked open, waiting for you to step through, smooth and steady. This tactic, it keeps you pushing, keeps you advancing no matter the scrapes life dishes out.

You know, there's a certain kind of calm that tags along when you know you got options. When you ain't boxed into one corner, the pressure drops a notch. You're set free to take them risks, push them boundaries, 'cause you got that fallback. That safety net, it sparks more bold, creative swings in your Plan A. It's all about balance—chasing your goals full-throttle while also keeping that conservative game plan tucked in your back pocket. And sometimes, Plan B? It might just shape up into something more fitting as you shift and grow, more in tune with your evolving game than your first draft.

Every move, every option, it's part of a broader strategy to make sure no matter what blockades you face, you got the agility to switch lanes and keep rolling. Life ain't no straight shot, and success ain't a clean, direct path—it's a maze of turns and what-ifs. Having a slew of plans, that's like holding a ring of keys to various doors. You might not swing 'em all open, but knowing you got the means, that's where the real power lies. And nephew, it's not a bad idea to have a Plan C and Plan D waiting in the wings, too. Abundance baby, never limitations. *As Uncle delved deeper into his tale, the backdrop of the club's sultry atmosphere painted a vivid canvas. A waitress glided by, her tray perfumed with the tangy zest of citrus cocktails, momentarily cutting through the dense musk of the nightlife. Nephew couldn't help but wonder if this was her only hustle.*

Look here, nephew, stacking your paper from different avenues ain't just smart, it's essential. You don't wanna be caught with all your eggs in one basket, not in the hustle, not in life. Take it from Phoney Tony's downfall, young blood.

In this game, you betta juggle or struggle—**diversify** or die dry. Betting it all on one gig can leave you broke and busted when the wind shifts. Spreading your bets, that's how you stay stable when the game gets wild. More streams, less stress, that's the key to keeping your wallet fat and your mind at ease. In the business world, it's like offering more than one hustle under the same roof. Diversify your dealings, and you create more ways to win. Never ride one wave—oceans of opportunity await when you got more than one hustle on yuh plate.

Being adaptable in the game means you can shift gears quick, spot new opportunities, and jump on 'em before they slip away. Keep your eyes on the market trends and what you're good at, nephew. That's how you spot the next money move before it's on everybody else's radar. You gotta be creative, think outside the box. Innovate, and you can turn even the craziest ideas into cash cows. Look at cats who done it right—those who've switched up their hustles and padded their pockets without missing a beat.

First off, assess what you got, your skills, your resources. Knowing your strengths sets you up to exploit 'em. Start building your portfolio piece by piece, mix it up with ventures that complement each other, so when one's down, another's up. Do your homework, nephew. **Market research** tells you where the money's moving, what's hot and what's not. Always **measure the risk**, see how much you could lose and decide if the juice is worth the squeeze, baby. Good **financial planning** keeps you from going under when you're juggling more than one hustle. It's about keeping the cash flowing right. They call it **long term sustainability.**

Allocate your resources smartly—don't throw too much at one thing. Balance your spend to keep all your ventures healthy. Balance your time and money like a pro. Over-investing in one area can starve your other hustles. That's like given' one broad to much attention and the others start to get jealous and blow up yuh spot. Check every dollar and every deal. Track it like a blood hound. **Performance checks** keep you in the know, so you're never flying blind.

Speaking of options, young blood, let me lay it out for you in terms more familiar to you, since you a wallstreet head. Options are like them golden tickets in the finance game of stocks and bonds—giving you the strategic edge to buy (calls) or sell (puts) stocks at set prices before time runs out, yuh know. They're your way to hedge bets and protect your stack, using less cash to control more value, and even making money upfront by writing options like covered calls.

They give you the power to call the shots but you gotta diversify to stay alive. Here's the deal: options demand sharp strategy. You gotta mix up your plays with **spreads, straddles, or synthetics** to keep ahead. Remember, these moves are high stakes; they're as risky as they are rewarding. And don't sleep on those expiration dates—missing one can blow your whole game up. Whether you're investing in cryptocurrencies, big names like Microsoft, Apple, and Google, or diversifying across the **S&P 500**, it's all about spreading your bets to manage risks. Risks come with the game, but a player who fly high need to always pack a parachute.

In fact, in your line of work nephew, technology is a game-changer, helps manage those risk and all those income streams without breaking a sweat. Get the right tools to keep tabs on everything. A.I. Agent's and Automation's like having a loyal soldier in each of your hustles—keeps things running smooth while you focus on expanding. Online platforms are doorways to new markets. They easy to enter, and the reach? Infinite. I got potnuhs who going crazy with the online peep shows and subscription based pimpin. Stay sharp on tech advances—they're your best bet to stay ahead in this fast-paced game.

When you ready to **scale**, do it without diluting what got you here. Keep the quality and up the quantity. Never stop learning, never stop growing. Skills are your arsenal, and you gotta keep 'em sharp and stacked. Know how to balance growth without tipping over. Look, sticking to one hustle might seem easier, but diversifying? That's where the real legends are made. Broaden your horizons, and watch your empire expand beyond what you ever thought possible. Or else, you can alway's get you a gig here with Tony.

Mid-discussion, a deep bass line from the R&B track the DJ switched to reverberated through the plush interiors of Club Velvet, matching the gravity of Uncle's lessons. As the mood lighting subtly shifted to a softer hue, laughter and cheers from a nearby group blended with the crescendo of music. Meanwhile, the sharp clink of ice in whiskey glasses punctuated Uncle's points, syncing with the low hum of intimate conversations that filled the shadowy corners of the club.

At the end of the day, the rundown is: Authenticity beats façade, consistency trumps occasional wins, and seeing through the smoke to grasp the reality, and make sure you got multiple hustles, diversification, and several offerings—that's the backbone of both street smarts and boardroom tactics. Options is the name of the game. Throw dice on multiple tables; some lose, some win, but you play on because a hustler's horizon ain't just wide—it's played with multiple money maps.

I wouldn't care if you worked at 'Mack-Donnels,' you betta have you a weekend job at the Taco spot too and cuttin hair when you get off from there. Diversify with several options.

Never be a one trick poney. I wasn't. Me and my hoe's had several tricks up our sleeves to get that cash flowing like the nile river up to Pharoah. The most trap I ever checked in one night was sixty thousand and it wasn;t because of no hooker shyt, but it came from a hooker.

Variety is the spice of life in fact it's the cornerstone to intelligence. You gotta blend expansion with consistency and adapt strategically to stay ahead in this game—whether you're dodging pitfalls in the streets or climbing ladders in the sky-scrapers. This mix, it's what keeps you relevant, respected, and real in the eyes of your peers and your prey; it's your armor and your strategy, all rolled into one.

Pulling lessons from both the corners and the cubicles, that's where you find the gold—applying the grit of the street to the gloss of the boardroom, staying solid in your game no matter where you play. It's about that consistent hustle, keeping your tactics tight and your goals in sight, whether you selling ideas or inching through corporate red tape.

Now take this game I've laid out, and run with it. Apply these insights to your own hustle, make moves that marry authenticity with dependability, variety and smarts, and watch how far it takes you. Don't just nod along, act on it! Use what you've learned to cut through the noise, stand out in your field, and build something that's real—something that last, that others can bank on.

The speakers pulsed like distant thunder—slow, steady, and deliber-ate—shaking the air just enough to remind you you were deep in the heart of somewhere slick. The scent in the air was layered—top note dank, gaseous green, middle note ambition, and a lingering base of

*too many choices made after midnight. Unc and Nephew, still posted
in the cut—corner booth, low light, high visibility.*

*That VIP placement, not too loud, not too deep, just right for
watchin' everything unfold without being part of the show. From their
perch, they clocked every player, pretender, and paycheck-drainer
moving across the floor like chess pieces on shag carpet. Just moments
earlier, they'd dapped up an old friend working security—once a
major player in the game, now reduced to patting down pockets and
watching exits.*

Unc sipped slow from his glass, eyes tracking the room.

"Neph," he said, voice low but firm, "I ain't sayin' it to clown
him. But you see what I'm sayin' bout Tony the tiger, right?
That's what happen when all your bread got one oven. No
backup. No blueprint. No system. You stop eatin' the moment
the stove go cold."

Nephew nodded, eyes serious now. Like Tony Robbins
already said, your level of success will rarely exceed your level of
personal development, and Warren Buffett already told you the
more you learn, the more you earn. Unc leaned in. "So here's
what you do if you serious 'bout never endin' up countin' tips
when you used to count stacks." He cleared his throat, then laid
it down smooth:

"First off get—**Multiple Streams of Income** by Robert G.
Allen. That one? Classic. Teaches you how to build income
pillars, not just paper routes. Royalties, investments, passive
bread—real foundational sauce. That book? It'll rewire how
you think about earnings.

Next—get that: **Unscripted** by MJ DeMarco. That one
heavy. He break down how the nine-to-five been lyin' to us
since we was in diapers. You wanna build a lane that pays you

while you sleep? That book show you how to create value and own your output, not trade time for crumbs. Like my man Myron Golden say, buy back your time instead of selling it, and for cheap at that. It's your time and you want it now.

After all that, then you ready for **The E-Myth Revisited** by Michael Gerber. That one right there gon' teach you systems. Systems, Neph! That's the only way you scale. Otherwise, you just self-employed and tired, not truly free. You want a biz that run without you? Gerber gon' show you how. If I could teach the world one thing, it would be the truth of systems and models and how they are the only way to success. I'd make Negus tattoo the word's **'systems and models'** on they forearm so they never forget.

Now when you done absorbin' that—wrap it all up with **The 10X Rule** by Grant Cardone. that's your cherry on top. It's your 'no-excuse' playbook. It's loud, it's bold—but it's the push you need when you start makin' excuses instead of makin' moves. That book? It remind you to think bigger. Always."

Nephew let it all marinate, lips pressed tight in thought. "Damn, Unc. You just dropped a syllabus."

Unc chuckled, gravel in his tone. "Nah, I dropped a mirror. You lookin' at your future self if you apply it. Get these books. Read 'em. Highlight 'em. Live 'em. You master what's in those pages? Ain't a bag in the world you can't create—or protect."

Forty-One

KNOCKIN (or Blockin')—Taking Yours in this Competitive Game

They're either gunnin for your gains or gummin up your lanes—whether they out for acquisition or annoyance, choose your battles wisely 'cause energy vampires can be costly and timely.

*N*estled behind the hills on the serene shores of a lake, Uncle's log cabin offered a respite from the relentless pace of city life, where the only ripples were on the water's surface. Inside, the cabin was alive with the old and rich aroma of cedar, intermingled with the subtle scent of pine from the surrounding forest, creating an atmosphere that was as warm as it was inviting.

Uncle, a sage in both the game of life and every table where skill outshines luck—be it dice, dominoes, cards, or consoles—was deep in a spirited chess match with an old hustlin' partner, eyes sharp like he was still bettin' rent money on the outcome. *Their laughter mingled with the ambient tunes of Parliament Funkadelic playing from an old record player, while cigar smoke lazily swirled around the room. In the kitchen, the gentlemen's lady friends, wine glasses in hand, chatted animatedly about the latest department store fashion line as they prepared a meal.*

As Nephew creaked onto the wooden porch, he glimpsed through the open window a scene of relaxed rivalry. He stepped inside, placing the blueprints for a new building project he and Uncle were partnering on next to the chessboard. "Watch this move, young blood," Uncle chuckled, casting a sly grin across the board at his friend. "Back in the day, when we was still teenagers, I knocked this old fool for his bottom chick—smoothest play I ever made. And now, he's trying to knock me for my queen, thinking it's payback time."

With strategic finesse, he blocked his friend's aggressive advance. "Just like I'm blocking him here, you gotta block that real estate competitor of yours trying to jam you up with his courthouse connections. Maybe you should knock him for that pretty little secretary of his and that courthouse connect. You say your game is A1, right?" Shiiih, show and prove.

This banter was more than simple jest; it set the stage for a deeper lesson on 'Knockin' and 'Blockin,' strategies not only vital to chess but crucial in the grander game of life and business. As the chess pieces clicked in the background, Uncle's tone shifted to something more grave, "Let me break it down for you, nephew. Whether it's on these squares or in the streets, knowing when to knock and when to block can make or break your game."

The serene backdrop of the lake, shown through the open windows, the haunting echo of loons in the distance, blended with the crackle of the fireplace and the gentle rustle of leaves through the trees, provided the perfect setting for Uncle's lessons.

Let me bless you with this certified 'G' real quick. One thing you best never forget—ain't nothin' in this world built to last forever. Even if it's death that does you part, everything got an expiration date. In this life, the game is yo wife. That's why you gotta remember it's got to be mack-aroni, not matrimony when it comes to your attachments to anything. You ain't married to no broad, no job, no deal—you married to the game, 'cause in this life, the game is the only wife that'll never leave you, long as you keep breakin' bread and keep her fed. Ain't no love in this game either, just lease agreements.

The most diabolical part in it all though, young blood, is somebody always plottin' to knock your hustle, lookin' to peel you for all you got. Some folks don't eat unless they takin' food off another man's plate. Don't tast good enough if they ain't take it from somebody else. They get they rocks off like that—get a kick out of it. That's just how the game go. If they can't knock you for your assets, they schemin' to block your rise, throwin' shade, startin' whispers, or throwin' obstacles in your lane just to slow you down. And why? 'Cause they ain't got the heart, the skill, or the vision to build their own castle—so they try to burn down yours. Or they dead-sca'ed you gon' do them how they do you if you was fully healthy—that's called self projection.

Knockin'? That's when another pimp sidestep in and snatch your girl—not 'cause she faulty, but 'cause he slid in with smoother game, painted a better picture, or just caught her slippin'. That's headhunting, street edition. In corporate terms, it's like when a rival company poaches your top employee—offering better perks, a shinier setup, and promising a fast lane to the good life. Strategic, bold, and always personal.

Now blockin'? Whole 'nother beast. That's a hater's move—runnin' they mouth, tryna downplay your name just to shine up theirs. Throwin' shade on your rep hopin' to slide in where you already got traction. In the game of pimpin', that's textbook blockin'. They ain't got the charisma to pull her direct, so they whisper in her ear, tryna make you look weak or unworthy. In business or your social circle, it's the same—they'll talk sideways to your supporters, twist the facts, and poison the well just to knock your hustle. That goes down in the office or the warehouse floor all day everyday.

But real ones? We don't trip. We upgrade the aura. Make the glow so undeniable, so magnetic, that no knockin' or blockin' can dim the light. When your presence speak louder than they lil' narratives, the game speaks for itself.

I can remember a time when I got peeled for a broad; my motto was I got to replace her by knockin' two more. I wasn't just sittin' there lickin' wounds. Nah, I was out there, turnin' loss into double the profit. 'Cause A pimp with no plan is just a trick with a scam. See, competition is the heartbeat of the hustle—keeps your instincts sharp, keeps your game polished, whether you flippin' on the blade or flippin' deals in a boardroom. Business ain't nothin' but street hustle in a tailored suit. You either expandin' your empire or fendin' off the ones tryna invade it. But understand, nephew, real players don't just muscle up, they strategize. They don't just push weight—they push positions.

Now peep this—healthy competition? That's the fire under your ass that makes you run faster, think smarter, move slicker. Ain't about crushin' your rivals—it's about runnin' your own race so cold that they can't keep up. Look at them cats who started out buildin' in a basement, flippin' ones and zeroes, now they Kings of Silicon Valley. They didn't just outlast the game—they outgrew it, and now they writing the code to your reality.

But here's where you gotta watch your back—**interference**. Some fools don't compete, they sabotage. They ain't knockin' to take your spot, they blockin' to make sure you never reach it. Treatin' you like black wallstreet back in the day. These the ones settin' up false charges, runnin' smear campaigns, lockin' doors before you even get a chance to knock. And in this life, nephew, it ain't always the strongest that wins, but the one who knows how to sidestep the traps and keep movin'.

Now let me warn you—play too dirty, and it's gon' catch up to you. Yeah, you might win the battle, but you gon' lose the war. 'Cause reputation? That's your currency in this game. Once folks can't trust your name, you worth nothin'—not on the street, not in the boardroom, not anywhere.

Back when I was doin' my thing, interference wasn't lawsuits and corporate blockades—it was a cat sendin' one of his girls to spy on your trap, a rival spreadin' dirt on your name, or a snitch whisperin' sweet nothings in the law's ear. Same game, different board. And the best way to beat that? Stay two steps ahead. Anticipate the hate. Move before they even think to block you. That's the kind of player who don't just survive the game, but runs it.

And, nephew, don't just pick allies—cultivate 'em. 'Cause one day you gon' need a lifeline, and the folks you fed gon' be the ones who pull you up. Build your squad not just with muscle, but with minds. Iron sharpen iron, but weak men dull the blade. If they ain't makin' you sharper, stronger, richer in game or in gain—cut 'em loose.

And watch them energy vampires, nephew. The ones always takin', never givin'. They eat off your plate, but ain't never put a crumb down for you. They keep your phone ringin', but ain't never brought a dollar through the door. Leeches, parasites—foolish liabilities. Learn to spot 'em early, and cut 'em off quick.

Keep your eyes peeled for the snakes in the grass, those slick cats who whisper sweet nothings but plan dirty somethings. It's the quiet moves that tell the loudest stories. You gotta set your terms, mark your territory. Show 'em where the line is, and make it known you ain't playing when it comes to crossing it. Make it crystal, nephew. Lay down your laws clear and loud, so there ain't no room for misunderstandings or mischief.

As the chess game neared its strategic climax, the crackling sound of the fireplace added a cozy, rhythmic undertone to the cabin's atmosphere. Outside, a gentle wind rustled through the leaves, bringing with it the fresh, damp scent of the lakeside woods.

This mingled with the occasional laughter and clinking of glasses from the kitchen, where the lady friends had just opened a new bottle of red wine. The rich, robust smell of the wine filled the room, blending with the smokier notes of Uncle's Cognac dipped cigar, creating a layered tapestry of scents that underscored the evening's lessons in strategy and foresight. The playa-potnuh got a few good moves off, but had no idea of what was in store.

"Use what you know," *said Unc*, "to spot trouble long before it knocks on your door. Use every piece of info like a weapon. It ain't just about having knowledge; it's about how you use it to play the game smarter. Always have a backup plan, then have a backup for the backup. The game loves to throw curveballs, and you gotta be ready to swing. Every move should push you closer to your crown. If it ain't making you bigger, better, or badder, it's wasting your time. Ain't no crown for a clown who let the game get him down, yuh dig."

Roll with those who strengthen your hustle. Allies should amplify your strengths and fortify your weaknesses, that's real power. Build your mind tough like armor. Life hits hard, but you gotta hit back harder and keep stepping. The game waits for no one. Take your knocks, learn your lessons, and bounce back like you're made of rubber.

Distractions are the enemy of greatness. If they can't attack you, they gon' try to distract you. Stack your chips high, keep your squad tight, and your intel right. You need a fortress, not just a fence, to keep you in the game. Every deal, every double-cross, every victory, and every loss has a lesson. School yourself daily. The game evolves, and you gotta evolve with it. Flexibility ain't just physical—it's mental too.

At the end of the day, nephew, this whole game is about strategy. Know who you runnin' with, who you runnin' against, and who's tryin' to trip you up just for the hell of it. If they knockin'—play to win. If they blockin'—play to outmaneuver. And if they just hangin' on, ridin' your shine without addin' to your grind—kick 'em to the curb like a mutha-phukn herb.

That's the truth, nephew, straight no chaser. In this hustle, you gotta be slicker than the slickest and smoother than the smoothest. Remember, every hustler's got their day, but a smart hustler makes every day count. You gotta keep your mind on the vision, or else be a player reminiscing. Time's the ultimate player in this game, and she waits for no man. So, make sure yuh head on a swivel and your eyes on the prize. Every player and every play got a purpose. Whether they're boosting you up or setting you back, understand their angle and stay two moves ahead, if not three.

Life's a serious game of high stakes, and the bets are your dreams, your peace, your future. But the good news? You're the master of your fate, the captain of your soul out here. You decide how to play your hand, when to hold tight, and when to fold. Make every decision count, every move a testament to your cunning and control. This game don't wait on nobody, and it damn sure don't show love to fools. Play smart, play strong, and always play to win 'cause if the game ain't first, then the bag gon' be worse.

*As the chess game continued, Uncle's old friend casually reached into his bag and pulled out a well-worn copy of **"The Prince" by Niccolò Machiavelli**. Sliding it across the table towards Nephew, he grinned, "You might find this enlightening. It's about power and strategy, using methods that ain't for the faint-hearted but necessary for those looking to really play the game at its highest levels."*

Uncle nodded approvingly, his eyes twinkling with a mix of nostalgia and mischief. "That book," he declared, "taught me a few tricks back in the day. Perfect for when you're dealing with folks trying to knock your hustle."

He then leaned closer, lowering his voice as if sharing a secret. "And when you're done with Machiavelli, I got a couple more for you. You should dive into **'Barbarians at the Gate: The Fall of RJR Nabisco'** by Bryan Burrough and John Helyar. It's a real-life saga of a corporate takeover that'll school you on the art of war in the boardroom."

"Also, check out **'Competition Demystified'** by Bruce Greenwald and Judd Kahn," he continued, tapping the chessboard thoughtfully. "It simplifies all these complex strategies into something you can really use to guard against those trying to encroach on what's yours." Even Highschool ninjas should be able to understand that one so ain't no excuse for not readin' that one.

As he spoke, Uncle moved a pawn forward, a sly smile spreading across his face.

"Remember, nephew, every move here," he gestured at the chessboard, "mirrors those big moves out there in the world. Learn the strategies, anticipate your opponent's moves, and always stay several steps ahead if you wanna set'um all on fire—If yuh ism ain't hot, your bankroll gon' rot—Checkmate Negus.

Forty-Two

Pimp Peep Game—Lames Just Complain

A disciplined mind paves the way for a prosperous grind, and when a pimp is wise, he can pimp through all space and time.

S *tepping into the plush corridors of his nephew's high-tech recording studio, Uncle couldn't help but emit a low whistle, thoroughly impressed by the sleek, state-of-the-art setup before him. Feel like I'm on the mothership bwoi. The walls, meticulously lined with high-quality acoustic panels, and the latest recording equipment gleamed under the soft, ambient lighting—a clear testament to his nephew's ambitions and significant financial investment in his musical venture. As Uncle toured the space, vivid memories flickered through his mind—nights long past spent in the company of legends like Rick James, Ike Turner, and Sly and the Family Stone, where the air was thick with creativity and the palpable promise of chart-topping records.*

Amid the nostalgia, the session was alive with energy, buzzing with a mix of eager young talent. Though they were experiencing technical difficulties, Nephews' engineers assured them they'd be back up and running in a few moments. *Uncle was in his element, dispensing nuggets of hard-earned wisdom, when Nephew's homie, a brash young artist with undeniable talent and an ego to match, began to disrupt the flow with his loud assertions.* His interruptions, although meant to showcase his confidence, were actually lowkey disrespectful—slicing through the harmony of the studio session with a punch of dissonance and an air of self-righteousness.

Seizing the moment as a critical teaching opportunity, Uncle shifted his tone; he adopted the sharpness of a seasoned player who had commanded the streets long before most everyone in the studio swam in they daddies sack. With a firmness born of experience, he checked the young artist, asserting the hierarchies of respect that are learned but often forgotten in the eagerness of youth.

The room fell silent, the air charged with tension and sudden insight, as the homie, visibly chastened, stepped back to absorb the lesson from someone who had walked the path before him and knew its twists and turns.

Man, let me lay it down for you like this— a wise man listens and a fool interrupts. Whether you pushin pleasure on the blade, booger sugar in the shade or cuttin' deals in high-rises, with disguises, the game don't change. It's all about holding your cards close and peeping the scene. The real players? They ain't the loudmouths blowing up the spot; they're the cool cats who watch, wait, and swoop in only when the iron's smoking hot.

Man, real macks, they get it done, jack. No excuses, just pure hustle. You see, a true man steps into the arena ready to handle whatever life throws his way. Ain't no room for whining or bitching; that's for the weak. These soft cats? They wouldn't know **accountability** if it walked up and slapped 'em in the face. Always playing the blame game, dodging responsibility like it's some kind of disease.

Say, blood—I've heard a few generic bar's about pimp shyt—ya'know from rappers and such. But, real pimpin live by a code. When things don't go as planned, the pimpin' ain't out there pointing fingers. Game gone look at itself and figure out the next play. It's about owning your moves, good or bad and taking responsibility for your own game. That's how you grow. Yuh grow through what you go through. That's how you lead. Cats stuck making excuses, they ain't moving nowhere—they just spinning their wheels. But the true leaders, the real macks? They out there setting the pace, carving out paths, and laying down legacies. That's the real game, youngsta.

You gotta master the art of timing, know when to lay low and when to strike. It's all about using patience, silence, and wisdom when you makin' moves day by day. Every play you run, it gotta be calculated, like you're holding all the cards and waiting for just the right moment to lay 'em down. This ain't just about hustle; it's about playing smart and knowing the field—poker face gotta be elite.

Whether you hustling on the streets, in the booth, or navigating the shark-infested waters of corporate life, patience ain't just a virtue or nice to have—it's your sharpest weapon. Like a chess master, a true businessman—whether he's working corners or corner offices—watches silently, waits for that moment when the other side slips, shows their hand. That's when you strike, turning what looks like a tight spot into your next big win.

Silence is also one of them things that turns up the pressure without saying a word. You ever notice how a well-placed pause in a conversation makes the other person spill their guts? That's power right there. Using strategic quiet like a chess move gives you control over the game, lets you dictate the pace without tipping your hand. It's like making silence do the heavy lifting, letting the tension build till the other side cracks. That's how you use patience and silence like a true hustler, keeping your strategy tight and your outcomes in sight.

As Uncle's universal wisdom filled the room, the soft hum of the studio equipment in the background lent a sacred quality to the space, like a church where the faithful gathered to hear the sermon.

A pimp absorbs the game, while a simp just complains, too busy whining about what he don't have instead of learning how to get it. See, a true boss be watchin' like a hawk, while the busters just all talk, running they mouths but never running a play. In the complex game of life, observing quietly and acting wisely separates the successful from the bystanders. The ones who move in silence, stacking their wins, always end up ahead of the ones making noise just to be heard and flashing just to be seen.

Wisdom ain't just knowing the game—it's knowing when to play your hand. A wise man catches the lesson, while the chump keep guessin', fumbling opportunities because he won't sit still long enough to understand the bigger picture. Meanwhile, a real player peeps the scene, a joker spills the beans, giving away too much too soon and exposing himself as a fool. The difference between winning and losing ain't just talent—it's discipline, patience, and knowing when to keep your mouth shut.

Man, when you step into any room, you gotta understand the power dynamics playin' out. It's all about who's holding the reins without making a big show of it. Like, you see that cat lounging back with a calm demeanor while everybody else is puttin' on a performance, hustling to impress—he readin' the room? That's your key player. Power ain't always where the noise is; it's often with the ones who got that quiet confidence, who don't need to prove nothin' because they already know they got their game locked down. They be on they, 'what's understood, ain't got to be explained type time.'

Now, about reading the unspoken—that's an art form, ya dig? When you movin' to loud, you make it easy for other's to read you like a book. It's like this: everybody's chattin', right, but the real conversation's happening in the silence. Who avoids eye contact, who's trying too hard to be heard, who's sitting back just taking it all in? Those silent cues tell you who's comfortable, who's insecure, and who's the alpha. In truth, a lion don't care about the opinion of no lamb. It don't argue or negotiate with one either. So there's no need to try to impress one.

I wan't to encourage everybody in here to pick up a couple of books on body language, I got two that you'll find real useful. The first one is '**What Every BODY is Saying**' by Joe Navarro. Dude's a former FBI counterintelligence officer, so he knows his stuff. And the other one is '**The Definitive Book of Body Language'** by Allan and Barbara Pease.

Bof'um solid for understandin' what folks are really saying with their gestures. Trust me, it's game-changing stuff. This skill is crucial, 'cause knowing this lets you navigate the scene smoothly, positioning yourself to interact with the right folks who actually make the decisions, not just the ones bumpin they gum's. That's the game within the game, my man.

Now, at them parties and social mixers or when deep in personal talks, the same rules apply. The heavy hitters, the real influencers, they ain't the ones jabbering all night. Nah, they soaking it all up, tuning into the low-key dynamics, figuring out who's holding the reins and who's just along for the ride. By catching the undercurrents, a sharp player positions himself as the go-to, the bridge everybody gotta cross. That's how you pull strings without even tugging hard. When that third eye is open, that's how you avoid gettin' caught swimmin' in pools of baby oir'l.

And here's where it gets real: Power ain't always where you think it is. It ain't in the noise; it's in the silence, the unsaid behind the scenes. It's about readin' the faces, catching the cues that ain't made for words. This kind of deep reading sets you up to steer things smoothly, lining up folk's wants with your needs without them even catching on they're being led.

When you leading the pack, whether you dealing street-wise or suit-wise, it's all about that perception game. You lead not just by barking orders but by radiating that charisma, making every soldier in your squad feel seen, valued. That's the stuff that builds die-hard loyalty, that amps up the play and cranks out success. Charisma can shine without a sound.

The slickest leaders are often the ones who speak least and think most. They know—real game is played in the quiet spaces where strategies are whispered, not shouted. In every sit-down, every face-off, it's the listener who walks away king. Let them talk, spill their plans, while you soak it all in. This kind of active listening cuts through noise, finds solutions that speechifying never could.

Feedback? Man, that's pure gold for those wise enough to dig it. Welcoming the heat, sifting through the noise for nuggets of wisdom, that's how a true leader sharpens his game, stays steps ahead of the street and the studio or boardroom alike. It's the leverage game baby-boy. Leveraging stretegic silence against a ninja that's talkin' loud and ain't saying nothin'.

Yeah mane, keeping your cool—that's where the real power's at. The street teaches you fast: the head that stays cool holds the crown. Emotions? They gotta ride shotgun; they can't be driving the whip. If you ain't using every setback as a setup for a comeback, staying chill when the heat's on so you can think straight, how you gone come back harder and smarter.

When folks lead with anger and gorilla agression, impulsiveness takes the driver's seat. Reacting on a hair-trigger to lil bitty provocations can lead to rash decisions, overlooking whats down the long road for a quick emotional fix. That impulsiveness don't just mess with yuh head; it can mess up your whole life, leadin' to choices that might feel good in the moment but bring a heap of trouble down the road. And believe me, that kind of trouble can stick around for a long time, leavin' you wondering if that quick temper was worth it.

In the cool, dim light of the studio—usually alive with the bustle of creativity—a hushed ambience settled over the room.

The engineer was busy troubleshooting the mic setups and dialing in the sound quality, his focus blending with the quiet. The air, thick with anticipation and laced with the occasional crackle from the soundboard, felt like it was holding its breath. Everyone inside hung on Uncle's every word, captivated by the gospel of the game he laid down.

Now, let's talk about how this plays out with the people around you. When you quick to anger, it puts everyone on edge, creating a tense vibe that can poison personal and work relationships. If folks feel like they're walking on eggshells around you, trust me, it won't be long before they start walking away instead. And once that trust is broken, it's a tough road to rebuild what was lost, leaving you isolated when you might need support the most. How you gone go to war with no soldiers when the gang don't phuk with you no more. Nobody wanna be around somebody who always crashin' out.

We call'em "crash dummies," lacking the common sense they were born with; they're mere puppets, and we manipulate them like puppet masters. If you want to take a crash dummies girlfrien, simply provoke them into getting themselves arrested because, for them, maintaining a facade of respect is way more important than goin' home at night to lay up with that girl. Yeah I can trick a dumb ninja out his freedom faster than he buss with a certified 304.

They like children throwing temper tantrums, and triggering them is the easiest task in the world. They fall for it every time. These type of men are more emotional than bitches. Why you think the prisons are filled up. The slaver's who fill them know this. The prisons got two types of people, real ones and extremely sensitive emotional ones, and they out number the real ones.

In the dance of strategy, the real players distinguish themselves by their ability to listen beyond the words spoken. A player hears what's unsaid, while the naive are easily led, and fall for surface-level distractions that lead them astray. Meanwhile, a boss hears what's silent, a buster talks what's violent, using aggression where wisdom would suffice, failing to grasp the **power of restraint.** In every encounter, the opportunity to learn hangs in the balance; a real player learns quiet, while the foolish ignite a riot, missing the cues that lead to wisdom, opting instead for chaos that burns bridges rather than builds them.

The game, young blood, is universal. Lessons learned on the street corners fit just right in the real world. This here's about taking those hard-earned street smarts, flipping them into executive strategies for dominance and power. It's a call to keep learning, keep adapting, 'cause wisdom? It's not about dodging bullets; it's about turning every shot into a chance to shoot back smarter, stronger. Because remember, A player gone use his mind and a sucker just gon' whine—a pimp gone peep some game but a lame just gone complain'. Make sure you don't do the same.

Forty-Three

Can't Take a Square No Where

Heres the jewel, missed money is a result of mismatched moves. That's like dropping cash in the trash in a game with phukd up rules. Simply put—Cant phuk with folk who unequally yolked.

*T*he sun hung low over the east side, burning red over cracked pavement and faded murals that whispered stories of hustlers long gone. The city was still sweating from the summer heat, and Nephew's networking was lookin' real boss-like at the day party he'd just dipped from. The scent of hookah smoke and spilled Hennessy still lingered in the air like perfume from the streets. He stood just outside his whip, parked under the shade of a tired old tree, cooling off from the heat—and from the bass-heavy beats that had been pounding through his chest minutes earlier.

That's when his phone buzzed in his pocket. He pulled it out, saw the name, and smirked.

Unc.

"Where you at?" The voice came through steady, carrying that weight of quiet authority that let you know this wasn't just a check-in. "Eastside," Nephew replied. "Just slidin' outta this lil art function—cool lil day party at a fly lil gallery. Got the homie with me, bout to drop him at his rest in a sec though. What's up?"

"I ain't far. I'll drop him myself, then we gone meet my man up here at this country club. Reeeall boss man. Corporate man. Went from hustler to multi millionaire and all legit. I want you to meet him. Be ready." Click. No goodbyes, no extra words. Just orders. Nephew knew the drill.

Five minutes later, a sleek black maybach pulled up, the kind that whispered old money and new power. Unc rode clean—always did. The window slid down smooth as butter, revealing Unc's sharp eyes, scanning, assessing, reading the whole situation before a single word was spoken.

That's when he saw him. The homie, as nephew called him. Loud. A walking neon sign of everything Unc didnt really move with. Shirt glowing in the dimming light, costume jewelry stacked on him. The air around him carried that unmistakable aroma—sticky, potent bud, loud as the outfit, and eyes more red than the devil is—as Ye said.

Unc blinked slow. Looked at Nephew. And then Back at the homie.

"Aight, get in."

The doors unlocked with a soft click, and the homie wasted no time sliding in, making himself comfortable. Too comfortable. Not two seconds in, he reached in his pocket, pulled out a pre-rolled joint, and sparked his lighter.

Unc didn't even turn his head. Just spoke, calm but firm. "Put that out, young man." If you patient, I got you covered, best bud you ever smoked and as much as you want. Homie chuckled, the kind of laugh that said he didn't fully grasp the gravity of the moment. "C'mon Unc, it's just a lil' somethin'. Nothin' crazy."

Unc exhaled through his nose midway between the homies response, his patience already thinning and before he finished, said <u>"Either you puttin' that out, or I'm puttin' you out."</u>

Silence.

Then, without warning, Unc eased the coupe to a dead stop. Right there. Middle of I-285. Cars whooshing past, horns blaring, Atlanta heat still clinging to the pavement. Nephew swallowed and just held his head down. He already knew. Unc ain't never been about no nonsense.

Homie's eyes went wide, caught between disbelief and the reality of the highway soon to be beneath his feet. He hesitated—just long enough to see Unc's hand hovering near the door handle.

"Aight, aight, damn!" Homie grumbled, rolling down the window and tossing the joint out. Just as it disappeared into the wind, a state trooper rolled past in the adjacent lane, his gaze cutting through the coupe, a hateful scowl on his face like he was considering his next move. But he kept going.

Unc let the moment settle before shifting the gear back into drive, only to accelerate a few hundred yards and smoothly exit at the next off-ramp. He pulled into a QuikTrip, the fluorescent glow buzzing overhead as he parked, but not for his customary mac-n-cheese and coffee. Homie stretched, oh we gettin' some gas, shaking his head with a grin. "Man, I'd love to check out this boss ninja Nephew told me about. Sound like he on some real money moves."

Unc chuckled. Shook his head slow. <u>"Not likely—you gon' have to catch an Uber from here, young blood."</u> Nephew sighed, already

*knowing what was next. When the tires peeled out the parking lot
with the sound of skirrrt... No question, you already know how it
went down.*

Lesson number one: Can't take a square nowhere Nephew.
I'm talkin' 'bout rolling with folks who ain't cut from the
same cloth as you, thinking you goin' somewhere. That's like
putting regular gas in a Bentley—you just gonna end up on
the side of the road, all broke down like yuh man's there. It's
simple, really: Can't take dead weight on a money chase if you
wanna cross the finish line with a smile on yuh face. If they
ain't built for the ride, gotta leave'um on the side. That's your
Uncle's golden rule, straight up.

See, this game—whether it's pimpin', hustlin', or legit business—it's all 'bout who you ride with. Can't be teaming up with
cats who ain't on your level or don't share your hustle. That's
like droppin' cash in the trash, son. You gettin what I'm spittin'?
The path to power is paved by the hustlers that hustles every
hour.

You gotta vet your circle like you're the Secret Service and
they comin' for the President. Only roll with those who amplify
your game, not those draggin' down your flame. And I ain't
just talkin' 'bout no street corners; this wisdom's universal,
applicable from the grimy alleys to the glossy rallies. Your
circle's either a ladder or a cage; and if you don't choose wisely,
you'll never turn the page.

Can't phuk with folk who unequally yolked—plain and simple. If they ain't adding value, they just taking up space, costing
you more than just money. They costing you time, energy, and

more importantly, opportunity—the kind of stuff you can't get back. But see, a square don't care.

So here's the real, nephew. Every move you make, every hand you shake, it's gotta be calculated. I say it all the time, think chess, not checkers. Every piece you move, every player you engage, gotta be part of your grander vision, pushing you one step closer to that king status, yuh dig—cause when you run with the blind, you bound to fall behind.

You roll with squares? You end up circling the block, getting nowhere fast. But you build with kings and queens? That's when you start building an empire, marking your territory with more than just footsteps, but with goldmines.

If you roll with a crew of five, and all four of 'em is deep in video games, best believe you gon' be the fifth one holding the controller instead of the bag. You ain't out here stacking no paper, you out here pressing buttons, thinking it's the only way to level up. No disrespect to the gamers, but'f you got nine rich friends, nine times outta ten, you gon' be the tenth, 'cause y'all sharing a mindset. Now, this ain't to pass judgment; we all equal souls in the eyes of the Lord, but the reality is, if you got four square friends, guess what? You most likely gon' be the fifth square friend.

That's just the **law of proximity**, nephew—you the sum of the five people you spend the most time with. The company you keep will either push you to the top or hold you back from reaching it. So, peep game—if you wanna be the one changing the game, you gotta align with the players who gettin it, not the ones stuck in the same loop. Find yourself a circle that's all about gettin' to the gold and the goal, not just getting high and sittin dry. Ya dig?

Ayye, listen here, nephew—birds of a feather flock together, and that's the law of the land. Pimp negus hang with pimp negus, gangbangers hang with gangbangers, inmates? They run with inmates. Weed heads gone always hang with other weed heads, hoes hang with other hoes, junkies gone run with junkies, and entrepreneurs bang with other entrepreneurs. It ain't about judgment; it's about understanding the vibe you're putting out. It's called **resonance.**

If you roll with cats who stay on their grind, making power moves and stacking paper, you'll find yourself right there with 'em, eating at the table, making moves just like them. But if you run with the wrong ones—those stuck in the same place, playing the same games, chasing the same lil distractions—you'll be just like them: stuck, chasin yuh tail, spinning wheels, going nowhere hella fast.

The highway stretched out ahead, an endless ribbon of asphalt cutting through the sleepy expanse of trees, dark shadows shifting with the rhythm of the passing cars and tractor trailers. The Maybach glided effortlessly, almost floating above the road as the purr of the engine filled the cabin, a low hum that resonated deep in the bones.

Unc's hands gripped the steering wheel as he continued his sermon, his voice steady, almost hypnotic, cutting through the soft hum of the engine. The car swerved effortlessly, the leather seats cradling them like an invisible force that demanded respect. As he continued, his words didn't come with urgency, but with the quiet authority that only time and experience could cultivate.

Ain't no shame in the game, but you gotta recognize when your circle ain't elevating, but suffocating. You wanna rise? You gotta fly with eagles, not pigeons. You wanna be a boss? You better be around bosses. Plain and simple—your vibe attracts your tribe, so make sure you pick a tribe that's all about wealth, wisdom, and winning, and leave them squares sittin' in they chairs.

You see, if you're the smartest one in the room, you in the wrong room. If you want to level up your game, you gotta be surrounded by players who push you to grow, who elevate your mind and yuh hustle. So check your circle, nephew, and make sure you're running with the right ones, cause without the right ones, you ain't never gone have none.

Align with the like-minded, those riding the same wavelength, chasing the same dreams. That's how you elevate, how you innovate, and ultimately, how you dominate. Yuh crew is like family and together you runnin a race but it's a race you can only win with the right kinda kin. You tryin' to be like them Americans at the Olympics, led by Shakari Richardson, not Omari Rumpelstiltskin.

"Ayye, listen here, nephew. Real talk, It's so damn simple, man—I could rattle off book after book that'll get you right. Everything you need to know? It's already out there, sittin' in plain sight, waitin' on you to pick it up. The real question is, are you gonna soak up the game or stay stuck runnin with the lames?

Check this here out, when you get a chance, go pick up, **The Power of the Other** *by Dr. Henry Cloud.* That one breaks it all the way down—who you surround yourself with will make or break you. Right people? They'll push you, sharpen you, open doors. Wrong people? They'll drain you, doubt you, and dead your dreams before they even get goin'.

Then there's **The People Factor** *by Van Moody.* Straight-up game on how relationships shape your whole destiny. You gotta start choosing wisely, nephew. If they ain't pushing you toward your goals, they pulling you away from 'em. Ain't no in-between. The most powerful people move by building relationships. You tryna win? You gotta connect, collaborate, and cultivate a network that feeds your future, not just your ego.

Everytime I drop one of these titles, understand, I'm giving you a billion dollars worth of game nephew. And everytime you check some game from a brotha like the one we about to go meet at this here golf course, thats like a million moh dollars in the account, litterally.

As they pulled into the Black Oak Country Club, Uncle closed the build by saying,

"That's the lesson for today. School's out—but the real test? That's every day you wake up and hit the ground. Make sure you're moving right, moving smart, and moving with purpose.

He stepped out the car, adjusting his shades with a smirk.

"Now let's go check this man for some game—'cause it ain't told, it's sold... and I already told him I'd cover the first few holes."

Forty-Four

Confidence is Currency

If your ism ain't hot, your bankroll gon' rot cause bosses delegate and busters hesitate. A pimp with no presence is a lesson with no essence. Yuh gotta have a mouthpiece like a Uzi, for keepin it real and never bougie. Im'ma charm yuh' I ain't gone harm you.

*T*he auction house was a palace of wealth and art, the kind of place where conversations were as polished as the marble floors beneath their feet. Soft golden lights bathed the room, their glow casting a warm halo around the collection of timeless masterpieces. The paintings themselves looked like windows into another world—deep, rich colors that seemed to breathe life. Classic artists like Van Gogh and Monet, alongside contemporary legends like Basquiat and rising talents like Ismani Sun, transformed the event space into a surreal experience. The expensive scents hung in the air, mixing with the rich aroma of aged wine and the occasional whisper of soft laughter.

It all started when Nephew, half-joking one evening, mentioned how Uncle's money could do more than just sit in the bank. "You ever think about art, Uncle? I mean, like the billionaires do. Let your cash appreciate, you know, like a safe haven for your money. They put their's in fine art—sit back and watch the value grow." Nephew chuckled, but his words stuck with Uncle.

A few days later, out of nowhere, Uncle scooped him up and said, "I took your advice. I'm goin' to check out an art auction. Figured I might see how these folks do it—network, maybe even place a bid if the price is right. You comin' with me?" Nephew didn't hesitate. This was a whole new world to step into, and he wasn't about to miss it.

They entered the auction house and immediately felt the weight of the space. The gallery felt sacred, a place where decisions were made with the kind of confidence that came with money, power, and history. Uncle's eyes moved from painting to painting as they walked through the grand hall, his expression, a mix of admiration and curiosity. But it was the people in the room who seemed to hold a magnetic pull. It wasn't just about the art—it was about how they moved, how they owned every inch of the space with an energy that was undeniable. There was a rhythm to it, a silent agreement that everyone here belonged.

The auctioneer, standing at the front, commanded the room with a voice that resonated through the air like a seasoned conductor leading an orchestra. His poise was absolute, his words smooth and rhythmic, keeping everyone on edge. The bidders, unfazed by the prices climbing higher, didn't hesitate, never second-guessed their moves. It was as if they knew their worth without needing anyone to confirm it.

Uncle glanced over at Nephew, his voice low but filled with the recognition of something new. "I told you this would be something special. I see why the wealthy flock to these places. It's not just about the art; it's the confidence they move with. They know the game. They know their value." M's were being ran all the way up for a particular civil war piece called "Bloom" painted by a very mysterious and private newcomer to the art scene.

A quiet hum filled the air as an old man raised his paddle in the corner, his face unreadable, his eyes steady. The auctioneer's voice rose, "Going once… going twice…" and the room seemed to hold its breath. The man didn't flinch, didn't hesitate. The final bid was called. Silence hung in the air, then a slow, almost reverent applause. The man remained seated, his quiet smile telling a story of someone who had mastered the art of knowing exactly when to make their move—and when to hold steady.

Uncle turned to Nephew, his voice almost a whisper. "You see how they move in here? No panic, no rushing. Just calm, clear decisions. This is how the real players play."

Nephew stood there, taking it all in. The polished self-assurance that radiated from each person—how they knew when to push, when to step back, when to claim their space. He felt the weight of it all, a realization settling in: confidence wasn't just a skill here—it was the currency that kept this world in motion. Man, Nephew thought to himself… when you can take some colored oil splattered on a canvas and flip it into six racks—or six M's—off pure vibe and belief, yeah… you realize the con game is definitely the CON-fidence game? It ain't always what it is—it's what you make 'em feel it is.

As they left the auction house and slid into the car, the evening's experiences still hung in the air. On the ride home, the silence between them wasn't uncomfortable, but thoughtful. Nephew leaned back, pondering what they had just seen, and slowly, the question came out. "Uncle… you think I belong in spaces like that? With folks who move like they do?" His voice was quieter now, as if asking the question out loud made it more real.

Uncle glanced over, his eyes softened with understanding. "Nephew, confidence is like a muscle. The more you flex it, the stronger it gets. You see those folks? They're no different than you—they just believe they belong. And that belief? That's the difference. You can be in any room, any space, once you learn to move with that kind of confidence. And like clockwork, the lesson began to pour."

Look, confidence ain't just a feeling—it's a **currency**. You can be rich in it or broke in it. You ever seen a cat walk in a room and *command* attention without saying a word? That's because they're rich in confidence. It's like stepping into a store, but instead of cash in your pocket, you've got swagger, authority, and presence that people just gotta respect. You can't pay for that at a bank. That's pure, raw capital.

A boss knows this—when you got the right amount of confidence, your presence is the transaction. Your words don't just float in the air; they land. They hit. They make waves. So, when you roll into that meeting or that negotiation, what you bring with you is way more than a suit and tie. It's that *energy*, that magnetic force that draws people to you. It's confidence that lets you buy influence without ever opening your wallet—but just like cash, it's got to be backed by somethin'.

See, it ain't about manipulation—it's about influence. A boss don't chase, he just create space—let the world come to his place. We ain't out here to exploit, we out here to connect, build, and elevate. There's a fine line between using charm for good and crossing over into exploitation. Now in the pimp game that line can get blurred because you got P's with heart, P's with smarts, and P's that talk shyt and fart, everybody gotta play they part. Some P's just swing in trees, eat banana's and can't fathom settin' a bihh free. Let God be the judge.

If you using your charm to help people level up, you're playing the game right. If you using it for selfish gain, that's a busta move. So, wield your charisma like a blade—but one that cuts only to help, not to harm, nephew. People can feel when you're authentic, when you're being real with them. Ayye, dig this, player—influence is the new power, and the one who got influence? He runnin' the whole show.

Why you think they droppin' $7 million just to slide a 30-second Super Bowl commercial in front of your eyes? Same reason these rappers gettin' million-dollar deals just to sell you on lifestyles they ain't really livin'—it's all about influence, baby. They spend millions to catch your eyes—if you can't see the game, you the one being hypnotized. this is an attention economy.

But here's where the sauce get thick—I can't influence you if I don't believe in my own product. See, game ain't just talk, it's gotta be *sold* with confidence. If I don't stand on what I'm preachin', you ain't finna buy it. That's why I always say—I gotta SELL this game, not just TELL it. 'Cause with no confidence? You ain't sellin' nothin', you just out here talkin', and talk without belief don't cash no checks, ya dig?

Listen, a pimp with no presence is like a Lambo with no engine. All style, no substance. If you ain't got that magnetism—that presence—you ain't really running nothing. You're just out here playing at life—might as well be invisible. You could know every strategy in the book, have all the credentials, but if you ain't got that commanding presence, you ain't gonna get no respect, simple and plain.

People don't just pay attention to facts—they pay attention to *you*. Can you hold a room with just your aura? Can you stand in front of a crowd and have them hang on every word you say? And then make'um break they-self and transfer they wealth. That's presence, and it's priceless. In business, and in life, you need to stand out. Not just to be noticed, but to be respected, revered. People don't just want information—they want connection. They wanna follow someone who makes them feel something real. That's power in its purest form.

Whether you pushin' courses, spittin' seminars, or breakin' a whole auditorium out they pockets in one day—for millions while givin'em game to go run up they own millions—there's one ingredient you can't finesse, flip, or fake—and that's Confidence.

See, you can't make 'em shop wit'cha if you don't stand tall on your own energy. Ain't nobody buyin' weak game, and ain't nobody signin' up for no shaky sales pitch. You gotta lace 'em so good they feel like missin' out on 'You' is missin' out on they bag. That's the difference between a player and a perpetrator—a real boss don't convince, he just make it make sense.

People always ask, "what make a person want to sell they body and give a 'P' all the profits. I tell'em, first off, A real ho don't need convincing—she already knows what time it is. She ain't new to the game, she true to the game, long before a pimp even pull in her lane. A ho gonna choose—either up or down, but she gonna choose. A real ho wants real pimping like peanut butter wants real jelly.

They say a pimp's place is in a hoe's face so when you see a pimp poppin' and choppin' up game, he's just running a campaign, trying to get elected but peep game. Pimping ain't a title—it's a mindset. It's the only game where you win using your brain. If you ain't got confidence in yourself, why would she? A shark could grow eight feet in a fish tank, but 80 feet in the ocean—because it's all mindset. Pimping is instruction—when you stop instructing, she starts self-destructing. But you got to have confidence to run them correct instructions.

Everybody with real wealth knows that your **network is your networth,** and more than ever now people are racing to find mentors that can chop game up so fine that a few word's can make you buss a penny into a dime so you can 10X yo' shine. People will pay top dollar for that pristine game. I heard Master P' once say he had to pay MJ's lawyer twenty stacks for a few words of game on percentages and turned that game into the most unheard of deal in music history grossing him damn near half a billion dollars.

That attorney couldn't have ran point on that play if he didn't have the confidence to sale that game. Percy couldn't have led a whole army on that tank if he didn't have the confidence to do it. He couldn't have pushed his first hit, "Bout-it," without the confidence. When some one ask me why a hoe sell tail and take her profit and sock-it to a pimp pocket, it's because his confidence game is all the way up like Fat Joe going to the Presidential suite in the Waldorf Astoria to sell Prince Akeem a bag of powder. Confidence is and has always been yuh currency nephew.

If you can sell her mind the dream of an experience that money couldn't ordinarily buy, then what value is her money to her? Even a dying rich man knows that his money is worthless if he can't buy the experience of more life or more time to keep runnin' game. The experience that I sell is worth more than your lil money can even afford—so you'll give me as much as you can, trying to pay off the debt for this game I exchange. Cause' If you can get even a little piece of this confidence game I got, you'll wake up in the morning and say, I believe I'm gonna make it.

When you deep in yo' bag of confidence, you move like a king who done already claimed his throne—ain't no doubt, ain't no debate, it just is what it is. You ain't thinkin' 'bout it, you just 'Be'ing' it. Walkin', talkin', stackin', mackin'—it flow like water 'cause it's second nature. You speak with authority. If your voice don't boom, your pockets won't bloom—speak with conviction or settle for doom.

See, when you brushin' yuh hair, takin' a dump or even chompin' down on them lemon pepper wings, you ain't second-guessin' how to do it—aint no special technique. Ain't nobody bout'a tell you how to do what you been doin'. You grab that wing, twist that bone, and get to work—clean plate, full belly, no crumbs left behind. Somebody try to tell you, "You eatin' that wrong," you look 'em dead in the eye like they talkin' crazy. 'Cause when you know, you glow—and when you glow, they know. Ain't no maybe in yuh' motion, just pure devotion.

Let me put you on, nephew—they call it a **confidence loop**, but really, it's just mastery in motion. See, when you do somethin' so much, so often, so sharp, it ain't even effort no more—it's instinct. You ain't thinkin' 'bout it, you just executin' like a natural-born boss. That skill get so crisp, so cold, you could do it blindfolded and still shine like a chandelier in a penthouse. That's when it crystallizes in yo' brain—turn from practice to habit, from habit to mastery, from mastery to straight-up dominance.

The formula is simple but the discipline is rare. Focused work, structured grind, and intentional hustle—that's the alchemy of supreme confidence. Anything you do long enough, hard enough, you gon' lap the next man without even tryin'. That's why you see cats talkin' like, "How you gon' tell me? I wrote the book on it." That's the kinda confidence that make the room move when you walk in. It's that 'stay ready so you ain't gotta get ready' kinda swag. Ain't no hesitation, no contemplation—just domination.

Look here, nephew, let me drop some real game on you—if you got the mind to write down everything you wanna do, you already halfway there. Now, if you practice just a lil' bit, a few times a week, consistently, it's like slowly charging up a magnet. At first, it's just a little pull, but keep juicin' it up, and eventually, your magnetism gon' be so strong, folks ain't never seen nothin' like it.

I'm talkin' 'bout workin' on your stage presence, media game, the way you command a room—get them public speakin' chops sharp like a razor blade. Stay ready for anything—adaptability, executive presence, charisma so thick, it drip when you talk. And don't forget the storytellin'—'cause a mouthpiece without a story is like a Cadillac with no gas, nephew, it ain't goin' nowhere. Everything I just mentioned can be studied and applied as a learned behavior. It can be integrated as a confidence loop.

Now, let's talk about that negotiation and persuasion—the real game, the real power. Yeah, I know that's a whole feast to devour, but peep this: You can learn it like a game, flip it like a hustle, and master it like the king you supposed to be. All of them skills I just dropped on you? They're teachable, they're learnable, and when you plug 'em in with repetition, they supercharge your competence so your confidence becomes extra magnetic. You gotta walk it like you talk it. If you scared to invest, you ain't really ready to flex. A broke mindset can't cash no checks.

Do that, nephew, and your magnetism gon' be on a hunnid—so strong, you won't even need to chase nothin'. Opportunities gon' come lookin' for you. And that confidence? It'll shoot straight past the stratosphere, nephew—gone—outta here—galactic-level glow-up. The shift is here, and you better recognize it. Street hustlers built empires on grit, hustle, and that raw confidence that gets them in the door. But now, that same energy is being repackaged for the mainstream. It's the same game, with another name.

Look at tech moguls today—they ain't just selling products; they're selling their presence, their vision. They've built personal brands that'smore powerful than they businesses. In a world full of cookie-cutter, corporate-clad leaders, it's the ones with that underground hustle mentality who are changing the game. In the world of influence, people aren't just selling courses anymore, they're selling communities and social networks.

Look here, nephew, you know I'm always gonna leave you with some real resources to get that mind right, ya feel me? So as soon as you get a chance, put these gems on your wishlist and make sure you study 'em, cause they gon' put you in the game like a pro.

Make sure you check out *Jordan Belfort*, **"The Wolf of Wall Street"**—you think he built his empire on luck? Nah, fam, he built it with a mouthpiece. It's about selling yourself so smooth, people can't resist doin' business with you. That persuasion? It's a straight weapon, nephew, learn to use it like a pro. And what's that other one, oh yeah—*Robert Cialdini,* **Influence**—this book is like a playbook on how to get people to say yes. Whether you negotiatin' with the plug or askin' for that raise, understandin' the psychology of influence is key to gettin' what you want. You can flip that influence into power, nephew.

Ayo, for'real-for'real, if you tryna level up that confidence ASAP nephew, peep **Radical Confidence** by Lisa Bilyeu. Then, go cop **Unstoppable Confidence** by Kent Sayre. It's all about them no-nonsense moves to smash insecurities, embrace flaws and handle anything that come yoh way. You might laugh now, but both of these gon' have you movin' different, no doubt. Knowledge is the key son, to keepin' yuh game tight, yuh money right, and every move shinin' like time square city lights.

Yeah, nephew, definitely get a look inside all of those when you get a chance, cause believe it or not, this type of shyt will sharpen your skills and take you strait to the top. Billion dollar rooms if you can handle it, yuh dig.

Forty-Five

If You Knew Better, You'd Do Better

Success ain't a mystery, it's all in yuh grind, With knowledge in your pocket, you're bound to shine . Knowledge is power, and power's in your grasp, Master this game, and you can make it last.

*T*he holiday gathering at Uncle's lake house, was in full swing *this year. A sprawling log-styled home that looked like a mini mansion nestled on the edge of the quiet hill side on a few wooded acres was the perfect place for privacy. The aroma of roasted turkey, creamy mac-n-cheese, and collard greens filled the air, blending with the subtle hint of freshly baked sweet potato cornbread. It was New Year's Eve, and the sixth day of Kwanzaa, called Kuumba. Christ-mas had been at Aunt Judy's house this year, and Thanksgiving at Grandma's.* The kids were buzzing, counting down to the fireworks Nephew had lined up over the lake—nephew made sure to drop a bag and get the good stuff. From Uncle's vantage point up on the hills, you could see both the lake show and the city skyline lit up with fireworks of its own.

The living room was alive with chatter, laughter, and clinking glasses as family members—some freshly reunited after more than a year—caught up on life, while the fireplace crackled in the background like an old friend chiming in on the joy. *The usual conversations ran deep: who passed away, who was locked up, who had a baby, and who had fallen off. Old family traditions mixed with new generations, but some stories never seemed to change.*

Nephew sat back on the couch, glassy eyed and just a little tipsy off the Tequila his eyes scanning the room, listening to the familiar sounds of a family gathering—a mix of love, frustration, and memories. It felt different this time. He'd been coming to these family functions for years, but this time, things were different. Last year, he came in low, feeling lost and with his confidence shaken. But now? Now, he had something to show for his time away, and Uncle's mentorship had turned his world around.

*He'd gone from hustling on the streets while working corporate, dabbling in a few entrepreneurial ventures and real estate mishaps, as well as a few successes with trading, to acquiring land, investing in commercial real estate, founding start-up's, and building his own empire. The difference? Knowledge. The knowledge that when you know better, you grow better and become a go-getter. He understood it now. runnin' and gunnin' in the streets, and or suites, just hit a lil different when you're standing in your **sovereignty**.*

As the evening wore on, the conversation shifted, and Nephew's cousin pulled him aside. With a sigh, his cousin started talking about his recent struggles—how he'd lost his apartment, his girl, and his sense of direction all in one fell swoop. Nephew could feel the weight of the words, but he also felt a sense of déjà vu, a feeling of "this ain't nothing new." It reminded him of the dark place he had been in not long ago. What good is the game if you can't pass it along. A King ain't a King if he can't make another King, Nephew thought to himself.

Cousin's voice was heavy, but it didn't seem to carry any real intention to change. Every other word was an excuse, a reason for why things didn't work out. It was the same story he had told himself over and over again. That self-talk script that manifested the reality he said he didn't want but fed every day. Nephew looked over at his Uncle, sitting on the far side of the room, holding court as usual. He saw the look in his eyes—calm, knowing, and wise. Uncle had given him the tools, and it was up to him to put them to use. Now, it was his turn to pass that wisdom on.

After attempting to no avail for what felt like hours, Nephew took a deep breath, looked his cousin in the eye, and let the weight of his words sink in. "Man," he began, his voice steady but firm, "I'm gonna tell you something that might sting, but it's the truth. You can lead a horse to water, but you can't make 'em drink." He paused, feeling the tension in the air, then let out a loud sigh. "If you knew better, you'd do better."

The room seemed to quiet down as everyone in earshot stopped and listened. Nephew could feel his energy draining, like trying to pour water into a glass that wasn't ready to hold it. His cousin's eyes were deflecting, just like they always did, and there was that familiar resistance, that unwillingness to accept responsibility for his own failures. On top of that, every time a notification on his phone beeped, it harvested his attention.

Nephew turned to his Uncle, his voice softer now, almost pleading. "Unc, talk some sense into this man. I'm out of energy." Uncle didn't need any prompting. He'd been watching the exchange from

his spot by the fireplace. Uncle's words, when they came, were slow
and deliberate, like each one had been carefully chosen over the years,
honed by experience. But for now, Nephew had done his part—he'd
shown the mirror, now it was up to the cousin to look into it. Uncle's
approach would be far more rugged.

You gon' have to take some accountability, lil' Neph. All
this free game sittin' right here in your lap, and you still out
here makin' excuses. That's on you. It's hard to believe a young
player, with access to a solid plan, would ever fumble the bag
on purpose. If they knew better, they'd do better, and that's real
talk.

Knowledge is power, and wisdom? Wisdom transforms action, makes you move with purpose. Whether you pimpin',
hustlin', operatin' in square business, or just levelin' up social-
ly—elevation always starts with education. You gotta be aware,
so you can execute like a boss. The right information? That's
the key to changin' your mindset, refining your strategy, and
stackin' success like you supposed to. Know the game, play the
game, and win the game, that's the only way.

Let me drop something heavy on you that'll change how
you move forever. In the pimping game, knowledge aint just
power—it's protection. You got to be a one man intelligence
agency out in that concrete jungle. A seasoned player understands the power dynamics of influence, the importance
of presentation, persuasion, and positioning. Big pimpin say,
"Church is in session every damn day—game don't stop, it evolves."

Meaning, adaptation is key. If a player keeps making the same mistakes, it's a clear sign he hasn't learned the lesson yet.

The same applies in street hustling—from small-time hustles to building empires, those who rise do so because they soak up game from OGs, read the terrain, and move accordingly. If a hustler only sees fast money and not the long game, he's doomed to fail. But if he learns the laws of **leverage, risk management**, and **wealth preservation**, he can transition from hustler to investor, from player to boss. From square to sphere and from lame to fame.

See, the reason folks stay stuck is 'cause they don't know no better. But when you know better, you grow better. That's why wisdom is the first thing you gotta get. A fool just react, but a wise man? He peep the play before it even unfold. He know the difference between motion and progress. He know how to move with purpose, not just run in circles lookin' busy. That's you lil nephew, you runnin in circles, chasin' yuh tail on a hamster wheel from hell.

Check this out though, wisdom alone won't get you to the bag, lil nephew. You can't just be out here takin' whatever comes your way; you gotta make **calculated moves**. A sucker move off emotions and **impulse**, a real boss move off **foresight**. You gotta set the play up so smooth that by the time they even realize what happened, you already countin' the wins. "Now, ask yourself—are you strategizin', or just reactin' to whatever comes your way? Crashin' out with unstable emotions like a crashout dummy, or you usin' your mind to make every move a calculated move?

Now foresee this. The first strategy in wisdom you need to adopt is the one where you realize the power of accountability.

Remember that word from earlier? Making excuses ain't gon' change nothin' in your life. That's what lil' emotional children do—then they grow up to be impulsive adults, crashin' out with temper tantrums just like they did as kids. A real man don't make excuses. No matter what you become in life, you a man first. A real man takes accountability for his actions once he becomes aware of them.

The moment you realize you on some bullshyt—and you man enough to be honest with yourself ('cause a lotta grown men love to lie to themselves and listen to their hurt emotions instead of their mature mind)—but if you got any intelligence about yourself, the moment you see and know what's really goin' on, even with your own actions, you gotta man up, take accountability and correct it immediately. The sooner, the better—less you stay stuck in a cycle of sucka-hood. You can't grow in sucka-soil.

Look around you—do you see more suckas or more bosses when you out in public? Well, now you know why. Suckas don't know how to take accountability for their actions and decisions.

Peep game, 'cause this part separate the real from the ones who just talkin'—you gotta master adaptation. The game change every day. What worked yesterday might leave you broke tomorrow. You think the coldest hustlers, the real business minds, or the top-level bosses stayed on top by bein' stuck in one way of doin' things? Nah, nephew, they adjust. They see what's comin' and shift before they get caught slippin'. Big moves, big money, all in the mix, just masterin' the game, aint no need for tricks. They say the the definition of Insanity is doing the same thing over and over again and expecting different results.

Ayy, listen up likl nephew, success ain't about just workin' hard, it's about adaptin' and executin'—so you can talk shyt, swallow spit and live rich—cause kings aint suppose to lift a finger, instead they send the bitch. And by bitch, I mean you delegate so you can celebrate.

Robert Kiyosaki, in **Rich Dad Poor Dad,** puts you on major game, tellin' you that financial literacy is the secret to breakin' out the cycle of livin' paycheck to paycheck. His book, **Cashflow Quadrant** gives you the blueprint on how to set up a life of delegation. Most folks out here ain't struggling 'cause they lazy, nah—it's 'cause they don't know the rules of the money game. If they did? They'd be investin', not just spendin'; they'd be ownin', not just rentin'; they'd be buildin', not just consumin'. Knowledge is the power that flips the script, nephew. Knowledge ain't just a tool, it's the key to the gate, unlockin' yuh fate, so you can elevate.

Once you got the knowledge and the plan? Ain't nothin' left to do but execute. This where most folks fold, 'cause they sit around talkin' 'bout what they 'bout to do but never actually do it. The difference between dreamers and doers? Is Action. Ain't no power in potential if you never pull the trigger. Closed mouths don't get fed, and stagnant feet don't eat. Slow motion is better than no motion, yuh dig.

Now, once you start movin' right, the streets, the business world, hell—*everybody* gon' start to feel your influence. Even yuh lil musty girlfriend gon' say, " theres something different about you." When your name ring bells, when your presence shift the energy in the room, that's when you know you got somethin'. You ain't gotta force people to listen when your game speak for itself. That's how real players move—they don't chase, they attract.

But let me put you up on real sauce: power is the next level. And I ain't talkin' 'bout flexin' for the 'Gram or actin' like you runnin' somethin' when you barely holdin' it together. I'm talkin' about real, undeniable power—the kinda weight that make moves *for* you. When you speak, things shift. When you decide, doors open. When you say "go," things get done. That's the difference between somebody who's just in the game and somebody who run the game.

At that moment, Lil Nephew's phone buzzed again—another notification about something and somebody somewhere that had nothing to do with his come-up or the empowering mentorship moments others would've had to pay for. "Man, put that sh*t on airplane mode," Uncle barked before picking up right where he left off, while Big Nephew excused himself to start gathering the fireworks—just as Aunt Louise hollered from the kitchen, "Y'all boys alright in there?

Now, the coldest cats in history, the real masterminds, they understood leverage. Nephew, let me tell you somethin'—you don't get rich off workin' harder, you get rich off workin' smarter. That mean takin' what you already got and flippin' it into somethin' bigger. That mean utilizin' connections, resources, and knowledge to create more opportunities. The ones who last in this game? They don't just win once, they set it up so they *keep* winnin'. They put winning on automation. The book, "**The 4-Hour Work Week**', drops that game right in yuh lap. Power gets you that kinda' leverage.

The power to leverage situations leads us to ownership. Now, this where boys get separated from men. 'Cause see, a lotta folks comfortable just makin' money—but the ones who really get it, they wanna own the money. They wanna own the businesses, own the real estate, own the brand, own the *name*. 'Cause when you own it, can't nobody take it from you.

When you don't own nothin', you always gon' be workin' for somebody who do. You wanna own whole systems. Aint no such thing as a billionaire—just executors and beneficiaries who leverage the control of billion dollar systems. You want that kind of knowledge in yuh dome, and wisdom in yuh tone, so you can move like a king, settin' the game on a throne.

Once you an owner of a system, you now have the potential to elevate yourself and do better. You ain't just tryna survive no more, you tryna *thrive*. You level up so high that the problems that used to stress you out ain't even on your radar no more. You ridin' a wave so high above sea level that you transcend mere mortal activities, you feel me. You start movin' like the elite, playin' on a whole different board, with a whole different set of rules. And once you reach them levels, the only thing left to do is set up somethin' bigger than yourself. I'm talkin' levels so high, you'd think they made a mistake, 'cause when you know better, you can lift up the whole state.

That's where legacy come in. Baby bruh you don't just wanna be remembered as somebody who had a lil' money and a few nice things. You wanna be the name they speak when they talk about how the game changed. You wanna be the reason the next generation move smarter, build bigger, and go harder. 'Cause if you ain't leavin' nothin' behind, then what was the point of it all?

The night went on, some with the itis some with room for more food—the energy of the room constantly shifting with each new book acquired at the spades table. Nephew, looked around at his family. Each face, young and old, was a reflection of choices—choices made long before they ever had a chance to learn what they knew now. Some people, he thought, would never get it. But others? Others might just take the lessons of life to heart.

Let me break it down for you, lil nephew. When I say **"If you knew better, you'd do better,"** I'm tellin' you that ignorance is the real chain that keep you stuck. Knowledge? That's the key to unlockin' them higher levels. From the block to blockchain, on to the boardroom and global networks, the game don't change, nephew—it's just the scenery that's different. You feel me? The real hustlers? They learn, they adapt, they execute. That's how you flip them street smarts into global influence, takin' it from the corners to the corners of the world.

Now a days you got rappers and entertainers who went from street hustler to billionaire mogul because they applied knowledge at every stage. They understand that the real game is ownership, not just moving product. Their evolution is proof that when you learn better, you earn better. Game recognize game, no matter where you play it. So, nephew, I'ma ask you again—is you playin' the game, or is the game playin' you?

Now, fully sauced up on the Henn, Uncle made a promise to the whole crew who had gathered around to soak up the game, "I'm gettin' everybody here a copy of **Think and Grow Rich** by Napoleon Hill for your stocking stuffer next time I see y'all, cause all y'all need to get yuh mind right, take flight and claim your birthright.

He paused, giving a nod like he'd just made a move on the chessboard, then added, "Now, where's the bathroom at? I gotta drain the pond."

Forty-Six

You Gotta Pay The Cost To Be The Boss

Real players move like chess, cool and calculated, but the cost to be boss? Yeah, that's highly underrated. See, the throne ain't free, you gotta bleed to lead—stack green and stay clean, that's a boss player's creed.

*T*he boat rocked gently on the lake, the golden glow of the setting sun reflecting off the rippling water. A cool breeze carried the scent of pine from the distant tree line, blending with the rich aroma of Nephew's smoke as he exhaled slowly. The water lapped against the hull in a steady rhythm, a quiet counter to the chaos always running through his mind. He stretched his legs, letting the steady movement soothe the tension coiled in his chest. "Man, I needed this," he muttered, watching the horizon shift with each ripple. "City moves too fast—this right here clears my head."

Uncle popped open another beer, the crisp hiss cutting through the quiet. The aluminum can gleaming in the fading light with beads of condensation slipping down the side. "That's exactly why I moved out here," he said, leaning back as if the lake itself carried his worries away. Nephew had promised to come out fishing for months, always putting it off, saying he wasn't a fan of sitting on the water with a pole in his hands. But now, out here in the quiet, away from the relentless pull of the city, he started to understand the appeal.

He sighed, reeling his line in absent-mindedly. "My business took a hit unc, and I don't know how to bounce back. I'm putting in the work, but it feel like I'm stuck in place. The grind is nonstop, but the results? Slow." He shook his head, watching the water ripple as his lure cut through it. "I've already pulled in a couple 'M's' this year, and it's barely March. A few years ago, that number was just a dream. But I was supposed to have ten Ms stacked by summer. Right now, it don't even feel close." I ain't tryin' to be ungrateful, but this shyt get hard sometimes. And then I'm tryin' to finish writing this book and thats taking forever.

The boat swayed as Uncle shifted, taking a slow sip before setting the can beside him. The water lapped against the hull, unbothered by the weight of Nephew's frustrations. Crickets had begun their evening symphony along the shore, their song blending with the distant call of a loon.

"No matter how much I grind," Nephew muttered, staring at the endless stretch of water, "the finish line just keeps getting further."

Uncle gazed at the horizon, like a man who'd paid every due and knew the price of the throne, his eyes heavy with memories of battles won and lessons learned. "That's how it is, mane—it be's like that sometimes. The cost to be the boss is hefty, and it don't get paid all at once—it's daily payments in time, patience, and sacrifice. But when you finally own it? You'll know it was worth every dime."

—and with that, came the game.

See, p*ayin' the cost to be boss,"* aint no body saying that cause it sound cool, that's gospel in the game—a sermon in and of itself. That line been ringin in the culture since James Brown laid it down in *'The Boss',* and ever since, every real hustler, from the streets to the suites, done lived by it. See, the game don't bless you with no handouts—whether you bangin, you a pimp, a hustler, or a CEO, you gotta put in that work, make them sacrifices, and take them risks if you wanna sit on top. Rappers been screaming it, entrepreneurs been preaching it, and every real player know—power ain't free, it's earned. The cost of the throne is paid in flesh and bone.

Now, regarding this here concrete jungle, the real bosses done paid dues in blood, sweat, and game. You think Iceberg Slim ain't go through hell before he wrote the blueprint? You think these street kings ain't took them risks, played the chess moves, and built their empires brick by brick? This game is a cold one, and the tax to be on top ain't cheap—whether it's dodging them jackers, staying two steps ahead of them laws, or keeping a firm grip on your operation. Ain't no free rides in the underworld, and only the sharpest, most disciplined players make it to that elite level.

You gotta have a plan, man. You plan yuh work and work yuh plan. A vision without a plan is just a hallucination. Now, flip it to the boardroom, and the same rules apply. You think these billion-dollar bosses got to the top off luck? Nah, they put in them 10,000 hours, they bet on themselves when nobody else would. They sacrificed sleep, relationships, and damn near their sanity to build them empires. Sometimes dreams don't work if the work don't hurt. Hard work hurt, but lazy make it worse. Grant Cardone talk about it in his book **The 10X Rule**—success ain't for the lazy, it's for the obsessed. Every decision, every risk, every late-night grind session? That's the cost. And if you ain't willing to pay it, you ain't ready to lead. Leadership can be lonely, but so is losing.

And let's not forget about the personal game. See, everybody wanna shine, but don't nobody wanna put in the work. You wanna be in shape? You gotta sacrifice them late-night snacks and put them hours in at the gym. You wanna master a skill? You gotta say no to distractions and stay locked in. David Goggins done told y'all in his book, **Can't Hurt Me**—greatness comes with pain, discipline, and sacrifice. Society loves to put the spotlight on success, but they don't never show the grind behind it. That's why the real bosses, the ones who truly paid the cost, move different, they talk different, and they live different. 'Cause once you done put in that work, once you done earned your throne, can't nobody take it from you—provided you move accordingly, like a boss, and not voluntarily forfeit it by moving like a goofy.

Now dig this—every real boss knows that before you get to sit on that throne, you gotta put in work, you gotta make sacrifices and take some risk, right? But sacrifice means cutting off dead weight—friends, habits, comfort—because not everybody can go where you headed. Risk is stepping into the unknown, betting on yourself when nobody else will, knowing losses are just lessons in disguise.

See, too many folks wanna shine, but they don't wanna grind. Success ain't free, and the game don't respect no lazy hustler. You want that money, that power, that status? You might have to bleed for it—cut off them distractions, them so-called friends who ain't bringing no value, them late nights of partying when you should be plotting on your next move. A true boss don't complain about the weight on his shoulders—he carry it like a badge of honor.

And **Responsibility**? That's the tax every head honcho pay for being in charge. Ain't no real player out here dodging **Accountability**. When all eyes on you, you got to be true. Im talkin true to the game. If you fail, that's on you. If you win, that's because you handled your business like a real general. You see, the weak ones, they fold when the pressure hit, but a boss? A boss stand ten toes down, take that loss on the chin, and come back stronger. That's why the game only got room for the real. You wanna be at the top? Then act like it—because responsibility ain't optional, it's the price of the ticket.

Let's be real, every empire got a foundation, and that foundation is respect. You want people to follow your lead? Then you better make sure you worth following. A weak leader gotta force folks to listen, but a real boss? He don't chase power—he becomes power. The ones who last in this game don't just bark orders—they inspire, they make people wanna be down, they turn their name into a brand that hold value. They stack it, flip it, and make 'em all wish they did it. That's the difference between a fraud and a king—one beg for the throne, the other build the kingdom around him.

Power and success ain't about how loud you talk or how many people you boss around. Real power is **earned**, not given. You see, a sucka demands respect, but a boss commands it. Whining and beggin' for respect is the sucka way all day, but the way you command it is by staying solid, handling your business, and making sure your name hold weight in every room you step in no matter where you at in the process. The coldest game is, the more power you got, the less you gotta flex it.

Here's the thing though nephew, ain't no player ever made it to the top by playing it safe. The game don't bless the timid, it bless the bold. If you scared to lose, then you already lost. Every real boss took a gamble at some point—flipped his last dollar, walked into a deal not knowing if he'd come out winning, put his name on the line for something real that he could feel. The difference between a leader and a follower? The leader got the guts to bet on himself—and that's chuch-atta-hunnid. If you scared of the heat, then get out the street. Ain't no reward without no risk, so if you out here tip-toeing, you might as well step aside and let the real ones slide.

The smartest bosses don't just jump off cliffs blindly though—they calculate their steps, they know when to go all in and when to fall back. Every risk gotta come with a plan, every play gotta be strategic. Im talkin Strategies mo' sharp than a blade in the dark. The ones who last in this game don't just take chances—they take smart chances. That's why the real kings keep winning while the suckas keep falling off. Ain't no safety net in this world, so you either make your move or you get moved on. The choice is yours, but remember—scared money don't make no money, and hesitation is the quickest way to lose the game.

Nothing great comes without a price, whether in the streets, business, or personal life. What separates those who thrive from those who fade is the willingness to pay that cost without thinking twice and keep'in it moving.

Imma lay on you some real shyt—Now I ain't no Albert Einstein, but I'm dead serious when I tell you—time is in the mind. One of his coldest quotes that stuck with me though, is: *"Time and space are modes by which we think, not conditions in which we live."* You gon' have to meditate on that one for yourself. See, if you put yuh hand on a hot stove for a minute, it'll feel like an hour. Sit with a pretty girl for an hour, it'll feel like a minute. That's relativity." Why am I tellin' you this? 'Cause an animal don't know no calendar time—but a human does. And even then, a human don't understand **deep time**—but a cosmic-level mind, a real boss, just might.

I know you think ole Unc be drunk, and ramblin' off that yak, talkin' sideways—but hear me. You say you a king, right? Then stop looking at your success through the eyes of an animal locked in time. Because some kings measure time in decades—and other plans are measured in centuries. **Strategic patience** and a commitment to shaping your future over an extended period through meticulous planning is the diabolical work of a mind that belongs to a boss of bosses. Not just a king... a kingmaker. A king of kings.

Strategic patience. Meticulous planning. Playing the long game. That's the diabolical work of a mind built for legacy. See, success is like a good stock—you sit on it, nurture it, until the interest on it's value alone makes you wealthy. But you'll never cash in if you quit before you even get your feet wet, yuh dig? That's the art of the compound, young pimpin'. Master that—and you won't even think about this stuff you talkin' about, 'cause time'll start working for you.

I said all that to make one single point, Nephew: you can't give up when you this close to the goal. Too many men quit just feet from the finish line—not because they wasn't built for the win, but because they couldn't see how close they already was. They let doubt creep in, let exhaustion whisper lies, and dropped the ball in the red zone. That moment of quitting? That becomes the memory they replay for life. And some don't ever recover from it—mentally, emotionally, or spiritually.

Remember what yuh man's Thomas Edison said on that poster down at the office: "Many of life's failures are people who did not realize how close they were to success when they gave up." That quote hit different when you livin' it. Sometimes the biggest test comes right before the breakthrough. So even when the road feels long, and the results feel slow—keep showing up, keep stacking, and keep pressing. 'Cause success don't always come dressed in celebration. Sometimes it shows up quiet... right after you decide not to fold. Pimp up and get to it lil negus. You gotta pay the cost to be the boss—yuh diiiigg.

Forty-Seven

Only A Fool Trips On What's Behind Them

Scared money dont make money and experience is expensive—yet you gone have to spend to ascend because what you sow, you reap—so plant yuh seeds deep, and don't look back when you on that track.

F or context: The former Vice President, now CEO, had once been the gold standard in his industry. His methods, meticulous and artful, had earned him accolades and a reputation as a rockstar in the business world. He built his empire on personal control—doing everything himself, delegating nothing, convinced no one could match his level of excellence. But the market had evolved, and his business needed to evolve with it. Customers wanted innovation, efficiency, and adaptability, but he was stuck in the past, clinging to the glory of his old ways like a security blanket.

As the years passed, his company lagged behind. The world kept moving, and he was still selling a product no one cared about anymore. His refusal to delegate left him burnt out, overwhelmed, and unable to keep up. Once-loyal employees now exchanged weary glances, watching him chase past successes that no longer applied. The market had moved on, but he hadn't. The victories that once defined him had become a weight around his neck, and his pride wouldn't let him cut it loose.

That brings us to the present. He's slumped at a midtown bar, drinking himself into a stupor, mumbling about the good old days and talking reckless. The dim glow of bar lights flickers against the rows of half-empty glasses, the air thick with the scent of spilled liquor and lost time. When Nephew and Uncle walk in, they spot him instantly. Nephew feels a pang of sympathy.

Despite this senior executives coldness toward Nephew's rise in the company, before nephew bounced, Nephew couldn't ignore the fact that the man once looked out for him, put him on game, and opened doors when he needed it. Gratitude doesn't disappear just because circumstances change.

The ice in the VP's glass clinked as he swirled it absently, staring into nothing, signaling for another. His once-commanding presence now slouched under the weight of regret. Seeing him like this—drowning in his own failures—Nephew knew he was on the edge of doing something reckless, something he wouldn't be able to take back. Before things could spiral further, Nephew turned to Uncle.

"We should talk to him," he says. "Before he throws away every-thing he's got left."

The VP looks up, his eyes glassy but still sharp enough to catch Nephew in the doorway. A smirk tugs at the corner of his mouth as he raises his glass slightly.

"There he is—the golden boy," he slurs. "I was on a hot streak just like you once. Had the world at my feet." His voice is thick with liquor and the weight of a man still chasing ghosts, clinging to a past that ain't coming back.

"Alright, that's enough," Nephew says, stepping closer, his voice firm but steady. "You're too focused on what used to be. The game don't stop moving just because you do." He glances at Uncle, knowing this is where real game needs to be spoken. "Right, Unc?"

Unc steps forward, adjusting his hat, his expression unreadable but his presence undeniable. He exhales slow, letting the moment settle before speaking, voice smooth as leather and solid as stone.

"That's right, nephew," he says, locking eyes with the VP. Then he leans in slightly, his tone shifting—low, deliberate, carrying the kind of weight that can wake a man up.

"Now let me tell you somethin'."

A real player in the game of life learns quick—the past ain't nothin' but a chain 'round the ankles, and the ones draggin' it along move too slow for the game. A fool'll sit up in the cut, pressin' rewind on old losses like he can change the script. Maybe he got double-crossed, maybe his bottom chick ran off with the bankroll, or maybe the law came knockin' too early one morning—but all that cryin' and rewindin' don't put a dime back in his pocket. The only thing that matters in the game is the next move, 'cause if you stand too long reminiscin' on the last one, you gon' get knocked out your position. Ain't no room for yesterday when today's lick is right in front of you. Stay stuck, stay struck—move smart, move up.

That drag of old mistakes, it got more men buried in the gutter than bullets ever did. Beef distracts, regret breeds doubt, and lost money has you actin' outta desperation instead of calculation. A real player knows the past ain't somethin' to mourn—it's something to learn from. Every dollar and every deal fumbled was tuition in the school of the game, and every betrayal was a lesson in trust. If you walk around mad about what you lost, you ain't lookin' hard enough at what's ahead to win. A hustler with his eyes on the past is like a driver watchin' the rearview the whole time instead of the road ahead—the only thing waitin' for him is a wreck. That's why real bosses shake the past like a bad habit and keep their eyes on the next stack.

Stock tickers scrolled in neon green across one screen, while slow-motion slam dunks and endzone celebrations lit up the other above the bar. Behind it, the bartender moved with muscle memory—wiping down the counter with one hand, already reaching for the next glass with the other.
The half-faded CEO leaned back, eyes squinting like he was trying to decode hieroglyphics mid-happy hour.
"Son... what the hell is your uncle even talkin' about?" *he said, a crooked smile breaking through his confusion.*
He made a slow, swirling gesture to the bartender, the universal sign for keep 'em coming, then jabbed a finger toward Nephew and Unc.
"Line a couple up for them too," *he added, still squintin' like the math wasn't mathin'.*
Then he turned back to Unc, eyes glossy with liquor and life weariness.
"Look, man... it's too cryptic for where I'm at right now. I don't need riddles—I need roadmaps.

What he didn't know was that while Unc directed his commentary to the down troddin exec, uncle was really giving the game to his nephew and using this man's life as an example.

"Just tryna gauge where your head's at—see if it's even worth the energy to juice up your spirit." said Uncle before continuing in a more aggressive tone. "I speak directly to the subconscious mind and ain't no bigger sucker than a man stuck in his own yesterday. The game only respects forward motion—whether you fall, fumble, or get flat-out finessed, it don't care 'bout your tears, only your next step. Weak ones fold when things go south, cryin' 'bout what they shoulda done, Woulda-shoulda-coulda! But a real boss, a cat with some steel in his spine, knows the only way to make it is to shake that dust off and keep movin'. The minute you let the past hold you hostage, you become a victim in a game that only rewards survivors. Hustlers sometimes hesitate, but bosses suppose to elevate—one gets left, the other levitates. You don't wanna be the man who find's himself staring at the bottom of a shot glass before blowing his top.

It ain't just the streets—this rule applies whether you slangin' a product, flippin' a hustle, or climbin' the corporate ladder in a suit. Every loss got a lesson inside, but too many fools cry over the cut without peepin' the wisdom they paid for. You gotta take that knowledge, tuck it in your pocket, and keep it pushin'. Real players, the ones who make it long enough to touch power, ain't lookin' back at nothin' but what's next. 'Cause the past ain't a place to live—it's a place to pass through. A fool reminisces; a boss reinvests.

Some people get too comfortable in them comfort zones, think the good times suppose to last forever. Their muscle memory gets soft—all it knows is ease and entitlement. They go from alpha to beta overnight, from king to pawn. Most never recover, so they might as well accept their new position as the loser in their own game—the one they wrote the rules to.

When a player stays stuck on yesterday, he's blind to tomorrow. Iceberg Slim learned that the hard way, sittin' in a cell with time to kill and regrets stackin' up like unpaid debts. He saw how too many of his own kind got lost in the rearview, replayin' the past 'til it swallowed 'em whole. He knew every mistake, betrayal, and lost dollar was just the cost of learnin' the game, but what set him apart was that he didn't let it make him bitter—he let it make him better. He peeped the angles, saw the traps, and when it was time to switch lanes, he ain't hesitate. That's why he survived where so many fell. A player stuck in the past ends up a relic, while a boss who evolves becomes a legend.

That lesson stretches far beyond the streets. A boss, a real one, knows the past is just a classroom—you take the knowledge, but you don't stay sittin' in the same seat. Business cats, hustlers, even everyday grinders, they all got two choices: stay cryin' over what went wrong or get busy buildin' what's next. The ones who make it big, who rise up and stay up, are the ones who know that every 'L' was just an investment in a future win. The past ain't where the money's at, the power's at, or the future's at. That's all ahead, and that's where a boss keeps his eyes. Yesterday's problems don't pay today's bills—so why waste time on what's already spilled?

The game don't change, just the players and the playing field. What started in the alleys and backrooms now moves in boardrooms and stock markets, but the rules stay the same—adapt or get left. Cats like Daymond John came up out the grind, flipped street hustle into corporate muscle. But to do that, he had to unlearn some things that kept him alive in the trenches but would've held him back in the big leagues. See, the paranoia, the cutthroat survival instincts, the "watch your back at all times" mindset? That works when dodgin' jackboys and shady deals, but in the corporate game, a different kind of finesse is needed. A boss gotta know when to let go of old habits, when to trust, when to pivot, and most importantly, when to stop fightin' yesterday's battles so he can conquer tomorrow's empire. Play small, stay small—adapt big, stack big.

That's the fork in the road where most hustlers crash—they stay movin' like the past is still the present, lettin' old grudges and street codes block new money. But the sharp ones? They keep their eyes forward, always lookin' for the next move, the next level. The lesson is simple—success ain't sentimental. It don't wait on nobody stuck on yesterday. A fool beefs over a block he don't even own, while a boss owns the whole damn city. The ones who make it out the streets and into real power, they're the ones who understand evolution is the name of the game. The world don't pay for what you used to be—it pays for what you become. Step up or step off, 'cause the future don't wait for no man.

Nostalgia's a tricky trap—it make a man romanticize old wins so much, he forget to chase new ones. Too many players get stuck relivin' yesterday's hustle, blind to the money movin' right in front of 'em. A real boss know that past shine don't pay today's bills, and old game don't always work on a new board. The ones who stay winnin' are the ones who respect the past but refuse to live in it. Nostalgia sweet like honey but sticky like a web—stay in it too long, and you trapped in a life that already passed you by. Can't stop the new growth, and change is the only constant.

See, the power of adaptation is the ability to evolve with the game, shiftin' strategies and mindset to stay ahead of the pack. When you stay flexible, you're ready for whatever the game throws your way, and that's how real players turn obstacles into opportunities. A real one move with the times, 'cause standin' still is just waitin' to get left behind. The game don't wait on nobody—either you switch up and stay sharp, or you sit back and watch the next man take your part.

Cryin' over what's already gone won't get you back in the game; only way to win is to take what you learned and double back stronger. Embracing failure as a lesson means lookin' at every setback as a blueprint for success, a chance to refine your hustle and level up. Instead of sittin' in regret, you flip the script, takin' the wisdom from that loss and turnin' it into fuel for the next play.

A fool sit around replayin' the past, wishin' he could run it back—but a real one take that same energy and flip it into somethin' new. Regret aint good for nothin', but reinvention? That's how you turn yesterday's failure into tomorrow's fortune.

Back in the day, the ancient folks called it **stoicism**—a mindset built on discipline, control, and movin' with logic over emotion. The Stoic, cats like Epictetus and Marcus Aurelius, believed that a man can't control the world, only how he respond to it. They preached that pain, loss, and setbacks ain't meant to break you, they just test if you built for the next level. A weak mind fold under pressure, crumblin' at the first sign of struggle, but a real player stand tall, usin' the pressure to sharpen his game.

See, stoicism is the art of control—knowin' you can't stop the storm, but you sure as hell can decide how you walk through it. It's about discipline over emotion, strategy over reaction, and learnin' that setbacks ain't nothin' but steps to the next level. When the world test you, you either break or you boss up—only the solid ones keep pushin' when the road get rough, 'cause they know every storm eventually passes. Only the strong is still standing when the sky clears.

By now, the exec had quietly hit record on his phone, and even the bartender—who started out just within earshot—was full-on ear hustlin', locked into the conversation. The bottle they were sipping had unofficially become the group bottle, courtesy of the bartender himself, who started throwin' back shots too, figuring this slow part of the day could use a little fire. Neph's former exec said, "I see what you're doing here—you're really talking about me so he doesn't end up like me. But in that, I've come to some clarity of my own. Please, continue."

Maintaining Forward Momentum is the name of the game, player. You can't afford to pause or hesitate when the world's always movin' fast; one minute you on top, the next, you're forgotten if you ain't still pushin'. Every step forward builds on the last, like stacking bricks to a castle—don't matter how small the move, just as long as you keep movin'. In the streets or in business, staying in motion is the only way to stay relevant. The moment you stop, others will pass you by, and they ain't gonna look back to help you up. So keep your feet movin', stay focused, and make every step count, 'cause time don't slow down for nobody.

You got to stay fluid like money and liquid like honey. You get what I'm sayin'? You already know, If money ain't movin', it ain't valuable—it's just sittin' there, collectin' dust like a rusty old chain. You see, money don't grow when you hoard it, it grows when you flip it and work it. When you make it multiply. A real player knows that stagnant cash is the same as dead weight, just waitin' to drag you down. And we are a lot like money.

Smart money stays in motion, whether stocks, real estate, or even a new campaign and rebrand, it's always workin' to bring back more. You don't want to be the one watchin' opportunity pass you by while you clutchin' onto old bills. That's how you get left behind—keep your energy flowin', and it'll flow back to you tenfold. Liquidity leads to longevity—literally and figuratively. Let that current of succes flow right through you like it's liquid electricity riding on a vibration of success.

If your flow seems to be gettin' stuck like swamp water in a clogged pipe, it's time to shake it up. Clear the blockages and flush the lines—'cause a cleanse is in order. All of nature works like that. When a volcano builds too much pressure, it erupts. When your gut backed up and all impacted and shyt—literally—it's either gon' explode from the inside and kill you, or you gon' run a cleanse and flush the funk out before it take you out.

I'm about to drop some heavy, heavy references on you. Some of my personal classics that'll light up your inner game. Write'um down. First, you gotta read **The Four Agreements** by Don Miguel Ruiz, then **The Alchemist** by Paulo Coelho, and **The Power of Now** by Eckhart Tolle—you see, those cats break it down real smooth—they talk about shedding the weight of the past, embracing the present moment, and forging ahead toward the future. And then you throw in Malcolm Gladwell's **Outliers**, which flips the script on success, showing you that it ain't just about where you from, but what you do with what's in front of you. Ive already given these to my nephew, these suggestions are for you gentlmen and ill keep reiterating them and reminding you everytime we have a conversation untill I know you've digested them.

Now to pull it all together—and I only mean this if you *dead serious* about changing your circumstances—what you gon' need to do is straight up become the world's coldest stoic. I'm talkin' about unshakable, untouchable, Zen-warrior type calm. You might even need to get hypnotized or somethin', start rewiring that mind until you *believe*—can't nobody out-stoic you, feel me?

Start by pickin' up **Meditations** by Marcus Aurelius. That man was a whole emperor, runnin' Rome while still scribblin' down reminders to stay humble, stay disciplined, and not trip over nothin' outside his control. One of his coldest lines was ? *"You have power over your mind—not outside events. Realize this, and you will find strength."* See, that's pure unadulterated game.

Then get your hands on **Letters from a Stoic** by Seneca. He was breakin' it down in letter form—how to live good, stay level-headed, conquer fear, and keep your peace intact even when life tryin' to swing on you. That one's like therapy from a real OG.

Bottom line: if you can master *that* mindset? Man, ain't a storm in life that can shake you. Never forget, only a fool trip's up on what's behind'em.

Forty-Eight

Loyalty is Royalty

Faithfulness in fellowship is the richest of rewards—devotion paves the path and commitment lace the craft.

The breezy hum of the funeral home's air conditioning provided a quiet backdrop to the somber gathering. Outside, the late afternoon light filtered through the heavy curtains, casting a muted glow across the room. The low murmur of voices, the soft rustle of tissues, and the faint sound of footsteps echoed, but nephew and uncle stood near the back, separated from the crowd of mourners.

Nephew, his hands clasped in front of him, stared at the casket of his uncle's old friend, a man who had once been like a loyal brother to Unc, in both business and life. His face was drawn with a mix of grief and contemplation. It wasn't just that they were saying goodbye to a friend today—it was the loss of someone who had shown him what true loyalty looked like. The game can be a treacherous environment to navigate—and it's damn near impossible to do so without loyal comrades. *Nephew had always heard about loyalty in theory, but today, standing in the quiet of the funeral home, the real weight of it hit him.*

"*Life don't stop, nephew,*" *his uncle muttered, his voice a low growl, a tone that was both comforting and firm.* "*We say our goodbyes, but the lessons stick with us. This here's a man who never crossed me—not once. Loyalty, that's how we built what we built. But now, it's your turn to understand the plan. Let's talk.*"

Nephew's mind flickered to the betrayal he had faced recently. A partner in one of his startup companies had made promises that fell apart the moment things started to get tough. The moment the pressure came, his partner folded, cut corners, and tried to make deals behind his back. It stung in a way that nephew wasn't prepared for.

"*Man—Unc,*" *nephew started, his voice edged with frustration.* "*I had a partner who I thought had my back, but the second something went wrong, he threw me under the bus. Tried to sell me out for chicken change—thought it would help him get ahead. Just—damn the company!*"

Unc nodded slowly, his gaze fixed on the casket. "*I see. I know that sting. Hell, I felt it more times than I care to admit. But here's the thing, nephew—loyalty ain't just a handshake, it's a lifestyle. You let a disloyal 'mo-fo' in yuh circle, you might as well be inviting the devil into your house. They'll betray you at the first opportunity. The thing is though, they can't get in unless you invite them in first, so remember that part.*

He paused, his eyes narrowing as if weighing his next words carefully.

Nephew frowned, glancing around at the solemn faces in the room. "*But how do I fix it? How do I know who's really loyal? I don't know if I can trust anyone anymore.*"

His uncle's jaw tightened, but he let out a soft breath, his voice thick with experience. Caught between the weight of passing on hard-earned wisdom and the grief of losing a friend who was like a brother, Unc stood glassy-eyed, doing his best to hold it together. Though his voice remained steady, the pain was there—quiet but undeniable. He began laying down the game with the same measured cadence he always used, the same stoic presence that had guided Nephew through countless lessons. But this time, something was different.

Nephew noticed it—the slight tremble in his breath, the heaviness behind his words. He wasn't used to seeing Unc like this. Still, he didn't say a word. He just listened, trying not to let on that he saw the cracks in the armor. Because even now, in the face of loss, Unc was teaching him something priceless.

This man right here was a stone cold P. Certified to the highest degree, yuh dig. See, In pimpin' and hustlin', hell, even in the highest echelons of the corporate world, loyalty ain't no accessory—it's the whole uniform. You can't wear the crown if your circle ain't solid. See, the game is built on principles, and rule number one? Ain't no room for backstabbers, turncoats, or disloyal squares. When a player puts a family together under one program—flyin under one flag, he ain't just lookin' for beauty—he's lookin' for belief, he's lookin' for discipline, he's lookin' for commitment. 'Cause a weak link? That'll sink the whole ship.

As far as the gangstas go, Look at the legends—they built empires, but when that loyalty crumbled? So did the dynasty. 'Cause the second you let a snake slither in, it ain't long before you feel the bite. Pimpin' Ken said it best in **Pimpology: The 48 Laws of the Game**—you don't force loyalty, you inspire it. It's always choice over force. A true boss don't demand respect—he commands it.

Now, don't get it twisted—this ain't just street talk. Loyalty runs corporate America the same way it runs the block. You ever wonder why brands like Apple, Nike, Tesla got folks lining up like it's the first of the month? That ain't just product—it's loyalty. They built reputations so strong that folks rep 'em like the set. That's the same principle a real player uses to keep his stable tight—give 'em something worth following, worth believing in, and they gon' ride for you till the wheels fall off.

Some of the richest men in the world, with the most popular brands—those cats didn't just build companies, they built movements. They knew that vision fuels loyalty and loyalty fuels legacy. Simon Sinek broke it down in the book, **Leaders Eat Last**—real leadership ain't about barking orders, it's about inspiring commitment. 'Cause a team that's loyal? That's a team that makes history.

But dig this, nephew—before you can expect loyalty from others, you gotta be loyal to yourself. See, some folks sell they soul for a quick come-up, but a real one? He stands on his principles like they made of marble. That's what 50 Cent and Robert Greene were preaching in **The 50th Law**—the ones who win big? They the ones who stay true, even when the odds are stacked against 'em.

Don Miguel Ruiz gave the game in the book called **The Four Agreements**—keep your word sharp, keep your actions tight, and never go against the code. Michael corleon said it too, never go against the family. 'Cause at the end of the day, the coldest betrayal ain't from outsiders—it's when you betray your own destiny.

Nephew stood still, letting his uncle's words sink in as he eye'd Unc's friend's daughter—making a mental note to console her later. *He thought about his company, about the people he had trusted, and how the one disloyal partner had shaken his belief in the business world. He thought about his uncle's friend, a man who had never once wavered, who had stood by his uncle through thick and thin. That was the kind of person he needed to surround himself with.*

Now, check game nephew—the rules ain't changed, the players just moved the chessboard. What used to be street tactics is now corporate strategy. What used to be reputation on the block is now brand loyalty on social media. I learned that from my lil cousins in Chi town. See, real ones know that networking is just a digital version of street alliances—same principles, different platforms. Guys like Nipsey Hussle and Young Dolph took what they learned in the trenches and flipped it into wealth, ownership, and generational success. The world ain't never stopped hustling—it just learned how to wear a suit while doing it.

Now, if you really wanna get into it, there's three ingredients to what loyalty is, according to ole Unc. And they are **Respect, Honor, and Trust.** Without 'em, you just got a whole lotta talk with no foundation.

First things first—respect is the first law of the game. If a man don't respect you, he don't value you, and if he don't value you, he ain't never gonna be loyal to you. That's why a real one don't beg for respect—he commands it, he embodies it, he walks like it, talks like it, and moves like it. See, respect ain't about fear, it's about presence. When a boss steps in the room, he ain't gotta announce himself—the energy shifts, 'cause real power speaks without words. The moment you compromise your respect—by being weak, by acting out of character, by letting folks walk over you—you done already lost the game. 'Cause trust and honor? They built on respect, and without that? You ain't got nothin'.

Now, honor? That's what separates the bosses from the busters. A man without honor is like a ship with no rudder—he gon' drift wherever the wind blows him. But a real man? He got a code, a creed, a foundation. See, when you live by a set of principles, folks know exactly where you stand. Ain't no switchin' up, ain't no backpedalin', ain't no shakin' hands today and stabbin' backs tomorrow. Honor is **integrity**. Honor is **consistency**. Honor is standing on your word even when it ain't convenient. And most importantly? Honor is never betraying the ones who put their trust in you. 'Cause in this game, your word is your bond, and when your bond is solid? That's when folks ride for you.

And last but not least, nephew—trust. See, you can have all the talent, all the money, all the game in the world, but if folks don't trust you? You a lonely man, playboy. 'Cause trust is the glue that holds everything together—your business, your relationships, your legacy. If folks can't trust your word, they ain't gon' follow you. If they can't trust your vision, they ain't gon' invest in you. And if they can't trust your loyalty, then you ain't nothin' but a liability.

That's why real players move in transparency—we don't make empty promises, we don't burn bridges we might have to cross again, and we sure as hell don't play both sides of the fence. Ain't no false flaggin' round here. 'Cause once that trust is gone? It's gone for good, and ain't no gettin' it back. Loyalty is the currency, but trust is what you really cash in on. The loyalty you deposit is what keeps the bank account full, but the trust is what earns you the interest.

So understand this—Respect. Honor. Trust. That's the trinity of loyalty, the holy grail of game, the three-piece suit of success. Get them three locked in? You'll be unstoppable.

Nephew hadn't realized he was staring at the same pretty young woman from earlier until she looked up and their eyes met. Her somber face, streaked with tears, softened into a faint smile. He gave a small nod, as if to say, *everything's going to be okay.*

Unc turned nephew around, guiding his gaze back to the casket. Nephew's heart clenched. The truth of his uncle's words felt heavy, but also like a beacon in the dark. He wasn't just learning how to navigate business; he was learning how to build something that could last, something that wasn't just about profit but about real relationships, about trust and honor.

Now that you know what loyalty is really made of, let me put you up on a formula for testing if a person's a real one. The Loyalty Formula, or the three T's as I call it: *Time, Temptation, and Trials.*

First there's **Time**—'Cause Loyalty Ain't Proved Overnight. The thing you gotta understand, nephew, is that loyalty ain't instant—it's tested over time. See, anybody can play the role for a season, but time always exposes the truth. A real one stays ten toes down whether the sun's shining or the storm's rolling in. Watch how they move when there ain't nothin' in it for them. When you up, they smiling in your face—but when you down, do they still show up and stick around? Or do they disappear like a ghost in the wind? Loyalty don't fade, it deepens. So if somebody only solid when it's convenient? They ain't loyal, they just **opportunistic.**

Now here's the real stress test—**temptation.** Will They Sell You Out for a Better Offer? See, loyalty ain't about what folks do when everything's good, it's about what they do when they got options. A loyal one stays down even when the opposition dangles somethin' shiny in their face. Whether it's money, status, power, percieved freedom or a slick-talking enemy whispering in their ear. A disloyal person gon' fold the moment the price is right. But a real one? He don't auction off his integrity. He knows that what's built on loyalty lasts, but what's built on betrayal crumbles.

And lastly, **Trials** because *Pressure Will Reveal Their True Colors.* If you really wanna know who's loyal? Put 'em through some pressure. 'Cause understand this—fire don't destroy gold, it refines it. When the heat gets turned up, when the walls start closing in, when the stakes get high—how do they move? Do they stand strong beside you? Or do they start lookin' for a backdoor exit? A real one don't panic, don't switch up, don't start singin' like a bird when the pressure's on. Loyalty means they ride with you, not just when it's easy, but when it's necessary.

The Bottom Line, next time you tryna figure out if somebody loyal, nephew, put 'em through the test: Time, Temptation, and Trials. If they stand tall through all three? That's royalty right there. If they crack under pressure, switch up for a better offer, or only rock with you when it benefits them?

Then they ain't never been loyal to begin with. 'Cause at the end of the day, loyalty ain't just a word—it's a lifestyle.

And since we dealin' in threes, nephew, let me lace you up with the real rewards of loyalty—'cause when you got real ones ridin' with you, holdin' you down through time, temptation, and trials, what you build ain't just temporary—it's eternal. See, loyalty don't just keep you solid; it elevates you to Power, Influence, and Legacy.

Real power ain't just about what you can do—it's about the team you got behind you. When you surround yourself with loyal ones, your power multiplies, 'cause you ain't out here fightin' every battle alone. You move like a general, and your squad moves like an army—everybody on the same mission, no weak links, no snakes in the grass. When a king got loyal knights, his kingdom stands strong. And best believe, in this game—whether it's the streets, business, or life itself—power ain't about flexin', it's about fortifyin'. You got loyal ones? You never stand alone.

In them corporate towers, you got more snakes then a little bit. Let a head hunter come trying to grab one of your best coders for ten stacks more per year. Some of them already have they bags packed just to learn, they gone get treated like shyt, and dont have the same flexibility when they use to work with family and was in line for a promotion that would have blown that ten stacks out the water. Loyalty is rare.

That man in that casket was my co-defendant once upon a time—and trust me, they don't make-em like that no more. We went into business once with this blond haired European, and the Op's thought they could poach him with more money. We thought for sure he was gone switch out. Guess that man said—the devil you know, cause he stuck with the gang. Between them two—that's when I really learned what it meant to really have a loyal ass team, cause lawd knows, them bitches I was dealin' with came a dime a dozen. Well some of them cause the way I ran my program, loyalty was a prerequisite to receiving this top tier game.

Together, however, we became powerful. Power is one thing, but influence? That's when your name rings bells even when you ain't in the room. A man with loyalty behind him don't have to force his way into spaces—his reputation moves before he does. When people know you solid, when they trust your word and respect your name, doors open for you that money can't buy. That's how kings, bosses, and legends are made. Influence don't come from talkin' loud—it comes from standin' on principle, time and time again, until the world takes notice.

Empires fall when betrayal creeps in, but when you got loyalty at the foundation, what you build outlives you. Whether it's a brand, a movement, or a family dynasty—loyalty keeps it alive for generations. That's why real ones play for the long game. They don't just chase quick wins; they set the stage for something greater. When you move with loyalty, you don't just make history—you create it.

So remember, nephew—Power, Influence, and Legacy ain't bought, they earned. And the only way to lock 'em in? Loyalty. Yeeesss.

As they stood in the quiet room, surrounded by the weight of loss and legacy, Nephew knew that the lesson he was learning today wasn't just about business—it was about life itself. And he would carry this lesson with him, as his uncle had carried his own, through every decision, every relationship, and every challenge ahead.

"Now run back everything I just told you Nephew, so I can see if you was payin' attention to me or that lil slim thick, chocolate, cherokee lookin gal, "said Uncle.

Forty-Nine

Team Work Make The Dream Work

Priests need nuns, doctors need nurses, and ho's need pimpin—Why?—Cause pimpin' an hoe'in is the best thang goin, and that's on all the teams out there collaboratin', innovatin', pollinatin' and celebratin'.

*T*he night was alive with the buzz of high society at a private affair. The super yacht cut through the moonlit waters, its sleek white body reflecting off the shimmering sea like a silver arrow. The air was thick with luxurious scents, mixed with the salty breeze of the ocean, as the who's who of the music industry and Hollywood mingled in crisp white tuxedos and glamorous white gowns far away from the prying eyes of the common man.

The soft sound of waves against the hull was drowned out by the thumping bass of the live band playing on the upper deck, its rhythm filling the air with an electric energy. The yacht's crew moved seamlessly, like a well-oiled machine, their pristine white uniforms gliding through the chaos of guests, trays of champagne balanced expertly on their hands, all in sync just like the synchronized swimmers performing in the pool beneath the stars.

Every detail was meticulously arranged. The wait staff navigated the crowded spaces like pros, offering drinks and drugs to the guests with polite smiles while avoiding the occasional misplaced elbow. From the bartenders to the sound engineers, everyone had a role, and the timing was perfect—no one missed a beat. The aroma of fresh hors d'oeuvres eatin off of naked bodies wafted through the air, mingling with the sound of laughter, caged tigers and clinking glasses.

The scent of saltwater mingled with the crisp undertones of fresh seafood, drawing guests to the buffet spread. In the shadowed corners of the yacht, beneath the flickering lights, the elite engaged in acts so decadent and unmentionable that the common man could never fathom the like's of such acts.

The lines between power, pleasure, and secrecy blurred in a way that only the highest echelons of fame and fortune could pull off. Movie stars and tough guy entertainers, all engaging in career ending acts. Pleasurable, sadistic, and ritualistic seemed to be the order of the night—and all who engaged were complicit.

Backstage, however, the tension was palpable. The band, once a tight-knit ensemble, had fallen apart under the weight of egos and jealousy. Creative differences had festered like a slow poison. The lead guitarist's fingers were still tingling from the last strum, his mind racing with frustration. His brow furrowed, the beat of the music still reverberating in his chest, but his words barely hung in the air, drenched with disdain.

The drummer was pacing back and forth, tapping his sticks against his leg, unwilling to let the silence settle in. The bassist, arms crossed, leaned against the wall, barely hiding his contempt. They had been a *team once. Now, there was nothing but tension and silence between them.*

Meanwhile, in the lavish VIP lounge, stood Uncle, Nephew, and a few of their cohorts—all in sharp white suits, Unc with a glass of scotch in hand, and Nephew with a sharp, inquisitive gaze and a pin joint—stood in quiet observation—looking as if this is not what they had in mind. They had been on this yacht long enough to see the spectacle of people pretending to be in sync, though the crew members were, just as the band had once been. Their conversation was casual, but their words carried weight as they watched the chaos unfold. Nephew, wide-eyed and eager, leaned forward.

"Unc," he asked, "how does something like this even work? Everything's so smooth. Look at the waiters, the dancers, the swimmers—they're all on point. But the band? They're a mess."

Uncle, whose eyes scanned the scene with an experienced calm, took a slow sip from his glass before answering. "It's all about teamwork, son. Look around, every single one of these people knows their role. They're not thinking about themselves; they're thinking about the bigger picture. It's that kind of alignment that makes everything work. At the top, sit's a circus master orchestrating it all."

As the lights flickered slightly above the dance floor, the chaos backstage reached a boiling point. The argument between the band members grew louder, their voices like knives cutting through the perfect harmony outside. Uncle continued, undisturbed by the commotion. "These people here, they're working together because they know that the success of the night relies on every piece fitting perfectly. One person drops the ball, and it all falls apart. The band? They forgot that. They caught up in their egos, each thinking they're the star. But the real magic happens when everybody plays their part."

Nephew watched the chaotic breakdown of the band's conversation, the egos clashing in the back. "But don't they know the whole show could fall apart without them all pulling together?" Imagine if the wait staff started unraveling like this.

Uncle smiled, his voice rich with experience. "Exactly. It's the same in life, son. Whether it's on a yacht or in the streets, when the team falls apart, the dream dies. You need a crew that's tight, that trusts each other, and that's what keeps things running smooth—like that team out there making sure everything's in place."

As the chaos raged on in the back, the rest of the yacht sailed through the night, everything running like clockwork—a perfect team, just as Uncle had explained. The team on deck had no room for ego or discord; each person was there for the bigger vision. It was clear: success came not from individual brilliance but from the power of the collective.

<u>"Look here Nephew,"</u> and with those three famous words from Unc, the lesson began.

(in a whiskey slurred tone) Lemme splain somethin' to ya. When pimpin go hoe'less and doughless, he got one type of ism on his mind, and thats, I need a gang of ho's cuz teamwork gone make this dream of mine work. A dream is just a thought 'til you put a team behind it. One man can make a move, but a team can make a movement. The ones who last, the ones who rise, they don't do it dolo—they got a squad, a system, a structure. It's chess, not checkers; how many time I got to tell yuh—every piece got a role, every player got a goal.

Ain't about ego, it's about execution. The ones who win know how to delegate, elevate, and appreciate. You can't run the whole show and expect the curtains to stay up. If everybody play they position, the vision comes to fruition. A team ain't just bodies in the same space, it's minds on the same page. The playmaker ain't the same as the closer. The visionary ain't the same as the strategist. Everybody got a part, and the game falls apart when folks try to do what they ain't built for.

Think of co-op, that's when a crew comes together, stacks the paper, and runs the bag up as one. It ain't about one person feastin' while the rest starve; nah, it's about everyone gettin' their fair share. The power of a co-op is in that collective strength—when you combine resources, knowledge, and talent, you create somethin' bigger than any one individual. The whole team moves together, you pull together for better deals, real opportunities, and support. It's about makin' sure everybody eats. When the team's united, that's when real power shows up—together, we rise.

You ever seen a squad where everybody wanna be the boss? That's a setup for a loss. You need people who know how to lead, but also ones who know how to support. The right team ain't about who's loudest, it's about who's effective. When everybody stay in their lane, the whole team gain.

A big school of fish? They move as one, baby. When danger hits, they scatter in sync, confusing the predator. Alone, they easy pickin's, like takin' candy from a baby, but together, they can't be touched. What about a herd of gazelle on the savannah? They stay tight. When a lion comes for them, they work together to outrun the threat. It's about that unity, movin' as one to survive, that group shield is their only weapon.

That's how yall youngsta's need to be movin in them sundown towns. Strength come in numbers. Even lions huntin' them gazelle's know there's power in teamwork. They hunt in pairs, flankin' and strategizin' for the perfect strike. In the wild, survival is all about movin' together and trustin' your crew. You don't see no gorilla out in the jungle by hisself. It's gone be a silverback alpha leadin' and a whole gang behind him—eatin on some bamboo shoots or somethin.

The streets taught the game before business schools gave it a name and nature taught the streets. Every real operation got structure—who watchin', who movin', who collectin'. You think major corporations don't work the same? The CEO ain't running ads, the marketers ain't doing security, and the investors ain't packing boxes.

Most can't see the forest for the trees but you gotta see the bigger picture—get a birds eye view, whether in business or if you hustlin', a scattered team is a sinking ship. The ones who build to last got roles, strategy, and organization. A dream with no structure is just wishful thinking.

Shiihh, What do you think the draw to gang-bangin' is? It's about belonging, being part of something bigger than yourself, with a team that's got your back. The dream's the same: to have people by your side, movin' forward, pushin' you higher depending on the type of gang that is. The difference is, gang-bangin for some, keeps them stuck in the struggle, trauma bonding—while positive teamwork takes you to a place where everybody wins.

In the streets, that loyalty and sense of togetherness feels real, even if it's the wrong kind of real for those that end up in prison or with dead homies. But when you realize that same loyalty and teamwork can be channeled into something positive—like building a business, a community, or a movement—you start to see how it's all connected. That's the magic—teamwork making dreams come to life, not just surviving, but thriving.

A lotta squads crumble 'cause folks assume instead of articulate. Pride keep people from asking questions, ego keep people from taking direction. But the dream only works when the team got one mind, one mission, and one method to make it happen. Everybody wanna be self-made 'til they realize every empire was built by many hands. Ain't nobody ever truly did it alone—not the hustlers, not the moguls, not the legends. Even the coldest lone wolves got a pack somewhere making sure they eat.

This whole "I don't need nobody" mentality? That's a fast-track to failure. Even the best ideas need investors. Even the hardest hustlers need distributors. Even the biggest bosses got consigliere whispering game in they ear. Most people would rather have 100% of nothing than 10% of everything. Sure you might start a business and own 100% of a thousand dollars a month, but imagine sharing 5% of a hundred million dollars per month between twenty partners.

Partnerships elevate power. If two minds think sharper than one, imagine what five could do? The ones who get ahead ain't the ones trying to outdo each other—they the ones outworking the world, together. Imagine a family household that understood this, that's like a mini corporation. If they could take emotion, religion and romance out the equation and just get to the bag and set up a legacy, everybody could eat for generations. Travel the globe first class while their children learn foreign languages and go horse back riding. Folks would rather they children walk through ghettos to a limited future before they understand this game I'm droppin'.

A weak mind sees a rival, a strong mind sees a resource. A fool wanna' compete with everybody, a visionary wanna collaborate. Ain't about who got the biggest shine—it's about who can keep the lights on the longest. I already said it once, one can make a move but a team can make a movement. Ms. Hill said it best when she said, " it aint bout what you cop, its about what you keep. Now marinate on that for a spell.

Ain't no dream working if the team hurting. One weak link can break the chain, one bad vibe can throw off the whole grind. Everybody with you ain't for you. Some folks show up for the win but fold when the struggle hit. What's the purpose in wasting your time if you planning to lose based on how you move. You don't need yes-men, you need real ones. You don't need dead weight, you need go-getters. If they don't add to the vision, they subtract from it. And subtraction ain't never been part of the formula for success—unless it was subtra tin the canser.

When the money come in, it gotta move right. A greedy leader gon' starve his team, and a starving team ain't got no reason to stay loyal. A real boss makes sure everybody eat, 'cause when the team full, the mission push forward stronger. Selfish hands fumble bags. Generous hands multiply wealth. The ones who think short-term stack, but the ones who think long-term build. You want a dream to work? Make sure the whole team got a plate at the table.

Every dream gon' hit roadblocks, every squad gon' face setbacks. The difference between the ones who win and the ones who whine is simple: adaptation. A team that can pivot, shift, and adjust when things ain't smooth is a team that can't lose. You ever seen a great quarterback? He don't panic when the play change—he adjusts. He moves the ball, he shifts the strategy, and he makes it work. The best teams got that same energy. They don't complain, they adjust the game plan and keep running plays. Now—can you do dat.

If the dream ain't shared, the work ain't fair. Everybody on the team gotta believe in the vision, 'cause a house divided can't stand. If one man chasing success and another just chasing checks, the whole thing gon' fall apart. They on two different teams with two different missions. One at work just to get a check at the end of the week, he don't care if the business failing or succeeding, no loyalty, and he gon' jump ship at the first sign of trouble. The others gonna make sure the whole ship gettin renovated, upgraded and elevated for triple the cashflow thats being generated. The real ones align their mindset before they align their money. 'Cause if the minds ain't right, the grind ain't right. And if the grind ain't right, the dream ain't taking flight.

Talk is cheap, execution is the only expense that matter. Everybody love the idea of success, but most don't love the work that go with it. The ones who win ain't just dreamers—they doers. A team can plan all day, but if ain't nobody moving, ain't nothing happening. Execution is everything. Execution is everything. Execution—Is—Everything. The ones who act get ahead. The ones who wait watch others win. A team moving as one is unstoppable. The dream ain't just yours, it's ours. When every piece is in place, when every role is respected, when everybody puts in the work—that's when success ain't a question, it's a guarantee.

It ain't just about working hard—it's about working togeth-er. 'Cause a dream alone is just a fantasy. But when the right team lock in, that's when it turn into reality.

Now listen—If you' really serious about takin' your game to the next level regarding that team for the dream mindset, you gotta check out this book right here—Gary Vaynerchuk's **Crushing It.** Gary Vee, is the king of hustle. *Crushing It* ain't just about grindin' solo, it's about building your team, movin' together, and turning your passion into profit. It's about taking your story, flippin' it, and building an empire with the right crew by your side.

Now, if you really wanna understand why your cousins and them find it so hard to think on that team-type time, you might find the answers you're looking for in a book called **Yurugu** by Marimba Ani. POWERFUL. Yurugu, originally known as Ogo in Dogon mythology, is described as moving with anxiety, impatience, and disharmony—traits that sabotage unity before it can even get started.

All of these books drop serious game on how success ain't about doin' it alone—it's about building your team, trustin' the process, and working together to make that dream come true. Albeit, some of these insights might be too powerful for an undeveloped mind to fully comprehend. A calcified pineal gland aint gone even begin to understand whats in these books. *At this moment, the boat began docking. As Unc and Nephew passed the window of a room below deck on their way out, Unc muttered, "About time," while Nephew shook his head, replying, "Can't wait to get off this death trap." Through the window, they caught a glimpse of the ringmaster disciplining the band members from earlier with sharp, open-handed slaps.*

Fifty

Break Bread

Game that's given ain't game that's gone—it's game that's grown. The sauce ain't lost when the recipe's taught.

*T*he choice had come down to two contrasting sanctuaries: Kyoto, Japan—a timeless haven of luxury ryokans, whispered silk robes, manicured private gardens, and tea rituals steeped in centuries of mindful silence—or Bali, Indonesia, specifically Uluwatu, with its breathtaking cliffside resorts, infinity pools spilling dreamily into endless azure seas, and outdoor stone showers beneath lush tropical skies.

Unc was seriously contemplating uprooting himself altogether, longing to settle somewhere peaceful and less crowded—a serene place to dive deeply inward, seeking what he called "monk mode" to sharpen his spiritual gifts. As he often mentioned, at his stage of life, there was little left worth pursuing besides mastering the mastery within.

Nephew, always eager and observant, invited himself along on the scouting mission to Bali to explore potential properties, sensing his uncle could use the youthful assistance. Unc didn't protest; in fact, he warmly welcomed the vibrant energy and technological ease of *a younger mind, someone to manage the digital devices and decode cultural nuances of their new surroundings.*

Yet, paradise was interrupted sooner than expected. Unc fell feverish, the vibrant hues of Balinese sunsets dimming in his eyes. Secretly, he'd been waging a quiet war against an unseen enemy—colon cancer. He'd always disliked hospitals, refusing to burden others with his battles, but as they hastily booked their return flight, regret weighed heavier than their luggage. Perhaps he should have heeded the subtle warnings whispered by his body.

Back on American soil, nephew convinced Unc to release his stubborn pride and admit himself into the sterile yet reassuring embrace of a hospital room. Settled amid the quiet echo's and rhythmic beeping of medical monitors, nephew took a seat beside his uncle's bed. True to form, despite the IV drip anchoring him firmly to reality, Unc's eyes sparkled with familiar mischief and unwavering resolve.

His voice carried strength beyond illness as he launched into another timeless sermon filled with game, wisdom, and street poetry—reminding nephew, with comforting certainty, that no matter the storm, he always found his way back to calm waters. "You know me, I'm gon' be aahite regardless—Imma always land on my feet nephew," said Unc. "But check this out. Here's some news you can use.

Always lace the next so the game stay blessed, 'cause when the game stay blessed, your legacy reflects success—knowdom-Sayin'. I mean shiiid, sometimes, bosses take losses.

But for real though—real one don't hoard no knowledge, they plant seeds. They don't just eat—they feeds. The same hands that reach up should reach back, 'cause the chain is only strong when every link stay intact, yuh dig?

A selfish hustler is a short-lived one—fools who hoard end up poor, but the ones who share, stay prepared. Look at the greats—the ones who built empires didn't do it alone, they put folks in position. A lion don't eat alone—he lead a pride, and they feast together. A king with no kingdom is just a man with a fancy chair, and a boss who can't build others is just a buster with a title. If you want yuh name to live, you gotta teach the game to give.

Breaking bread ain't just about dollars—it's about dividends of wisdom, interest in influence, and stock in strategy. 'Cause money can be spent, but knowledge can be flipped forever. A fool spend a dollar, a player invest a dime, and a boss plant a seed that pay out over time. You see, wisdom ain't taxed, but ignorance got the highest fee. That's why the sharp keep teaching, and the soft keep reaching.

Some cats afraid to lace the next, thinking it take somethin' away from them. That's that weak-minded, small-time, nickel-and-dime mentality. Real ones know—game shared is game prepared. When you build folks up, you don't lose power, you multiply it. That's how dynasties form. That's how history remembers you. That's why bosses sit at tables, while suckers stand outside tryna peek in the window. Ain't no scarcity in the game—only scarcity in mentality. It's enough to go around for everybody. See, a bucket of crabs fight to stay at the bottom, but a school of fish move as one and own the ocean. You gotta decide—do you want to stunt in a small pond, or flow on the big wave?

But don't get it twisted—breaking bread don't mean feedin' the undeserving. Some folks want the meal but won't put in no work. A lazy hand don't get no plate, and a greedy mouth get cut off quick. You gotta peep the difference between who's an asset and who's a liability. See, a wolf pack move as a unit, but a leech just ride the wave 'til the well run dry.

And let's not forget—whether it's tithe or tax, tribute or toll, the strong gotta look out for the weak. Ain't no real boss that don't give back, 'cause the game ain't just about flexin'—it's about foundation. You think them old-school hustlers built all this just for themselves? Nah. They built so the next generation could run farther, climb higher, and stack bigger. If you ain't investing in the next, then you ain't really invested in success.

Even kings pay tribute—whether it's to the streets, the people, or the principles. The hand that gives is the hand that receives, 'cause when you hoard, you starve, but when you share, you expand. gone ahead and watch an episode of hoarders and see what I'm talkin' bout. That's why the real ones leave legacies, while the selfish leave cautionary tales. You want to be remembered? Then break bread. You want to be forgotten? Then keep it all to yourself and watch how fast the world moves on without you.

So what's the play? You finna build a table or beg for a seat? You finna lead the feast or fight for scraps? 'Cause understand this—bread don't break itself. You either slice it up and serve the game, or sit back and starve with the lames. Boss up, lace up, and make sure your name ring bells long after you gone.

Real kings leave recipes, not empty plates. Now it's time for me to pass the plate and keep the game great.

A soft knock at the door gently pulled them back into the hospital room's muted glow, antiseptic air mixing with the distant hum of quiet footsteps down the hall. Nephew glanced up, breaking the pause,

"Yeah, I got you Unc, say less. I feel like you tryin' to tell me something though, shoot strait. what's on your mind?"

"Nothing's on my mind but choppin' up game per usual, nephew—but I do wanna roll a seven with you real quick. If anything ever happens to me—not now, but someday, whether it's next year or ten years from now..."

Nephew interrupted gently, "Come on, Unc, don't even talk like that—you gon' live forever."

"I hear you, I hear you," Unc said firmly, "but listen, this is serious. If I go, I've named you trustee of my estate. My son would run it into the ground, so I set up a hundred-million-dollar life insurance policy to keep things solid. Your job is to make sure my instructions are carried out exactly as I lay them out. Here's the move: put the same hundred-million-dollar policy on everyone who was at the family reunion. Aunt Beatrice doesn't have much longer, so you'll probably see another hundred million from her soon. In fact, given how our family's living, we might lose a few more over the next ten years, do to diabetis and god knows what else."

Unc leaned in closer, eyes steady. "Every time one of us crosses over, the estate—which is essentially the family trust—gets a big payout. Each bag goes into the trust fund to keep it growing. Every new birth will also get insured, so the cycle keeps running perpetually for the next hundred years. Between these death benefits and a stipulation that nobody gets any assistance unless they're actively studying investment strategies and contributing to our family portfolio, the trust will eventually grow into billions."

"Every child born into this family will be a trust-fund baby, raised with privileges reserved for royalty—top-notch education, elite healthcare, world travel, and luxury vehicles before they're even sixteen. By the time they hit thirty, they'll know enough to run a whole country. But nephew," Unc said, his voice low and steady, "I need you to make sure it gets done. Can you dig it?"

"Don't trip, nephew, it's a strait lick with a crooked stick—you ain't gotta approve, authorize, or deny no special requests or extra handouts. It's an incentive-based trust; meaning they'll see distributions only for specific moves: college, marriages, cribs, rides, chefs, travel—you know, quality-of-life upgrades—but no real dough directly in their hands. Otherwise, they liable to lose their minds and blow it all. Sure, they'll get a lil' pocket change for wastin', but everything else? Provided top-shelf, cream-of-the-crop style. Just some fly pimp shit straight from the game, designed to keep the whole family locked in and focused on the bigger picture." Can't lock in to make a billion dollars if you stressed, taking the bus and going to work everyday for 12 hours. Naw, Imma' buy they time back. So do that for me neph.

"You damn right," Nephew responded without hesitation. *Unc was in high spirits, treating it like a minor setback—and truth be told, it showed. He figured a couple months of healing, then maybe that Japan trip could be the perfect celebration.*

Nephew said his goodnights and headed back to the rest, already planning to return first thing in the morning. The blacktop freeway stretched quiet before him, the late-night air mostly empty, save for a few scattered tractor trailers. He cruised five over the limit, coasting easy with the road to himself, thoughts drifting—until his phone rang. He tapped the answer button on the steering wheel. "Hello?" he asked, half-curious who'd be calling at this hour.

It was the hospital.

Just that fast, Unc had crossed over—called home to join the realm of the ancestors.

Epilogue

Unc's passing hit us like a Mack truck—and quite by surprise. One day he was making plans and the next, he was gone.

The closed casket funeral was a beautiful homegoing, full of color and character—more celebration than sorrow, just the way he would've liked it. Old friends, distant cousins, and quiet nods filled the chapel like echoes of a life well lived, told through memories that made folks laugh one minute and wipe their eyes the next. Nephew had kept his word, seeing through every one of Unc's final instructions with care and precision. Knowin' Unc was a private man, Nephew kept quiet about his passin'—figured anyone outside the family would just have to find out on their own.

One overcast afternoon, while gathering a few final items from Unc's lake cabin, Nephew noticed something on the shelf beside a worn copy of **The Prince** by Niccolò Machiavelli. Half-buried under a fine layer of dust sat one of nephew's old phones—the one he thought he'd lost but had actually left behind after upgrading. He picked it up, thumbed the cracked screen, and to his surprise, it still had a bit of juice left in it.

The room was quiet, wrapped in the scent of aged wood and distant pine, as sunlight slipped through the trees in fractured beams—casting a warm, ghostlike glow across the space, like the past gently nudging him to pay attention.

He'd almost forgotten: this was the device he used to take notes and or record entries—thoughts, voice memos, passing moments—usually when he had an idea he didn't want to forget or when Unc was dropping certifie game. Whether it was during phone conversations, riding through back roads, casting lines off the dock, or waiting in some quiet airport lounge between cities.

The files were still there—grainy audio clips, notes jotted down mid-thought, fragments of conversations that now felt like sacred texts.

As Nephew listened and scrolled, each entry pulled him deeper into the rhythm of Unc's voice, like echoes from another realm. The moment was bittersweet. His eyes welled up as he revisited those words—not just hearing them, but feeling them. It was like sitting with Unc all over again.

What follows are a handful of those entries—saved, scattered, and stitched together—fragments of wisdom, raw and unfiltered, recorded in quiet corners of life. These aren't just notes. They're remnants of a legacy.

Fifty-One

The Game is the Game—It is what it is.

ENTRY: 21 / JULY 1st 11:01 AM

Look here, nephew... lemme lace you with somethin' simple but heavy: *the game is the game.* Ain't no sugarcoatin', ain't no do-overs. You sign up? Then you signed *all* the way up. No partial participation. No crying when the storm hit after you danced in the devil's drizzle. It is what it is.

You choose the streets? Cool. Then know that steel talk louder than words, and trust get measured in seconds. You choose the boardroom? That's cool too. Just know them handshakes ain't always deals—they be daggers sometimes, dressed in smiles. Whatever game you pick, just make sure you know the *rules.* And once you know 'em? Play to win, or don't play at all.

See, fools want the fruits but fear the fight. They love the perks but duck the price. But real ones? We own our choices. Ain't no excuses, no finger-pointin', no "what had happened was..." If I fall, I own it. If I rise, I still stay humble, 'cause I know the same game that blesses you will test you the next day, just to see if you *really* learned the lesson.

Too many want to be players but can't even handle the bench. You wanna wear the crown? Then carry the weight. You wanna eat? Then wash your hands in blood, sweat, and strategy. 'Cause in the game, ain't no refunds. And the bill always come due.

Now lemme give you a little story to lace this up. I once knew a youngin' out west—sharp dresser, smoother talker, swore he was built for the life. He wanted the thrill, the power, the fast money, the fast women... but not the responsibility. Thought the game was a costume he could throw on and off depending on the company he kept. One night, he ran up a play that wasn't his to run—stepped on toes, made promises he couldn't keep, and when the fallout came, he tried to cry foul. But the streets ain't a sandbox and this ain't preschool. The OGs didn't feel sorry. They just reminded him: "The game is the game, homeboy." And when the dust settled, all he had left was a lesson—and a limp—plus other things i'd rather not even speak on.

That's the cold, hard gospel right there. You can't cherry-pick the perks and duck the pain. The streets don't come with refunds, and the hustle don't have a suggestion box. If you sign up for the race, understand the track comes with hurdles. Ain't no magic undo button when it don't go your way. You can't scream victim when the game responds to the energy you brought into it. If you played foul, expect foul calls. If you move with integrity, the rewards gon' come—maybe slow, maybe silent, but they come.

And look, even outside the streets—this apply to every lane. In business, in relationships, in legacy-building—whatever your "game" is, you gotta respect the field. The rules ain't always fair, but they real. You either play it like a professional or get played like a fool. It ain't about what happens to you—it's about what you do with it. That's why real bosses don't panic when it rain—they just switch coats, adjust the umbrella, and keep walkin'.

So the next time life smack you with a plot twist, don't pout. Pivot. Adjust your crown, square your jaw, and keep movin'. The game ain't meant to be fair—it's meant to be *played*. And if you gon' play, play cold, play clean, and above all... play conscious.

Bottom line, nephew? If you step in the arena, don't flinch when it gets gritty. Cause the game don't care 'bout how you *feel*. It care 'bout how you *move*. You chose the game, so play it with pride. Own your wins, wear your losses, and don't ever let the bitterness of the moment make you forget the honor in the journey. The game is the game—it don't owe nobody nothin'. But if you come correct, it just might crown you king.'

Fifty-Two

Charge It To The Game

ENTRY: 16 / JULY 18th 8:11 AM

L et me tell you somethin', nephew—when you in the game, any game, from the corners on the streets to the corner office suites, you gon' take a few hits. That's just part of the admission fee. You gon' get lied to, played on, overlooked, maybe even backstabbed by somebody you put on. And when that moment come—and it will—you got two options: cry about it like it's the end, or charge it to the game and keep steppin'.

See, real ones don't cry over spilled loyalty. We mop it up, learn the lesson, and move sharper. If Shorty switched up on you? Charge it. When your homie ghosted soon as you hit a slump? Charge it. When your own blood don't support you till strangers do? Man, charge it to the game. That's the price of elevation—every level got a toll. I aint saying don't handle it, but charge off them emotions.

A boss don't keep receipts on betrayal—he just keeps record in his mental ledger. No need to broadcast your pain to folks who secretly clap when you hurtin'. Keep it player. Because every setback is a tuition fee in the University of Game. You either pay attention or pay again.

Let me give you a quick one, lil bruh—back in the day, I broke bread with a partner who smiled in my face and siphoned my sauce behind my back. Took my connects, used my lingo, even tried to flip my lady—ninja tried to destiny switch with me. For a hot second, I wanted revenge. But Unc ain't no emotional crash dummy. I laughed, poured up somethin' brown, and said, "Charge it." 'Cause see, revenge keep you broke in spirit. But elevation? That's the real payback. I elevated so high, they all got swept up in my dust by default. I didn't even have to lift a finger, let's just say gods universe handled it.

But here's the thing: you gotta develop that unshakable calm, that ice-water-in-your-veins cool. Everything don't need a response—some things just need distance. Some folks expose themselves for free; all you gotta do is give 'em time. And when they do, don't trip—just charge it to the game. See, when you refuse to charge it, you don't just hold on to the loss—you finance it. You start payin' interest on pain. You swipe your spirit for grudges and bitterness, and next thing you know, your soul in emotional overdraft. People think debt is just financial—but nah, nephew, you can owe energy, owe peace, owe clarity, and be behind on all them payments.

You ever met somebody still mad over something that happened ten years ago? That's a broke soul. That's a bankrupt heart. That's somebody livin' in emotional Section 8, barely gettin' by because they never wrote that loss off. They try to make sense of betrayal like it's refundable, but it ain't. Life don't issue refunds—it issues receipts. And if you can't let that go?

You gone live poor in every way—psychologically, spiritually, even physically. Stress got folks lookin' older than they mama, walkin' around with hunched backs from burdens they shoulda left at the curb.

Sometimes the smartest move ain't revenge—it's Chapter 11 for your sanity. File emotional bankruptcy, pack up your peace, and relocate your soul. Maybe that look like movin' to another city, blockin' some numbers, switchin' your route, or changin' your number—whatever it take to bail your spirit out. That's survival, playboy. That ain't weakness—that's wisdom.

Know when to stop while you ahead—cut your losses, charge off the account, and don't go into debt over some nonsense. If the balance ain't bringin' you value, why keep payin' interest in stress? Chalk that shyt up as tuition in the school of hard knocks. 'Cause see, energetic poverty is a mortal sin in this game. It make you easy prey, a magnet for more chaos. And what we don't do is stay broke tryna pay for what already hurt us. If it already cost you your peace once, don't keep makin payments. Just charge it—and move like a man who know the value of his energy.

So when life throw shade, betrayal, or setbacks your way, don't fold up. Don't get stuck rewinding the scene. Take the hit, learn the playbook, handle yuh business, and move forward wiser, colder, and cleaner. Because the longer you dwell, the deeper you sink—and we don't sink over hear, potnuh. We swim. We stride. We stay laced.

That's the cost of the game, and if you gon' play, you better know how to pay like you weigh. Pay in peace. Pay in silence. But whatever you do—never stop playin' the game.

Fifty-Three

If The Game Don't Change You, You Ain't Playin' It Right

ENTRY: 07 / JUNE 15th 8:07 PM

Ignorance ain't bliss—it's bankruptcy. Fools stay the same, but the wise rearrange. See, enlightenment elevates, but ignorance incarcerates. If the game don't leave scars, you just spectatin'. If the hustle don't stretch your mind, you just clockin' time. Ain't no growth in the comfort zone, and ain't no championships won from the sidelines. This ain't hopscotch, baby—it's high-stakes poker. And if you ain't playin' for keeps, you just watchin' chips slide across the table.

The real players get tested, invested, and battle-born. If you still think the same, move the same, and react the same as you did five years ago, you ain't in the game, play boy—you in the stands. Same hustle, same muscle, same struggle, same trouble—if that sound like your life, you ain't risin', you just runnin' in place. Real hustlers evolve, real bosses adapt, real men transform under pressure. This ain't no kiddie pool hustle—this deep-water swimmin', swimmin; with the sharks—and if you can't hold your breath, you drownin'.

The game got a price, and the cost ain't just money—it's mindset, it's muscle, it's makin' peace with pain and turnin' L's into lessons. You either pivot or perish, boss up or back out. 'Cause in this world, if you ain't changin', you gettin' changed. Every loss carves wisdom into your bones, every betrayal chisels caution into your soul, and every victory stamps resilience on your spirit. If the furnace don't burn you, it don't brand you. If the storm don't shake you, it don't shape you.

Pressure make diamonds, but it also bust pipes—so which one is you? You gon' crack when the stakes get high, or you gon' level up? The game don't wait on no man to catch up, and life don't throw no pause button when you behind. You either transform, or you turn obsolete—no in-between. A weak man whine, a wise man refine, a real boss redesigns.

A hustler who never shifts his strategy is a hustler who stays stuck. It's like drivin' the same route every day and expectin' new scenery—don't work like that, playboy. You gotta switch gears, shift lanes, flip scripts, and stack chips. If the board change, the moves gotta change too, or you checkmated before you even know it. Ain't no cheat codes, ain't no shortcuts—just grind, wisdom, and adaptation. A sharp blade don't stay sharp by sittin' still—it need friction, it need action and movement, it need steel to stay real.

See, a caterpillar don't argue when it outgrow the cocoon—it just become the butterfly. A snake don't cry when it shed its skin—it just slide smoother. But some fools wanna hold onto the past, scared to outgrow old habits, too stubborn to let go of what don't serve'em no-more. That ain't growth, that's stagnation—and stagnation is just death in slow motion.

If the game don't test you, it don't respect you. If it don't humble you, it don't need you. And if you still the same after all these rounds? You wasn't really playin', you was just passin' time. Real bosses leave the game different than how they entered. Whether it made you sharper, harder, wiser, or colder—you ain't the same man who walked in. 'Cause if you are? You ain't been playin' this game—you been playin' yourself.

No fire, no forge. No struggle, no story. No risk, no reward. Stay sharp, stay swift, stay movin'—or get left like last week's news.

Fifty-Four

Don't Hate The Player—Hate The Game

ENTRY: 31 / AUGUST 20th 3:33 PM

S ee, most folks get caught slippin' 'cause they too busy pointin' fingers at the one playin and not the board bein' played on. But don't hate the player—hate the game. 'Cause a real one just movin' through the rules that already existed before he even showed up. The hustle been in motion—the streets had laws long before your feelings had opinions. You mad at me for dancin' in the rain, but I ain't the one who made the storm.

You got women hatin' the ex who played 'em, but never questionin' why they keep signin' up for a bad boy or a system that rewards looks over loyalty. Dudes cryin' foul in the fourth quarter, mad the dealer got all the chips, but never learned how to shuffle they own deck. The game cold, but it ain't personal. The dice don't care about your dreams. The cards don't flinch when you fold. So why get mad at the man who mastered it?

I done seen fools blame the shark for swimmin' in the ocean, like it was supposed to move like a goldfish. But the game don't bend to your emotions—it respects strategy, resilience, execution. You can't guilt-trip the rules. You either adapt, evolve, or get played like background music. See back in the day, when they saw me comin' , it was like a parade on the blade. Why they was mad at me though, just cause I had it made.

Hatin' the player just means you ain't learned the rules yet. But if you really wanna win? Study the game. Observe the board. Respect the hustle, even if it ain't yours. And if you feel like the game unfair? Cool. Then build your own game. Start your own table. Set your own rules. But until then? Play smart, play sharp, and stop cryin' when somebody play it better than you.

You got men out here simpin over some coochi-cat, ready to kill the whole block cause they girl got knocked. Why not take that same energy and level up to rock star status? Just cause another playa knew what to do and outshined you, that's supposed to be they fault cause' they player-fly. You buggin' on they thuggin, and if you don't level up, it's gone keep hapening.

Now let me break it down even cleaner—if a predator huntin' in the jungle, and the prey get caught slippin', the predator ain't evil—it's just good at what it do. So don't be the prey complainin' about the predator. Be the one that learn how to move differently. Watch the patterns. Learn the terrain. Master the rhythm of survival, master the game.

You'll notice I suggest books to damn near everybody that ask me for advice. Solid ones. Game-packed. But you know how many actually go read 'em? Hell, I'd say maybe 1 outta 10—if that. They don't even scan through 'em, let alone listen to the audiobook while drivin' or doin' laundry. Nah, they got every excuse in the world why they "ain't got time." But somehow, they got all the time for gossip, Netflix, IG scrollin', or some drama bonding.

The game be gifted to 'em multiple times a day—but they ain't payin' attention. Then they got the nerve to hate on the one that is payin' attention and winnin'—talkin' slick 'bout the muthaphucka who runnin' laps around 'em like it's magic. It ain't magic. It's discipline, study, and application.

I was tellin' this young lady just the other day—if you really wanna understand your man and his hatin' ass family, go pick up **The Secret Language of Birthdays** or **The Complete Book of Astrology**, or better yet, some solid psychology books so you can master the game of personality. She nodded, said "OK" like 30 times. You think she cracked a book open since? Hell naw. Not even a peek at the table of contents. And that's the problem.

Everybody say they want game, but only a few actually show up to class. Then they got the nerve to hate on the ones who do show up for class—the ones who study the game for winning it. Call 'em nerds, squares, tryin' to clown 'em… but guess what? Them same "nerds" end up bein' they boss, callin' the shots, signin' the checks, and makin' decisions that affect their whole life.

Ain't that somethin'? Instead of respectin' the one who mastered the board, they throw shade—like it ain't the game itself that's been chewin' 'em up. Yeah, youngsta… if you out here hatin' on the player, but not the game? That's a fools move.

Especially when you smack dab in the middle of it—just like an avatar in the Matrix, with no memory of divinity—thinkin' you got free will, but you movin' like a programmed pawn. You betta get right… before you get left.

Fifty-Five

Ain't No Refunds In The Game—Make Sure You Cash Out Right

ENTRY: 21 / MARCH 10th 9:52 PM

L ook here, nephew—when you swipe that card called life, just know: ain't to many reciepts and refunds. This game don't come with a return policy. Once that decision go through? It's posted. Ain't no manager to complain to, ain't no store credit for bad behavior. You break it, you bought it. You play it, you pay it.

See, life is like a high-end boutique with no price tags. You don't always know what the cost is up front, but trust—it's coming out your account eventually. Might be peace, might be time, might be energy, might be your damn soul. So you better know what you investing in and make sure it's gon' pay dividends, 'cause you can't go cryin' for a refund once you realize the return on that shyt is pain and regret.

You don't get to fumble through the game reckless, and then act surprised when the tab hit like a freight train. Naw, the game don't pity fools. You eat what you kill, you sleep in the bed you made, and you wake up to the consequences you brewed. That's why I always say: make sure you cash out right.

I'm sure you've seen somebody who had it all in they hands and left the table broke? Played a good hand, but got greedy. Got caught up in the bluff, forgot the rules. That's how folks end up bankrupt in life—emotionally, mentally, and spiritually. The game ain't evil, it's just exact. It keeps score whether you watchin' or not.

Let me tell you something—when the game is done, and it's your time to cash out, you don't wanna be sittin' there askin', "Where did all my time go?" That's the worst kind of broke—when you ain't got no peace, no passion, no purpose… and no time left to get it back. Man, I know so many 'P's' and playas that use to be up. At the playa's ball, lookin' like they belong on the Tonight Show—yuh know, Hollywood shyt. If you see'um now, they look like the Crypt Keeper—figuratively and literally. Some in the grave; some look like they need to be in the grave. Hollywood to Halloween-looking face, ass.

So listen when I tell yuh, every move you make better be laced in intention. Don't just play to play—play to win. Play to grow. Play to build. 'Cause when the curtains close and they call last hand, you either walk out with wealth in wisdom or poverty in regret.

Peep game: Time, lil bro, is the coldest currency you got. And the thing about it? It don't fold, it don't jingle, and you can't stack it under your mattress. Once it's spent—it's spent.

Gone like a whisper in a windstorm. And most folks? They broke in time before they broke in dollars.

I done seen old G's in hospice beds cryin' 'cause they realized too late they was rich in potential and poor in execution. Chasin' thrills. Chasin' likes. Scrollin' for hours on bullshyt. Beefin' with folks that never built nothin'. They traded a lifetime of greatness for a season of distraction.

You ever notice how time don't feel the same depending on what you doin'? Scrollin' Instagram? Hours fly by. Sittin' with your dreams and fears? Feels like forever. That's 'cause time bends to attention—what you give it to, it multiplies. And if you ain't careful, you gon' look up one day grey, tired, with a body that don't cooperate, wondering what you did with all that fire you once had. That's that soul-deep poverty, youngblood—the kind no money can fix.

So don't just watch the clock; be the reason it ticks. Master time like you master game—strategically, with purpose. 'Cause at the end of the day, the real flex ain't how much you made; it's how well you spent your seconds. I know you heard the one about, if you could take a million dollars right now, would you take it? And then they ask, what if the catch was you could have it but you would have to die first thing in the morning? Would you still take it? With that, the question arises: so which one is more valuable?

Remember this, A king who don't guard his time dies a slave to his distractions—A king who don't guard his time—A king who don't guard his time. So cash out right—or stay poor in spirit forever.

Fifty-Six

A Pimps Love Is Like No Other

ENTRY: 13 / JUNE 22nd 12:45 AM

M an I was sharp as a tack back in the day. When I get yuh, I got yuh. My presence alone made'um flow like the Nile River—and they ain't get no complaints outta me because I knows the wetter the better. I use to run the game up somethin' like this:

I'd tell'um—You got to believe in me, baby; This love ain't built on fairy tales and false promises—it's laced in luxury, locked in loyalty, and wrapped in real game. This ain't just a choice; it's a chance at a championship opportunity.

A golden ticket to a love that elevates, motivates, and cultivates your finest self. See, a pimp's love ain't like no square's love, 'cause a square loves you in potential, but a pimp loves you in comfort and confidence. A square holds your hand, but a pimp holds your future. A square gives you romance, but a pimp gives you a roadmap.

Now listen, I ain't talkin' about no weak love, no whisper-sweet-nothings love, no "let's see where this goes" kinda love. Nah, baby—this love's got structure. This love's got vision. This love ain't built on emotions that shift with the wind—it's set in stone like commandments, carved in game like scriptures. You rock with me, and you gon' feel the love every time the bag touches your hand, every time the doors open in front of you and every time the world bows to your presence. 'Cause when a pimp loves you, he invests in you.

See, a pimp's love ain't poetic, but it's prophetic. I see your future before you do. I see your glow before you shine. I see your potential before you recognize your own power. And I ain't gon' let you settle for less, 'cause less ain't even an option in my world. You ain't just a woman; you're a work of art—priceless, timeless, flawless. But see, baby, even the finest diamonds gotta be polished. Even the baddest rides gotta be maintained. You ready to shine, or you just wanna sit on the shelf? 'Cause a pimp's love puts you in position, but you gotta play the part.

I love you like a champion trains his fighter—I coach, I guide, I elevate. I love you like a king loves his kingdom—I protect, I provide, I proclaim. I love you like the ocean loves the moon—pulling you towards something greater, keeping you in constant motion. This ain't no surface-level infatuation—this is elevation.

But understand this, baby—a pimp don't love like a beggar; he loves like a boss. He don't chase; he chooses. He don't cry; he cultivates. If you got faith in my game, my guidance, my greatness, then you gon' live a life you ain't never imagined. But if you hesitate, if you doubt, if you question the crown? Then, baby, you ain't fit for the throne.

A pimp's love don't suffocate; it stimulates. A pimp's love don't limit; it liberates. A pimp's love don't beg; it builds. 'Cause when you rockin' with me, you ain't just holdin' my hand—you holdin' history in the makin'. So tell me, baby—you ready for this kind of love, or you still playin' in the kiddie pool? 'Cause a pimp's love is like no other... but only for the ones who can handle it—now, can you dig it baby.

To think, I was spittin that righteous game before I even truly knew what love was. In one word, Love is sacrifice.

Now I've matured and my love is based in freedom and quite unconditional. Aint no attachments cause that's the root of suffering yuh dig.

Now look here, youngblood—ole Unc don't like to get too mystical on ya, but, borrowing from the polyamorous nature of the pimpin—let me lace you with a little evolved enlightenment. Y'see, back in the day, my love was poly by profit—multiple women, multiple streams, all roads leadin' to the bag. The heart beat to the rhythm of currency, and the connection? That was transactional, baby.

Love was logistics, not no lofty emotion. But I done grown, traveled a few inner landscapes, and what I found out? The real game? It's energetic. Love is currency—and you best learn how to circulate it with intent, not just spend it on pretty faces and pillow talk.

These days, I ain't just pimpin' for paper—I'm pimpin' for purpose. The love I move with now? It's spiritual. Sacred. Intentional. Every moment I spend with my woman now is an investment in both our souls. We building altars, not just lifestyles. See, true connection don't just stimulate the body—it elevates the spirit. A real one know: if it ain't nourishing your growth, it's draining your light. And love that don't evolve is just lust with long legs.

Now check game—freedom inside love? That's the boss-level understanding. I ain't tryin' to chain her, and she ain't tryin' to trap me. We both move like sovereigns, choosing each other every day without possession. That's trust on a whole different frequency. That's love that lets you breathe and still hold space. She walk her path, I walk mine, but we stride in sync—never steppin' on each other's toes, always pushin' each other toward higher versions of ourselves.

And let me say this, 'cause it's real: emotional depth ain't no weak man's game. You gotta have the strength to hold her tears and still be honest about your own wounds. This grown-man love? It's built on transparency, not territory. Ain't no shame in showing your vulnerabilities sometimes." We done built a temple between us—a sacred space where we speak truth, even when it's ugly. That's the real power, nephew. That's love with structure and sanctity.

But the coldest revelation I ever came to? Love is a mirror. It reflects all the parts of you—especially the ones you try to hide. The insecurities, the trauma, the fear of not being enough. But instead of runnin' from the reflection, we face it together. Her eyes show me my gaps, and I fill 'em not with ego, but with evolution. That's self-discovery with a partner who got you spiritually spotted, like a gym trainer for your soul.

So hear me when I say: love is the ultimate transformation. If it don't challenge you to grow, it's just comfort wearin' a disguise. A queen gon' test your crown, not to disrespect you, but to make sure it still fit. And you? You gotta be willing to shed old layers to stay aligned with the throne.

Now don't confuse none of this with weakness. I'm still the same Unc who know how to turn a cold situation into gold. But this version of me? He move different. He move like he know love is sacred geometry. He know her body ain't just pleasure—it's prophecy. Her presence ain't just warmth—it's wisdom. And together? We co-create a kingdom and queendom where both of us rule and neither of us shrink.

So if you really wanna learn love, youngsta, don't just look at how many you can pull. Look at how deep you can go with the one who see your soul and still choose you every time. That's game beyond game. That's heaven on Earth, right there in your living room.

In short, what I'm sayin' is this, youngblood—real love ain't just sweet talk and skin contact, it's soul work. It's a catalyst for self-discovery, a mirror that reflect who you is and who you could be if you stop runnin' from your own growth. It's a journey of transformation, not just two bodies layin' up, but two spirits stretchin' each other toward they highest selves. It's a dance of autonomy and unity, where you don't lose who you are but find new steps in harmony.

You lead when needed, you follow when wise, and y'all move as one without ever dimmin' the other's shine. And above all, it's love as a spiritual practice—a daily discipline where intention, presence, and respect lay the bricks for somethin' sacred. You gotta navigate emotional complexity with grace, not avoidance. Embrace the hard convos, sit with the discomfort, 'cause that's where the gold at. You feel me? If love don't elevate your frequency, it ain't divine—it's just distraction. So treat it like the temple it is, or don't step inside at all.

If I had to recommend just one book that breaks down the spiritual, dimensional, and elemental nature of what I'm talkin' about, it'd be *The Twin Elemental Effect*. Real talk, that book should be goin' for a rack—it's that heavy. Most folks can't grasp it 'cause it's written from a fourth-dimensional consciousness. It don't cater to no average mindset—it's advanced game for advanced minds. But like the old heads used to tell me, when the student is ready, the teacher will appear, yuh dig?

Fifty-Seven

Upgrade or Fade

ENTRY: 3 / MAY 14th 9:00 PM

L evel up or get left behind. In a world that stays in motion, you either steppin' up or steppin' out—because stagnation ain't part of the equation; only elevation secures your station. Staying the same won't win the game—true players evolve and adapt because transformation is the test of elevation.

See, what you got to remember is, as a Mack thinketh, so is he—your reality is just your mentality in motion. A king with no foresight is just a pawn in hindsight. The sharpest blade ain't the one that sit on display; it's the one that stay sharpened, stay tested, stay ready. 'Cause in this life, if you ain't upgrading, you downgrading—if you ain't elevatin', you evaporatin'.

Success don't wait, and greatness don't negotiate. You got to put in the work to stay in the worth, 'cause the game only rewards those who evolve. A shark that stop swimming drown, and a hustler that stop grindin' gets ground down. The only thing guaranteed in life is change—so you either ride the wave or get washed away.

Don't nobody wanna pay no fool, don't nobody praise the stagnant. The world don't care about what you used to be, only about what you becoming. That's why bosses move forward, never backward. A broken clock might be right twice a day, but a stopped player don't ever get paid. You can't expect front-row seats with a nosebleed mindset. You can't demand VIP treatment while thinking like a scrub. The price of success is constant evolution, 'cause yesterday's game won't win today's championship.

And watch how you walk, 'cause the crowd you keep can cripple your climb. Some folks ain't meant to rise with you—some are elevators, others are anchors. If they ain't helpin' you build, they busy tearin' you down. Too much dead weight, and you won't take flight.

The weak chase comfort, but comfort breeds complacency, and complacency breeds poverty—not just in your pockets, but in your purpose and yuh process. A real one knows that pressure makes diamonds, while the soft crumble like week-old bread. Every level got a devil, but only the sharpest rise to meet the challenge.

Evolution ain't optional—it's survival. You think the wolves worry about the sheep? You think the sun asks permission to shine? If you play small, you stay small. If you scared of heights, you stay grounded. There's a reason the lion don't ask the gazelle how it feels before it eats.

Look around, playboy—technology flip the script every ninety days. That's right, every quarter, the game get a patch, an update, a whole new rulebook. We went from telegrams then telephones, to internet in under a century. Now it's AI, VR, AR, and now they talkin' 'bout brain chips and biotech with computers small enough to party with your blood cells. Six-G and satellites got folks connected across time zones like they sharin' a duplex. If the world changin' that fast, what make you think you can stay the same and still compete? You either evolve with the tools or get replaced by 'em—because the game got no sympathy for the slow adapters.

So what's the move? Upgrade, elevate, renovate—or fade. 'Cause one thing for sure, two things for certain—the game keeps playin', with or without you—so yuh betta not let it catch you hurtin.

Mack up, stack up, and stay laced—'cause if you ain't changin', you rearrangin' your own downfall.

Fifty-Eight

Don't Negotiate Cooperate

ENTRY: 22 / MARCH 12th 11:59 PM

Aint no debates when I dictate—compliance is key, and obedience is what I need to see. This ain't a democracy, it's a hierarchy—kings don't argue with pawns, and bosses don't barter with busters. See, in this game, the sharp lead, the soft plead, and the weak get left to bleed. If you ain't built to follow direction, then you ain't fit to ride in this section. A Mack don't explain, he maintains. A boss don't convince, he commands. You either with the program or you the problem, and problems? They get solved quick around me.

See, a ship don't sail with two captains, and a kingdom don't stand with two kings. The second you start debating your position, you already losing it. A real leader lay the law, and the wise follow suit—'cause hesitation breeds elimination. You want the game? Then respect the chain of command that is, or get left in the land of the lost. Ain't no time for backtalk and backpedalin', 'cause if you ain't movin' forward, you just takin' up space.

A Mack move with precision, a trick move with permission. Ain't no room for doubt when the blueprint's been laid. See, the difference between a boss and a worker ain't just the pay-check—it's the posture. A real one command the room, while a weak one beg for space. There ain't no "ifs" or "buts" in this lane—just execution and elevation. A leader don't need a round table to prove he in charge—his presence alone set the standard. When a lion steps in the jungle, he don't need an introduction—the roar speak for itself.

Some folks act like the game a debate club, like the rules is up for discussion. Talking back to the game is like arguing with the wind—pointless, breathless, and foolish. You can bark all you want, but at the end of the day, the storm still gon' move you. The smart ones recognize the current and ride the wave—they don't fight the tide, they finesse the flow. You want to be in the winner's circle? Then understand, leadership don't debate—it dictates.

Now peep this: submission ain't weakness, it's wisdom. If you think the sun negotiates before it rises, you got the game twisted. If you think the lion holds a meeting before the hunt, you must be the gazelle. Real ones move with authority, and only the foolish question a proven formula. See, you gotta learn to follow before you can lead, and if you ain't willing to follow game, you damn sure ain't ready to give it.

That's why fools stay broke and bosses stay paid. 'Cause real ones don't waste energy arguing over principles—they execute 'em. You ever see a shark ask permission before he take a bite?

Exactly. Game recognize game, and hesitation gets you nothin' but starvation.

So what's the play? You gon' follow the ism or fall into schism? 'Cause out here, it ain't about how loud you talk—it's about how well you listen. The game don't reward the rebellious, it praises the disciplined. Cooperation is the key to elevation, and obedience is the shortcut to success. You can fight the current, or you can ride the wave—but remember, the ones who resist the flow drown the fastest. So lace up, wise up, and recognize the order of operations. 'Cause the game ain't askin'—it's tellin'.

Obey, comply, or step aside—'cause negotiations ended when the game started. and that's to all my mentees.

Fifty-Nine

Birds of a Feather, Flock Together

ENTRY: 49 / DECEMBER 23rd 4:25 AM

B ig game rolls in Packs so run with hustlers or get left with busters and derelict muthaphukas—because if there's nine, you the tenth.

Look around, man—the proof is in the people. Hustlers run with hustlers, scholars roll with scholars, and suckers? They huddle up like pigeons on power lines, chirpin' but never takin' flight. Every man moves in a pack, whether he knows it or not. Gamblers post up with risk-takers, hoopers keep courtside company, and pimps? Well, you ain't never seen a real one sittin' at the table with squares. See, energy attracts its own kind, and the world is one big sorting process. You might think you stand alone, but best believe—your surroundings tell your story before you even open your mouth.

Take a stroll through the city and peep the scene. The rich congregate at the country club, the broke at the liquor store. The visionaries swap ideas over dinner, while the complacent complain at the corner. The hustlers hit the pavement, the lost souls hit the church or the couch—depending on if it's Saturday or Sunday. The bosses build, the bums beg. Ain't no mistake in the movement—people gravitate toward who they are. A doctor ain't posted with dropouts, and a tech mogul ain't killin' time with couch potatoes. The game is designed that way.

So what's the move? You gotta ask yourself—who are you, and who do you wanna be? 'Cause if your surroundings ain't showin' the life you want, then you sittin' in the wrong section. Wanna be a millionaire? Find the ones who talk investments over brunch, not excuses over cheap liquor. Wanna be a world traveler? Then you need to break bread with folks that book flights, not just fantasize about 'em. Whatever your goal, whatever your dream, there's a pack for that, and they ain't waitin' on you to catch up.

See, too many folks stay stuck 'cause they scared to migrate. They think loyalty means stayin' in the nest, even when the nest is burnin'. But real loyalty? That's loyalty to the vision, to the mission, to the elevation. You gotta break away from the broke mindset, from the stagnant circles, from the folks who say "yeah—one day" while you tryna make today the day. Ain't no growth in a garden full of weeds, and ain't no success in a squad full of setbacks.

A lion don't ask sheep for strategy, and a king don't sit with jesters for wisdom. If you the smartest one in your circle, you sittin' at the wrong table. The game is about levels, and elevation don't come with hesitation. Sometimes you gotta leave behind the homies who still partyin' every weekend while you out here buildin' wealth. Sometimes you gotta distance yourself from family members who don't understand the hustle, 'cause not everyone got the vision. That's the price of greatness—separation from stagnation.

And don't think it's just about money. It's about mindset, about movement, about growth. Even in the streets, you got different types—real players politickin', strategizin', buildin' empires, while crash dummies runnin' in circles, makin' the same mistakes. The difference? One crew is thinkin' five moves ahead, while the other ain't thinkin' past the weekend. And trust me, who you move with determines where you end up.

The fastest way to change your life? Change your circle. Upgrade your conversations, upgrade your connections—upgrade your habits. 'Cause whether you know it or not, you're a reflection of who you keep around. If you run with nine broke folks, you bound to be the tenth. If you surround yourself with nine bosses, well, you already know what's next.

So, what's it gon' be? You tryna fly with eagles, or scratch with chickens? You tryna build with kings, or joke with jesters? 'Cause the reality is simple—birds of a feather flock together, but only the strong take flight. Find your tribe. Or get left behind.

Sixty

Hood Rats and Gnats

ENTRY: 38 / JANUARY 12th 8:09 PM

Too much baggage and too much damage don't bring me no progress, just more problems to manage—excess baggage turn first-class flights into fights, and I dont need no turbulence on my way through life. A king don't break his back haulin' dead weight, and a hustler don't waste his fate on no featherweight. See, real players move light, stay right, and keep their minds in flight—while hood rats and gnats buzz 'round, spreadin' mess, blockin' blessings, and beggin' for a lick they ain't built to stick.

It's like flies to honey, mosquitoes to blood—these hoes don't love you, they love what you can do for'em. You shine too bright, they swarm too tight, and next thing you know, you swattin' drama left and right. But check game—real bosses don't let pests stress. We spray game like Raid, cut suckers like blades, and keep them energy-drainers far away. 'Cause in this world, you either ridin' in the driver's seat, or you playin' chauffeur to a backseat bum.

A hood rat don't build, she break. She don't invest, she infest. She a drain, not a gain—a setback, not a step up. Like a broke watch, she stay stuck on past time, talkin' 'bout what she deserve when she ain't put in no work. Always schemin', always screamin', always plottin' on a come-up that don't involve no real hustle. She wanna sip the champagne but never pop the bottle, wanna count the money but never make a dollar. Once pon a time my motto was, I don't shame'um, I claim'um. But after a life time of that goofy shyt—my mentality now is, I don't shame or blame but you definitely not finna come up off of my fame so save that weak game for a lame.

Frustrating and itrritting like gnats? Oh, them lil' naggin' nuisances? They ain't got no purpose but to pester. No power, no paper, no position—just petty problems and pointless opinions. Always in the mix, but never in the money. Always got a story, but never got a strategy. They hang around bosses hopin' for drips, but a real player don't let leeches sip. If you feed a pest, they just come back hungrier—best to starve 'em out and let 'em find their own feast.

See, the wise know the rule—let a fool chase a fool, but let a king choose his queen. If she ain't addin' to the kingdom, she subtractin' from the throne. And if she more headache than help, she belong in the wind, not in the whip. Ain't no room for rats in the palace, no space for gnats on the plate—and definitely no free rides on the first-class flight.

So what's the move? Fan 'em off, boss up, and keep your circle elite. Ain't no king ever built an empire swattin' flies—let them pests buzz elsewhere while you stack, shine, and climb.

Hood rats and gnats? Shoo, fly, shoo—is how I do! Ain't got no sugar for ya, ain't got no seat for ya, ain't got no time to entertain ya. Stay blessed, stay bossed, and stay away from the nonsense. And remember, always lettum kno—I can't do nuthin for yuh mane.

Sixty-One

Elevation Requires Separation

ENTRY: 61 / APRIL 19th 1:22 PM

Everybody ain't meant for the penthouse—you gotta leave some in the lobby. A bird can't soar if it's tangled in chains, and a hustler can't climb if he's draggin' the dead weight of yesterday. You want the view from the top? Then you gotta drop the baggage, cut the chatter, and shake off the hands that been holdin' you back.

See, some folks is like ankle weights—you keep 'em around too long, and you wonder why your steps feel heavy. They don't push, they pull. They don't lift, they lean. They don't inspire, they expire. Some folks is born for the sidelines, yet they swear they tryna play the game. But a real one know—you either elevate or you evaporate, 'cause dead weight don't levitate.

Ain't no shame in lettin' go of what don't grow. Sometimes that mean sacrificin' the crew you came up with, 'cause loyalty to a losing team just make you another loser. Sometimes that mean steppin' back from family, 'cause bloodline don't mean shared vision. And sometimes, the hardest truth of all—you gotta separate from yourself. That old version of you, the one who played it safe, the one who made excuses, the one who feared the risk—bury him, mourn him if you must, but don't resurrect him.

See, great minds discuss ideas, average minds discuss events, and small minds discuss people—so ask yourself, what kind of mind do you got? You tryna build blueprints or gossip about who fell off? You tryna mastermind moves or sit in the peanut gallery, whisperin' about who's winnin'? Champions focus on victory, suckers focus on spectators. Just look across your social media timelines, and you'll see who and what I'm talkin' about.

You can't carry first-class dreams with coach-class discipline. You can't teach altitude to folks afraid of heights. You can't expect million-dollar moves from nickel-and-dime mindsets. That's why bosses move different, why real players walk solo. You ever wonder why most billionaires are up before 4:30 A.M.—or why millionaires pay beaucoup cash on education when half of'um couldn't stand school and probably dropped out? It's a mindset thang.

Look around—eagles don't flock with pigeons, sharks don't school with dolphins. You tryna swim with whales, but you still wadin' in puddles. You say you want penthouse views, but you surround yourself with basement thinkers. You still entertainin' small talk when you supposed to be makin' big moves.

Growth ain't comfortable, but comfort don't grow you. Elevation ain't easy, but easy never built empires. The higher you go, the thinner the air, 'cause the top ain't made for crowds. Ain't no traffic in the sky. Ain't no benchwarmers in the Hall of Fame. Ain't no gold medals for participation.

So, what's the play? You tryna climb or you tryna cling? You tryna lead or you tryna linger? 'Cause one thing for sure, two things for certain—you can't fly while draggin' folks who was never meant to leave the ground.

Penthouse moves don't include basement minds. Cut the cord already, climb the heights, and never look back. Now tell 'em—i'll meet you at the top… or not at all.

Sixty-Two

Message In Ya Motion

ENTRY: 55 / JULY 17th 7:02 AM

E very gesture I make, every step I take, tells my tale and each move is a chapter, written in swagger. Every gesture is a lecture, every step is a scripture—walk like a king, or crawl like a fixture. The way I move ain't just for show, it's a sermon on stride, a doctrine in drive. Before I say a word, they already heard—through the tilt of my brim, the swing of my limb, the way the light catch the gems on my wrist when I spin. See, body language ain't just talk, it's translation. A fool stutters in his steps, but a boss? He let his pivot paint the picture.

Ain't no cappin' in cadence, no frontin' in footwork. You either glide like a shark or stumble like a mark. A lion don't tiptoe through the tall grass—he let the jungle know he comin'. A real one don't beg for respect—his aura collect it like a debt, and it's past due. Ain't no refunds on weak presence, and the game don't do layaways—you step correct, or you step aside.

See, the streets peep before they greet. The game reads before it speaks. The way you carry yourself dictates whether you get the bag or get left holdin' receipts. A fool fumbles 'cause he ain't got poise, and a player pivots 'cause he always got poise. You ain't gotta say you solid—your posture gon' say it for you. The tilt of your chin, the roll of your wrist, the way you hold your frame like a temple instead of a tenement? That's the announcement. You ain't a boss 'til the room bow without words.

Ain't no press conferences in power moves—real ones let the silence speak. If you gotta scream that you the man, you already lost the plan. Let somebody else do it for you. A general don't yell orders—he simply speaks, then he moves, and the soldiers adjust. A king don't plead, he decree.

Body language is currency, and if you broke in your stance, don't expect to cash out in conversation. A weak handshake is a bounced check. A shaky stance is a signed confession. The way you move before you talk tell 'em whether you came to own or owe. 'Cause if you walk unsure, you negotiate from the floor. If you move with hesitation, the wolves smell supper. But if you flow like you own the land, they assume you do. If you command space like a throne belongs beneath you, they lay down the carpet before you even ask.

A hustler moves with grace, a sucker moves with haste. 'Cause when your motion match your mission, the world step aside or step in line. You gotta walk like you done it before, even if it's your first time. Yuh man's Neville Goddard say move like you already know what the end look like. So, what's your stride sayin'? What's your posture preachin'? 'Cause before you open your mouth, the world already heard you.

Sixty-Three

Game Don't Wait, So Why Should You?

ENTRY: 57 / NOVEMBER 24th 3:00 PM

L et me lace you with some quick gospel, young-blood—game don't wait, so why should you? Opportunity don't come with no RSVP, and success damn sure don't wait on nobody to feel ready. While you sittin' around second-guessin', talkin' 'bout "timing ain't right," the game already movin' ten paces ahead. Life ain't no dress rehearsal—this the real show, and curtain call don't come with a warning.

See, hesitation is a cousin of defeat. Every time you pause, doubt creepin' in the back door like a thief. Every time you stall, somebody else already steppin' in the role you was built to play. Time don't take tea breaks, baby—it's tickin', it's movin', and if you ain't movin' with it, you gon' find yourself left behind, lookin' out the rearview mirror wonderin' what coulda been—like an artist kicked off coulda-been records.

Every time you pause when you should pounce, you lettin' fear take the wheel and faith ride in the trunk. You see, the brain wired to protect, not to prosper—it'd rather keep you safe than see you shine. That's why hesitation feels like caution, but really? It's just fear in a fitted cap, lookin' like logic. The moment you stall, opportunity move on to the next hustler who ain't scared to shoot his shot. Life don't always hand out trophies to the most prepared—sometimes it reward the one bold enough to jump, even when his boots still muddy. So tighten up. You thinkin' too long and talkin' yourself out the throne.

I ain't never seen a predator wait for the jungle to get quiet? Nah, he move when it's time to eat. A boss don't need the stars to align—he light his own fire and create the constellation. You wanna win? Then move like you built for it. Ain't no extra credit for potential, only for performance. That idea you got? That dream you holdin'? That plan you keep sayin' "one day" to? That's today's business, not tomorrow's fantasy. Sometimes your product hit when it's a market fit, and sometimes it's all about first to market—just gotta roll the dice, and hope you come out nice. Don't hurt to be super prepared either though, with some practice and experience—knowm-talkin-bout?

Point is, I done seen too many players get played by they own procrastination. Sat on gold 'til it turned to rust. Missed the train 'cause they was too busy packin' imaginary bags. Let me say it plain: the game don't wait for your healing, your clarity, your confidence—it just keeps goin'. Either you build the plane mid-flight, or you sit on the runway til the weeds take over.

Procrastination just self-sabotage dressed in slippers. It's the art of steppin' over your future to comfort your feelings in the moment. See, the average cat ain't lazy, he just emotionally avoidin' the weight of what needs doin'. He'll scroll through drama, binge on distractions, tell himself he "work better under pressure"—but what he really doin' is protectin' his ego from the possibility of failure. He scared that if he try and flop, he gotta face himself. So he delay, distract, and detour—never realizin' he playin' himself outta time, opportunity, and greatness. Like Doc Pychyl said, it ain't a time issue—it's emotional regulation. It ain't that he can't start—it's that he can't stand to sit with discomfort.

But here's what Unc gon' tell you: the price of procrastination ain't paid in hours, it's paid in identity. Every time you push somethin' off, you chippin' away at your self-respect. You teachin' yourself you can't be trusted to follow through—and that's how grown folks end up with childlike confidence. You lose the ability to show up for you. And before long, your dreams turn to dust and you out here bitter, watchin' other folks cash in on the life you was too scared to show up for. So start ugly. Start unsure. But damn it—start. Your future self gon' thank you, but only if you stop leavin' him broke with overdue ambition and bankrupt potential. Time ain't waitin', and neither is the game.

So what you scared of? Failure? That's part of it. Lookin' foolish? That's the price of elevation. But trust me, you'll feel worse watchin' somebody else do what you knew deep down was yours to do. Game don't wait—so why should you? Every second you delay is a seed not planted, a bag not secured, a lesson not learned.

Bosses make moves, not excuses. Hustlers stay in motion, not emotion. So lace up, tighten your pivot, and step like the throne already got your name etched in the crown. Time gon' keep tickin'—the only question is, will it tick in your favor or tick past you?

Pull the trigger already, youngsta. Not later. Now.

Sixty-Four

Commit or Quit—B'yuch

ENTRY: 69 / NOVEMBER 19th 7:17 AM

Ain't no half-steppin' in this game—either you all the way in, or you already out. See, you can't climb that hill standin' still, and you can't win the race tip-toein' in place. The game don't reward hesitation, it don't cut checks for contemplation. It's all about execution, 'cause ideas without action is just empty conversation. You either buildin' or you foldin', but one thing's for sure—if you ain't movin', you losin' and you in a world of confusion.

A hustler don't wait for the stars to align, he get up and grind. A boss don't hesitate, he delegate and dominate. See, commitment is currency, and indecision is debt—the more you stall, the more you owe. You think millionaires sit around just thinkin' about it all day and all night? Nah, they act. They move, they adjust, they risk, they grow. But the ones still talkin' 'bout what they "gon' do" been gon' do it for ten years and still ain't done a damn thing. The kind of woman I know? Look at men who can't commit as phuk-boys, and stand up men see woman who can't commit as "three-oh-foh's" with corns on they toes and skeet's in they teefs.

It's real simple: **commit or quit.** Ain't no "try," ain't no "maybe," ain't no "one day." You either in, or you out. 'Cause let me tell you somethin'—this game don't cater to cowards, and hesitation ain't nothin' but self-doubt in disguise. You got to be married to the mission, loyal to the hustle, faithful to the elevation. Ain't no side-flings with success—you can't just flirt with ambition and expect to birth results. You got to stay down 'til you come up.

See, folks love to start, but how many really finish? Yeah they get active, but how many push through when the struggle get thick, when the road get rough? Anybody can say they want it when it's easy, but when the weight get heavy, that's when the truth get told. The weak fold, the real hold. That's why you see so many quitters, but so few winners—'cause the climb separate the fakes from the greats.

You ever seen a cheetah halfway commit to the hunt? A shark halfway commit to the kill? You either devour, or you starve. Simple. So, what's it gon' be? You tryna feast, or you tryna fast? 'Cause the table got plenty plates, but they only get served to the ones who show up ready to eat.

Success don't wait for nobody. Opportunities don't check your schedule. The ones who win ain't necessarily the smartest, the strongest, or the most talented—they just the ones who refused to quit. They locked in, and stayed in. See, life gon' test you. The game gon' push you. But pressure only busts pipes if the pipe is weak—otherwise, it make diamonds.

Commitment, youngblood? That's the grown man's game right there. Ain't no halfway in greatness—either you marry the mission or you just flirtin' with failure. See, psychology'll tell you commitment starts where motivation ends. It's discipline that show up when the hype clock out. And let me tell you, most folks treat their goals like situationships—show up when it's convenient, ghost when it get gritty. But the real? They lock in like a pit with purpose. 'Cause commitment don't just mean stickin' with somethin'—it mean becoming somethin'.

It's what separates the dabblers from the dominators. You don't get the crown by playin' part-time king. So if you ain't gon' show up for it through the rain, the drought, the setbacks, and the silence? Do yourself a favor—don't even start. The game only rewards the ones who never renegotiate with their purpose.

So what's the play? You tryna level up, or you tryna lay low? You tryna cash out, or clock out? 'Cause the road to the top ain't paved with "I mights" and "I'll trys"—it's built with I wills, I dids, and I'm still standing on business muthaphuka.

So **commit or quit—bihhhht.** But don't waste the game's time with that in-between shyt.

Sixty-Five

Pimpin Forever, Simpin Never

ENTRY: 80 / FEBRUARY 28th 12:05 PM

Listen up, player—this here's real game, no fakin', no mistakin': I'm talkin' boss tactics over basic actions—Imma reign with game and avoid the pain of lames. Pimpin' forever, Simpin' never. We movin clever—and smooth through stormy weather. You either stackin' or slackin', ballin' or stallin', and if your game's tight, you steady risin', and never fallin'.

Ain't no room for simpin', only winnin'—every loss a lesson, every setback a blessin'. Understand me now: you either pimpin' strong or simpin' wrong. Be wise in how you roll—cause the power's in your soul. Too many lost to basic ways, trapped in a simpish daze. But the boss knows better, keeps his shoes laced tight—eyes on the prize, always ready to strike.

A real pimp sees through lies, moves with precision—makes calculated decisions with immaculate vision. Lames complain about the pain they feel, but real ones deal, adapt, and keep it trill. So lace your game proper, player—ain't no stoppin' a boss who's locked in with game sharper than a razor. Rise above the noise, maintain poise, and never lose sight of your choice.

Remember, the world's your chessboard, every move strategic—stay authentic, never pathetic, always magnetic. Keep it pimpin', not simpin'; make your game prolific, your hustle terrific, and your moves specific. That's the game, youngblood—stay official, not superficial. Keep your mental essential, your hustle influential, and your style presidential.

Now dig this deeper, let the words seep in—real pimps don't sleep in; hustle never weaken. You see, life's a gamble, better handle it wise—no surprise, when you rise, leave 'em wonderin' how you survive. A real player don't stumble on the small things, never trip on what the past brings, just keep stackin' chips and flash platinum watches and rings.

Understand clearly, only fools get weary; the pimpin' stay focused, eyes never teary. Navigate the game like a captain steers ships—smooth seas or rough trips, mouth sealed, tight lips. Real talk, your silence is louder than noise—actions speak volumes, power poised. Keep your circle small, your standards tall—weak links break chains, real bosses don't stall.

Pimpin's a mindset, not just cash and clothes—real game glows, bright as hell and it shows. Keep your purpose defined, sharpness refined—hustle and grind, leave your worries behind. A simp cries tears when the pressure applies; a pimp adjusts gears, never compromise. Move cautious, make your steps precise; never gamble twice without checking the dice.

Never underestimate the hustle's longevity; the game rewards skill, patience, and integrity. Keep your moves solid, never chaotic; smooth, exotic. Always remember—simpish ways cost yuh dearly, pimpish ways think clearly. Stay fresh, step lively, build wisely, speak timely. Walk tall, never crawl—if you're gonna play the game, play to win it all.

Everyday pressure only sharpens a boss, turns coal into diamonds, no loss in the sauce. Watch the snakes closely, keep enemies near—never driven by fear, vision crystal clear. Move wise, minimize your distractions, maximize your interactions, multiply transactions. Remember, life's chess, not checkers; strategize carefully, never settle for lesser.

Lastly, let the wisdom settle deep in your mind—stay defined, refined, always one-of-a-kind. When challenges knock, let your actions talk. Move calculated, elevated—never outdated, always upgraded. Keep your circle tight, your shine bright, your hustle right, and your future in sight.

Now that's game, and I'm handing it over to you so stay forever true, cause one thangs for certain slim, real bosses shonuff do.

100 OF UNCLES
FINEST RANDOM ISMS

- Stay prayed up and paid up.
- Feed the need, so the game can breed.
- Pass the plate, keep the game great.
- The sauce ain't lost when the recipe's taught.
- This Ism is ethier in yuh or it's on yuh.
- What you give grows, what you hoard folds.
- Lace 'em right, they'll shine bright.
- Game shared is game prepared.
- Real game never die, it just multiply.
- Elevate your team, so your legacy gleam.
- Build the bridge, don't block the ridge.
- A pimp with no plan is just a trick with a scam.
- A ho with no vision gon' make a bad decision.
- A boss with no hustle gon' struggle like a puzzle.
- If yuh game ain't tight, you ain't living right
- If the ism ain't deep, you ain't playing for keeps.
- Slick tongue's with no funds ain't impressing no ones.
- If she choosing for a chain, she ain't built for the game.
- Mouthpiece like a Uzi, keep it real, never bougie—Don't waste it on chelsea choosy.
- A ho that don't listen ain't built for this mission.
- A trick with no bread is just a fool who's misled.
- A ho in rebellion gon' cost you a million.
- You ain't a king if your words don't sting.
- A fake pimp on the blade is just a mark getting played.
- No crown for a clown who let the game get him down.
- A player that sip an dip, gon' soon lose his grip.
- If your ism ain't crisp, she gon' slide in the mist.
- A ho who's structure aint great gon' fluctuate.
- If you chase her, you erase her, real game ah replaces her.
- If the game ain't first, then the bag gon' be worse.
- If your ism ain't hot, your bankroll gon' rot.
- When the ism ain't sharp, yuh hustle fall apart.
- Take my money, take my ho's just please don't take my game.
- A sucker in disguise gon' get taxed like a prize.
- If you flex only for the fame, you ain't built for this game.
- A boss without discipline is a pistol with no trigger.
- Money move fast, but the broke move last.
- Loyalty's rare, like a pimp with no flair.
- When your presence hit the room, let it boom—ain't no need to assume.
- You mackin' like a poet, but the money gotta show it.
- A hustler with no strategy is a muthaphukn tragedy.
- A weak mind fold, a strong mind mold—turn pressure to diamonds and double the gold.
- Lion's don't beg, they claim stake—when you know you the prize, you don't wait on fate.
- The real don't beg, they attract—confidence is the magnet that keep the bag comin' back.
- Power's in your reach, wisdom's in your soul, knowin' how to hustle's how you stay in control.
- Good game speaks to your soul, when you master it, it'll makes you whole.
- Don't just hustle for now, hustle for the long haul, keep on hustlin' till the game answers your call.
- Get the knowledge, get the game, take the crown, wear the name.
- There's mo loyalty in the ho house than in the chuuch houwz.
- Ho hustlin' vs real pimpin'. is diabolical work. If you sked then go to church.
- I don't explain, and a bith-bett-not complain.
- If you get in yuh feels fuh deez ho's you start makin' deals wit deez ho's. Nevah discount yuh pimpin.
- They act like butchers who love to carve—they wanna eat and see me starve.

- Ain't no time for crime, only time for shine.
- Take these tools and jewels, stay cool and try not to break the rules.
- May yuh next move be yuh bes: move—Mr. Smooth.
- Broke minds whine, but rich ones climb.
- Put it in the streets and see if you get beat.
- A ho's heart is a treasure, so don't let her play you for pleasure.
- When you're a true player, you don't need a script, you just flip the script.
- Real recognize real—if they ain't recognizing, they blind.
- If you keep yuh circle tight, the game'll never bite.
- Trust your hustle over the shine—it's all about the grind.
- Keep your eyes on the bag, and the bag'll keep its eye on you. Chuch at a hunnid.
- A boss don't beg, he just flex—and watch'um respect what's next.
- Get up, get out, and make 'em shout—cause you the one they can't do without.
- Hustlin' ain't a job—it's a way of life. Your grind should be your only shine.
- Let yuh money pile and yuh teeth smile-cause' it's a muthaphukn lifestyle, ya dig.
- In the game, the only thing guaranteed is change.
- A real hustler knows how to pivot, talk about plan A,B&C, oh he live it.
- If yuh ism ain't sharp, the game'll break your heart.
- Every loss is a lesson, but the game still a blessing, so I ain't stressin.
- You ain't winning unless you're grinning from the beginning.
- Time's money, so make every second count. You get what you give, so give it yuh all.
- Every step you take should elevate your stake and the higher you climb, the smoother the grind.
- Don't just hustle hard—hustle smart and never stop your hustle, just adjust the muscle.
- Always stay ahead, don't wait to be led.
- Get yuh mind right, and your hustle'll align right.
- Get yuh mind right and yuh moves uh feel light.
- Get yuh mind right, and your stack will ignite-kaboom!
- Stay in your lane, and never beg for the fame.
- A real mack never craves—he just waves.
- Success ain't a trend, it's a lifestyle you defend.
- The hustle don't stop till the money drop.
- Keep your foes close, but your hustle closer.
- If you ain't learnin, you ain't earning.
- If you wait too long, you'll miss the song.
- If you pockets don't shine, that mean its time to grind.
- Broke minds whine, but rich ones climb, and they game card don't decline.
- Never let your ego cloud your hustle—always stay humble.
- The game sometimes speaks in silence—only the real hear it.
- A mack moves with precision, leaving no decision to chance.
- Never chase a hoe; that block the money flow.
- Hustle with a purpose, or the game'll curse ya
- Only the strong survive in this game, the weak just complain.
- Hustle hard, and make 'em respect your game from the start.
- If you checkin major trap, you gon see me clap, even dap, i aint no hater.
- Prove yo roots before I lace yo boots.
- If she can stomp down on the blade, survive and get you paid, she earned her stay.

Core Strategic Themes and Lessons
Interwoven Throughout the Narratives

- Leadership Presence
- Persistence
- Adaptability
- Knowledge Transfer
- Profit Focus
- Financial Necessity
- Priority Management
- Risk Analysis
- Self-Regulation
- Resourcefulness
- Authenticity
- Strategic Alliances
- Financial Discipline
- Lifestyle Alignment
- Opportunity Cost
- Directional Focus
- Proactivity
- Resilience
- Wealth Building
- Consistent Growth
- Strategic Silence
- Authority Establishment
- Foundational Success
- Transparency
- Strategic Patience
- Proactive Thinking
- Entrepreneurial Mindset
- Resource Flexibility
- Operational Efficiency
- Balance and Strength
- Peer Recognition
- Financial Focus
- Persuasive Communication
- Competitive Edge
- Respect Enforcement
- Attraction Law
- Quality Focus
- Confidence
- Management change
- Critique Management
- Knowledge Power
- Urgency
- Adaptive Growth
- Loss Management
- Outcome Focus
- Future Focus
- Value of Loyalty
- Innovative Leadership
- Network Dynamics
- Growth Separation
- Effective Leadership
- Preemptive Reputation
- Nonverbal Communication
- Generosity
- Exclusive Offering
- Service Excellence
- Damage Control
- Visionary Thinking
- Entrepreneurial Freedom
- Continuous Improvement
- Strategic Execution
- Self-Sufficiency
- Skill Mastery
- Decisiveness
- Authentic Foundation
- Authentic Value
- Strategic Positioning
- Learning Orientation
- Opportunity Maximization
- Strategic Compatibility
- Investment Savvy
- Emotional Intelligence
- Market Stability
- Collaborative Success
- Mental Control
- Pimpin

FROM SOME ISM & HOE'ETRY
COMES A PIMPS SORCERY
LACED IN POETRY
SEASONED IN GAME
PAID AND BOUGHT
JUST SO YOU CAN GET A LIL
TASTE OF A PIMP'S THOUGHTS.

~Unc

PIMP JOURNAL
INDEX & NOTES

PIMP JOURNAL
INDEX & NOTES

PIMP JOURNAL
INDEX & NOTES

PIMP JOURNAL
INDEX & NOTES

PIMP JOURNAL
INDEX & NOTES

PIMP JOURNAL
INDEX & NOTES

PIMP JOURNAL
INDEX & NOTES

PIMP JOURNAL
INDEX & NOTES

PIMP JOURNAL
INDEX & NOTES

PIMP JOURNAL
INDEX & NOTES

PIMP JOURNAL
INDEX & NOTES

PIMP JOURNAL
INDEX & NOTES

PIMP JOURNAL
INDEX & NOTES

PIMP JOURNAL
INDEX & NOTES

PIMP JOURNAL
INDEX & NOTES

PIMP JOURNAL
INDEX & NOTES

PIMP JOURNAL
INDEX & NOTES

PIMP JOURNAL
INDEX & NOTES

A MIND STATE MOVEMENT

THE OFFICIAL GAME OF YOUNG MILLIONAIRES

ALSO FEATURING EXCLUSIVE APPAREL

FOR MORE INFO & INSTRUCTIONS VISIT
WWW.MONKEYMONKMASTERMIND.COM

WELCOME TO THE OFFICIAL MONKEY MONK MASTERMIND GAME PAGE. PREPARE YOURSELF FOR AN EXHILARATING EXPERIENCE OF STRATEGY AND COGNITIVE HIERARCHY. IN THIS GAME, PLAYERS WILL ENCOUNTER THE CAPTIVATING INTERPLAY BETWEEN THE DOMINANT MONKEY MIND AND THE WISE MONK MIND, AS THEY STRIVE TO ASCEND IN CONSCIOUSNESS TOWARD OPERATING FROM THE HIGHEST MIND'S PERSPECTIVE, CALLED THE MASTER MIND... IF POKER, SPADES & UNO HAD A POLYAMOROUS BABY, IT STILL WOULDN'T BE AS FUN AS MONKEY MONK MASTERMIND. PREPARE YOURSELF FOR AN EXTRAORDINARY JOURNEY TOWARDS ENLIGHTENMENT AND ENJOY THE UNPARALLELED EXCITEMENT THAT MONKEY MONK MASTERMIND UNLOCKS. YOU, YOUR FRIENDS, YOUR FAMILY, AND YOUR TEAM WILL EVOLVE WITH EACH HAND. PRE ORDER YOUR DECK NOW ALONG WITH EXCLUSIVE APPAREL AND BE THE FIRST AMONGST YOUR CIRCLE TO REPRESENT THIS MASTERMIND MOVEMENT.

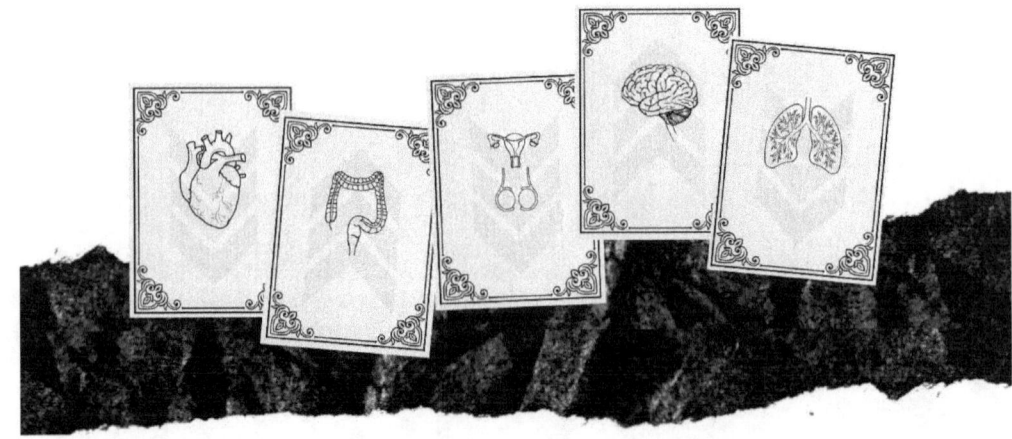

Authors Page

Author, speaker, and relational strategist Kushaqxi brings street wisdom into sharp focus with 50 Pimp Philosophies for Enrichment in the Game of Life—a groundbreaking blend of life lessons, business game, and poetic grit. Known for his narrative approach that fuses storytelling with strategic insight, Kushaqxi draws from lived experience, urban philosophy, and timeless truths handed down from Unc—a fictional yet deeply symbolic mentor whose voice echoes through every chapter.

From The Twin Elemental Effect to his renowned "Polyamorously-Celibate" framework, Kushaqxi has challenged norms and redefined personal evolution with fearless creativity. His current work is no different—bridging the gap between the streets and the boardroom, between raw instinct and refined intellect.

When he's not decoding power moves or hosting workshops on psychological strategy, Kushaqxi can be found nurturing his land through organic arboriculture, raising a family at home, or inspiring minds through social media and speaking engagements. His mission? To elevate the culture, one philosophy at a time—turning lived wisdom into legacy.

OTHER BOOKS BY THE AUTHOR

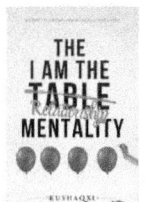
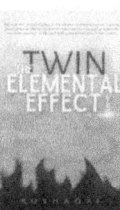

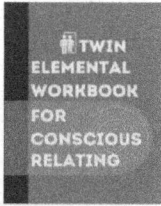

ALSO COMING SOON:

POLYAMOROUSLY CELIBATE:
An Advanced emo-tech model for
spiritual and social development.

FRIEND ZONE MASTERY:
Why a fleet of platonic wing(wo)men are far more
valuable than a torrent of limerent entanglements.